THE
RULE
OF
THRE3

THE RULE OF THREE

ERIC WALTERS

SCHOLASTIC INC.

ISBN 978-0-545-84300-3

Text copyright © 2014 by Eric Walters. All rights reserved. Published by Scholastic Inc., 557 Broadway, New York, NY 10012, by arrangement with Farrar, Straus and Giroux, LLC. SCHOLASTIC and associated logos are trademarks and/or registered trademarks of Scholastic Inc.

12 11 10 9 8 7 6 5 4 3 2 1   15 16 17 18 19 20/0

Printed in the U.S.A.   40

First Scholastic printing, January 2015

Designed by Andrew Arnold

For Anita, my wife, my world, the person from
whom all the blessings in my life flow

THE
RULE
OF
THRE3

"Can't you keyboard a little bit faster?" Todd asked.

We were in the computer room during study hall, our second-to-last class of the day. Not exactly where I wanted to be, but there were worse places to be than hanging with my best friend—even if we were working on *his* essay.

"It's not the speed of my fingers that's slowing us down. I can only type what you say. And you're not saying anything," I answered.

"Come on, Adam, I'm counting on you to fill in the blanks on this thing."

"It's *your* essay."

"Don't you want me to pass?" Todd cajoled.

"Of course I want you to pass."

"Then you'd better get busy, because that whole *passing* thing isn't likely to happen if you don't contribute."

"You wouldn't need my help if you didn't wait until the last minute to do your homework, you slacker," I said.

"It is *not* the last minute. This isn't due until final period."

"Which is in forty minutes," I replied.

"That's my point. It won't be the *last* minute until thirty-nine minutes from now. If I handed it in *now*, technically it would be *early*."

This was Todd logic at its finest. He was almost impossible to reason with but totally impossible not to have a laugh with. The freshman girls seated on either side of us in the computer lab seemed to agree as they started giggling.

"Please don't encourage him," I said.

"And now you don't want me to be encouraged. What sort of best friend are you?" Todd demanded. "If you ladies want to offer me encouragement, please feel free."

They giggled again. This was obviously becoming more about him trying to impress them and less about helping me help him avoid flunking another assignment.

"Why didn't you just do this last night?" I asked.

"I was worn out from football practice. Physically and mentally. You'd have been worn out, too, if you hadn't quit the team."

I snorted. "I didn't *quit*. I just didn't try out this year."

"Same thing."

"It's not the same thing. I chose flying lessons over football."

"What kind of normal sixteen-year-old chooses flying lessons over anything?"

"One who wants to be a pilot."

"Just like Daddy."

"Sure." My father was a commercial pilot for Delta. He had been in uniform at the breakfast table and said he was heading to O'Hare this morning. I knew he would be taking off on his return flight soon, so he'd be home in time to read with the twins before they went to bed.

"Personally, I'd rather be like your mother," Todd said.

"My mother is a woman," I pointed out. "And I gotta tell

you that picturing you in a dress, heels, and makeup is a bit unnerving."

"First off, I want to be a police officer, like your mother. Second, the idea that you are picturing me in a dress, makeup, and heels is *more* than a bit unnerving," he replied. "Just how long have you been fantasizing about me as a woman?"

Once Todd got started it was hard to turn him off.

"Excuse me!" Todd called out. Everybody in the lab turned to face him. "How many people find it disturbing that Adam has been picturing me as a woman?"

Lots of hands went up.

"Ignore him, please!" I protested.

"Adam, don't be ashamed, embrace your feelings!"

"Let me know when you're done, Todd."

"In this day and age it's important that all of us accept you for what you are and how you feel. In fact, I take it as a compliment that you fantasize about me."

"I don't fantasize about you!"

"Don't be embarrassed. I'm sure you're not the only one who fantasizes about me." He turned to the girl on one side. "Right? You must admit I've entered your dream world at least once or twice."

She stopped laughing and looked like she was choking on something.

"Don't be shy," he said. "Embrace your feelings, too. *Live* the fantasy and you could become part of the total Todd experience."

She turned beet red, gathered up her things, and practically ran away. The other two girls beside us pretended to ignore us now.

"Nice," I said.

"Mean, possibly. Fun, tremendously. That's why God created high school—so kids in older grades could torment kids in younger grades."

I knew that Todd could be neither embarrassed nor contained. He was as relentless as an avalanche. All I could do was redirect him.

"Since when did you decide you wanted to be a police officer?"

"Recently. I decided it would be cool to run around with a gun," he said.

"The fact that you don't have a gun right now is at least a small blessing for all of us."

"I'll ignore that crack—but if I had a gun I would force you to play football."

"Like I said, I have no time."

"You could have time for both football and flying lessons if you didn't *waste* so much time on school. That's *my* solution."

"And just how is that working out for you?" I asked.

"It would be going extremely well if *somebody* would stop giving me a hard time and help me finish up this essay."

"Let's just get it finished. I have to get out of here right after school. I have a flight lesson."

"Okay, Orville Wright," he said.

"Hey, better Orville Wright than Orville Redenbacher. Three more lessons and then I solo."

"When you get your license, do you know who I want to be the very first person up in the air with you?"

"You?"

"I was thinking anybody *except* me!"

The two girls to my left started giggling again—as well as a couple of other people in the lab.

"You better not insult the man who has your future at his fingertips or—"

The lights suddenly went out, the computer screen went blank, and everybody in the lab collectively groaned as we were thrown into darkness.

"What happened?" I wondered.

"Power failure or something. More important, did you at least save my essay?" Todd questioned.

"I saved it . . . a few minutes ago. It's almost all there."

"But I need *all* of it there! What am I going to tell Mr. Dixon?"

"You'll tell him about the power failure."

"He won't believe me!"

"Of course he'll believe you. The lights are out everywhere, so I think he might have noticed." I gestured to the darkened hall. "This isn't just a power failure in the computer lab. Besides, I'm sure everything will be back on soon," I said.

"Soon may not be soon enough, and he won't believe me that it was almost done. You have to tell him!"

"Why me?"

"He'll believe *you*! You hand in your assignments on time, you never skip class, you do your reading, and you're always polite to teachers. You are *such* a suck-up!"

"It's called being responsible."

"Suck-up . . . responsible . . . different words for basically the same—"

"Hey, my computer is down, too," the girl beside us said.

"*Everybody's* computer went off," Todd said. "Computers need a magical substance called *electricity*." He turned to me. "Today's younger generation doesn't understand much."

"I understand that this is my laptop and it has a battery," she said.

"The battery must be dead."

"But mine went down as well," another boy said.

"Mine, too," a girl at the other end of the lab added. All of them were on laptops.

"Well, that's because . . ." Todd turned to me. "Well, Adam?"

"How should I know?"

"Didn't you win the science fair last year?"

"That was for designing a two-seated ultralight, not because I know everything about electricity."

"Come on, you know everything about everything. I wouldn't let you do my homework if you didn't. Can we go and find Mr. Dixon and explain to him about my paper?"

I wasn't going to do that. But I did want to see what was going on. I gave a big sigh and got to my feet.

———————

The halls were filling with kids. The only light was coming from classroom windows and scattered emergency lights running on batteries. Classes had ended unexpectedly, and everyone was streaming out. There was a lot of laughing and loud conversation as kids enjoyed an early break.

"Can I have your attention, please!" a deep voice boomed. "Please, everybody, stop where you are!" It was our vice principal yelling through a handheld bullhorn. "We need everybody in the gym for a brief assembly!"

There were groans from the crowd.

"I say we head for the doors," Todd said. "In this commotion there's no way they're going to be able to stop us from leaving."

"What about the assembly?"

"And you wonder why I call you a suck-up?"

We headed down the stairs, only to find two teachers at the exit deflecting the river of students toward the gym.

"So much for leaving," I said. I knew Todd was disappointed, but I really did want to hear what they had to tell us.

We went with the flow. The gym was dimly lit with just a few emergency lights. It was already crowded, and I felt a little claustrophobic as we pushed in. The bleachers were filled to capacity and we were herded onto the court, shoulder to shoulder. I was grateful to be taller than most everybody else. Did they really think they could cram fifteen hundred kids into this space?

"My phone isn't working," Todd said.

"You know there are lots of dead spots in this school."

"No, I mean it's as blank as the computer screens." He showed it to me.

"Your battery is dead. Your phone needs that magical substance called electricity to—"

"My phone is dead, too," a girl said.

"Same here," somebody else added.

All around us people who had overheard were pulling out their phones. There was a chorus of disbelief and upset. It was strange how they seemed more upset about their phones not working than there being no electricity.

I pulled out my phone, just to confirm things. It was off—as per the school rules—but when I pushed the button to turn it on, it remained blank. I knew my phone was fully charged. The cell phone towers probably needed electricity to work. Is that why we weren't even getting a screen? No, that didn't make sense. Even without the towers there should have been power to run other apps.

"Can I have your attention!" Our principal was on the stage with a bullhorn. "Please!" he called out. "We need everybody to listen carefully . . . Please stop talking!"

There was a murmur of conversation that faded to a semi-silence, an acceptable level of cooperation.

"As you are all aware, we have a power failure," he started. "We're assuming that it's probably countywide, as there is a complete breakdown in telephone service, both landlines and cell phones, which must be related to the power failure."

The crowd noise went up as those who hadn't noticed previously all pulled out their cell phones to confirm what he'd said.

"Quiet down, people! The sooner we can finish here, the sooner you can all go home!"

A cheer went up from the crowd and then applause.

"Silence, please!" The noise faded. "Whatever the issue is, I'm confident it is being addressed and will be corrected shortly."

For some reason I had a feeling it wasn't going to be so simple. I was still thinking about why the batteries in the laptops had gone dead.

"We've decided to cancel final period today and let you all go home early."

A cheer went up from the audience once again.

He raised a hand to quiet everyone. "You can stay here in

the gym to wait for the buses. If you're driving or walking, keep in mind there will probably be no functioning traffic lights, so please be careful. Dismissed."

There was an even bigger cheer as we all started for the exits.

2

The flood of students spilled out through every available door of the gym. With my dad away, I guess this meant I was picking up the twins at the elementary school, as I knew my mother would be asked to stay on duty with the power out. They'd be keeping all officers on duty, and as captain of the precinct she would be tied up completely until this was resolved. And since no power meant no flying lesson, my afternoon was pretty much shot anyway.

"Do you need to get anything from your locker?" I asked Todd.

"Nope. I guess that essay for Dixon will be due tomorrow, but we have study hall beforehand to finish it up."

"I have to give you marks for being consistent."

"All I need is a ride home. Hey, do you see her?"

"Keep your voice down," I hissed. "I see her."

Just exiting the building ahead of us was Lori—holding hands with Chad. I felt myself cringe. Something that nice shouldn't be touching something that bad. I didn't dislike many people, but Chad was in that group. A rich, snobby, squinty-eyed lacrosse player two grades ahead, he didn't like me either. As Todd had pointed out more than once, it didn't take a genius to figure out I had a thing for Lori. So far she hadn't noticed, or if she had, she pretended that she hadn't.

"I don't know what she sees in him," I said.

"Let's ask her. Hey, Lori!" Todd screamed.

Lori and Chad turned around, and I wanted to find a rock to crawl under.

"I was wondering," Todd called out as we caught them. "We were *both* wondering—"

"What you got on the history test!" I exclaimed, cutting him off. Lori, Todd, and I had the same third-period class.

"An eighty-nine," she said, and flashed us a smile. I felt my feet get mushy.

"That's great," Todd said, "but I was really wondering—"

"If you wanted to join our study group for the finals," I broke in again. Todd laughed but I ignored him. "I know it's early, but it's important to get these things sorted out."

"Umm, that would be great," she said.

Chad shot me a dirty look. He was neither impressed nor deceived.

"Good. See you tomorrow. Come on, Todd, we better go now."

"But—"

"If we don't leave now, somebody is going to be *walking* home, if you understand what I'm saying."

"I understand. Okay, then, let's get going. See you two *ladies* tomorrow."

Lori smiled, and Chad scowled but was smart enough not to say anything back. Todd was younger but bigger, and he had a well-earned reputation for being quick-tempered, tough, and willing to fight just about anybody. It wouldn't have helped Chad's cool to be beaten up by a guy two years younger. They walked off.

"I think that's part of the answer to your question," Todd said, gesturing to Chad's BMW.

"I don't think so. She's got too much going for her to be impressed by somebody's car. You'd have to be pretty shallow to let something like that influence you."

"Hey, watch what you're saying. If he wasn't such a complete tool, *I'd* become his friend just to ride in that car. Look at the piece of junk you drive."

"It's not junk, it's a *classic*." I unlocked the door.

"A classic is a '57 Corvette, not an '81 Omega," he said.

I reached over and unlocked his door. "It's a '70-something Omega and it *is* a classic. By definition, any car that's older than twenty-five years is a classic. Do the math."

"I won't be doing any math until next semester, when I have to take it as a subject."

I turned the key and the car groaned but didn't want to start. "Come on, come on."

"I bet you Chad's car will start," Todd said.

"So will mine."

"She'd better or I'm going to have to try and hail down Chad and get a—"

The engine roared to life. I adjusted the rearview mirror, got ready to back out, and . . . saw only people standing by their cars. I eased out and for once wasn't fighting to edge my way through other cars. No vehicle was moving. Not one. Kids were opening car hoods all over the place. What was happening? I stopped and rolled down my window. There were voices, but no engines racing other than mine.

"This is weird," Todd said. "What's going on?"

"I'm not sure."

I put the Omega into park, and Todd and I climbed out. All of the cars were dead except mine. Then I saw an old beat-up minivan slowly inching through the crowd.

"This can't be happening," Todd said. "It's not possible that all the vehicles in the parking lot stopped working at once except for two old wrecks."

A thought jolted me. "It's the computers."

"What have the computers got to do with the cars not working?"

"A modern car has more computers on it than the space shuttle. If something has shut down the computers in the school, they must have shut them down out here in the parking lot."

"And your car, because it's as old as the car Fred Flintstone drove, doesn't have any computers," Todd said.

"Exactly." I had a brief flash of what all this meant. This was bad. Really bad. "We have to roll. We need to pick up my brother and sister. Get back in the car."

"Hold on—that still leaves you one empty seat," Todd said. "Lori!" he screamed, his voice cutting through the rising tide of voices that filled the parking lot. She was standing next to Chad's car and turned to face us.

"Can we give you a ride?" he yelled.

She smiled, nodded, and came toward us—but not before giving Chad a little kiss goodbye. That made my skin crawl.

Todd held open the passenger door, she climbed in, and he got into the back. This was great, I thought, that she was right here and—

But then my head snapped back to the present. Whatever was happening might be kind of serious—at least more serious than the principal was letting on. Either he was trying to downplay things or he didn't know . . . Wait . . . He didn't know about the cars or he wouldn't have mentioned us all driving home or getting on the buses.

"We've got to make one stop to pick up my brother and sister."

"Of course. I just don't understand what's happening," Lori said. "This is all so unreal."

"I think it has to do with computer systems," Todd said. "Cars have lots of computers in them. Well, except for old cars like this one."

I shot Todd a look in the mirror.

"That's what Adam thinks, anyway," he said.

I nodded. "The computers control everything. Fuel pump, transmission, electrical system, power brakes and steering, locks, windows." We started moving, and everybody stared at us as we rolled by. They looked confused, amused, and worried. At the exit, there were no other cars waiting to turn out.

And then the three of us looked beyond the school lot.

"What a sight," Todd said.

The entire road had become a long parking lot. There were clusters of cars at lights—lights that weren't working. Standing around the cars were more people—equally confused, but also angry-looking. An old truck—again almost as old as my car—rumbled along slowly, weaving past the stalled cars like they were pylons. The driver looked at me and waved. I gave a little wave back as if we were members of some secret club. I moved over to the far side of the road to get around cars that had clumped together blocking the way. This was eerie.

"So you think this is some sort of computer problem," Lori said, "like a virus?"

"Yeah, a virus of some kind. A *bad* virus."

"But how was it spread so that it infected the cars?" Todd asked.

"I have no idea. Maybe through the airwaves."

"You mean like Wi-Fi and the Internet?" he asked.

"Well, maybe that's how the computers at school got infected. But the car computers aren't hooked to the net. Maybe it spread through the GPS, or satellite radio, maybe even OnStar systems," I suggested.

"That makes sense. Almost every car has one of those," Todd agreed.

"But not all of them. It has to be something else as well." And then the answer came to me. "*Every* car has a radio. It could be through AM or FM radio signals. That could be how the virus arrived and then infected the computer systems."

"Do you know what this reminds me of?" Todd asked.

I had no idea. This was like nothing I'd ever seen or heard about.

"What?" Lori asked.

"This is going to sound stupid."

"Look around," I said. "Compared to what's happening, nothing could sound stupid."

"It reminds me of one of those movies where the only human beings in the world drive around in a car with zombies chasing them." He paused. "Okay, now tell me if that isn't stupid?"

I shook my head. "Not stupid. I think I even understand."

I came up to an intersection, easing through the stalled vehicles, my progress marked by looks of awe or surprise from those standing beside their disabled rides. I'd gone from driving an old piece of crap to piloting an object of wonder.

3

Rachel and Danny followed me out the doors of their school. The principal had been thrilled to have me take them. He had hundreds of kids with no school buses and almost nobody to pick them up. Taking two fourth graders off his hands made his job that much easier.

The kids were still thinking it all had to do with the power going off. I was positive the power going off wasn't the cause of the problem, but the *result* of the problem.

"I hope everything is still blacked out tomorrow," Danny said. "It would be sort of like a snow day without all the snow."

I laughed. Maybe it really was nothing serious and I was overthinking all of this and it would be fixed in a few hours. That made sense. Power failures happened, and then things were repaired. That's how it worked. Except then, when the lights went out, there usually was a storm or something, knocking down power lines and causing outages. I also knew this was more than just about the power, but I didn't say anything. There was no point in worrying the twins by opening up questions when I didn't have answers.

"Our teacher told us about a blackout that hit the eastern half of North America a few years ago," Danny said.

"I kind of remember that," Lori said. "It was freaky and a little bit scary."

"You have me and Adam, so there's nothing to be ascared of," Todd said.

"Ascared?" Danny asked. "Who taught you how to talk?"

"Great, I'm being disrespected by a fourth grader," Todd said.

"A smart fourth grader," Danny said.

Rachel laughed. "Not that smart."

"Do you think this blackout could be that big?" Danny asked me.

"I'm not sure about anything," I said.

"Our teacher said that it took three days to fix that big one. Maybe there won't be school for the rest of the week," Danny said. "Wouldn't that be amazing?"

"That *would* be amazing," Todd agreed.

Nothing could be more amazing than what we were witnessing. People had started to abandon their vehicles as they realized that they weren't going to start up, that there was no way to call for help, and that even if they could make a call there was nobody to help them since the emergency vehicles would be stalled, too. People who would have been sitting in their cars were on their feet walking. This was strange to see, because nobody in our suburbs ever really walked anywhere.

There were streams of people hiking down the middle of the street—more obstacles in my way. Most people just looked at us, but others waved and a couple stuck out their thumbs to try to hitch a ride from us.

"There's another car!" Danny screamed.

Another old junker was coming toward us. The driver leaned out his window and waved to us. As he came to a stop I pulled up beside him and halted when we were window to window.

"Old car," I said, pointing at his vehicle.

"We're the only things that seem to be running. How far have you come?" he asked.

"Only a couple of miles."

"And is it like this all over?" he asked.

"As far as we've seen. Where are you coming from?"

"Milton. I've been driving for thirty miles, and it's like this everywhere I've passed through. I figure the only way my wife is getting home from work is if I get her."

"She's one of the lucky ones who'll get a ride home," I said. "Be careful."

He gave me a strange look.

"You know, drive carefully . . . There are so many abandoned cars," I said—but that wasn't what I'd meant, and I think he knew it. I had an uneasy feeling about the way people had been looking at us as we passed. There was something in their eyes, especially the last guy who tried to wave us down. He looked angry when I didn't stop.

The other driver headed off in one direction and we drove in the other.

"How *are* people going to get home?" Todd asked.

"I guess they're going to have to walk."

"Where's Dad?" Rachel asked.

In the rush of everything I hadn't even thought of that. I looked at my watch and did a quick transposing of time. "He's halfway across the country, on the ground in Chicago. His flight isn't scheduled to leave for another hour."

"So he's okay, right?" Rachel asked.

"Of course he's okay. He's millions of miles away," Danny said. "Probably none of this is even happening there."

"I'm sure he's good," I said. "You know Dad. Nothing fazes him. He's probably just worried about how we're doing."

We continued driving, leaving the last of the houses behind. Lori lived on one of the few remaining little farms on the edge of our suburbs. I'd seen more and more of those farms turned into new subdivisions. I figured it wouldn't be long before her farm was gone, too.

"You live way out here?" Danny asked.

"It isn't that far. My family's been there forever. It's the farm where my father and his father were born."

"What's it like to live on a farm?" Rachel asked.

"I love it. We have lots of space and cows and horses and—"

"You have horses?" Rachel asked.

"Three."

"I love horses!"

"Then you have to come and *ride* sometime."

"Could I do it today?"

"Not today," I said, before Lori could answer. "We need to get home."

"But today is the perfect day," Rachel said. "It's not like we can watch TV when we get home."

"Another day," Lori said. She turned to me. "Your sister is adorable. You have to promise you'll bring her back."

"If he won't, I'm sure my mother will," Rachel said.

"No, I'll do it!" I said, cutting her off.

Todd started chuckling from the backseat. He knew what I was thinking.

"There's my dad!" Lori said.

In the middle of a big field alongside the road was a man on a tractor pulling a plow. Trailing behind the machines, landing in the newly turned ground, a flock of gulls gobbled up whatever grubs were being unearthed by the plow.

Then I realized that the tractor was *functioning*. I guessed it was an old tractor.

We turned up the dirt lane leading to the farmhouse. It was a bumpy, pothole-filled ride, and I slowed down dramatically to stop from bottoming out. My suspension wasn't that great at the best of times, and with this many people in the car it was much more of a problem. I had already felt the extra weight in the turns, and acceleration had been even slower than usual. Todd always joked that my car could go from zero to sixty in under ten minutes.

I stopped at the end of the lane. As Lori climbed out I put the car in park, but I didn't turn it off. I just didn't want to risk it not starting again.

"The tractor your father is driving—is it old?" I asked.

"Really old. He doesn't trust new when old still works."

My theory was holding up.

"Thanks for driving me home, Adam," Lori said. She touched my arm lightly, which sent an electrical charge through me. At least *that* power grid was operational.

"Um, no problem. So I guess we better get going."

"But you are coming back, right?" Lori said. "You know, for Rachel to ride a horse. You could even join us."

"I could do that. See you later."

With the twins and Todd shouting back and forth to see who could say the loudest goodbye to Lori, I gave her a final wave and then turned the car around and went back up the lane. When I got to the road, I stopped and instinctively looked both ways for traffic that wasn't coming.

"I still don't know why I couldn't go riding today," Rachel said.

"Not today, kid. Maybe I could bring you back tomorrow."

"You don't even like horses," Danny said.

"It isn't Lori's horses that he's interested in," Todd said.

"Shut up, Todd," I warned.

"Is that any way to talk to your best friend, who arranged for Lori to even be in the car to begin with?" he asked. "Rather than saying 'Shut up, Todd,' shouldn't you be saying 'Thank you, Todd'?"

I took a deep breath. "Thank you, Todd."

"Now, was that so hard?" Todd asked. "It's no wonder that I find *you* so adorable."

4

I maneuvered through the dead cars in the intersection leading into our neighborhood. Off to the left sat the gas station. There were a few cars parked there, and a big gas tanker stalled at the pumps. I'd meant to stop on my way home and get a fill-up, but I knew that couldn't happen now. My gas gauge showed half a tank—it always showed half a tank because it was broken—but I knew I had a lot less than that. I hadn't expected to drive Lori home.

We turned off Erin Mills Parkway and drove past the little strip mall at the top of the neighborhood and down the hill leading to our houses. Everything looked so normal. I rolled slowly along to our street.

There was one car at one side of our driveway—my father's. My mother's truck was with her at the police station, and she'd driven him to the airport before her shift had started. Her car was newer and wasn't going to get her home. Then again, I didn't think she was going to be able to leave the station right now anyway. I pulled in next to my dad's car and we all climbed out.

"Hey, Adam!"

I turned around. It was our neighbor Herb Campbell.

"Look," Todd said under his breath. "It's James Bond."

"Not quite 007," I said quietly.

Herb walked over. He always walked quickly for a guy his age—he had to be almost seventy. He'd moved in next door about a year ago. He said he was retired from working for the government and had been stationed in embassies around the world. My father *loved* that. As a pilot he'd flown all over, and the two of them were always talking about places and politics and people. Herb was a handyman type and seemed to have every tool in the world. He'd lent his tools—and suggestions—as my dad and I had worked on the ultralight plane we were building in our garage. Herb was always friendly and helpful.

And he made me nervous.

Most of the time he was just Herb, our neighbor, but then you could see there was something else, and you got the feeling that he was looking right inside of you. It wasn't a grumpy-old-guy kind of thing, like a geezer yelling at kids to get off his lawn. I watched him when he didn't know he was being watched. He really *studied* people. It was the same way my mother and every other cop I'd ever met looked around, scanning the room, checking things out. Herb never said much about his job to us, even when he was asked direct questions. He just said he'd been a paper pusher—but I had a feeling there was more to it. A lot more. Didn't spies work out of embassies? How crazy a thought was that? I'd only ever mentioned it to one person—Todd—and he never let me forget it.

"What's it like out there?" Herb asked.

"Pretty quiet," I said. "Nothing is moving."

"Nothing that has computers," he said. "Obviously, your car is old enough to still work."

"Sometimes older is better," Todd said.

"I've been saying that for a while," Herb agreed with a smile. "It's just good to see you made it. Even with a car that works I was worried that you might not be able to get home."

Herb did take an interest in our family. All my grandparents had been gone for years, and he was kind of the only older guy I knew. Because he had nobody else, my mother had started inviting him to join us for holiday meals. My dad joked that she always took in strays.

"It was a little tricky, but it wasn't that big a deal. I'm sure it'll all be fixed pretty soon," I said, trying to sound reassuring.

"Optimism is a fine quality," Herb said.

"We spoke to a guy who said it was the same in Milton," Todd said.

"This is not a standard power outage. This is something very different. Something a little bit bigger than that," Herb said. He turned to my brother and sister. "I have a generator, so there's electricity at my house. If you two are interested, you can go over to watch a DVD and have a cold drink."

"That would be great," Danny said.

"You might want to even dip into the freezer and make yourselves an ice cream cone."

The twins weren't going to say no to that offer. He waited for them to leave before he continued.

"I was on the radio and—"

"I didn't think radios worked," Todd interrupted.

"My shortwave radio. I have an old tube set. Completely

analog. Those with digital sets are going to be out of luck. And broadcast stations—AM, FM, satellite—are all off the air."

"Herb is a ham radio operator," I explained. I pointed out the tall aerial that rose above his roof.

"I've been on the horn for the last hour. With the power down, most of my contacts are out of operation. I've reached a ham with an old set in Detroit. It's the same situation there."

"And in Chicago?" I asked.

"Probably . . . Wait . . . Is that where your father was flying today?"

I nodded. "He took off early this morning and was scheduled to fly out this afternoon."

"When this afternoon?" Herb asked. "When was he due to fly out?"

There was an urgency in his voice, and then with a jolt to my heart I realized why. "This would affect airplanes as well, wouldn't it?"

"I don't know for sure. Let's not jump to any conclusions. When was your dad's return flight today?"

I checked my watch. "He'd be in the air by now . . . but he would have been on the ground when it hit, if it hit at the same time there as it did here."

"It hit Detroit at the same moment as here, so Chicago would've gotten it at the same time, too."

"Then he's fine, right?" I asked.

"I can find out more about the general situation at night, when my signals can travel farther," Herb said. "I hope I can connect to more hams."

"So this is big," Todd said.

"Very big," Herb confirmed. "Adam, I was wondering if you could do me a favor."

"Sure," I said.

"I need a ride."

"I don't have much gas," I said, looking for an excuse to stay put.

"It's not far."

I should have just said no. Now it was too late.

"Todd, could you stay with Danny and Rachel?" I asked.

"Do you really think they need a babysitter?"

"I was hoping they'd watch *you*," I joked.

"You could join them at my place," Herb suggested.

"Do I get ice cream, too?"

Herb smiled. "Just go in. Lock the door behind you."

"And I won't talk to strangers or—"

Herb reached out and put a hand on Todd's shoulder. "I'm not kidding, son. You lock the door behind you and watch the twins. This isn't a request. Understand?"

"Yeah, sure."

There had been that sudden change in Herb—the sort I'd seen before. Todd had seen it, too. In a flash he'd changed from a friendly old duffer to somebody different, almost dangerous.

Todd entered Herb's house as we climbed into my car. I was relieved when it started right up again.

"Where are we going?" I asked, backing out of the driveway.

"Not far. Just go to Burnham Drive."

There were more people in front of more houses now,

clustered together, talking. With nothing to do inside, they were drawn outside, probably looking for answers that none of them had. I got the sense that Herb had more of an idea than anybody else. How many people even knew how widespread it was?

"What do you think caused this?" I asked.

"Obviously computer related, but you knew that. And computers control most of the things that control our lives, from the power grid to your ability to text that girl you're interested in at school."

He was wrong. Even if we had power I couldn't text Lori, because I hadn't yet been brave enough to ask for her number.

"How long do you think it will take to fix?"

"Days is a given. The question is how many days, or weeks."

"You don't really think weeks, do you?"

"Speculation is just like rumor. I don't know if anybody knows the real truth, and that's what leads to both danger and opportunity."

"I don't understand."

"Rumors can cause panic that leads to desperate and dangerous actions. As for opportunity, it's still there until people more fully realize what's happening. That's where you're driving me, to take advantage of an opportunity."

"If you need food, we have plenty at our place."

"Thanks, Adam, but I am well stocked. I even have a good supply of extra gas to run my generator."

"Maybe we should be coming to you for stuff," I kidded.

"You know your family is always welcome," he said. "You're good people."

"You're good people, too," I said, as lame as that sounded. What else could I say?

Except for the parade of walkers and a few bicyclists, I was the only thing moving on the road. We were the center of everybody's attention. I almost felt guilty, driving while everybody else was hoofing it.

Suddenly, a man jumped off the curb in front of me, waving his arms wildly. I swerved, easily avoiding him. He yelled out a stream of swear words that came in through the open window as we rolled along.

Up ahead, the intersection was partially blocked with stalled cars and people milling around the vehicles. There wasn't really a clear path. I slowed down, but then Herb leaned over and placed a hand on my horn. It blared out a warning and people slowly moved to the side, some of them shooting resentful looks our way.

"Just keep going," Herb ordered.

We passed right through the gap.

"It's important not to stop," he said. "You can't help them. Just keep driving."

"Where *are* we driving to?"

"Jamison Pools. At that little shopping center down Burnham toward the bridge."

"But you don't even have a pool."

"It's all about opportunity."

"You're going to *get* a pool?"

"Of course not. Your parents let me use yours whenever I want. You know where the pool place is, right?"

"I know where it is. I just don't know *why* we're going there."

"To purchase chlorine."

"Again, you don't have a pool," I said.

"Chlorine is a very essential chemical and one of the few things I don't have in stock— Look, more vehicles!"

Up ahead two motorcycles were coming toward us. They were small, and one of them looked more like a twelve-year-old's dirt bike than a street-legal machine.

"That makes sense," Herb said. "I started my snowblower, lawn mower, and rototiller and they all worked because they don't have computers. Do you still have your old minibikes?"

My old-school minibikes probably had smaller engines than his lawn mower. "Yeah, but one hasn't worked since last summer."

"It can be fixed."

Up ahead was the little strip mall with the pool store. We pulled into the parking lot. More people were standing around their vehicles—many of them peering into their engine compartments. I pulled to a stop right in front of the pool place, with everybody watching us roll in.

"Lock the car doors behind us," Herb said.

We got out and Herb grabbed the door of the store. It was shut tight.

"Damn!" Herb said. "We'll have to go someplace— No, wait, there's somebody in there!" He started pounding his fist against the glass.

A man appeared. He turned the latch and cracked open the door.

"We're closed," he said, and started to pull the door closed.

Herb grabbed it and kept it open. "I just need to make a quick purchase," he said calmly.

"Sorry, but without electricity there are no credit cards and no cash registers working."

"How about straight cash?" Herb pulled out a wad of bills that made my eyes go wide. "You don't want to turn away business, do you?" He also offered the guy a big smile.

"What do you want?"

"Could we talk about that inside?" Herb asked. "I'm not feeling comfortable out here with this much cash in my hands."

I glanced over my shoulder. We *were* being watched.

The man allowed us in. Herb locked the door behind us.

"Stay by the door," Herb said to me quietly. "Keep an eye on your car."

I nodded.

"So what do you need?" the man asked.

"Chlorination tablets."

"You came out *today* to get those?"

"Yes. Tablets, sticks, or crystals, whatever you have."

"I have a special on one-inch tablets right over there. How many containers do you want?" the man asked.

"How many do you have?"

"This is a pool store, my friend."

"I want to purchase as many containers as two thousand dollars can buy."

"Seriously," the man said.

"Didn't that money look serious to you?"

"But why would you need that much?"

"Do you want my money or don't you?" Herb asked.

"Of course, but how are you going to haul all that chlorine away?"

"You're going to help us get it into his car," Herb said, pointing at me.

"I'd be happy to do that, but— Wait, you have a car that works?"

"Are you here to make a sale or to play twenty questions? Let's work out the details and get loading."

Herb and the man started to discuss numbers. I was more interested in what was going on outside the store. Lots of people seemed to be looking and pointing in our direction. It was starting to concern me.

"Grab a couple of buckets," Herb called out.

"Yeah, sure."

There was a big display of twenty-five-pound plastic containers stacked in a pyramid. Herb and I each grabbed one per hand. The salesman took one and then unlocked the door with his other hand.

"That's not a very big vehicle," he said as we stopped beside my car.

"Hopefully big enough for forty-two pails," Herb said. "Let's start with the trunk."

I put down the pails, pulled out my keys, and opened it up. The trunk was big and empty.

"I'll start loading, and you two hustle out with the rest of the buckets," Herb ordered.

Back and forth we went, two pails at a time, putting them down and letting Herb load them up.

"What *is* he going to do with all this chlorine?" the pool store man asked me at one point.

"I have no idea."

"He's okay in the head, right?" he asked. "I don't want anybody to accuse me of taking advantage of some poor old-timer."

"Don't worry about him. I have no idea why he wants it, but he's got his reasons."

We grabbed another load and headed out. Herb now had the trunk and backseat pretty well loaded. He'd popped some buckets open and was jamming individual plastic-wrapped packages of chlorine to fill in the spaces between the other pails.

"We have to squeeze them in wherever we can or they're not going to fit," he explained.

"I still don't know why you want this much," the man said.

"I'm planning on having the most disinfected pool in the world. How many containers to go?"

"Eight more, I think," the salesman said.

"They should all fit in if I do this right. Adam, you help me finish up these while he gets the rest out here."

The salesman headed back into the store as Herb opened up another pail.

"Hey there," somebody called out behind us.

Herb and I turned around. A group of men had broken away from the crowd and were closing in on us. They were middle-aged, and three of them were wearing suits and ties—hardly threatening-looking under normal circumstances, but this wasn't normal and there was something edgy about them.

"That car runs," the largest man said.

"Yep, it does," Herb said.

"Look," one of the others said, "we all need a ride."

The others nodded in agreement.

"Everybody needs a ride today," Herb said.

"We have money."

"We don't want your money. And we can't help you. Already got a full load. Sorry."

"Gramps, I'm trying to be friendly about this," the big guy said.

He took a couple of steps forward and the others followed along, fanning out slightly. Each of them had an air of desperation.

"First off, I'm not your grandpa," Herb said. "And second, you're not being that friendly. Please leave us alone."

"Look, old man, there's six of us and we need your car. One way or another we're going to—"

Herb brushed back his jacket to reveal a pistol in a holster. They all froze in place—and so did I.

"You're pulling a gun on us?" the big guy demanded.

"Not pulling. Showing you this weapon that I have a permit to carry and know how to use."

The guy laughed. It seemed a nervous laugh. "So what are you doing, *threatening* to pull a gun on us?"

"If necessary."

There was a matter-of-fact tone to Herb's response that made him sound scary. His voice was so calm and cool that I almost felt the chill.

"You shouldn't fool around with a gun; somebody could get hurt," the man said.

"Back off, friend, or somebody *will* get hurt." Herb pointed a finger directly at the big man who had been doing most of the talking.

The man laughed again. This time it was definitely nervous.

"You can't go around threatening people," the man said.

"You can't go around threatening to steal a car," Herb replied. "Have any of you ever tried this kind of stunt before?"

"Of course not!" a third man protested, and the others mumbled in agreement.

"Then don't let a few hours of inconvenience without electricity make you do something you'd never do, something you're going to regret as soon as things start working again."

Right before my eyes the men's stances wilted, their expressions softened.

"It's just that we're worried," one of them said.

"It's only reasonable to be worried," Herb said.

"We didn't mean any harm," a man who hadn't spoken before explained.

"We're just trying to get home to our families," another added.

"I understand, but there's no point losing our heads, is there?"

The big man looked down at the ground. They'd gone from acting like a mob to looking like a bunch of embarrassed little boys.

"Don't worry," Herb said. "This is just going to turn out to be nothing. An hour or so and it'll be sorted out."

"You think so?"

"We've all lived through power failures and computer glitches before. No big deal, right?" Herb asked.

Again, general agreement.

"You could wait," Herb said, "but why don't you lock up

your cars here and start walking? The sooner you get moving, the sooner you'll be home to make sure your families are fine."

They started muttering among themselves and moving away. I didn't care where they were going; I was just glad they were leaving.

"And good luck!" Herb called out. "I'm sure everything will be all right."

They turned, waved, and kept going. I let out a big sigh of relief.

"I didn't like that," I said.

"People can act pretty strange when things don't go normally. Let's finish loading up," Herb said.

Quickly we filled the car with the last of the chlorine and climbed in. Before I turned the key I had another small panic attack. *What if it didn't start?* But it turned over on the first try, and the engine roared. All around people turned to look.

"Put it in gear and let's get out of here," Herb said.

I didn't need to be told twice. I backed out and then headed for the street.

"What made you change your mind about it being over soon?" I asked.

"I didn't. I was just trying to calm the situation. Of course the weapon helped."

"I can't believe you're carrying a gun."

"We live in dangerous times. A lot of embassy staff had to have one."

"Even paper pushers?"

"You bet. In some countries embassy staff members are

the prime targets for kidnappings and terrorist attacks. Just read the newspaper."

"But you're retired."

"I guess I just got used to having it. I'm legally registered to carry a sidearm."

I supposed he had no reason to lie to me about this—although I'd mention it to my mother.

"I'm just glad they didn't challenge my bluff about the gun," he said. "There was more danger that I'd shoot my foot off than hit one of them."

"You have a gun but don't know how to use it?"

"I had some training, but it was a long time ago."

"You seemed pretty confident," I said.

"I'm a pretty good actor. That's a lot of what diplomacy is about."

If he didn't know anything about guns, then he *was* a good actor back there in the parking lot. Or maybe he was acting right now.

"Do you think they were really going to try to steal my car?"

"Don't be so surprised. Situational ethics can take root in a very short time."

He could see from my expression that I had no idea what he was talking about.

"It's simple. The way people act, what they believe is wrong or unethical, changes because of the situation. None of those men woke up today thinking they'd try to steal a beat-up old car from a kid and an old man. Things change, especially when a mob mentality sets in," Herb said.

"Six of them hardly makes a mob."

"It's not the numbers but the attitude. The situation set the stage for their action, provided the fuel, but the big guy was going to be the one to ignite them. Always take on the big dog when you're attacked by a pack."

"They were people, not a pack of dogs."

He smiled. "Of course, but I've learned the two have some things in common."

"Was that part of your embassy work?" I asked. "Taking on the big dogs?"

"Part of life."

His cryptic responses were driving me a little crazy. "So all embassy staff have to be trained to carry weapons?"

"You're no stranger to firearms either. Your mother is a police officer, and don't you have long guns in your house?"

"We have a couple of rifles." We had three, actually, and a shotgun, secured with the ammunition in a lockbox. The first thing my mother did when she got home every night was to lock away her service revolver in that box. Then I realized he'd avoided answering my question by asking me one. "So some of the places you worked and lived were pretty dangerous."

"Danger is a relative thing."

"But compared to here?"

"Almost every place in the world is more dangerous than here. Living in this incredibly wealthy country dulls people to the realities of other places."

"And those other places?"

"I've been stationed in countries where there was virtually no infrastructure or rules. No effective police, spotty communications, virtually no transportation, no running water, no electricity." He laughed. "Sort of like it is right here, right *now*."

"But this is different—it's only temporary."

"It's only temporary *after* it's been fixed."

"But it will be fixed," I said.

He didn't answer.

"Right?"

"Of course it will. It's all a matter of time. Are you still wondering about the chlorine?"

Again, he was changing the subject, but I *did* want to know about it.

"Do you know about the rule of three?" he asked.

I shook my head.

"It's an expression that has to do with emergency survival situations. You can go without air for three minutes, without water for three days, and without food for three weeks," he explained. "Beyond that, you're dead. In controlled doses, chlorine, the stuff that you put in your pool to kill bacteria and algae and keep the water clear, can make contaminated water fit for drinking."

That made sense.

"With the power going out, the entire system for maintaining fresh drinking water is gone. Not only can't they sanitize the water, but they can't deliver it. That all relies on pumps."

"But why would you need this much of the stuff?" I asked— and then I realized why. "You think this is going to last a long time, don't you?"

"I don't *know* that," he said. "I just know that it's better to have something and not need it than to need it and not have it."

"But this much?"

"I hope I don't need it. And if the computers start working again soon, then I guess I'll have to get myself a pool."

5

The old windup alarm clock I'd set woke me
from a deep sleep with its grating ring. It was two-thirty
in the morning.

I was surprised I'd managed to get any sleep with all the
things rumbling around in my head. I had passed out on
the couch. Somehow it seemed better to be downstairs—
between the front door and the twins. Was that protective or
paranoid?

My eyes strained to see. There was no light from the little
nightlight in the main floor washroom, no glowing lights from
the printer or TV or DVD player. Our home computer was
dead in the corner; the thing I'd spent so much time on was
totally useless. Not even any glow coming in from the street-
light near the end of our driveway. It was complete darkness.

I got up, still dressed and wearing my shoes. I shuffled
through the room, trying not to bump into anything. Why
hadn't I put the flashlight on the coffee table instead of the
desk across the room? I inched my way over and felt around
until I found the light. Flicking it on was reassuring and trou-
bling all at once—it was a blazing reminder about what was
happening.

The twins were upstairs, sleeping. My mother wasn't home.

Not long after Herb and I had gotten back from the pool store, she'd sent word with an officer on a bicycle that she was all right and occupied, and that I was to sit tight.

The officer she'd sent, Brett, was a rookie. Brett said she was posting officers all around her precinct. He was assigned to patrol our neighborhood.

Did Mom really think that was necessary?

Herb was also going to stand guard at the top of our street, where Powderhorn Crescent met Folkway Drive. I didn't think that was necessary either, but still it was strangely reassuring. I'd set my alarm so I could go out and see if he was okay.

I followed the flashlight beam over to the front door. I went to turn the lock and hesitated. After a moment I reached into the umbrella stand behind the door and pulled out a baseball bat. Then I opened the door, stepped out, and locked up behind me. The twins were asleep; it wouldn't matter if they were alone for a few minutes.

A shiver went up my spine. It was much cooler outside. I guess closing and locking all the windows last night had really kept the heat in. My footsteps against the pavement seemed loud because everything was so silent. There were no cars on the highway a few blocks away, no trains in the distance or planes in the sky. No random sounds escaped from open windows, no breeze rustled the trees. There was nothing except the sound of insects, and even they seemed quieter than usual.

I breathed deeply. There was a heavy scent of barbecue hanging in the air. Every home had barbecued for dinner. Propane or charcoal grills still worked. With freezers defrosting and people worried about spoiled meat, there had been a feast in every backyard. We barbecued, too. At least I tried. Dad was the expert griller, but I managed not to burn the thawing burger patties too badly. Didn't stop Danny and Rachel from complaining, though.

The sky above was streaked with thousands of stars that we never usually saw at night. It was kind of strange to see them all—I was so used to streetlights. With no other light to block them, the stars were amazingly bright. Together with the half-moon on the horizon, they bathed the street with soft, gentle light. It was brighter out here than it had been inside the house. I wasn't even sure I needed the flashlight—although it made *me* more visible. I didn't want to surprise Herb and risk being shot by a paranoid old paper pusher with a gun that I thought he only pretended not to know how to use properly. I really did have to talk to my mother about this.

Then I smelled Herb's cigar. I recognized the smell that often drifted from his backyard. Down the street, at the corner, I saw the ember of that cigar.

"Herb!" I shone my flashlight on him.

He waved and I walked over. He was in a lawn chair in the middle of the intersection. A bike, leaning on its kickstand, was beside him.

"Going to play a little baseball?"

I'd forgotten I was carrying the bat. "Yeah, wondered if you wanted to play."

"Night games don't work so well unless the lights do. What are you doing out here?"

"I thought you could use some company."

"I've had company all night as people have limped their way into the neighborhood."

"Have there been a lot?"

"Quite a few. Sitting here I can hear people coming from a long way off. I've biked out to meet them. The last few walked all the way from the city."

"That's thirty or forty miles. That would have taken them—"

"Most of the day and half the night," Herb said.

"And they've been all right?"

"Most have been exhausted and confused, but relieved at finally getting home—and eager to see their family members. They're all hungry and thirsty. I've given each one a bottle of water." He tapped a nearly empty case of water at his feet.

"That's nice of you."

"Most need it, but it also calms them down so they can talk. With all the local communications down, word of mouth is the only way I can know what's happening out there."

"And?"

"There have been acts of kindness. Some grocery stores have been handing out bottled water and pieces of fruit. Other people have given jackets and shoes, lent their bikes."

I got the sense he was telling only half the story. "But not everybody has been so nice, right?"

"Not everybody. There's been some looting of stores, electronics and valuables taken, rumors of jewelry store robberies. One guy who lives on Stonemason was mugged at knifepoint—he's pretty shaken up. I even heard about a couple of buildings that were on fire."

"Has anything happened up at our mini-mall?" There were a few stores over by the gas station.

"It's all safe. At this stage, one police officer making himself visible is assurance that everything will be fine."

"This stage?"

He didn't answer right away. "Adam, as long as people think things are going to recover quickly they won't panic."

"But you still don't think things are going to get better anytime soon."

"Here's the problem. It's not just that the lights are out and all our computer screens are dead. It's also all the computer-controlled tools and equipment that are used by first responders like police and EMS and fire departments to help people recover in an emergency. Like the vehicles to transport food and medical supplies. Or the trucks and tools used by the electric company to fix power outages. None of that's working."

"And you think people will act differently once it doesn't get fixed right away."

"Everything changes when people are desperate for water, food, when they're scared for the well-being of their children."

"But that couldn't happen here. We're too . . . um . . ."

"Civilized?"

I nodded my head.

"Civilized behavior is nothing more than a thin veneer. Once that's peeled away it can get ugly very quickly. I've seen it close up."

I didn't know what to say.

"You probably don't believe me."

I shook my head. "No, it isn't that I don't believe you. It's just that I hope you're wrong."

"I do, too." He paused. "In the morning I'll run a line over to your house so you can have electricity from my generator."

"That would be great. Maybe we won't even need it by then. I can hope."

"It's good to have hope," he said with a grim smile. "Right now I should go up and make sure our young police officer is doing fine. You should probably head back inside."

"I could wait here until you get back—that is, if you think it's necessary to have someone here."

"I wouldn't be out here if I didn't think it was." Herb climbed onto the bike. "I won't be long. Remember that discretion is the better part of valor."

"What?"

"Sometimes the bravest thing to do is run."

Herb rode away, getting smaller and darker until he vanished. I went to sit in the lawn chair and then stopped. I decided I'd feel better on my feet. I looked up and down the street and then for good measure did a complete three-sixty.

I started pacing into the intersection and then back again. Twenty steps up and twenty steps back. I rested the bat on my shoulder like a rifle. A rifle would have made me feel better. I *could* have a rifle. I knew where the key was to our gun cabinet, and I could be back here in a few minutes. But I wouldn't do that. I wouldn't give in to Herb's paranoia. There was no need for a gun—or even a bat.

I heard something from down the hill. It was somebody

coming, dragging their feet as they walked. I could hear them a long way off, just like Herb said. After a while, I could make out a faint image. It was one person. I retreated a few steps and circled around the chair until it was between me and the person. That didn't make any sense, taking refuge behind a piece of plastic lawn furniture, but somehow it still felt reassuring.

The man's head was down and he was moving slowly. He hadn't even noticed me yet. Wait, it wasn't a *he*—it was a woman and I recognized her. It was Mrs. Gomez from up the street.

"Hello," I called out as I turned on the flashlight.

She screamed and jumped. "Don't hurt me!"

"I'm so sorry! I didn't mean to—"

"Leave me alone!"

"It's *me*, Mrs. Gomez, it's *Adam*, Adam Daley, from down the street." I grabbed a bottle of water and took a few steps toward her.

"Adam . . . I'm so glad it's you." Her voice was hoarse.

"Here, take this." I handed her the water. She tipped it back, draining half the bottle.

"Thank you. I'm so thirsty and my feet hurt so much."

I panned the light down. She was shoeless and her feet were bleeding.

"What happened?"

"My heels were no good for walking. I came all the way from the city."

She looked like she was going to fall over. I took her arm, holding her up.

"I'll help you get home."

I led her up the street. Her steps were small and strained. "How'd it go out there?"

"Not good. I saw a man being mugged. For most of the time I stayed in a group, mainly women and a couple of men who were walking this way. It just seemed safer. One by one they dropped off as they reached their homes or had to go a different way. Nobody else was coming this far. I've been by myself the last hour. I was *so* scared."

"I'd be scared, too."

"I just wanted to get back to my family."

"Your husband and kids were out on the street earlier this evening. They were worried about you."

She started crying. We neared her house. She pulled out keys and tried to put them in the lock, but her hand was shaking so badly she couldn't do it.

"Let me help."

As I went to take the keys the front door opened up—Mr. Gomez rushed out and swept her into his arms. From behind them the kids appeared and they threw themselves at their mother, all four of them hugging and crying.

I felt awkward and started to walk away.

"Adam!"

I turned back.

"Thank you so much," Mrs. Gomez called out.

"Yes, thank you for bringing her home!" her husband said.

"I didn't do anything. I just walked her from the corner. I have to get back now."

"You're watching the street?"

"Herb is with me."

Mr. Gomez came out and shook my hand. "I'll get my

wife and kids settled, and then I'm going to come watch, too."

"It's all right—we can handle it."

"No, it's important that we pull together. I'll be there."

"Thanks." It would be good to have another person. Even if none of this was really needed.

6

I opened up one eye and then the other. I
was back on the living room couch, where I'd crashed after
Herb had sent me home for the night. Sunlight streamed
through the windows. There were soft voices and strong smells
coming from the kitchen. The voices were too quiet to make
out, but the smells were unmistakable—coffee and bacon.
Did that mean that we had electricity again? I looked over to
the DVD player—no little red light glowing meant there was
still no power from the wall sockets.

I got up and shuffled toward the kitchen. Before I'd
rounded the corner to see, I could make out Rachel's and
Danny's voices—and Mom's.

"You're home!" I said from the doorway.

It wasn't just Mom and the twins, but Herb and that officer, Brett, all sitting at the kitchen table.

"Good morning! Glad to see you're not sleeping away the
whole day," my mom said.

I looked at my watch. It wasn't eight yet. "It's not that late.
Besides, I was up most of the night."

"And your mother was up *all* of the night," she said.

"That makes two of us," Herb said.

"Three," Brett added.

"Come and sit down, have some coffee and breakfast," my mother said.

I noticed the extension cord leading in through the sliding glass door, snaking across the floor and up onto the counter, where it was connected to a toaster, the coffeemaker, and an electric skillet. Obviously this was the line coming from Herb's generator. I poured myself a nice hot cup of coffee and then put a few strips of bacon and a couple of pieces of toast onto a plate.

"How are things?" I asked.

"Considering all the potential for problems, things are going well, especially since I was short so many officers."

"Why so many?" I asked.

"Some have a long drive to work, so there's no way they could report for duty. With others I suspect that they were worried about their own families and stayed home."

"I can understand that," Herb said.

"So can I," my mother agreed. "I'm fortunate not only to live close but to have Adam to look after the kids."

"We don't need babysitting," Danny said.

"Yes, we do!" said Rachel. They were on the opposite sides of a lot of issues.

Herb smiled. "I'm just saying I understand these officers wanting to protect their families."

"I couldn't go home even if I wanted to," Brett said. "My parents are out west, and my house is well over an hour's drive."

"You're welcome to stay here as long as necessary," my mother said.

"I really appreciate that, Captain. I know a couple of the guys are sleeping at the station."

"And I'm grateful for that," my mother said. "We can't leave it unmanned."

"Brett did a fine job last night. It was helpful to have an officer standing post," Herb said.

"There are actually three others from the precinct who live right here in the neighborhood," my mother said. "And they've all reported in for duty."

"What if they didn't?" Herb asked.

"I'm sure they'll come. All three are veterans and—"

"I mean, what if you assigned them to patrol in this area instead?"

"Then I'd be down three more officers that I can't afford to lose."

"Not lose—*reassign*," Herb said. "With those officers, along with Brett, this whole area would be completely under control."

"And other areas would be less under control. I can't do that," my mother said. "I'd be accused of acting in the interests of my family and not of the whole community."

"Isn't this neighborhood a big sector of your precinct?" Herb said. "Four patrols could protect hundreds of houses, a couple thousand people, the stores and their supplies, the fuel at the gas station."

"Four officers on foot couldn't patrol all of that," Brett said.

"But four *patrols* that were mobile could," Herb said.

"What sort of transportation do you have in mind?" my mother asked.

"There are bicycles of course. And older vehicles as well as minibikes and dirt bikes that are still working. You could even double the coverage by allowing each officer to be partnered with a civilian. Sort of like Neighborhood Watch, but on wheels."

"That would certainly make it more doable," my mother said. "Although, obviously, none of those civilians involved in patrols could be armed."

I wondered how she'd feel about me carrying a baseball bat—or Herb packing heat.

"Only those legally registered to carry a firearm should be doing so," Herb agreed.

"Yes, people like yourself, who are licensed," my mother added.

So she already knew about his gun.

"Actually, I was thinking of borrowing your car today, Adam," my mother said.

"Sure thing," I said, even though the idea of somebody else—even her—using my car made me uneasy because it had always stalled out when other people tried to drive it.

"But I've thought better of it. Your car isn't reliable, and you seem to be the only one who can make it go. I'll figure out another option."

"I'll scout around the neighborhood if you'd like," Herb said. "Take an inventory of working vehicles."

"That would be appreciated. We could try taking an inventory here, and if it worked I might be able to apply the same thing to other parts of the precinct."

Mom was being completely relaxed and straightforward with Herb. I got the feeling that she really did appreciate his help around our neighborhood, while she considered her whole precinct.

"And since I'm looking I could also be trying to find some people who could establish nighttime checkpoints at key locations in the neighborhood," Herb said. "It would give your officers reassurance to know that their families are safe while they're out on patrol. Of course, I'd only do that with your permission."

My mother nodded. "I understand the reasoning for everything you're suggesting, Herb, but at this point I don't think it's necessary."

"Okay," he said. "But if you change your mind, I can put things into operation quickly."

"That's good to know," my mother said. "Thank you for thinking this through."

I was grateful she wasn't giving in to paranoid thought or overreaction. After all, the power hadn't been out for even twenty-four hours. It would be all right soon enough.

My mother got up from the table. "I'm pretty sure that I won't be back until tomorrow morning at the earliest. Adam, I know you'll look after your brother and sister while I'm gone."

"Do you want me to drive you to the station?" I asked.

"That would be wonderful. It *is* a long walk."

"If you don't mind I'd like to go along with you," Herb said. "Just to keep you company."

"I need to get some things from the station, so I should go, too," Brett said.

"There's enough room for the four of us," I said. "It would be okay to leave Danny and Rachel for a while, right?"

"For a while is no problem," my mother agreed.

"No problem," Danny said.

"A *little* while," Rachel added.

———————

I turned the key and my car started right up. Strange, but it seemed to be working better than it usually did. It was now pretty loaded down between the extra weight of three passengers and the working minibike and two trail bikes strapped into the trunk. My mother was going to have officers use them for patrol, and then she'd ride the minibike home at the end of her shift. Slowly I backed up, easing down the driveway so I wouldn't bottom out.

"I think your grandfather would be proud of how this old car of his is doing," my mother said with a laugh.

"I think we should all be proud of it," Herb said. "Sometimes things that have been retired can still do the job."

"I get the feeling you aren't just talking about the car," my mom said.

"You're right about that," Herb said, and we all chuckled.

I was surprised how many people were already on the street this early. Folks were outside talking in pairs or small groups. Normally the only people I'd ever seen at this hour were walking their dogs. Without exception, people stopped talking and watched as we passed by.

"This must be what it's like to drive a Ferrari or Lamborghini," I said.

"Especially since none of those cars would be working now," Brett said.

"Well, really old Ferraris would be working," I noted, heading west up Folkway toward the parkway.

I rolled through the stop sign at the top of the hill and looked over at the mini-mall. It didn't look normal at all. The parking lot was full of abandoned cars, and there were hundreds and hundreds of people milling about the stores.

"Are the stores open yet?" I asked.

"I'm not sure most of them are going to open at all," Herb said.

"Pull in," my mother ordered.

I cranked the wheel and we motored into the parking lot.

"Crowds this big make me nervous," Mom said. "We'll just stop and—"

There was a tremendous crash and the front window of the supermarket shattered into a million pieces. A roar went up from the crowd as it surged forward.

"Let us out!" my mother ordered, and I slammed on the brakes.

My mother and Brett jumped out. The two of them rushed toward the mob, which was pushing and shoving its way through the opening where the window had been. I watched Mom and Brett disappear into the store. I could almost feel the chaos from here. Things were out of control.

"Drive," Herb ordered.

"I'm not leaving!"

"You're not going anywhere. You just have to park and lock your car—hide it among the other vehicles—and then we can help."

"How can we—"

"Go!"

I pressed down on the accelerator, whipped around a corner and found an empty spot, pulled in, and turned off the engine.

"Roll up the windows and lock it," Herb said. His voice was calm again.

Quickly the windows went up and we climbed out, locking the car behind us. There was another tremendous crash, and I looked up to see that a second window had been broken, pieces of glass raining down, scattering the crowd before they rushed into the second opening.

"Stay right with me, Adam, right *behind* me," Herb said. His hand was on his pistol, still in its holster. As we rushed forward there were already people moving away, carrying cases of water and soda, arms full of cereal and boxes of cookies and bags of chips. There was a strange look on their faces, eyes wide open and glazed, like they were excited and scared and happy all at once. Where was my mother? Where was Brett?

There was a loud noise. "Get down!" Herb yelled.

He ducked and I did the same, almost hiding behind him.

"Is that gunfire?" A second shot rang out, and then a third. There was no mistaking that sound now. At once the crowd reacted—some froze in place and others started running. Herb stood straight while I still cowered, trying to hide behind him. I caught sight of Brett stepping out of the store through one of the shattered windows. My mother appeared in the second—there was blood flowing down her face from a cut on her scalp.

"Everybody stop!" my mother yelled. She aimed her gun in the air and fired another shot, and the entire crowd froze.

Brett was holding his revolver in one hand. In the other he had his baton. Herb had also unholstered his weapon. It was now in his hand by his side, his other hand cradling it, partially hiding it from view.

"Those inside the store need to leave!" my mother yelled out. "If you try to leave with stolen merchandise, you will be arrested and charged with looting and rioting. Get out and go home now!"

A man came out past her, and then another, and then a woman holding a small child by the hand. This woman had brought her kid along as she went into the store to loot!

People were leaving the store, but they weren't leaving the lot. If anything, there were more people coming, slowly walking toward the front of the store.

"This isn't over," Herb said to me quietly. "Come." We threaded our way through the crowd, and I noticed that his hand was now in his pants pocket, his pistol out of sight.

"We just want food and water!" a man called out, and the crowd reacted with a roar of agreement.

"This isn't the way to get it," my mother replied. Blood was dripping down the side of her face.

"Then what *is* the way?" somebody else yelled. The crowd was now becoming louder, pressing closer again.

"We have a right to food and water!" another person in the crowd yelled, and again the crowd reacted. They were going from crowd to mob again, right before my eyes. My mother wiped her face with her hand.

Herb stepped forward until he was standing beside my mother. He whispered in her ear a moment and she nodded. Then he spoke to the crowd. "Folks, you do deserve food and water. And I know how you can get it!"

"Let's hear it!" a voice called.

I wanted to hear it, too, but I also wanted to know about my mother. I sidled past Herb until I stood right behind her.

"Are you okay?" I whispered.

"Fine, just a little cut—nothing. A piece of glass. You know how head cuts can bleed." She turned to the crowd. "Let's listen to my friend here. His name is Herb."

"You'll all be able to purchase some water and food from this store," Herb continued.

"What if we don't have cash?" somebody called out. "We can't get any from the banks, and credit cards aren't working!"

"A credit system, an honor system will be arranged where some merchandise will be given out on the promise that you'll pay once power is restored," Herb announced.

"He's not authorized to make that offer!" a man exclaimed as he stepped out of the store. "I'm the manager, and he has no right to—"

"Shut up and listen," my mother snapped. She turned to Herb. "Go on."

"We need you all to stay calm and orderly," Herb said. "I know you're good people and want to do the right thing. Here's how it will work. There will be a line, and it will start over there, right by the sign on the street."

As one, the crowd turned and looked in the other direction. The entire mob had become a group of obedient children. Herb was controlling the group like a magician.

"I want you all to know that you have my word that things will be distributed fairly so that everybody who is present now in this parking lot will receive supplies."

I looked at my mother. Her quizzical expression mirrored

my thoughts—how is he going to do that? But he sounded so calm, so matter-of-fact that I believed him, and judging from the reaction, so did the crowd.

"Okay, slowly now, women with children and older people move forward and then in just a minute I want the rest of you to make an orderly line over there by the sign. And remember, we're all civilized people, and the best way to care for your family is to respect other people's rights to care for their families."

The crowd started reorganizing itself. A line was forming while old-timers and some women with kids moved toward us.

"He has no right to—" the manager started to say again, but my mother cut him off.

"Inside," she ordered.

He hesitated and then did what she said, the broken glass on the floor sounding under his feet.

"Herb, can you come in, too, and explain how this is going to work?" my mother asked.

"It's not complicated," Herb said.

She turned to Brett. "Stay out here—watch."

Brett stood on the sidewalk, and I followed Herb and my mother into the store. Along with the broken glass on the floor there were bags and boxes and cans and displays that had been knocked over.

"Listen, I know you're just trying to help, but you had no right to say those things," the manager said. He sounded anxious and scared.

"I'm Captain Daley, and I have the right in civil emergencies to do many things," my mother said. "And he is acting as my deputy."

Herb held out his hand to the man. "I'm Herb, and who are you?"

"Ernie Williams."

"Ernie, I know how difficult this all is. I can only imagine how you felt when those people crashed through your window and started rampaging."

"It was terrifying! I was afraid that somebody would have killed me if I tried to stop them."

"Mobs can get out of control like a forest fire. You had every right to be terrified, Ernie. If you tried to stop them they could have hurt you."

I noticed how he let the "hurt" part sink in.

"Please, don't get me wrong, I'm grateful that you stopped it, but what's going to happen when they realize that we can't do what you said?" Ernie asked.

"Oh, but we are going to do it," Herb said.

"I can't just give away food without people paying. It isn't my store—I'm just the manager!"

"Ernie," Herb said as he placed a reassuring hand on his shoulder. "Nobody is asking you to give things away. You're going to get cash where you can and enough information from people who don't have cash so that you can get them to pay later. Isn't that what a credit card does?"

"I guess it *is* sort of like an IOU."

"You're also only going to allow them to purchase selected items. Look around the store. With the electricity out there is a lot of food that's going to go bad today."

"It's a nightmare—what a waste of inventory," Ernie said.

"And you're not going to allow that to happen. You're going to turn these things that were going to be thrown out into profit for your company. You'll make your company money, and when this is all over the customers will remember you as the guy who helped keep their families fed. You're going to be a hero to everybody. They'll be loyal to your store from now on."

He put his arm around Ernie and walked him over to the opening so that he could see the line forming. "Wouldn't you rather be their hero than their victim?"

"But how do we do it?" Ernie asked.

"How many people do you have in the store to help you?"

"Usually more than a dozen. Today only two came in. Counting myself that makes three."

"And if you add in me and young Adam here you have five. And I recognized a few other people out in that line who can help. They can stay when I send everybody else home," Herb said.

"You're going to send them home?" my mother asked. "I'm not sure that's such a good idea."

"They won't be going empty-handed. Ernie, I want you to go to the back and get that thing from the deli that gives people a number to be served. Then you and I are going to go through that line out there and give each person a number. We're going to ask them to come back at a specific time. It's better to deal with people a few at a time, and by giving out numbers we get to know how many people are out there and how we have to divvy up the supplies."

"And we're only giving them some things, right?" Ernie asked.

"Yes, you're going to allow them to purchase all of the things that are going to go bad if they're not eaten. Meats that aren't completely frozen, dairy products like milk and yogurt and butter and ice cream, frozen vegetables that are thawing out."

"What about fruits and vegetables that will go bad?" Ernie added. "Can I sell those as well?"

"Now you're thinking. Let's also sell them a small quantity of bottled water if you run out of other liquids. There should be no sale of nonperishables—anything that's canned, boxed, dried, or otherwise packaged so that it can survive without refrigeration. Can you do all of that?" Herb asked.

"I can do it!"

"Good, then you get your people and we'll make it all happen!" Herb said.

Ernie rushed off.

Now there was orderly action inside the store and out in front. Brett was organizing the first group of shoppers into a line.

"That was amazing," my mother said to Herb. "The way you handled everything, *everybody*."

"Without you taking charge in the first place I couldn't have done what I did."

"It was like with those guys trying to steal my car yesterday," I said.

My mother turned to me. She looked shocked. I'd just made a mistake.

"It was nothing," I said. "It was more like a misunderstanding."

"It was more than that, but your son and I handled it," Herb said. "And together we can handle the situation here. We can keep this all under control for now, but once night hits it's going to get worse. We really could use those officers, patrols, and checkpoints."

She didn't answer right away. But after a few moments it was clear she'd changed her mind about his earlier request. "I'll have the four officers report here by six p.m. I'll leave it with you to connect them with their civilian partners and then figure out their patrol routes." She paused and smiled. "You already have the routes figured out, don't you?"

Herb returned the smile. "It's not just Boy Scouts who need to be prepared."

"You know, Herb, those people out there, I know a lot of them—they're my neighbors, people whose kids play soccer and baseball with my kids. I never would have guessed it could have turned so bad so quickly."

"Bad can happen in the blink of an eye."

"If I hadn't seen it I wouldn't have believed it. I'm grateful for your help here today. Perhaps we can talk later about how I might utilize your skills more."

"I'm at your disposal. Anything you need I'm under your command," Herb said. "Now, we better get you to the station. How's the cut?"

She put her hand up to touch it. The blood had stopped flowing but was still dried on her face and matting her hair on one side. "I'd forgotten about it. It's stopped bleeding."

"You should clean up. Your officers shouldn't see you that way," Herb said. "I'll work with Ernie to organize and then help with the food distribution. Does that sound like a plan?"

"I guess it's the best plan we have," my mother said.

7

The line was never long. They kept coming in small groups, sticking to the assigned times. Those who were early stood off to the side patiently, while those in line waited equally patiently.

After we returned from dropping my mom at the station, Herb and I drove to the house to get the twins and then came back and helped, giving out the items as Ernie totaled and either took money or an IOU from the customer. As the supplies on the tables outside the store dwindled, more were brought out to restock. Nobody other than us was allowed into the store. That was the way Herb had sorted it all out.

Everybody in line got the same things: a piece of meat of one kind or another, a dozen eggs, a carton of milk or a container of frozen juice, a couple of pieces of fruit, and either a half stick of butter or a container of yogurt. It was enough to keep a family fed for today and maybe part of tomorrow. It was clear that a lot of people hadn't thought about stockpiling food in their homes before this. We were lucky—my mother had done a big shopping the day before yesterday. I'd complained about bringing in all those bags. Now I was just grateful.

The grocery store wasn't the only thing open. The walk-in

clinic was seeing patients, and the pharmacy was selling over-the-counter drugs and filling some prescriptions. Like the supermarket, they weren't allowing customers in but were doing business from the front entranceway.

The variety store—which had sold out of batteries, flash-lights, and candles yesterday—was open for business, too. Milk, ice cream, and anything else that was going to melt or spoil was being hustled outside to be sold at a table. The own er was selling, reluctantly, at the regular cost. He had tried to bump up the prices, selling water and bread and everything else he had at three times the usual price. There was a lot of complaining, but people were desperate and were paying. That's when Herb stepped in.

Along with Brett he went over to talk to the owner. After-ward Brett told me about it. Herb had told the man, quietly, that aside from charges of profiteering that he'd personally make sure were investigated, nobody would forget what he'd done. Herb told him that they'd drive him out of business once things returned to usual—assuming he had a business. He said that nobody could be responsible if angry people broke his windows and looted his store. The prices came right back down.

The bakery sold off every single thing in the store. Unlike the guy at the variety store, they even sold bread and rolls at reduced price, as day-olds. I thought that showed class.

Maybe the strangest thing was that half the people were eating ice cream. The owner of the Baskin-Robbins, with Danny and Rachel thrilled to be helping him at the counter, was giving out small servings in paper cups. Since the black-out began, he'd been running his freezer off a gas-powered generator, but he was out of fuel and was giving up the fight. The ice cream was all going to melt, but the cones themselves weren't going to spoil. He told Ernie that it was almost all covered by insurance anyway, so he wanted to promote goodwill with his customers.

Between the children in strollers, wagons being pulled, kids on bikes, neighbors visiting in line, and of course the ice cream being consumed, it seemed like a picnic or a school carnival out in the parking lot.

Brett, looking official and I thought a little bit nervous, walked up and down along the pavement, one hand on his gun, the baton in the other. Part of me didn't think that was necessary. The other part remembered what had just happened. These people, my neighbors, had been rioting and looting. It was like a lightbulb being turned on and then off again. We had to keep it turned off.

Herb disappeared inside the supermarket for a while, sleeping on a couch in the staff lounge. Out of sight, but close enough to hear and act if something happened. Having organized everything, he said he needed to get some sleep and be ready for tonight. He was pretty old and had been going hard since the blackout began. After seeing him in action I couldn't help but wonder again what kind of paper pusher he had been.

8

"**We have to do this as quickly as possible,**" Sergeant Evans said. "It's going to be dark in less than an hour, so everybody has to be out on patrol by then."

Assembled in our living room were four police officers, Brett, Sergeant Evans, Officer O'Malley, and Howie; the four civilian partners, including Mr. Gomez; and me and Herb. I'd volunteered to be one of the civilian partners, but they felt it should only be adults. Besides, I guess I really was on patrol taking care of the twins. My mom was at the station. While we were trying to protect this neighborhood, she was trying to safeguard the whole precinct.

"I have to apologize for the motley collection of vehicles you're going to be using for your patrols," Herb said. On our driveway were three minibikes, a go-cart, two little gas-powered scooters, and two dirt bikes.

"It's a lot better than what we've been using," Sergeant Evans said.

"Might be fun to ride a go-cart," Brett added.

"Hey, rook; what makes you think you're getting the go-cart?" Officer O'Malley asked. "I was thinking that little pink scooter was for you."

The others laughed.

"Especially if we can slap on a couple of training wheels," O'Malley added.

"This *rookie* could ride with me anytime, O'Malley," Herb said. "The kid has handled himself like a veteran last night and today."

That stopped the laughing and Brett looked relieved, maybe even a little proud. Herb was being nice to Brett, but I got the feeling it was more than that. It was sort of like a coach talking up a kid who necessarily didn't hit so well so that the next time up at bat he'd have more confidence.

"There are two checkpoints manned by civilians," Sergeant Evans said. He pointed to a map of the area taped to our kitchen cupboard. "The checkpoints are here and at the top of the neighborhood, right by the intersection with Erin Mills Parkway, where they can watch both the stores in the mini-mall and the gas station."

"Both checkpoints have eight people," Herb said.

"Although they have bats or clubs, they were told not to engage anybody in a fight," Sergeant Evans explained. "They are to question anybody trying to enter the neighborhood, stop them if they have questions, and if necessary try to detain them until one of the patrols arrives."

"I'm a bit worried about somebody trying to loot at the mall," Herb said. "We need that carefully watched and patrolled."

Arrangements had been made to nail sheets of plywood over the broken plate-glass windows of the supermarket, and Ernie and another employee were staying overnight as watchmen.

"But that pharmacy is also a target, as is that gigantic gas tanker sitting in the station across the street," Herb said.

"He's right," Sergeant Evans said. "Howie, I want you and your partner to make sure you buzz through that checkpoint at least every fifteen minutes."

"Sure, Sarge, will do."

I knew Howie. He and his family lived in the neighborhood. He was big—almost gigantic—but he was a friendly giant who liked to joke around.

"Remember, those checkpoints can't possibly stop anybody coming in off Mullet Creek or through the woods, or even through the back of the school yard," Sergeant Evans explained.

"That's why one of the patrols needs to make regular passes through the field underneath the high-voltage electrical towers that buffers the houses from the highway," Herb added.

"My patrol will handle that," O'Malley said. "That field backs onto my house, so I know it pretty well. That's where I run my dogs and play catch with my kids."

"Excellent, but just remember we have fifteen hundred houses in this sector because we're going to patrol over to the other side of Erin Mills Parkway right to Winston Churchill and south all the way to Dundas," Sergeant Evans explained.

"Are there any civilian checkpoints in any of those other places?" Brett asked.

"Nothing," Sergeant Evans said. "We have to patrol those neighborhoods, but I want you all to remember where you live, where your families are."

Everybody silently nodded in agreement.

"I also want you to remember that I don't want any dead heroes. The only backup you have is the man beside you. If you can't control or contain a situation, you get away. Come back, get another patrol, but don't—I repeat, don't—attempt it alone. As for the civilians, you do what you're told, you just follow orders."

"You can count on it," Mr. Gomez said, and the others agreed.

"Now let's get going, and let's be safe out there."

Everybody got up and walked out of the room. Herb didn't move—he seemed to be lost in thought—so I stayed put as well. Finally he startled, almost as if he had just noticed they had left, and got up. I trailed after him out the door and onto the driveway.

The four patrols were mounting up. It was almost comical watching the eight men—four in uniform—climb onto or into the little vehicles. The engines started one by one, and the noise was overwhelmingly loud. None of this seemed real. Instead it was like a bad skit on *SNL* or that part of a parade where the Shriners drive those little cars among the floats. But in reality these were the men protecting our entire neighborhood and the neighborhoods beside and below it. All those houses and thousands of people were depending on four cops and four volunteers riding on things that could have been borrowed from a track at an amusement park.

In pairs they slowly started off. People were all out on the streets, some drawn by the noise, and as the group passed they started clapping and cheering. It *was* like a parade.

They reached the corner of Folkway Drive, and one pair headed up the hill toward the mini-mall. The two dirt bikes went off-roading straight north toward the field that held the high-voltage electrical towers alongside the interstate. And two other pairs went down the hill to the east end of Sawmill Valley Road, which looped around the opposite side of our subdivision. The exhaust fumes lingered in the air as the noise dropped off. In the absence of other sounds the high-pitched whine of the dirt bikes could be heard long after they'd disappeared, until finally that faded to nothing as well.

"We're in a lot better shape than we were last night," I said to Herb.

"We *have* to be better each night to stay even."

"Because you think each night is going to get worse, right?"

"Either things get fixed or they get worse."

He didn't need to say anything else. I knew what he was thinking, even if I wasn't ready to believe he was right.

9

The next morning I walked outside to check the weather. It was overcast and warm. I was glad we weren't having a cold spring this year, so heating wasn't an issue. Two little minibikes sat in the driveway. Brett was upstairs sleeping in our guest room. He'd told me before he turned in that none of the patrols ran into anything too bad. Maybe what had happened at the mini-mall was a one-time thing, I decided.

Almost on cue, Herb came out of his house.

"Good morning," he called out. "What would you think about a little drive?"

"Do you need more supplies for your pool?" I asked.

He laughed. "I might have a lot more chlorine than I need right now."

"So where are we driving to?"

"Just around. I need to see what's going on out there. Do you have anyplace in particular you'd like to go?" he asked.

"Well, I'd like to check on a friend."

"We could go out to her farm," Herb said.

I gave him a questioning look. How did he know what I was thinking about?

"I'm just not sure if I should go that far and leave the kids here."

"We could take them along," Herb said. "Rachel told me you promised to bring her horseback riding out there."

"I did, but I'm not sure what my mother would say."

"She asked you, and me, to watch them, so we'll watch them. She didn't say anything about watching them here."

"But is it safe?" I asked.

"It's safe. We could even bring along somebody else."

"I'm sure Todd would come," I said. "He's probably already getting restless."

"I was thinking Brett," Herb said. "Although we could bring them both."

"We could." An extra person would be good—especially one with a gun. I was allowed to be a little paranoid.

"How much gas do you have?"

"Not much."

"Good, because the gas station is the first place I want to stop."

"But the pumps don't work," I said.

"Gas can be siphoned up from the storage tanks. Tell the twins. Then you go and get Todd, and I'll meet you out on your driveway in thirty minutes."

———————

Danny didn't want to come, telling me that since he wasn't a girl, he wasn't interested in riding any horses. I wasn't a girl either, but a girl was certainly motivating me to ride a horse. I'd never actually ridden one before, but how hard could it be?

With Danny in tow, I'd gone down the street to Todd's

house. His mother was puttering in the garden and she agreed to watch Danny. He actually seemed happy to help her in the garden. Todd's father was in his woodworking shop in the garage and waved as I went in the front door. He was a banker by profession but a master craftsman with wood. Using hand tools, he'd made half the furniture in their house—including the bed Todd was sleeping in when I got there. I woke him up and he declined my offer by tossing a pillow at me, swearing, turning on his side, and pulling the covers over his head.

Herb and Brett were waiting as I walked back to the house alone. Rachel was still inside trying to find something horsey to wear.

"While you're waiting, I was wondering if we could take a look at your ultralight," Herb said.

"You have a plane?" Brett asked.

"My dad and I are assembling it, so it's not quite finished yet. I'll show you."

I opened the garage door. It sat on a trolley waiting for the wings to be added. I couldn't help thinking about my father, hoping that he was all right, wishing he was here to take care of us. Strange, but I felt like if he had been here that we'd be safer, somehow.

"Doesn't look like much," Brett said.

"You don't need much to fly," I said, suddenly feeling defensive. It wasn't just his words but the look on his face.

"You've flown it?" he asked in amazement.

"I've flown *in* one—it was a two-man ultralight just like this, and my dad was at the controls. You use them for training."

"That's right—your father is a pilot," Brett said.

"And so is Adam," Herb said.

"I'm still a few lessons away from my solo, but soon, you know, when things get back to normal."

"Your ultralight doesn't have computers, does it?" Herb asked.

"None. Everything is simple. It even runs on automotive fuel. It could get up into the air."

"You know, being able to fly would be a huge advantage," Herb continued.

I thought about my father again. If he was here we could get it into the air almost immediately and he could fly it. Then I thought about if the ultralight was with him. Even halfway across the country he could fly home in a few days, a week at most.

"All that's left is to attach the wings, and it could be up there," I said.

"Are they difficult to fly?" Herb asked.

"They're not that difficult if you already know how to fly," I explained. "You learn in a plane with a pilot, and then once you know what you're doing you can fly an ultralight."

"So, technically, you could fly this thing," he said.

"Technically, yes."

"Very interesting."

A chill went up my spine. Was he suggesting that I fly it? But then again, that was why Dad and I were building it, to fly it. Flying an ultralight without training was difficult, dangerous, and maybe even a little crazy, but I'd certainly spent enough time on an ultralight simulator and I did know the controls of this thing as well as any pilot except my father. I *could* fly it.

"But first things first—let's go for that drive. Brett, you're carrying, right?" Herb asked.

Brett, who was wearing civilian clothes, pulled open his jacket to reveal a badge on his belt and his service revolver in a side holster. "I try never to leave home without it."

"I'm ready to go!" Rachel called out as she rounded the corner.

"Then we better get going," Herb said. "We need to get back before dark."

Rachel climbed into the backseat of the Omega along with Brett, and Herb was in the passenger seat.

I was backing out of my driveway when somebody appeared in my rearview mirror and I slammed on the brakes. It was Todd, and he came to my open window.

"Are you trying to get yourself run over?" I asked.

"Not only can I move faster than your car, but if it did hit me it probably would have broken or stalled out," he joked.

"Don't insult the best car in the neighborhood."

"Think again. That judge over on Trapper Crescent has a '57 Chevy and Mr. Langston on Wheelwright drives a '66 Camaro. He gave my dad and me a ride yesterday."

"Okay, fine, *one* of the best cars in the neighborhood."

"I changed my mind. I'm coming along," Todd said. "Once you woke me up I was instantly bored. If I'm not careful my mother will have me working in the garden or babysitting your little brother. Parents are so much easier to deal with when they go away to work."

Before I could even think to answer he pulled open my door, shoved my seat forward so that I was squished into the steering wheel, and climbed into the back.

"We're going horseback riding," Rachel said.

"Fantastic. I hate horses, but I'm feeling a little claustrophobic."

I was happy enough to have him along, and not just because he was my friend. Another person, another big person, could only help.

We rumbled up the street and past the mini-mall. With the exception of the plywood covering two of the windows of the supermarket, it looked normal. I knew Ernie would be open for food distribution later that day. It would follow the same pattern. Nobody would go hungry in the neighborhood, and because of the system Herb had put in place it would all be orderly.

The checkpoint was just up ahead. They'd taken patio furniture from the nearby houses and set it down in the middle of the intersection. There were lots of people there—more than the eight men assigned—women and children, including a few kids riding bikes and some playing Frisbee. It was like they'd set up a picnic in the middle of the street.

"Quite a little street party going on," Herb said.

"Do you want them to stop?" Brett asked.

"No, it's probably better this way. More people being there provides more protection. Let them enjoy."

I tapped on my horn and everybody turned to us. A couple of the men on the line waved, and then four others picked up a picnic table and moved it out of the way so we could pass. I eased through the intersection and turned into the gas station. I drove around the big tanker truck and went to pull in beside one of the pumps.

"No, park it right in front," Herb said.

I came to a stop beside the entrance. Herb climbed out. He had a big smile on his face and waved to the man inside, who gave a little wave and a nervous smile in reply.

"Open the door!" Herb called out. "We need a fill-up."

Reluctantly the man came to the door and opened it a crack. "Sorry, but without electricity there are no pumps."

"We could siphon up the gas, and of course we'd pay. Straight cash." Herb produced a thick wad of cash from his pocket.

"With that amount of money you could buy half the gas in that tanker truck!" the man exclaimed.

"It's probably a stroke of bad luck for you that that truck was here when everything stopped working."

"It's not my truck, but now it's like I'm responsible for it."

"And it's bad enough that you have to be responsible for all of the gas in the holding tanks below. How big are your tanks?"

"Between regular, ultra, and diesel they can hold almost twelve thousand gallons."

"What's in there now?" Herb asked.

"Close to ten thousand. I don't even know why the truck was here to begin with. My tanks weren't low enough to need a refill."

"This fuel makes you a target for looters and vandals," Herb said.

"That's why I've been sleeping in the building. Somebody has to watch it."

"I guess so. Now let's get some of that gas in our tank."

———————

We drove away and the man waved and offered a big smile. Herb and the gas station manager had used a piece of garden hose and a foot pump to siphon the gas from the holding tanks and into my car. While that was happening Herb had talked to the man, Mr. Singh, about buying more gas—much more gas—had gotten to know him, and had offered for the sentries at the intersection to help watch the station and for the police patrols to go past regularly. He'd also gotten a candy bar for each of us.

Herb had done a lot more than just fill my tank.

10

"Slow down," Herb said, "but keep rolling."

I eased my foot off the gas pedal.

Brett leaned over the seat and I braked lightly as we came up to a burned-out vehicle right in the middle of the road.

"That's what we call a barbecue," Brett said. "Somebody torched it."

There was nothing left but the blackened metal skeleton of the car's frame.

"But why would somebody do that?"

"Some people are just stupid and looking for kicks," Herb said.

"How would they even do it?" Rachel asked from the backseat.

"It's easy. They pry open the gas tank, stuff a piece of cloth in, light the end on fire, and then run like hell," Brett explained. "I saw another one last night. I'm surprised we haven't seen more."

As we passed by, an acidic burning smell seeped into our windows.

"What would happen if somebody did the same thing with that gas tanker up at the service station?" I asked.

"It would be quite the show. There'd be a huge explosion

with a deadly fireball and shock waves that would knock down nearby buildings. We need to do something about that tanker," Herb said.

"We could bring it into the neighborhood," I said.

"But wouldn't it be better to take it farther away from our houses, not closer?" Rachel asked. She sounded anxious.

"Adam's right. If it's in the neighborhood it can be protected by the patrols and the checkpoints so nobody can get to it," Herb explained. "Besides, it would guarantee that we have a source of fuel for the patrols for a long time."

"How much gas do you think eight or so little two-stroke engines and a few cars need?" Brett asked.

"And how long do you think we're going to need them?" Todd asked.

"I guess I'm just being a silly old coot about all of this. It's really just a safety precaution," Herb said.

They looked a bit reassured, but I had a feeling that he'd revealed too much and then backtracked. He was lots of things, but a silly old coot wasn't one of them. I couldn't help but wonder if he'd heard more news on the shortwave that he hadn't shared.

We crossed Highway 403 on the overpass. Below us were lots of abandoned cars. The overpass took us across the sort of unofficial boundary between the suburbs and the countryside. Lori's farm wasn't far from here, but it was like a different world.

We continued down the road until we came to the lane leading to the farm. I turned and slowed to a crawl even though I felt like racing up the drive to see her. Up ahead a hay wagon blocked our progress. We coasted to a stop right in front of it. I turned off the car and Brett, Herb, and I climbed out. Herb asked Todd to stay in the backseat with Rachel until he gave the all clear.

"I guess we walk the rest of the way," I said. "Maybe I should honk the horn to let them know we're here."

"I think they know that already," Herb said. "Just wait."

The words were hardly out of his mouth when I caught a hint of motion off to the side. It was Lori's father—he was walking toward us carrying a shotgun, barrel toward the ground. Herb didn't seem surprised to see the weapon, though I saw Brett's hand move closer to his holstered side-arm.

"Say hello, son," Herb whispered.

"Hey, Mr. Peterson, my name's Adam. I'm a friend of Lori's."

The man stopped and stared a moment, then waved, and everybody relaxed.

"I recognized the car from when you dropped her off," he called out. "I have to apologize for the gun. I don't usually greet people armed like this. But at the moment you can't be too careful."

He introduced himself as "Stan" and he shook hands with everybody. He did look sort of like a Stan.

"Completely understandable," Herb said. "That was pretty smart to have the trip wire on the lane."

What was he talking about?

"As we drove in I saw it before we rolled over it," Herb explained.

"It's attached to sleigh bells up in the house," Mr. Peterson confirmed.

"Always good to know if somebody's coming," Herb said. "Just like it's wise to be armed. Both Brett and I have guns with us, and Brett here is a police officer. Now, Mr. Peterson, could you do me a *big* favor and ask your wife to lower her weapon? It's always a little unnerving to have a high-powered rifle trained on you."

He'd seen something else we hadn't seen.

Mr. Peterson nodded. "Susie, it's okay!" he yelled. "Come on out."

From the other direction a woman carrying a scoped rifle stepped from behind a bush. She looked like an older version of Lori.

"I have to apologize again," she said, "but we have to be careful."

"No need to apologize. It's just being wise given the circumstances," Herb said.

Lori came rushing out from behind the hay wagon. "I told you it was just Adam!" she said. "There's nothing to worry about—he's my friend."

She threw her arms around me and gave me a big hug. I was so shocked I couldn't even think to hug back.

"Really, pointing a gun at my friend," Lori said to her father.

"You need to be suspicious of anybody coming down your driveway," Herb said.

Her father shook his head. "Sixteen and they think they know everything."

"Well, at least there's a cure for that," Herb said. "Getting older."

He turned and gave a wave at the car. Todd and Rachel

climbed out and came over. Lori gave Todd a hug, too, and I introduced my sister to her parents.

"We had some other company last night," Mr. Peterson said. "I had to fire off a couple of rounds."

"What happened?" Brett asked. Slipping instantly into cop mode, he pulled back his jacket to reveal his gun and badge.

"It was probably just some people looking for food, but I can't take any chances."

"And you fired at them?" Brett asked.

"Not *at* them, just to warn them, chase them away. Of course this morning I see that I didn't fire fast enough. There are half a dozen chickens missing."

"Are the horses all right?" Rachel asked.

"They're fine," Lori said.

"The horses and the cows stayed in the barn with me last night," her dad said. "I guess I have to take the chickens out of the coop and put them in there as well."

"Did you come to go horseback riding?" Lori asked Rachel, who smiled and nodded.

"Would that be all right, Dad?" Lori asked.

"Of course. I just don't want the two of you going too far from the house without somebody to watch you."

"I could go with them," Brett volunteered. "That is, if you have a third horse."

"They do have three!" Rachel exclaimed.

"Actually, I thought that maybe . . ." I started to say.

"It would be wonderful to have you go along with them, Brett," Mr. Peterson said before I could finish. "It may sound paranoid, but it'd be comforting for me to know that they had a police escort. You know how to ride?"

"I was born and raised on a farm," Brett said. "I learned to ride a horse before I learned to ride a tricycle. I may be a cop now, but I'm a hayseed at heart."

Mr. Peterson laughed and put an arm around Brett's shoulders. "Then it's even better to have you around. Come on, son!"

He led Brett, Lori, and Rachel away to the barn; Todd and I trailed behind.

"I figure that isn't *exactly* how you imagined this was going to play out," Todd whispered. "Very smooth on your part, *very* smooth."

"Not another word or you're going to have a long walk home."

Rachel looked happy but a little nervous on top of her horse. Lori looked comfortable—and beautiful. Brett looked like he was on a poster for some cowboy-style cologne from Ralph Lauren.

"Lori, I want you to stay away from the woods and the trails that are close to the road," Mr. Peterson said.

"Yes, Dad."

"And listen to Brett here."

"*Okay*, Dad," Lori said.

The three of them set off, leaving the rest of us out in the yard in front of the house.

"I think we might have some pie in the kitchen, right, Susie?" Mr. Peterson said.

"Freshly made in the farmhouse's original woodstove, and

still steaming," she said. "Enough for everybody to have at least two pieces."

"That would be great!" Todd said.

"Actually, why don't you go inside and have a piece, maybe even a second." Mr. Peterson turned to me. "Lori mentioned that you're handy with tools."

"He's good with *almost* everything," Todd said.

I ignored the crack. "Herb is pretty good, too," I added.

"I've got a problem with one of the mowers and could use help fixing it. Could you two give me a hand?"

"Our pleasure," Herb said.

Todd headed off to the kitchen with Mrs. Peterson, and Herb and I followed Mr. Peterson. Not only wasn't I going to spend time with Lori, but I wasn't even going to get any pie.

"It sounds like things are getting tough out there," Mr. Peterson said as we walked along. "I was hopeful that a police officer would have more information."

He'd been asking Brett all sorts of questions as they were saddling up the horses, none of which Brett had answers for.

"You know, Adam's mother is Brett's commanding officer," Herb said.

"Really?" Mr. Peterson said, sounding surprised. "I'd like to ask her if she could send some patrols out this way."

"I know she'd want to help, but your place is beyond her jurisdiction and she's pretty short-staffed," I said.

Herb let out a big sigh. "I don't want to be the one to bear bad news, Stan, but let's be honest, there are no signs of anything being restored. There have been assaults and looting, and the police are pretty well powerless to do anything."

Herb wasn't saying anything Mr. Peterson didn't already

know. "I told my wife we can't count on anybody except our-selves," he said.

"Farmers are pretty good at being self-sufficient. You have plenty of water, right?"

"We have a well we use whenever there's a problem with the regular water supply."

"Excellent. I want you to know that I have lots of chlorine and I can give you enough to make your drinking supply safe for consumption."

He'd emphasized the word "give," but I could tell he was going into negotiating mode. What was he after now?

"I really appreciate your offer," Mr. Peterson said. "Very neighborly, but our water is completely safe for drinking."

"And you have enough?"

"There's enough for us, our animals, and even our vegeta-ble garden."

"That's one of the things I miss by living in the suburbs," Herb said. "My folks lived out in the country and we always had a garden when I was growing up. We grew most of what my family needed for the year."

"Our kitchen garden here is probably a lot bigger than that. My wife cans and preserves some, and we have a cold cellar for potatoes and carrots. It provides for us all year, and we sell the excess at a stall at the top of the lane all through the summer season."

"I assume you have at least one functioning tractor," Herb said.

"Yeah, how did you know?"

"You didn't drag that hay wagon down the drive without a tractor. You have a generator as well?"

"Yep, we do."

"It's the rare farm without one. Obviously, be careful with lights at night," Herb said. "With no other lights out there, you'd be visible for a long way."

"That's good thinking," Mr. Peterson said.

"That may have been how those people found you last night. Think of moths to a flame."

"We'll be careful of that tonight."

"Water, livestock, and food don't just make you self-sufficient—they make you a target. This is a lot of property to defend, although there are things you could do to make it easier for yourself."

"Such as?"

"For starters your hay wagon on the driveway needs to be moved."

"How come?" I asked. "It stopped us from driving up to the house."

"There aren't enough moving vehicles to have to worry much about that," Herb answered, then turned back to Mr. Peterson. "Your biggest worry is somebody using it as cover to open fire on your house."

Mr. Peterson looked startled. "I hadn't really thought of that."

Who would have—other than Herb? I didn't know whether to be impressed or worried that he was being a little too paranoid again.

"And I noticed those bales of barbed wire behind the barn. Those could be used to put up some additional fencing around the back of the house and garden to provide a perimeter defense."

"That would be good if I had the manpower to put it up. There's only me, my wife, and Lori."

"Would a fourth set of hands help?" I asked.

"What do you have in mind?" Mr. Peterson asked.

"I could stay and work on it today."

"You'd do that?"

"Sure, if it would help," I said.

"Well, I believe it would. Thank you, son."

"Herb could take my car and drive everybody else home when the riders get back."

"It might not work to have somebody come out and get you later today," Herb said.

"I could stay the night, if that's okay with you," I said to Mr. Peterson. I was happy to help him, but I didn't think he needed to know I was also more than happy to have some time with his daughter.

"That'd be just fine. Do you think your parents will be all right with this?"

"They'll be fine," I said. I told him about my dad being halfway across the country, and Herb said he'd look after the twins. He'd also talk to my mom when he saw her. And then he said something I didn't want to hear.

"Adam, I'm not sure if leaving just you here is the best idea," Herb said. "If four would help, then five would be better. Do you have space for two overnight guests?"

"You'd stay, too?" Mr. Peterson asked.

"I've got to get back, and so does Brett, but I don't think anybody would mind if Todd stays on as well. I can let Todd's parents know when I get home."

I minded, but what could I say? Having more help

suited Mr. Peterson just fine. If Todd hadn't been inside stuffing his face with pie, I knew exactly the look he'd be giving me.

"It's settled, then," the farmer said. "Now let's go take a look at that mower. It's been giving me fits."

11

"Can we talk?" Herb asked me later, after the riders were back and the others were in the barn, helping them put the horses away.

"What's up?" I asked.

"I want you to be careful," Herb said.

"Don't worry."

"You know I wouldn't leave you here if I didn't feel it was safe."

"I just hope my mother thinks the same thing."

"She'll understand. And don't worry about Rachel and Danny. You know I'll watch over them tonight."

"Okay."

"I spoke to Mr. Peterson to let him know he can count on you. I also told him I was giving you this." Herb pulled out his little snub-nosed pistol.

I drew away slightly.

"The safety is on. You know how to use it, right?"

"Yeah, but I can't take your gun."

"If you don't take it, I don't think I can leave you here. Just ask Mr. Peterson where you can keep it today. And make sure you carry it tonight."

I took it from him. It felt frightening and reassuring all at once.

"But what about you? Don't you think you might need it?"

"I have a second weapon with me," he said. "I always have a backup just in case."

Of course he did, I thought, as we swapped the holster from his belt to mine. The holster was compact, and the gun was concealed under my jacket. It felt so heavy as we walked back to join everybody else that I was certain everyone would notice it, but nobody seemed to. I handed my car keys to Brett.

"I still think it would be better for me to stay," Brett said.

"You have to go out on patrol tonight, Officer," Herb said.

"That's true. Duty calls," he said, acting like a big cheese.

I gave Rachel a hug, while Brett thanked Mr. and Mrs. Peterson for a great visit. I got the feeling he was laying it on pretty thick, and I definitely didn't like the way Lori was looking at him.

They got into the car with Brett behind the wheel. It just seemed wrong to have him driving—as wrong as it was for him to even be looking at Lori. Rachel waved out the window as they started away. We watched until they made the road, turned, and were gone.

"So what now?" Todd asked.

"Now we get down to work," Mr. Peterson said.

Despite thick work gloves, the barbed wire still got through, puncturing or scratching my skin. There was no good way to handle the stuff.

Todd and Mr. Peterson were ahead, driving posts into the soil with a big sledgehammer. They alternated who held the stake and who wielded the hammer. I could feel the pounding running through the ground and up my legs. They were moving pretty fast, driving the posts just deep enough to support the wire but not deep enough to stay upright very long. There had to be a sacrifice made here—strength and depth versus speed and distance. With any luck, by dark the whole north and west sides of the barn and house would be fenced, leaving only two approaches to be guarded.

I hammered the third staple into the post, trapping a strand of the wire in place. I removed a glove and wiped the sweat off my forehead. The sun was almost directly overhead and blazingly hot.

"Looks like you're falling behind." Lori was standing there holding a tray with a pitcher of lemonade and three glasses. That looked really good. She looked even better.

"There are two of them and only one of me," I said.

"Maybe you don't have time for a glass of lemonade."

I put down my hammer. "I think I better find some time."

She poured and handed me a glass. "This is so nice of you and Todd to help."

"I'm the nice guy. Todd's only here because of the pie."

"Seriously. I hope with you here my father will be able to get some sleep tonight. He's hardly slept since this all started," she said.

"I guess none of you has gotten much sleep."

"Not much. I must look hideous."

I looked her up and down. "I wouldn't say hideous."

She smiled.

"Now, horrible or haggard, those words would fit."

She reached out and gave me a playful smack on the shoulder.

"Careful now, don't go abusing the hired help."

She laughed and then suddenly stopped. "You know, that's the first time I've laughed in a couple of days. This has been hard, really hard." She suddenly looked like she was going to lose it.

"Just remember that you all can sleep well tonight and we'll take care of things."

"That's tonight, but what about tomorrow night and the night after that?" Lori asked.

"Tomorrow things might be fixed and this will be over."

"Do you really think so?"

"Why wouldn't it be?" I asked.

I think we both knew it was a lame but reassuring lie.

"Could you stay another night?" she asked.

"Maybe." But probably not. My mother wasn't going to be happy about this. Doing it without asking was the only way I was here tonight.

"If you can't come back, maybe somebody else can. Your friend is very nice," she said.

"Todd is actually a pretty good guy."

"I meant Brett."

"Brett isn't that nice," I blurted out.

She looked surprised by my reaction. I was more than a little surprised myself, considering I barely knew the guy.

"I mean, he's not my friend. I guess he's a nice guy, but sometimes it's hard to tell. Some people confuse fake manners and a fancy car for nice."

"Fancy car?" she asked. "Just who are we talking about?"

In a blink of an eye I'd moved from Brett to Chad.

"I could be talking about a lot of people," I said, trying to back away.

"You haven't ever liked Chad very much, have you?"

I'd said too much already, but since I'd started I went on. "I guess I just don't like his *type*," I said.

"And you think that Brett and Chad are the same type?"

"Not exactly. Brett is a grown-up who's old enough to be your, well, much *older* brother."

"And Jeremy?" He was the guy she had dated before Chad. "You didn't like him either, did you?"

"I figure you yourself didn't like him much, because you broke up with him."

"So you think I've been interested in the wrong type of guy?"

"That's not for me to say."

"Have you ever thought that I'm dating the *wrong* guys because the *right* ones haven't ever asked me out?"

"I've sort of, you know, thought about that."

"Maybe it's time to stop *thinking* and start *doing*," she said.

Was she asking me to ask her out? That would be incredible, unbelievable and—

"Hey!"

We both turned around. It was her father.

"Are you planning on sharing any of that lemonade?" he yelled out.

"Oh, sorry, Dad!"

Lori took the empty glass from me. "All right, Mr. Nice Guy. I guess we'll have to finish this conversation later."

12

I walked up the driveway, slowing down as I approached the trip wire. I couldn't see it, but I knew which trees supported it. I stopped just short, leaned over, and reached out until I brushed my hand against it, making sure I didn't disturb it and trigger the bells. I just wanted the reassurance it was there.

I turned to the right, retracing the steps I'd taken two dozen times before, walking sentry on the south side of the farm. Todd was doing the same on the east side. The other two sides were bounded by the fence. We hoped that the fencing would either stop any intruders or slow them down enough so that we'd hear them trying to get through.

The farmhouse was well set back from the road and hidden from view by stands of trees on both sides of the lane. The lane itself was rutted gravel and dirt, so narrow that at places the trees leaned over and met in the middle so that it seemed more a tunnel than a driveway. While most of the farmland was cleared fields, there were still some parts that had been left wild and rough—and could easily hide somebody coming toward the farmhouse.

Lori and her parents were inside sleeping. At least I hoped they were sleeping. If I were them, I didn't know how well I'd sleep knowing that Todd and I were the ones offering the protection. We both were carrying baseball bats, and of course I had the pistol Herb had given me, but nobody except Mr. Peterson knew that. Todd had tried to convince them to let us have guns, but Mr. Peterson hadn't given in to the idea. Maybe it would have made Todd more confident, but it would have made me less. A gun in his hands would have been a danger to everybody, including me and him. At least I'd fired a gun before. My mother had insisted that, since there were firearms in our house, I had to have some training as well as some time on the firing range.

If there was any sign of trouble, we were supposed to either run to get Mr. Peterson or make enough noise to wake him up and he would come out with his shotgun to help us confront the problem.

I was doing my best to keep my footfalls silent. That way nobody could hear me coming and I could hear somebody else's steps coming toward me. So far, all I'd heard were Todd's. He sounded like a moose breaking through the trees, but it was reassuring to know he was there. I stepped over some roots and came out from under the trees. It was surprisingly bright. I caught sight of Todd as he rounded the corner of the barn.

"So can you remind me again why I'm doing this?" he asked as we got closer.

"To help Lori's family."

"No, no, that's why *you're* doing it. Why am I here?"

"Because you're my friend."

"I must be a damn amazingly *great* friend to spend the entire night walking around in the dark carrying a baseball bat because *you* want to impress some girl."

"You are a damn amazingly great friend."

"I'm glad we have this figured out. She better be worth all of this."

"She is, I think."

"You better be more certain than just *think*. I'm out here helping you make brownie points and—"

We both turned our heads at the same sound. Somebody was walking down the lane. Actually, it looked like it was more than one somebody.

"Go and get Mr. Peterson," I said.

"Nope. There's more than one of them, so there should be more than one of us out here right now."

"Two of us isn't going to help much if there's ten of them. We need backup with a shotgun."

"I can't just leave you here by yourself."

I pulled the pistol out of its holster. Todd's eyes widened in surprise.

"But I thought it was agreed we wouldn't have guns," he sputtered.

"Herb made me take this. Mr. Peterson knows about it. Now go—they're getting closer."

Todd ran off, the sound of gravel crunching under his feet. I could hear them coming—not just their footsteps but their voices as well. There were definitely a lot of them. I had to get to the right position, and that meant going directly toward them, alone, in the dark, not knowing how many of them there were, how they were going to react, and whether they were carrying any weapons.

I took a step forward and had to use every ounce of determination to move the next step and then the next. They were getting louder as I got closer.

We had moved the hay wagon back to the barn, as Herb advised. But we'd replaced it with the tractor, which *we* could use for cover and move quickly if necessary. I came up behind it and I could see the intruders bathed in moonlight coming up the driveway. I tried to do a quick count, but their shapes and shadows blurred together—were there six or seven or five? It didn't matter, because I was outnumbered.

I hit the switch Mr. Peterson had shown me, and the tractor's headlights came on, freezing the uninvited visitors in place, hands shielding their eyes. There were seven of them, and they were carrying bats, clubs, and a hockey stick. They also each had a large plastic container. They crowded together under the glare of the lights like they were huddling for safety. I was hoping the lights alone would chase them away, but while they looked confused, even scared, they weren't retreating.

"Who's there?" one of them yelled out.

They didn't wait for an answer. They started walking forward again.

"Stay where you are!" I yelled out. My voice sounded shrill and unsure, but it stopped them again.

"Step out where we can see you," one of them demanded.

There was no way I was going to do that. They started inching forward again.

"You were told to stop moving!" Mr. Peterson stepped out of the trees, no more than two dozen feet in front of them, leading with his shotgun. He took a few steps forward, and they backed up the same distance.

"What are you doing here?" he demanded.

Todd came up behind me at the tractor. Off to the side I

caught sight of Mrs. Peterson in the shadows, holding her rifle.

"This is private property," Mr. Peterson said.

"We just need water," one of the men said, holding up a container.

"You just need to leave," Mr. Peterson said.

"Come on, mister, we need some water for our families."

"If you only need water, why are you carrying weapons?" he demanded.

"To protect ourselves," another man said. "It's getting dangerous out there."

"It's going to be more dangerous for you *here* if you don't move, right now! Get off my land!"

All except one of the men started to back off. "Look, I understand we shouldn't have startled you in the middle of the night like this," the man said. "But if you have any, I can't leave without water. My kids need it. Are you really going to shoot me for that?"

Nobody moved. Nobody talked. Somebody had to do something. I slipped my pistol into my pocket, where it was still handy, and stepped forward.

"Could you just put down the weapons?" I asked, remembering how Herb had defused the situations at the pool store and the grocery store. "Mr. and Mrs. Peterson, could you lower your guns a little as well?"

Nobody did what I asked, but I kept walking toward them. I put out my hand and did my best to smile. The man who was doing the talking handed the club he was carrying to another man and came forward.

"I'm Adam," I said as we shook.

"I'm Jim."

"How many kids do you have?" I asked. Herb always tried to bring a personal note into these conversations.

"Three. A girl and two boys. The boys are twins."

"My family has twins, too," I said. "Could you have your friends put down their weapons, please?"

They all did as I asked before he could say anything. I turned to Mr. Peterson. "Look, I know this isn't my farm, but what do you think about us filling up their containers with water for them?"

"That would be just fine," Mrs. Peterson answered before her husband could. "Nobody should be going without when we have enough to help them."

"Jim, how about if you put down the containers? My friend and I, we'll fill them up and bring them to you at the top of the lane."

"I can help as well," Lori said, her voice coming from somewhere behind me.

"But you all have to do us a favor: you can't be telling people where you got this from," I said. "If there's a stampede of people, this is the only water you'll get."

"And if we don't tell anybody, can we come back tomorrow or the next day to get more?" he asked.

I looked at Mr. Peterson. He seemed hesitant.

"I have an idea," Mrs. Peterson said. "What if they left their empty containers hidden in the bushes up at the top of the lane and we'd make sure they were filled and put back there?"

"Would that be all right, Mr. Peterson?"

All eyes turned to him. He lowered his shotgun the rest of

the way. "You all wait at the end of the drive. We'll get you the water. Then we will bring it out and show you where to hide the containers from now on."

"Thank you, thank you so much. In the meantime we'll figure out how we can return the favor, sir," the man said to him. "And, Adam, thank you."

13

The sun came up over the horizon. The light and the warmth were awesome after our night outdoors. I stood up and stretched, working out the kinks in my back. After a quiet few hours, Todd and I had decided to stop patrolling behind the fence sometime around three-thirty in the morning. I took up sentry duty in front of the house. Todd hunkered down by the barn.

Following the confrontation, just after the intruders left with their water, I felt my whole body get soft and mushy. It was the aftereffect of an adrenaline rush I didn't even know I'd had. Nothing else had happened for the rest of the night.

I circled around the side of the house and went to the barn. The door was shut and Todd was sitting on a chair, leaning backward, snoring, with the bat on his lap. I couldn't blame him for sleeping. I knew I'd drifted off a couple of times, once while I was standing.

But I wanted to get home before my mother did. It would be far better for me to explain things and for her to see that I was all right than to have somebody else tell her I was gone and get her worked up and worried until I returned.

"Good morning."

I leaped into the air. It was Mr. Peterson. He laughed and then tried to hide it.

"I guess I'm a little jumpy," I said.

"A little? You got some good hang time there."

"Maybe a bit more than a little," I said. "So I think we have to get going soon. Things are okay during the day, right?"

He nodded. "So far, but I'm not sure that means much."

"I'm sorry we can't stick around."

"I understand, and I'm grateful for you guys being here last night. Especially the way you handled things with those men. Polite and civil is better."

"As long as it works," I said.

"Those men were just trying to provide for their families, and I'm just trying to protect mine." He shook his head slowly. "But it's only day four. Somebody is going to get hurt or killed if this goes on much longer. I sure as heck don't want to be the one who gets killed, but I really don't want to be the person doing the killing either."

Those words bounced around in my mind. I was carrying a gun, but I certainly didn't want to use it. Could I point a weapon at another person and pull the trigger? I wasn't ready to think about something like that. I should be thinking about school, or what university I was going to in a couple of years, or flying lessons, or Lori—although she was probably thinking about Chad. Or Brett.

"I'm worried about my family, about how I can watch the place with just the three of us."

"I might be able to come back."

"And then I'd be worried about you as well. It wasn't right of me to put somebody else's son at risk."

"I volunteered. Look, I'm going to talk to my mother and Herb and see what they have to say. One of them might come up with an answer. I better wake up Todd now. We have a long walk ahead of us."

Todd groaned. "I am awake, and did you say *walk*?"

"Good morning, dear," I said.

"You didn't answer my question."

"We can't wait for somebody to pick us up. It's not that far. If we move fast, we can cover the distance in less than ninety minutes."

He got up, yawned, and stretched. "Unless you're planning on running instead of walking it'll take way over two hours."

"We might jog a little."

"Do we at least get breakfast before we leave?"

"I'll mix you up some fresh eggs and toast," Mr. Peterson said. "And then I can drive you on my tractor as far as the overpass."

"It's probably better if you don't leave the farm," I said.

"It's probably better if we don't have to walk all the way," Todd countered.

"He's right," Mr. Peterson said. "Besides, it's so early that nobody is going to be out yet, and if they are, well, I'll bring my gun."

———

Todd and I bounced along on the rear of the tractor, standing precariously on the hitch, facing backward. I'd never been on a tractor, and this didn't seem particularly safe. At least the trip wasn't any rougher than in my car. That probably said more about my car and the need for new shock absorbers than anything else.

The road was empty and deserted. Leaving early was smart, although I really didn't expect that we'd find anybody along this first section. It was after the overpass where the houses and apartment buildings started that we'd see people around. It was Saturday, although anything but a normal weekend. I just hoped most people would be still sleeping and those who were up and about wouldn't be causing any trouble. Mr. Peterson had lent us two baseball bats just in case, and of course I still had the gun.

I was thinking how this ten-minute ride had probably saved us a forty-five-minute walk when I saw something up in the sky to the south. It was a small plane!

"Do you see it?" I screamed.

Todd looked up to where I was pointing. Mr. Peterson had noticed, too, and brought the tractor to a stop. Todd and I jumped off. The plane had changed directions and seemed to be coming right toward us. I wondered if he'd seen us moving along the road and was as curious about us as we were about him.

"I think it's a Cessna," I said.

"But I thought planes couldn't fly?" Todd said.

"It's probably older, precomputer."

There was now no question it was coming right over us and was dropping down to have a closer look. It *was* a Cessna, an old four-seater. It closed in, so low that I could make out the pilot and the passenger beside him. Todd jumped up in the air, screaming and hollering and waving as the plane buzzed over the top of us. We stood there watching as it flew off, gaining height and then banking to return to the course it had been on before it saw us.

"It's great to know some planes are flying," I said. It gave me hope that maybe my father could find one of those and fly it back. The worse this got, the more worried I was—not just about him but about us being without him.

14

We said goodbye to Mr. Peterson and walked the rest of the way in an hour or so. We saw a few people outside their homes and apartment buildings, but they seemed to go out of their way to avoid us. Probably because that's what you do when you see two guys with baseball bats coming your way.

It was good to get past the checkpoint and into the neighborhood. I felt my whole body relax. It was almost like I hadn't realized how tense I'd felt until I wasn't tense anymore. I wasn't at my house yet, but still, this was home. I'd lived in this neighborhood almost my whole life. We were one of the first families to move into the subdivision. I remembered houses going up, the mini-mall being built, the stores opening, and those little shrubs and trees growing into real trees.

As we arrived home, the driveway was crowded with the peculiar little fleet of vehicles driven by the patrols.

"Looks like you have a full house," Todd said.

"It's not the worst thing. I'll get to find out more about what's happening, and there's less chance that my mother will yell at me in front of other people."

"How upset do you think she's going to be?" Todd asked.

"Hard to predict. I just hope she was too preoccupied with other things to be worried about me."

Todd headed home to take a nap. I was sure his parents would be glad to see him home safe and sound as well.

As I went through the door, I could hear voices in the kitchen. There was no point in putting things off any longer. I walked right into the room. Herb, my mother, and her four officers were sitting at the table. They turned to look at me as I entered. I nodded but worked hard not to make eye contact with my mother. I walked over and sat down at the table, acting like nothing was wrong. They stopped talking.

"Am I interrupting?" I asked.

"I was just getting ready to send somebody out to get you," my mother explained. She sounded like she was working on being calm.

"Mr. Peterson drove us partway with his tractor, and then we walked from where the 403 curved around and crossed over Burnham Drive. It wasn't far."

"Farther than it should have been," my mother said. "You shouldn't have been out there to begin with. But we'll talk about it later."

"Like I said, it's really my fault," Herb said. "I just didn't think there was going to be any major problem out there."

"And was there?" my mother asked, who was clearly not thrilled with Herb's decision.

I thought about the pistol in my pocket, the intruders, and Mr. Peterson threatening them with a shotgun. "Everything went fine."

She looked relieved.

"I was just trying to help them—the way I hope people are helping Dad if he needs it," I said.

I saw those words sink in. Her eyes looked pained and then softened. We seemed to have an unspoken agreement that if we didn't talk about him he'd be okay. I guess I'd broken our agreement.

I looked around the table. "So . . . how did things go on patrol last night?"

"Not great," Howie, the big officer, said. He'd always struck me as sort of a good-natured kid. Despite all that had happened in the last four days, he still had a smile on his face.

"I knew things were going to potentially be worse than the night before, but I didn't expect them to be that bad," Sergeant Evans reported. "Between the fires, the robberies, the looting, and the assaults, it's just getting out of hand. I don't mind telling you that I was afraid out there."

"If you're not afraid, you'd be an idiot," Howie added.

"I wouldn't mind being out there if I thought I was actually doing anything," Sergeant Evans said, "but we're useless. We can't stop anything from happening or fix it if it does. All we can do is watch and report."

"It's starting to feel like *we* need the protection," Brett added.

"Speak for yourself, rookie," Sergeant Evans joked.

"Weren't you the one saying you were afraid out—"

"Okay, gang," my mother said, cutting Brett off. "Look, everybody is tired and worried. How about if people go home, kiss your wives and kids hello, pet the dog, and just get some sleep? I've got to get back to the station. And you're going to be back on patrol in only a few hours."

They all agreed. After they finished their coffee and left, it was just my mother, Herb, and me around the table. If she was going to yell at me, this was going to be the time. Maybe that's why Herb spoke up.

"I heard some things on the shortwave radio last night that I didn't think should be for everybody's ears," Herb said.

"Do you want me to leave?" I asked.

"I think you should stay, Adam. Here's the deal. It's getting much worse in the cities. The bigger the city, the worse the problems."

"Have you heard anything at all about what exactly caused the outage, where it started, or why? Anything?" My mom looked hopeful.

"Only speculation. No concrete information. Mainly the few people I can reach are only talking about the results."

I listened as he told us about robberies, assaults, fires being set, and the streets becoming completely out of what the police could control. While he talked, I couldn't help but think of my father, in Chicago, being part of all of that. If Herb was right, Chicago would be one of the worst places to be.

"So it's all just breaking down," my mother said. "We have to hope that tonight it doesn't get any worse."

"In fact, you should expect it to get exponentially worse tonight," Herb replied.

"I was afraid you were going to say something like that," my mother said.

"Because of your job and training, Kate, you probably know the drill better than anybody," Herb said. "Either services will be reinstated and it will become much, much better, or they don't get repaired and each night will be a factor of five or even ten times as bad as the night before."

"I think I know what to expect," my mother said. "I just don't know if we can handle that. I hope you're wrong."

He shook his head. "I'd like to be wrong, but I've seen this before."

"Nobody has seen this before," I argued.

"Not here, but in places where I've been stationed. I don't expect the patterns to be different here. They haven't been so far. After three days is when things start to get hairy."

My mother looked worried, though not scared.

"Are you hearing anything official from any level of government?" Herb asked.

She shook her head. "A few hand-delivered messages from the chief. Both stations in his command are understaffed, with officers deserting to protect their families." She paused. "At a time when things are getting worse, my colleagues and I have fewer officers on hand. That's compromising our ability to contain the situation."

"The solution may be to try to do less," Herb said. "Your choice is to protect everything badly or protect some things well. What would you think about drawing back the patrols to only look after this neighborhood?"

"I can't do that. Not yet."

"Would you consider putting more civilians on sentry duty?"

"That we could do."

"And arming those civilians?" Herb asked.

She didn't answer right away. I wondered what she'd say if she knew I had Herb's pistol in a holster strapped to my waist.

"I don't think I have the authority to make that decision," she said.

"You're the only one who does," Herb said. "Although I understand why you wouldn't want to do that . . . at least not yet."

She shook her head. "Hopefully not ever. You know, Herb, I really appreciate what you're doing, the perspective you're bringing."

"I'm just trying to offer whatever insights I can to help you with the decisions you have to make. I guess I feel lucky I'm not in your shoes and grateful that you're there showing leadership."

"It feels more like partnership. I'm happy you're here. Thanks for all your input. I need to get back to the station. Adam, you're in charge of the twins . . . assuming they wake up."

"I'll watch them."

"And I'll help," Herb offered.

My mother got up and left the room, leaving Herb and me alone.

"So what really happened last night at the farm?" Herb asked.

"What makes you think anything happened?"

"You're not a very good liar even when you don't say anything. Was there a confrontation?"

"Nothing that we couldn't handle." I pulled the gun out of its holster and offered it to him.

"I think it's better if you just hang on to it for now."

"I don't think my mother would be happy about me having it."

"And how about you?"

I held the gun in my hand. I wasn't sure I wanted to give it back.

"I'm sure the Petersons appreciated your staying out there last night."

"I think they'd appreciate somebody going out there again tonight," I said.

"How many people do you think you would need to provide protection tonight?" Herb asked.

"Me and Todd could do it, plus of course the Petersons."

"That was *last* night. Each night they'll need more people until finally . . ."

"Finally what?"

"Something has to change. I'm just not sure what that change is going to be yet. You should go to bed, too, and we'll talk later. Hang on to that sidearm until then. If necessary, I'll talk to your mom about it."

15

I heard crying when I went upstairs. It was coming from behind the closed door of Rachel's room. I knocked at her door and the weeping noise stopped. "Can I come in?"

"Wait a second," my sister answered. I could hear the tears in her voice. "Okay, come in."

She was sitting up on her bed, and her red eyes squinted at me.

"Are you all right?"

"Of course I'm all right," she said. She attempted a weak little smile, and then she burst into tears again.

I rushed over and wrapped my arms around her. But this only forced more sobs out of her and she became louder—much louder.

"Rachel?" Danny rushed into the room. "What's going on?"

He looked at me accusingly, like I was the one who was causing her distress. I shrugged. Danny threw an arm around her as well. She tried to answer his question, but it sounded like a jumbled combination of sobs and mismatched syllables that I couldn't understand. But Danny seemed to.

"Dad is going to be okay, right, Adam?" he asked.

"Yeah, of course."

"But, but, he's alone," Rachel howled, and then dissolved into more sobs.

"He's not alone," I said. "He has his whole flight crew with him. There are a bunch of them, including his copilot, the engineer, and all of the flight attendants. They're all together, plus they have all the staff and crew at the airport down there to help them."

"That's right," Danny said. His face showed relief, and I realized that I wasn't just trying to ease Rachel's fears.

"I'm sure they're all taking care of each other," I said.

"Really?" she asked.

"He's probably just worried about us," I said.

"But why would he be worried about us?" Rachel asked.

I'd gone too far. I didn't need her to be anxious about what was happening here. "You know how he is," I said. "He's always worried about us even when we're *safe* and when there's *nothing* to worry about. We're completely *safe*."

I emphasized the words I wanted her to hear. That's what Herb did. And then I tried to distract them with a chore.

"I need your help, guys. I want you both to get up, grab some breakfast, and then go down to Mullet Creek and get some water so we can flush the toilets."

"I don't know why we need to go down to the creek when we have a whole pool of water in the backyard," Danny complained.

"Because Herb told us that's what we should do."

"Is Herb in charge?" Danny questioned.

"Of course not. He just knows some things from his job. He said that pool water is best to use for drinking. Even when it has to be re-treated it's still more pure. How about if

I go with you two to get the water? That'll be easier." I guess I'd have to find a chance to sleep later.

"That would be nice," Rachel said. She used her sleeve to wipe away the tears.

"Get dressed, eat, and then the three of us will go together. It'll be fun."

Danny shook his head. "Fun isn't what it used to be."

———————

We each carried two buckets. I figured six would be enough to flush the toilets for the whole day. Even without clean water coming in through the pipes, the toilets still worked. It was simple gravity—you poured water in the tank and then flushed, sending the contents of the bowl down the sewage pipes leading away from our house and toward the treatment plant and the lake beyond. I knew that no treatment was taking place. I couldn't help but think of what the effect would be of all that sewage flowing untreated into the lake, but right now I was more concerned about it sitting in our toilets if we didn't flush it.

We weren't alone walking for water. People who had always relied on water coming through their taps were now reduced to scooping water from the two creeks that ran through our neighborhood. Lots of people were either headed down to Mullet Creek or coming back up. You could see the strain in the arms and on the faces of those returning as they carried overflowing containers of water.

We nodded or said hello to people as we passed. There were many people who looked familiar but not that many I really knew. Of course I knew some of the kids from school or soccer or baseball, but I was almost shocked by how few people I did know when it came right down to it. And it wasn't just people a street or two over, but neighbors right on my street whom I'd never gotten to know before this. The last few days I'd seen people standing in front of their houses—I'd even joined a couple of conversations. Normally they were just little heads visible through their car windows as they raced past my house. Then they were either gone around the corner or disappeared into their garage and then into the house through an interior door so that they never even needed to appear in the outside world.

We came along the walking path that ran behind the houses and cut through the electrical-tower field to the closest little creek. It was hidden by a thin curtain of trees and weeds. Other paths cut through the brush, leading down to the water. A couple of kids ahead of us went down one path carrying their pails, and almost immediately a woman emerged carrying a bucket. She nodded to us as we passed. She was familiar-looking, but again I had no idea who she really was.

"This is like the nursery rhyme," Danny said.

"How do you figure that?" I asked.

"Isn't it obvious?" Rachel asked. "Jack and Jill went up the hill to fetch a pail of water."

"Jack fell down and broke his crown and—"

"We're going *down* the hill, nobody is breaking anything, and only another twin would think it was obvious," I said.

There were half a dozen people already at the creek—but

where was all the water? The creek, which was never big except after a rain, was flowing even less than normal.

"What happened?" I asked.

"There was more water yesterday," Rachel said. "It wasn't like usual, but it was much more than this."

There was just a small trickle of water, inching its way past the rocks at the bottom. People were gathered around the depressions where water was still pooling. They were using cups to scoop it up and then dump it into their water jugs and pails. We hadn't brought any cups. Maybe I could use one of the pails as a scoop. We squatted down and I sank the pail into the shallow water, using it like a ladle and then pouring it into one of the other pails.

"You know what this reminds me of?" Danny asked.

"Now what? I can't even imagine," I said.

"It's like one of those commercials, kids sitting in the dirt with no water in sight. You know, those international charities that sponsor children. Maybe we can get somebody to *sponsor* Rachel."

"At least somebody *would* sponsor me," she said.

I laughed even though I knew this wasn't something to joke about. If this creek dried up where would we get water from? What if this situation did go on for four more days, or four weeks, or four months? I guess we could start to draw water from the pool. It was clean and chlorinated. We could drink it, which was why we shouldn't be wasting it on the toilet. Was that why Herb didn't want us to use that water for flushing? Because he thought it could go on that long?

Then I thought about Lori's farm. They had water, lots of clean, fresh drinking water. I could bring out some containers, and that would be my excuse to go back.

Slowly we filled up the first five pails and then scooped out as much as we could into the sixth. That would be enough. We trudged back up the slope and along the path to our house. There were more people heading down for water. Was that what had happened to the flow? Were so many people in this neighborhood and others from upstream drawing water out of the little stream, pail by pail, that they were draining it? Was that even possible? But what else could it be?

"Wow, look at that," Danny said.

I turned. On the horizon was a thick black cloud rising into the sky.

"That has to be some big fire," Rachel said.

"Did it just start or didn't we notice it?" Danny asked.

"I'm not sure."

"Where do you think it is?"

I shook my head. "I don't think it's close. It looks like it's north of Eglinton, but really it could be farther and bigger. There's no way of knowing."

"You could drive there," Danny said. "You could drive us there."

"I'm not driving us anywhere. Let's get home."

"Mom is coming home today, right?" Rachel asked.

"Right. And when she comes home she might even know about this fire."

"What are you carrying?" Rachel asked.

"This would be water," I said, holding up one of the pails.

"I meant under your shirt."

"Nothing. C'mon, get busy." The pistol in its holster made a bulge under my jacket. I pulled my stomach in so that the gun was less visible. I knew I should have left it hidden under my bed as long as I was in the neighborhood, but I just felt better with it on me. As uncomfortable as it was to have it, I still felt more comfortable carrying it. Herb must really be getting to me.

"It certainly looks like something," Danny said.

"Maybe once the electricity comes back you can both have your eyes checked."

"That's not on the top of my list once things go back to normal," Danny said.

"What is on that list?" I asked, moving away from the original topic. I slowed down slightly to allow them to get just a little in front of me. I didn't want them to have another chance to look at the bulge under my jacket.

"Ice cream, a cold Coke, video games, and air-conditioning," he said.

"Fair enough. It was hot last night, especially for late April."

"I'm just glad this didn't happen during the summer," Danny said.

"You're right—it would be a lot hotter," I said.

"And we wouldn't be in school."

"You're not in school now," I pointed out.

"Exactly, but it's better to be *missing* school."

"I don't like to admit it, but he has a point," Rachel agreed. "But I like school—well, at least my friends from school."

"You still have friends from the neighborhood," I said.

"But I want *all* my friends."

Other than Todd I hadn't really talked to many people my own age except Lori, and I *was* going to see her again. I just needed a reason.

"Would it make you happy to go horseback riding again?" I asked Rachel.

Silly question. I smiled at the eager expression on her face and assured her I'd ask Mom as soon as I got a chance.

That night I was restless. After spending the whole rest of the day with the twins, trying to amuse them with endless board games, I had felt stuck inside. I lit a candle and read for a bit, but the whole time I worried that I was wasting the candle on a story that wasn't very good, so I finally just lay in bed in the dark, listening to the complete quiet, wondering what was happening out there.

16

Shortly after dawn, I heard motorbikes and a go-cart drive up and park in our driveway. The police officers were back from their patrols and meeting again in our kitchen.

I came downstairs and sat quietly in the living room, pretending to read a magazine. As my mother, Herb, and the four officers talked, I was trying to listen in on the conversation, hoping to find out what had happened during the night. So far there was nothing except small talk. I figured that soon I could just sort of saunter in, take a seat, and hope my mother didn't evict me. Until they got under way, though, it was probably safer to stay out here and hope they didn't realize I was within earshot.

Herb appeared at the doorway. "You want a coffee?"

I looked at him and shrugged my shoulders. So much for being forgotten.

"Come on in and get it, then."

I got up and followed him back into the kitchen.

The four policemen and my mother just nodded at me while Herb poured a cup of coffee and then gestured for me to sit at the table. I went to sit down but stopped and looked out the window behind them, where I could see smoke still rising on the horizon.

"It's hard to tell how far away that is," Herb said, gesturing out the window. "I don't suppose any of your patrols went in that direction?"

"No," Officer O'Malley said. "That's definitely on the far side of the Credit River, well out of our patrol areas."

"But that doesn't mean we didn't see a couple of things that had caught fire," Brett added.

"More than one?" my mother asked.

"Two on our patrol," Brett said. "Three if you include the car that was torched."

"And another one just south of Burnham," Howie added. "A small house fire—they were using a charcoal grill under the overhang of the deck and it caught. Luckily they were able to put it out with some handheld extinguishers."

"At least it was an accident," my mother said.

"Fires are going to be a problem if the weather continues to be this dry. Particularly in those town houses at the top of the neighborhood. There's no way to call the fire department, and even if you did they have no operational trucks or running water. A fire can get out of control really fast and spread to surrounding buildings," Herb said. "Do we have any firefighters who live in this neighborhood?"

"Yes, at least a couple," my mother confirmed. "Isn't your friend Greg's father a fireman?" she asked me.

"A fire captain," I said. "They live a couple streets over on Wheelwright."

"That's good to know," Herb said. "He'd also know if there are other firefighters living right here. I was thinking it would be really helpful if we could get some firefighters to do a door-to-door and talk to people, educate them about dangers around candles, indoor fires, and the use of propane."

"That would be helpful," my mother agreed. "I've been worried about that tanker sitting up in the gas station at the top of the hill."

"What if we were to secure the tanker?" Herb said.

"I think the checkpoint by the plaza does that to some extent. Are you suggesting moving the checkpoint farther out?" my mother asked.

"I'm suggesting the opposite—moving the tanker closer, right into the neighborhood." Herb paused. "Actually, to be fair, it was Adam's suggestion."

My mother looked at me.

"We could guard it better," I said.

"Is the truck working?" she asked.

"Dead as a doorknob, but I think I could arrange for it to be moved—of course, with your permission," Herb said. "I've gotten to know the owner of the station, and he'd be relieved to have it moved. If we brought it right into the neighborhood, we could guarantee its safety."

Brett asked the obvious question about how we were going to move a stalled eighteen-wheeler.

I knew Herb's answer and said it myself. "People. Lots of people. We're going to pull it."

"No, seriously, kid," Brett said.

"He's right," Herb replied. "All we have to do is get it over the crest of the road, and then it's all downhill. Hook enough people up to enough ropes, and we can do it."

"If you think you can do it, go for it, with my blessing," my mother said.

Herb nodded and was quiet. I figured he was thinking about the details. But after some more chatter from the other guys, Mom turned the meeting back to a report on their night's work.

"So how has it been having civilian partners along on patrol?" she asked.

"I think it worked out fairly well," Howie said.

"I like it. It would have been way eerie to be out there by myself," Brett said.

"What's wrong, rookie, afraid of the dark?" Officer O'Malley joked, and Howie and Sergeant Evans laughed.

"I think he's only showing wisdom," my mom said. "You have to understand that between your weapon and your vehicle you aren't just enforcing the law, you're a target for those wanting those two things."

There was a long silence.

"I know I wouldn't want to be alone out there," Herb said. "I was also thinking it's probably wise to ask us civilians to keep silent about what we see."

"Good point," my mother said.

"It's like being in a ghost town except with people, if that makes any sense," Sergeant Evans said.

"Yes, perfect sense," Herb said. "No lights, no noise, but you know that people are behind the windows looking at you."

"We did have eyes on us everywhere," the sergeant added. "The noise of our vehicles draws people out or at least makes them pull back the curtains to look at us."

"Did you notice any other vehicles on the road?" Mom asked.

"I pulled over a big old dump truck," Brett said. "When he stopped I noticed the back was filled with people. He was charging them a small fortune to drive them back out here from the city."

"It's nice to know that free enterprise isn't dead," my mother said. "Any other vehicles?"

"A few older motorcycles."

"And a couple of antique cars," Officer O'Malley added. "And of course there were lots and lots of bikes."

"How are the checkpoints working out?" Herb asked.

"I think they've really helped to keep things safe and controlled," Howie said.

"That's good to know," my mother said. "Any reports of looting or personal assaults?"

"We weren't really stopping to take reports," Brett said, "but there are three stores in the little plaza on the southeast corner of College Way and Maple that had their front windows smashed two nights ago. I talked to a couple of other owners, and they said they've been sleeping in their stores to protect them."

"That's all to be expected," Herb said. "As supplies of food and water dwindle, there will be more looting in the days to come."

"Jeez," Brett said. "I don't like to hear talk about days to come."

"Unfortunately, we have to be aware of that possibility," my mother said, "although that fact is best kept from the general population. Some things have to remain unreported."

"Are things being kept from us?" Sergeant Evans asked.

"Yeah, Cap, are we completely in the loop?" Howie asked.

"If I know, you know it," my mother said. "And I'm only working on guesses, not facts."

"She's right," Herb said. "We need to prepare for the worst and pray for the best."

"Okay. I'm going to turn things over to Herb for a minute. I have a feeling he has some other ideas about how we should be preparing." Going on five days of this mess, Mom seemed more open to Herb's input than ever.

Herb shifted in his seat. "Well, I was wondering about a few things, but only of course with your approval."

"Fire away, Herb," she said. "We're just talking now."

The first thing Herb suggested was setting up other checkpoints to provide additional security for the neighborhood.

"How many more?" Brett asked.

"Three." Herb got up and walked over to the map still taped to the kitchen cupboard. "Here, in the field behind the school, here where the walking path meets Erin Mills Parkway, and the third over in the electrical-tower field, where the creek passes under Highway 403."

My mom smiled. "I knew you'd given this a lot of thought," she said.

"I have," Herb said. "Which brings me to my second suggestion. Ideally, these civilian checkpoints would be manned either by people with some background in the military or by first responders."

"That would be ideal," my mother agreed.

"But the difficulty is that, just like we didn't know there was a fire chief in the neighborhood, we don't know who we have who fits into those categories and others. For example, we should be identifying doctors and nurses. What happens if somebody gets sick or injured? We can't be searching for somebody then, or lives might be lost."

"I know of a doctor who lives on Talbot Court," Sergeant Evans said.

"And my neighbor is a delivery room nurse," Howie added.

"Those are exactly the people we need to know about," Herb said. "But we need to know what everybody does who lives here. We can't afford not to know the resources we have at hand."

"Are you suggesting a census of the neighborhood?" my mother asked.

"Yes. There are four hundred homes in this little quadrant. We need to know who all of them are and what skills they possess."

"That would take a lot of time and a lot of manpower."

"We have people and we have time. It's better to give people a job to do than to leave them feeling helpless."

"My wife could help do that," Officer O'Malley said. "She's an accountant and just about the best-organized person I know."

"She'd have to be organized to keep you in line," Howie joked.

"You said it. If she had ten people to help her, she could get it done quickly."

"I'm sure she could," Herb said. "Especially if we can have people come to one location where they report to us. This morning we spread the word, and this afternoon we do the actual survey. To draw them in, we say that if they register, they can bring buckets and receive fresh drinking water," Herb suggested.

"And where will we get that?" my mother asked.

"With your permission, you're looking at it." He gestured

out the window to our pool. "It's clean and still has enough chlorination remaining to be fit for drinking. Would you agree to part with some of your water, Captain?"

"I think that would be the least I could do."

"It would be reassuring to people to see something was being done. Sometimes movement is as good as progress. People will be reassured that we're doing *something*."

"Okay, it's agreed, then," my mother said. "Let's divvy up these tasks. And then I think those of us who need it can get a little sleep before we get down to business."

17

Rachel and Danny had been put to bed early. We'd spent the day together, first playing some board games, then tossing a Frisbee, and finally I organized a baseball game on the diamond up behind the school. It was a good time—lots of our friends played—and for a while I almost forgot what was going on. It was relaxing to have it go away for a while. Maybe we could play again tomorrow.

Supper had been more of the same—semifrozen burger patties that I pulled out of our freezer and cooked on the barbecue. Danny looked like he was going to complain but was smart enough to keep his mouth closed. I couldn't help wondering when we had last filled the propane tank and how much was left and what would happen after that.

Now Mom and I sat around the table having a cup of tea by moonlight and a couple of candles. We still had the power line from Herb, but he'd turned off the generator for the night and so there were no other lights. If it hadn't been that we were sitting in the dark without any background noise of a TV or radio, it would have felt normal. Mom was drinking out of the WORLD'S BEST MOM mug I had made for her in a crafts class when I was seven or eight. She always said it was her favorite mug in the world. She was in her usual Mom clothing. It was almost hard to believe all of what had happened, and was still happening. Or, really, what *wasn't* happening. The area outside our doors was shut down. No, that was wrong. It wasn't just the area outside our doors—it was the entire country, maybe even the entire world.

Mom looked over at me. "How do you think your brother and sister are doing?"

"All right, I guess. I made sure they had a good day today. They're just worried about Dad."

"I know he's fine," she said.

"You can't know that."

"I know your father. He's so impatient he's probably left Chicago and is working his way back home instead of waiting for things to recover."

I *could* picture him walking home across the country, but I imagined him in an old Cessna. I shrugged, and Mom reached out to hold my hand.

"Neither of us can even think of him as not being fine. We have to be as reassuring as we can with Danny and Rachel."

I gave her a quick smile. "They are scared, but they don't understand how big all of this is."

"Nobody really does," she said.

"Herb has a pretty good idea." I looked at my watch. I'd asked Herb to come over. "He should be here soon."

"Do you know what he wants to talk about?" she asked.

"It was my idea. I asked him to explain things to us," I said. *"Everything."*

"It would be good to know all that he knows. He's been slightly ahead of the curve on things, knowing what was going to happen."

"He told me that this is like a chess game."

"Who does he think he's playing chess against?" she asked.

"Probably everybody, including us."

It wasn't long before there was a knock at the sliding door. It was Herb, and my mother waved for him to come in.

"How are you two doing on this fine evening?" he asked. "I brought over a box of canned goods that might come in handy."

He was all smiles, fresh clothing, clean hair, and a well-rested look. The only hint that things weren't all sunshine was the bulge under his jacket where I knew he had his pistol.

"Thanks for the pantry donation. We are starting to run low on some things. Do you want tea?" my mother asked.

"Sounds good." He sat down, and my mother put a cup in front of him. He smiled, then cleared his throat. "I've had a chance to go over the first day's results from the survey."

"And?"

Herb pulled out a sheaf of papers from the food box and placed them on the table. "There are four hundred and twenty households, and sixteen hundred thirty-seven people in the neighborhood," he said.

"I would have thought there would be many more than that," my mother said.

"Normally there are, but there were people away on business or holidays or who for whatever reason haven't been able to get home. For some people even twenty miles is an impossible distance."

My father was a thousand miles away.

"We need the people at the checkpoints to become more stringent in checking the identification of all people claiming to live in the neighborhood. We have to restrict entry to people who live here."

"I know the flow of people past our walls is becoming more pronounced," my mother said.

"It's all part of the flight from larger centers to smaller ones. Nobody can live for long in an apartment in the city, because they can't grow food or get water. They're fleeing to places where they think they can take refuge, find food and water. Cities that had millions will soon have hundreds of thousands and then become practically deserted."

"And a lot of those refugees are walking right past our neighborhood," my mother said.

"And we need them to keep walking. We can't take them in," Herb said. "As every place else deteriorates, we're going to be seen not only as a destination but also as a target."

"How do the patrols and checkpoints look tonight?" my mother asked.

"Thanks to the survey, it looks like we've been able to enlist four firefighters, two former military men, and three retired police officers who I didn't even know lived around here," Herb said. "We also have a couple of doctors on standby. Our checkpoints are more solid."

"The question is, are they solid enough?"

"We have to hope. I picked up a report on the shortwave last night from a ham in the Los Angeles area of a significant increase in violence, including murder, arson, and formal gang or group violence."

"But that's in the cities, not here, right?" I said.

"It's a wave spreading out from the cities. Whatever is happening there will happen here in time. If we know the trends, we can stay ahead of them."

"What are the next steps you think we need to take?" she asked.

"You're going to have to put more people out for security purposes."

"We don't have more trained people who I can trust in those positions."

"And having people you can trust is going to become even more essential," Herb said. "Have you given any more thoughts to arming civilians?"

"So far we've been effective with only the officers having weapons."

"That will change quickly, and when it does there will be loss of life."

"I hate to think that it's going to come to us having to kill people," my mother said.

"Loss of life isn't just going to be on the other side. We will have people killed. That is a certainty. We have to devise a plan to make sure that many more of those casualties take place on the other side."

"It sounds like you're talking about a war," my mother said. She sounded a bit shocked, and so was I. How bad did Herb think things were going to get?

"I am," Herb said softly. "Actually it's more like hundreds and hundreds of little civil wars are going to take place—which is, if nothing else, a contradiction in terms, because no war is civil. In fact, a civil war is even more evil because it involves not soldiers and strangers but civilians and neighbors."

My mother rubbed her hands through her hair. "I don't think it will come to that."

"I fear it will," Herb said.

"How can you be so certain of all of this?" I asked.

"I'm not certain of anything," Herb said. "Had I seen everything coming that's already happened, I would have been much better prepared."

"You're the best-prepared person in the neighborhood."

"Not as well prepared as I should have been. I never dreamed of a scenario this severe. This has the potential to be so much worse than anything I've ever seen before."

"What have you seen?" I asked.

He didn't answer.

"I know you worked in foreign affairs," my mother said, "but what exactly did you do?"

"I held a variety of posts and did a number of things in a number of countries."

I'd seen Herb do this trick before—he answered with either a question or an answer that didn't mean anything. I wasn't going to let that happen.

"Were you with the CIA?"

He laughed. "Why would you think that?" Again he was giving a question rather than an answer.

"It doesn't matter why I think that. The question is, were you a spy for *some* part of our government?"

"The term used in foreign affairs is 'operative.'"

"So were you an operative?" I asked.

"Do I look like I was a—"

"Are you going to answer or not?" I demanded. "Listen, you want us to be honest with you, so isn't it time you were honest with us?"

"I have never told you anything that wasn't true," he said. He sounded a little bit hurt, but I wondered if that was a technique to stop me from pushing further.

"That doesn't mean you *haven't* told us things that are true. I think that's what you've been doing, only telling little bits, moving us in a direction without telling us what's farther along in that direction."

"You are a very wise young man." He took a deep breath. "Unfortunately, by law, I'm not able to provide more information about my previous assignments."

"What law?"

"It's all classified," my mother said. "That's it, isn't it?"

Herb had the grace to look a little uncomfortable. "I can't even confirm or deny that. Unfortunately, at this time I—"

"Can you at least tell us if you've seen things deteriorate like they have here?" I asked.

He took a deep breath. "Much worse than they are here." He paused. "At least as they are today."

"But it's not today you're worried about—it's tomorrow," my mother said.

"Tomorrow isn't going to be the problem as much as three weeks from now. The thin veneer of civilization we are still clinging to will soon be peeled all the way back to reveal an ugly reality."

"You sound so certain, so *pessimistic*," my mother said.

"From what I've seen, I think I'm being realistic," Herb said. "In fact, what I'm thinking now almost verges on optimistic.

I think we can do something despite the odds. Bad things are coming, but we can compensate for them."

"How?" my mother asked.

"We have to become increasingly more organized as the world becomes more *dis*organized. The situation will *de*volve quickly so we have to *e*volve *more* quickly and continue to evolve, not just reacting to what's happening but anticipating it before it happens."

"Like you keep talking about chess, keeping a few steps ahead," I said.

"Exactly."

"And you think more people with weapons at the checkpoints is the next step," Mom said. "What's the one after that?"

"That's hard to tell."

"Hard to tell or you won't tell?" I asked.

"Everybody has secrets," he said. One hand gently touched the bulge over his gun as he looked me straight in the eyes. Was he threatening me or . . . I knew what he was saying. He'd given me a gun and I'd taken it, and my mother didn't even know. That was our shared secret, but that secret wasn't going to keep me from pushing further.

"There's nothing to stop you from telling us what you think is coming," I said. "What's the next step in this chess game?"

"You don't understand. With chess it's never just the next step, but six or seven steps ahead. And the foundations of those steps are right here," he said, tapping the papers he'd laid down on the table. "The most valuable resource we have is the people in this survey, knowing what skills they possess."

"Even if you won't tell us what skills you possess?" I demanded. "Maybe those skills, plus what you've seen, are the things we need the most to get through this. You need to tell us, tell my mother."

A small smile came to him. "Perhaps it is time for me to—"

He was interrupted by the unmistakable sound of gunfire.

My mother sat up straight. "Where do you think that's coming from?"

"It's hard to say with just one shot. It could be up by the plaza or—"

There was a barrage of gunfire, so many shots that I couldn't tell where one stopped and the next started!

Then silence. It was clear that this had been some kind of full-fledged gun battle, and that it had gone on right here in our neighborhood.

Mom jumped to her feet.

"I'll go with you," Herb said.

"So will I."

My mother gave me a worried look. "Adam, I need you to stay here with the kids."

"But I should come along, to drive you. Nobody can drive my heap better than me. You might not even be able to get it started."

"All right," Mom said. "As long as the door is locked, Danny and Rachel are safe."

Herb nodded in agreement.

I raced upstairs to grab my shoes and check on the kids. Luckily both of them were sleeping right through the excitement. I left Danny and Rachel each a sticky note in case they woke, and then I caught up with Herb and my mother as they were heading out the door.

Herb carried a big police flashlight. Both of them were armed with their holstered revolvers, and now my mother had our shotgun as well. I was glad to see this. When I had been putting on my shoes I decided to leave my pistol in its hiding place, since I didn't want to chance Mom finding out about it the wrong way.

She locked the door behind us, and we ran down the driveway just as the night exploded with another burst of gunfire. Whatever was happening wasn't over yet.

"Over there." Herb pointed south, toward the elementary school.

I was surprised it wasn't in the other direction, at the minimall.

We jumped into the car and once again she cranked, turned over, and came to life. I squealed out of the driveway, bumping down the ramp.

"Stay calm," my mother said. "Let's not run somebody down on the way there."

I started up the street and hung a turn, careful not to burn any more rubber. The streets and sidewalks were empty. I had thought that the gunfire would have drawn people out of their homes, but it seemed to have had the opposite effect. I rolled around a big curve, my headlights leading the way, but really I already knew by heart where every car was stalled out on the road, so I could almost have done it with my eyes closed. Just as I came up to a stop sign we saw the headlights of another vehicle racing toward us from the school.

"Pull over," Mom yelled.

I slammed on the brakes so hard we fishtailed.

"Turn it off and kill the lights!" Herb ordered.

My heart was racing and I felt like I'd had a sweat explosion. The other car roared up and then skidded to a stop right beside us. It was the Camaro with Mr. Langston at the wheel. He leaned out of the window.

"It's Mike Smith!" he yelled. "He's been shot!"

Herb turned on his flashlight and aimed it through the open window of the car. Mr. Smith was in the passenger seat, his hand clutching his arm, blood trickling through his fingers, his face an eerie white. He was staring straight ahead, as if he hadn't noticed us or the light shining on him.

"Did the checkpoint hold?" Herb yelled.

"There was gunfire everywhere, and all hell broke loose and—"

"Did the checkpoint hold or not?" Herb demanded.

"The patrols came back in time to chase the intruders away."

"Good," Mom said. "Now go straight to Dr. Morgan's home!"

He squealed off.

"Okay, Adam. Get us to the checkpoint," Mom ordered.

I started the car again but wished I was headed in the other direction. I'd never before seen anybody who'd been shot. That image was frozen in my head.

"Keep driving, but don't turn on your lights. If you hear any more gunfire, pull over and stop," Herb said.

Up ahead there was a cluster of flashlight beams dancing around, right where I thought the checkpoint should be.

"Those have to be from our men," my mother said.

"That's what we hope."

"Who's in charge here tonight?" my mother questioned.

"John Wilson," Herb said. "He's a retired police officer."

"That's good," my mother said.

"I guess we'll see how good," Herb said.

My mother ordered me to stop the car. When we halted, both she and Herb stepped out.

"Wilson?" my mother called out.

The flashlight beams fanned out in our direction, searching for us.

"It's me, the captain, and I have Herb and my son with me!" she yelled.

One of the men waved for us to come.

They climbed back in and we drove forward. In front of the elementary school there were a dozen men standing around. As we got closer I recognized most of them, including Howie and Sergeant Evans. They were standing over a man on the ground—no, there were two men on the ground, and in the thin light I could see that the pavement was stained with blood pooling out from beneath them.

I cut the engine, and Herb and my mother jumped out. I hesitated and then slowly got out, remaining right by the car as my mother and Herb rushed away. I was afraid to follow but more afraid to be alone. I ran after them.

Everyone started to talk at once until Herb and my mom

quieted them down and asked Wilson for a report. "They came from behind us and—"

"Are they gone?" Herb demanded.

"Gone?" Wilson said, almost like he didn't understand what the word meant.

"Have they left, have you driven them away?"

"Yes, yes . . . well, except for . . ." He gestured to the two men lying on the ground.

Herb bent down and put his hand against the pulse point on the neck of one man and then the other. "Both men are dead."

"By chance my patrol was almost right here when the shooting happened," Sergeant Evans said. "They were shooting at us and we had no choice."

"Of course you didn't," my mother said.

I stared at the two men on the ground. One was facedown while the second was on his back, his eyes wide open, reflecting light. I looked away.

"You said they came from behind," Herb said.

"They just appeared behind us, and when we tried to stop them they opened fire on us!" Howie said.

"There were five or six of them," Mr. Gomez said.

"Maybe more," another added.

"That's when Mike was hit!" Mr. Gomez said. "He was standing right behind me and then he was—"

"That's when we arrived," Sergeant Evans said. "We exchanged fire, and then they sprinted that way, toward the school. We chased them, two were hit—those two—and the rest ran. Some of them dropped what they'd taken."

Howie pointed to some canvas bags lying on the ground off to the side.

"We checked them. They contain some food, but also jewelry, some electronics. They must have robbed some of the houses. They died for practically nothing," Howie said.

"I've been on the force for fifteen years," Sergeant Evans said. "I've never had to even take my service revolver from the holster . . . and now . . . I did this." His voice cracked over the last few words.

"You didn't have any choice," my mother said. "They were a danger to everybody. You did what had to be done. Look, I want you to go to the doctor's house and see how Mike Smith is doing, and then I want you to go, have a coffee, just rest, try to go to sleep. Tomorrow, we'll talk."

He nodded his head. "Thanks, Cap. Would it be all right if I just went home instead?"

"Of course, go. See your wife, check on your kids."

"And know that because of you they're safe," Herb said. He reached out and took Sergeant Evans's hand and shook it. "Son, I know you didn't want to do this, none of us do, but you did the right thing. Tomorrow in the light of day you'll see that."

"Thanks . . . thanks so much."

Sergeant Evans walked away, leaving us behind. We stood there until we couldn't hear his footfalls any longer.

"I know this has been hard on everybody," my mother said. "I need some people here on guard, but if any of you think you need to leave, go and we'll take your duty."

"I'm good," one man said. "I'll stay."

"If it's okay with you, I think I do need to go," Mr. Gomez said. "I'm afraid I might throw up."

"No problem," my mother said. "Does anybody else need to go?"

Two more men put up their hands. They looked sheepish, embarrassed. I didn't know if I would have been brave enough to put up my hand.

"Go and get some food in your stomachs. We'll take care of things," my mother said. She turned to me. "Drive them home, and then you go home as well."

"But—"

"You have to go home. If your brother and sister wake up, they need to have somebody there. Besides, *I* need you to be there."

I understood without her saying any more. If some people had gotten through the guards and sentries and checkpoints to break into some houses, what was to stop them from breaking into our house?

"I'm not going to be home for a while," she said. "We have things to do."

"Including removing the bodies," Herb said. "Seeing them will only cause problems, upset, even panic among some people."

I knew how much it was upsetting me. I was working to avert my eyes, not look at them, but it was hard. It was like passing a car crash on the side of the highway.

"Okay, you need to get going," my mother said. "Don't wait up."

18

I knew I should get to sleep, but I couldn't. After checking on the kids I'd made a conscious decision to sleep on the couch instead of my bed, so I could be downstairs—between them and anybody trying to come into the house. Usually the couch was comfortable and I'd fall asleep watching TV. Maybe I couldn't sleep because there was no TV. More likely it had something to do with the fact that I had one eye and both ears open and had a gun tucked under my pillow. Then, when I did close my eyes, I couldn't escape the images I'd seen. How was any of this possible? How could things go so bad, so fast? Had it really only been last Wednesday that I was in school, typing Todd's essay in the computer lab?

I got up from the couch. I had to check the doors again. I wandered around the house—front door, garage door, side door, and then both sets of sliding doors. This house had way too many possible entrances, and that wasn't counting the large front window or the three big windows off the kitchen. If somebody really wanted to break in, there was practically no way to stop them.

The house was dark and quiet. I could have lit some candles or turned on a flashlight, but it was better to blend into the background of the other dark houses than to be a bea-con, a light leading people to a place where there was some-thing valuable to take. Still, I could have really used a cup of tea, except the generator was off and there was no power. It was for the best, I thought. We still had lots of tea, but we'd run out of milk and, worse than that, we were running out of sugar. Black was one thing, but I needed sugar in my tea.

Then I noticed on the table the sheets that Herb had brought over. They were the list of everybody in the neighborhood—the key to the next steps.

I picked up the pages and went back to the living room. I closed the door, sat down, and flicked on my flashlight. I looked at the first page.

It listed everybody in our neighborhood, street by street, their names written in very careful handwriting. All of the streets were arranged in alphabetical order, and then the people by their address on the street. I flipped through the pages until I came to our street—Powderhorn Crescent. I started going through the list. I only knew a few people by name, and hardly any by what they actually did for a living. Our street had teachers, a couple of IT people, two engi-neers, a dentist, a vet, four nurses, a paramedic, and a whole bunch of retired people whose former occupation was listed. So many people with different skills. Was this what Herb had meant when he said that the people were our best re-source?

I slid my finger down to our address. It listed my mother, myself, Rachel, and Danny. It didn't list my father. My stom-ach did a flip. He wasn't on the list because he wasn't here. He was halfway across the country. I wished he was here to help out, to care for us. I just wished he was here. I'd heard enough to know that it was dangerous, that terrible things were happening and he was out there without us, without anybody. I didn't even know if he was injured or— I stopped myself. I couldn't think like that. I couldn't *let* myself think like that.

Then I noticed that there was a faint mark in the margins beside our name. It was a letter "F" and it was made with pencil. I traced my finger down the list and found a second "F" and then a third. Did that mean family? We certainly were a family. But wait, there was another "F" and it was beside an address where there was only one person listed—he was an engineer, but he certainly wasn't a family. Then there was Todd and his parents—no "F"—and they were definitely a family.

I went from page to page looking at those marked with that faint but distinct "F." They were mainly families, because almost everybody in the neighborhood was a family, but not all—there were singles and seniors. It looked like an "F" was placed beside about ten percent of the houses or, really, the people.

I searched the list and my mind to try to figure out if there was anything that all of these people had in common. Maybe it was about the occupations of the people.

I scanned back through the pages. All of the police officers in the neighborhood had a mark. That must be it. Then I noticed that two of the doctors had a mark but two didn't. Of the six nurses only three were given an "F." There were two paramedics, the judge, two lawyers, some of the engineers, only a few teachers, two social workers, two pharmacists, and the vet. Every single person listed as a mechanic, contractor, or builder of some kind had the "F."

Was that it? Did the "F" have to do with a set of skills that were valuable? Maybe Herb should have put a plus mark or a star or something else. "F" was like they'd failed, and certainly that couldn't be the failure group. Those would be the people who had the most to offer if the technology didn't return.

I looked more closely at the mark by my family's names. There was a definite "F," but it looked like there had been more letters there and that the rest of the word had been erased, rubbed off. It was the same way with each mark—one letter and the following letters gone. If I could read what *had* been written, maybe the mystery would be solved, but I couldn't make it out in the limited light.

I lit a candle and then a second and a third. I was amazed how bright it was, and it took a few seconds for my eyes to adjust. I held the one page up close. It was obvious that something had been erased but I still couldn't see what it had said. I flipped through the pages, thinking maybe one hadn't been erased as well as the others. Page by page, I looked at each "F." It was a short word, no more than four or five letters, and the second letter was definitely an "a." It was like his eraser was being worn down as he went back through the list.

I flipped to the last page, went down to the bottom, found the last mark, and held it right up to the light. Tilting the page, I saw four letters, the last three mostly erased but still visible. It read "Farm."

"Farm . . . Why would he write 'Farm'?" I whispered to myself.

Then I realized why he was so interested in the Peterson farm, why he'd gone out there and asked so many questions, why he had acted so concerned. Safeguarding the people in this neighborhood was one step, but it wasn't the next. That involved the farm. I just wasn't sure how.

If sleep had been nearly impossible before, it had become completely impossible now. I had counted—there were 158 people with marks. That left over 1,400 without. Was Herb's plan for us to leave the neighborhood behind and go out to the farm? But what about everybody else? Without my mother and the other officers, without Herb himself, this neighborhood would soon be no different from every other place out there. The people who were left behind would be in danger. No, not just danger. If what Herb was saying was true, then a lot of them would die. And what about Todd and his family, the little girls and their mother who lived down the street, the Kramers, who had retired and were pretty old?

No, I had to be thinking wrong. Herb couldn't want us to just take off and leave them behind. He would have told my mother and me if that was his plan. Maybe he *was* going to tell us before the gunfire drew us away. He had started to tell us things. I couldn't make assumptions. I had to ask him, straight out. When he came back with my mother, I'd ask him and he'd tell me. I wouldn't settle for questions from him when what I needed were answers.

19

I startled awake. Somebody had come in the front door. The hair on the back of my neck stood straight up. I rolled off the couch and dropped to my knees. Reaching back, I grabbed my pistol from its holster under the pillow. It was probably my mother coming home, but I couldn't assume anything.

I stood up and silently made my way to the kitchen door and slowly opened it.

It creaked slightly but let in light. I peeked out. My mom and Herb were sitting quietly at the table, having a cup of coffee. I ducked back to the couch and tucked away the gun, then went to join them in the kitchen.

"Good morning!" my mother said. She sounded deliberately cheerful. I'd lived around her long enough to know that tone was a disguise. "Did you sleep well?"

"Probably better than either of you."

"And the kids?" my mother asked.

"Still zoned out, I guess."

"The sleep of the innocent," Herb said.

That sounded ominous. Not unrealistic, but ominous.

"How is Mr. Smith doing?" I asked.

"The doctor couldn't save him." Herb looked grim as he took a sip from his mug.

"He's dead?"

"We just came from the house. I told his wife." My mother's voice quavered.

"You handled it well," Herb said. "We should send over a social worker to talk to them. I should see who's qualified to offer counseling." He looked at me. "Do you have the survey papers?"

"I'll go and get them."

Maybe he thought I shouldn't have taken them and worried that I'd looked at them. I didn't care. I brought them back and handed them to Herb, who put them into his pocket.

"I've learned that there's a real role for counseling in traumatic situations. Death affects so many more people than only the one who dies," Herb said.

"Normally we have a whole team that meets with victims. I also think we should send somebody over to speak to Sergeant Evans," my mother suggested. "Poor man. It's hard to take a life, even if it's justified."

"It is. I know it's very hard," Herb said.

My mother and I both turned to him. I think we weren't the only ones surprised by what he'd let slip out.

"Yes, I've been in that position," he admitted. "The first time is the hardest, although it never gets easy."

"How many times have you . . ." I started to ask, then hesitated. "I guess that's not something you want to talk about. Sorry."

"There's nothing for *you* to be sorry about. I meant what I said to Sergeant Evans about doing what had to be done. I think that; I *believe* that. I *need* to believe that. So did you have a good look at the survey?"

"Yes, I did."

"And what are your thoughts?"

He looked like he was studying me, trying to figure out what I knew. I wasn't going to leave any doubt.

"I want to know about the farm," I said.

"I didn't know the farm was on there," my mother said.

"That isn't what Adam means, is it?" Herb asked.

I shook my head. "When were you going to tell us?" I asked.

"I started to talk to you about some parts last night before we were interrupted. I would have thought it was better to leave it for now, but maybe last night helped make the case for what I'm seeing."

"Are you two going to let me in on what you're talking about?" my mother asked.

"Certainly. Adam, would you like to tell your mother?"

"It's your plan, so you should tell her. Besides, maybe I don't even understand it."

"Adam, my guess is you understand it completely, but, as you wish, I'll outline it. Would it be all right if I topped up my coffee first?"

I quickly got to my feet and replenished both his cup and Mom's.

"Thank you. Let me preface what I'm going to say. Last night was unfortunate but completely and utterly inevitable," Herb said. "It was the fault not of the checkpoints or the security details but of the nature of the job they've been given to do. There are simply not enough people or weapons to patrol this area effectively and keep a perimeter defense."

"We haven't done badly so far, and each day we'll get a little better," my mother said.

"Unfortunately, getting a little better doesn't work when things are getting exponentially worse. The people who wish to exploit, invade, or violate this little pocket will become more organized, as well as more desperate. Last night was only the tip of the iceberg. We cannot stop a determined attack."

"We stopped them last night."

"Last night was nothing compared to what's to come. We can't defend this entire precinct or even this neighborhood," Herb said. He paused a moment. "It might be necessary for us to move outside this neighborhood."

My mother stared at him. "What do you mean?" she asked.

"At some point we might have to abandon the neighborhood and move to a place with more potential for water, food, livestock, and defense."

"Like the Peterson farm," I said. I turned to Herb. "Right?"

"Correct. The farm has sufficient water and land for growing food, but also could be secured more readily and completely than the neighborhood because of its relative isolation. We could defend that position and the people living there."

"There can't possibly be housing for everybody in the neighborhood."

"He's not talking about everybody," I said. "He just wants *some* people."

My mother turned to Herb. She looked shocked. "Is Adam right?"

"I went through the census of the neighborhood and

found people who have the skills, abilities, or aptitudes that will be needed if we are to survive."

"How many people are you talking about?" my mother questioned.

"About a hundred and fifty," Herb said.

"But there are over sixteen hundred people living here right now," she said.

"That's part of the problem. It's not just that the area is too big to defend but that there are too many mouths with not enough food, and too many people who don't have the skills or health to make a contribution to the collective good."

"You don't really think that we should or could simply pull up stakes and leave, do you?" my mother demanded.

"Certainly not at this stage. I'm just trying to be a good chess player and figure out the potential future moves."

"This isn't a chess game. You can't just sacrifice lives like they're pawns. What would happen to the people who don't go to the farm?" I asked.

"They will, of course, be free to continue to live either here or elsewhere if they choose," Herb said.

"It's not *where* they'll live, but *if* they'll live," I said. "If it gets bad enough to force us to leave, then without support a lot of them would die."

"If things go bad, then even with support a lot of them are going to die. I'm not acting to kill people but acting to have some people live."

"You said 'if' things go bad," I said. "You're not certain?"

He shook his head. "I'm not certain of anything. There are so many directions this could go that I need to try to think through all the options."

"Maybe we have to take it step by step," my mother said.

"You try to plan in advance, but you have to act step by step. Right now, today, it would be impossible to put in place a plan to relocate."

"I'm glad you understand that. I have a duty to protect these people."

"But, Herb, you think it might come to a point where defending them isn't possible," I said.

Herb nodded. "We can't change what's going to happen in the outside world. Decisions may have to be pursued that will make it harder for some people."

"People like the Stevensons from down the road, and Sally Briggs and her little daughter . . . And what about Todd and his family?" I asked.

"I know it's hard for you to even think about leaving people behind," Herb said.

"It's just not fair," I said.

"I gave up believing in that word a long time ago. This has nothing to do with fairness," Herb said. "It has everything to do with survival."

"What if we put up better walls and got more people to man the checkpoints?" I asked.

"The walls would help keep people out, but how would that supply food for the people inside? How long before the food up at the market will be gone? Do you know how much food it takes to keep sixteen hundred people alive?"

"I have no idea, but a lot."

"I know *exactly* how much," Herb said. "I did the calculations. And when it's gone, the people inside will no longer work together but will start preying on one another. If it comes to that, nobody survives. We might have to leave for some of us to survive. It's a necessary evil."

"But it's still evil," I said.

"A *necessary* evil. Desperate and ruthless times call for desperate and ruthless actions. The secret is to leave while there still is a choice. Right now we can feed and defend the neighborhood. If this continues much longer, we won't be able to do it."

"And you really think it will come to that," my mother said.

"Think, but don't know. If it gets to the point at which we're unable to either defend ourselves or provide food, it might be too late to leave. The farm could be overrun, destroyed, the Petersons gone or even killed."

That sent a chill up my spine.

"I'm not saying we should be leaving right now. The time is not yet here."

"And maybe will never get here," I said.

"I'd like that," Herb said.

"But you don't believe it. You think more people are going to die."

"I *know* more people are going to die. We have no control over that. All we can do is keep some of the people alive and work so that we're members of the surviving group."

"And you could walk away and let all those other people die?" I asked.

"I've done it before," Herb said, his voice not much more than a whisper. "I just hoped that I never would have to do it again." He got slowly to his feet. He suddenly seemed old. Placing a hand on my shoulder, he gave it a little squeeze. "I wish we hadn't had this discussion. It's just one of many directions that could evolve, options I can plot but not predict. I think we all hope it never will come to that."

His voice was quiet, and quivering. "I'm sorry to have troubled you both with the ranting thoughts of an old man."

"It's okay," my mother said. "We've all been under a lot of pressure."

"I'd be grateful if you didn't mention any of this plan to anybody else. It will only upset people . . . the way it upset you two."

"It will stay right here," my mother said.

"Thank you. I think I need to get some sleep."

Slowly he limped away, and out the door, leaving us alone.

"I know he's just trying to do the best for all of us," my mother said. "It has been a tremendous strain."

It had. That didn't mean he was wrong. He just didn't want us to think about it anymore or, worse still, tell anybody.

I had to clear my head. "I think I need to go for a walk."

"That would be nice. I wish I could go with you, but I need to get some sleep, too."

She stood and rested her hand on my head for a moment before leaving the kitchen. I stayed in my chair.

Maybe we'd never need to do what Herb was suggesting. Maybe we would. He was old, but nobody's fool. I couldn't help feeling he'd just put another chess move together with us watching, not even knowing there was a game being played.

20

It was early but not completely quiet in the neighborhood. I stepped out the front door, locking it behind me. People were already up and out, a lot of them carrying water containers, heading down to the creek. I remembered how low the water was when I went with Rachel and Danny before. What would happen if it didn't rain for a while or when winter came and the water was trapped as snow? Would there be water for us then? It was scary that I was even thinking that far in advance—winter was seven months away.

Of course, the Petersons didn't have to worry about water. Their well had enough water to provide for the whole farm and, if Herb had his way, for the people who would live there. One hundred and fifty people needed a lot less water than sixteen hundred. Hopefully, the well would be enough. Herb probably had the whole thing figured out when he was there, looking, talking to Mr. Peterson, and planning and plotting.

Plotting—that's what it felt like. I felt a surge of anger. Herb was plotting all of this behind the scenes. He was willing to sacrifice all of those people to make this work for us—for him. Would he be willing to sacrifice my family if he had to? Really, there was no doubt that he would. But then again, I'd sacrifice him if I had to for my mother or sister or brother, or my father. What about my father? If we were gone from here and he came back, how would he find us? He wouldn't know to go to the Petersons' farm.

I kept walking, nodding and waving to people but trying my best to keep to myself. Despite everything there was a certain civility in the way we were all treating one another. I'd actually gotten to know some of my neighbors better in the last six days than I had in the twelve years that went before. That only made it worse because now I was starting to know more and more of them as people, not just a face driving by. If Herb was right, if we did have to leave them behind, they'd be left without a leader, or a plan, or anybody to defend and protect them. It wasn't a question of how many were going to die, but how many would actually be able to survive.

This all reminded me of Todd talking about our situation being like a zombie movie. All around me, I was strolling through the walking dead. If it got worse, if we had to abandon the neighborhood, then most of these people were going to die and they didn't know it. I strained my mind trying to connect the real people to the names on the list.

I got to the end of my street and continued up Folkway, past houses, past streets, past abandoned cars that had been pushed from the middle of the road and parked off to the side. The lawns were still green and were still being tended. Gas lawn mowers still worked, and despite everything people were still cutting their grass. It was a strange little ritual, an attempt to stay normal in a world that was no longer normal. Flowers were starting to bloom after the warm April weather. Many gardens had been planted prior to all this happening, and the flowers didn't know there was anything wrong. They had soil and sun and enough rainfall to keep growing. Strange how the people who had planted them were in jeopardy, but the plants would continue to thrive. If only people had known what was coming they could have put in vegetables instead of flowers.

I came to the mini-mall. The stores were all closed. If it hadn't been for the boarded-up windows on the grocery store everything else would have seemed completely normal. I walked along, passing the stores, looking in the windows, thinking.

First was Baskin-Robbins, where I used to meet my friends for an ice cream or, when we were little, go with our parents after a soccer game. There would be a line right out the door, parents and kids in their uniforms and cleats, waiting and talking. For most of us it didn't matter how the game ended as long as it ended with ice cream.

Then there was my dentist's office, followed by the walk-in medical clinic and the pharmacy, and the veterinarian's office that had just opened. There in four spaces were all the medical needs of man and beast.

Next were the variety store, the bakery, the pizza place, the dry cleaners, and finally the grocery store. I pressed my face against a remaining window. It was hard to see far into the store in the gloom, but the shelves still looked pretty full. There was a lot of food in there, but how much? It looked like it could keep all of us supplied for a few months, but what about six months or a year? I was sure Herb had done all the calculations correctly.

I wondered if part of his plan for leaving the neighborhood was that he was going to take the remaining food off the shelves when we left. Would it be done in the dead of night? Would the remaining people figure out what was happening and try to stop it? Would our guns be turned on our neighbors? Even then, would it be better to die quickly with a bullet or slowly from starvation or disease or attacks by outside gangs? I turned away. I didn't want to think about what could be. Herb wasn't the only one who wished I hadn't figured it out.

I came toward the checkpoint. I recognized a couple of the men there, and we waved at each other. Sidestepping the checkpoint, I walked along the sidewalk down Erin Mills Parkway. Except for the abandoned cars, it hadn't changed. The pavement, the multiple lanes separated north from south by a concrete divider and a grassy median, holding light posts that no longer worked.

When I was a kid this always marked the western boundary of my world. This street was too big and busy and dangerous for me to ever think about crossing. In fact, then I hardly ever left our neighborhood. I had the stores at the mini-mall, my school, the soccer field and basketball court, the field with the big electrical towers where people ran their dogs, my friends, the playground, and the people who lived here. It wasn't big, but it had been my world—the highway to the north, Erin Mills Parkway to the west, Burnham to the south, and Mullet Creek and Mississauga Road to the east. Funny how those were the boundaries we were guarding.

And now Herb was saying we had to abandon it to create a new world in order for us to survive.

I went to step out onto the road and stopped. There was no traffic, but there was still danger. Out there, beyond this boundary that we'd drawn, there were things that could still hurt me. I suddenly wished I'd taken my gun with me. My routine had always been cell phone, wallet, and keys. Now I didn't need the cell phone or the wallet, but I did need a gun.

Herb's words kept running through my head: "decisions have to be made"; "you can't save everybody in the world"; "desperate and ruthless times call for desperate and ruthless actions." I knew we couldn't save the world, but maybe we could save everybody in *my* world. Then it came to me.

I started running, my legs moving almost as fast as my head. It was all downhill, and gravity was working in my favor. It was good that something was finally moving in my favor. I passed by people, running too fast to stop, too occupied to talk even if I did stop. I had to get home as soon as I could and tell Herb and Mom what I was thinking.

I slowed down as I came to Herb's house and then stopped. I needed to gather my breath and my thoughts. It was important for me to tell him my idea as calmly as possible. No feelings, no emotions, just an idea. I knocked on the door and there was no answer. I knocked again and Herb came to the door, rubbing his eyes. I'd forgotten about him trying to get some sleep. He motioned for me to enter. The hall was lined with paintings that he'd gathered in his time working around the world. My father always joked that it was like having a multicultural gallery in the neighborhood.

"We need to talk," I said.

"Sure, come on in."

"No, I want my mom to be there, too. Can you come back over . . . please?"

"Of course. I'll be right there."

"Thanks."

Inside our place I heard Danny's voice coming from the kitchen. He and Rachel were sitting at the table eating dry cereal and my mother was puttering in the cupboards. Obviously she hadn't gone to sleep. I needed my mother to be part of the conversation but I didn't want the twins to be involved.

"Hey, can you guys take your breakfast upstairs? I need to talk to Mom."

"Well, good morning to you, too," Rachel said.

"Yeah, good morning. Now go away. I need Mom, and Herb is coming back over."

"And who exactly elected you king?" Danny asked.

"Nobody." Just like nobody had elected Herb to be king and make decisions for them. "Please, guys, it's important."

"Was it so hard to be polite?" Danny said. He stood up and grabbed his bowl of cereal. "I'll eat and watch— Wait, there's no TV."

"Is it about Dad?" Rachel asked. Danny came over to her side. They both looked at me with a worried expression, and Mom turned around to stare at me, too.

"No, it isn't. I just need to talk to them alone."

"Why can't we hear what you're going to talk about?" Rachel asked.

"It's important, and it doesn't really concern you."

"If it's important, then it does concern us," Danny said.

Rachel looked like she was close to tears. I felt awful that I was the cause—no, the *trigger*—of that happening again.

"Rachel, you have nothing to worry about," my mother said. She reached out and placed a hand on Rachel's head.

"Please don't lie to me," she said. "I know we have lots to worry about."

"We're not stupid," Danny said. "We know things are bad."

"We just want to know how bad, and how much worse it's going to get," Rachel added.

My mother took a deep breath. She was stalling for time to try to answer a question that really didn't have an answer.

"Look, nobody knows much right now," I said. Maybe it was better to have a half-truth coming from me. "But I know Mom will tell you once things have sorted out a little. Okay?"

They both nodded. I had a feeling that while they said they wanted the truth, what they really wanted was a reassuring lie. I'd give it to them.

"You know that with Captain Mom living here nothing is going to happen to us." I smiled—a forced smile—and they both smiled back. I wasn't sure whether their smiles were any more genuine than mine or whether they were just agreeing to our little deal to provide and accept reassurance. I really didn't care. They got up and left the room, already engaged in an argument about gathering water.

There was a tap on the window and, before we could answer, Herb walked in through the open sliding door. He nodded a greeting to both of us.

Interestingly he didn't look as old and frail as he had only an hour ago. Was that because he got some sleep or was his looking old just part of an act, getting us to feel sorry for him? I didn't know, but I was sure he was capable of doing that. I'd seen him with people and watched enough to know what an actor he could be.

I now had the stage, but wasn't sure of the words in my performance. I sat down, trying to find the way to express what I was thinking. I wasn't sure of everything, but I knew where to start.

"I agree with the things Herb has told us," I said. "I know he's right."

Herb nodded. I thought I saw a slight reaction, a relaxation, in his neutral expression.

"The food in the store and in people's homes isn't going to be enough to last until this is over unless it ends really soon . . . and I don't think it's going to." I paused. "Just like I know we can't save everybody in the world."

"I'm glad you understand," Herb said.

"I understand that. I just don't agree with what you're saying we have to do and how we have to do it."

"If you agree with my premise, you have to agree with my conclusions," Herb said.

"No I don't," I said forcefully. "Just because things are desperate and people are getting ruthless doesn't mean we have to be ruthless. We don't have to abandon all of those people."

I braced myself, waiting for his response.

"Adam, I value your opinion and ideas. If you have a better plan I want to hear it."

"It's not really a plan as much as an idea of a plan."

"We need to explore all options. Tell us and maybe we can all fill in the blanks. Let's hear it," Herb said.

I was expecting him to argue, to tell me I was wrong, that I was nothing but some stupid kid, but not this.

Okay, now I had to speak. "I don't think we have to move to the farm. We can stay here."

"Aside from security issues, where would the food come from for all of these people?" he asked.

"Before all the houses were built here, this used to be a farm—the soil has to be good."

"Soil that's now covered with pavement and houses," Herb said.

"And a soccer field, school yards, the field under the electrical towers, the playground, the parks, and everybody's front yards and backyards. There are acres and acres of land, probably as much as there is at the Peterson farm."

"Most of those acres are fenced off into little sections," Herb noted.

"But they don't have to be. Those fences could be taken down, and that material could be used to build a perimeter fence that could surround the entire neighborhood. Why couldn't we grow food on all of that land the way the farm grows food?"

"The farm has a tractor and mechanization to help grow food," Herb said.

"But none of that is going to last. You said it yourself—the Petersons are going to be forced off, maybe killed, the place looted. What if we asked the Petersons to come here to live and bring all their equipment, to help turn the land into farmland and the people into farmers?"

"Even if we could grow enough food for everybody, that doesn't mean we can defend what we grow," Herb said.

"Putting up perimeter fences for defense would work only if you had enough trained people to guard those fences."

"We have enough people, and we have the skilled people who can train enough people." I turned to my mother. "You could train people, right?"

"I could train them, but I couldn't necessarily equip them. We have a limited number of weapons."

"There are a limited number of guns, but what about other weapons—things like bows and arrows and clubs and bats?"

"I don't think those would be very effective," my mother said.

"I've seen what a group of people with no more than machetes and clubs can do, for better or worse," Herb said. "Alternate weapons can be effective when mixed with trained personnel with guns, night-vision goggles, some body armor, and perhaps a mix of explosives."

"Explosives? Where are we going to get explosives?" my mother asked.

"We don't have to look any farther than under the sink, in the laundry room, or in the garages or backyard sheds throughout the neighborhood. Go on with your idea," Herb said to me.

Again, this wasn't the exchange I was expecting. He wasn't shooting down my idea but instead almost seemed to be supporting it.

"I know how essential water is," I said. "We have the two little creeks as—"

"They aren't a sufficient or reliable source for this many people and the agricultural needs to support—"

"They're just a starting point," I said. "The farm has a well, so what's to stop us from digging our own wells?"

Herb nodded. "I hadn't thought of that. The water table is fairly high here, close to the surface," he said. "We probably wouldn't have to dig too deep."

"It sounds like you think we could do this," my mother said.

"I think that what Adam is suggesting is *possible*. It would be very difficult, and perhaps not even the correct move, but not impossible. We have some tough decisions to make."

"No," I said. "I don't think it's up to us to decide."

"Then who should decide?" Herb asked.

"The people whose lives depend on it. Nobody made you or me king. We have to try to explain what's really happening out there, tell them the truth, and try to convince them that we have to do what we have to do."

"That's assuming we not only know what we're doing but that they would listen to us," Herb said.

"They won't be listening to us—we'll all be listening to one another. It'll be like Athens, people speaking their minds and coming to an agreed decision."

"You're putting a lot of faith in people not only to understand but to do the right thing," Herb said.

"People need to be involved. Desperate doesn't mean we can't be democratic."

Herb smiled. "You are very young."

"That doesn't mean I'm wrong."

"I didn't mean to imply that one meant the other," Herb said. "With age comes cynicism. Maybe I've seen too much to remain innocent or optimistic. I'm not even sure what I believe in anymore." His expression had gone from that neutral mask he usually wore to sadness—genuine sadness. "I entered my chosen profession because I was a true believer in freedom and democracy. Do you know what Sir Winston Churchill said about democracy?"

I shook my head.

"He said it was the worst form of government . . . except for all the others," Herb said. "I imagine the question is, are we simply trying to preserve life, or the way of life we claim we believe in?"

"Why can't we do both?" I asked. "What have we got to lose in trying?"

"We could lose everything. If people are scared or spooked or confused, they can do any manner of things. There are no limits to the depths of inhumanity. In trying to save more, we might lose all. Are you prepared for that possibility?"

I looked at my mother. She gave a subtle nod of her head.

"I don't think we have any other choice but to try," she said. "How do we start?"

"Carefully, slowly. There is no way to put the genie back in the bottle once it's out. We have to start with the right people."

"Who are the right people?" my mother asked.

"First would be the Petersons, to see if they'd be willing to move themselves and their equipment here. Without them, we have no chance to put this plan into action."

"I could go along with you to talk to them," I offered.

"I wouldn't dream of going there without you."

"And what would come next?" my mother asked.

"Nothing, yet. We have to wait for the right moment to

act," Herb said. "We're still too many steps away to talk to anyone else about this. We need to keep everything as quiet as possible. We can't afford panic. And in the meantime we have to be like a duck."

"A duck?" I asked.

"Calm on the surface but paddling like crazy where nobody can see it."

21

It had taken a couple of days to work through the details, but Herb and I were going to the farm to talk to the Petersons. After I told him about the plan to visit Lori and her family, Todd had insisted on coming along and for the most part I was just grateful to have him. Hanging with Todd, I could almost convince myself that things were normal. Of course things weren't normal. Each morning the patrols reported more and more going wrong just outside the boundaries of our neighborhood. I knew it wouldn't be long before all that wrong flooded in on us.

The day before, at Herb's suggestion, and with my mother's approval, Howie and Brett had been sent out to the farm to spend the night. It meant two fewer patrols in the neighborhood when things were getting worse each night, but there was no choice. If the farm fell, both Herb's plan and mine were gone.

I steered the Omega around abandoned cars on the roadway as we drove down Erin Mills Parkway.

"I guess at some point those cars need to be harvested," Herb said.

"Harvested?" Todd asked.

"They have gas in the tanks and tires that can be burned

for heat. Soon we have to begin to think about assembling a team to go out and gather resources."

"I could help with that," Todd said.

"I just wish there were fewer people in the neighborhood," Herb said.

"But aren't more people better?" I asked. "You know, more people who can defend and do work?"

Herb explained, "The larger the number, the harder it is to control communication, coordination, and cooperation."

"You mean like for the people running things, getting things done?" Todd asked.

"And having people get along. Larger groups create dynamics that can be difficult, even dangerous. People start arguing over what should be done, how it should be accomplished, and who should do it. The optimal number is less than two hundred, and we're eight times that—"

"Traffic up ahead," I interrupted, pointing out the windshield.

There was a truck rumbling toward us.

"Pull over to the side," Herb ordered.

I did what I was told. Herb pumped the shotgun on his lap, feeding the shells into the breach. I pulled out my weapon and placed it on my lap.

"I still think I should have a gun," Todd said.

"And you're still the only one who thinks that," I said.

The truck slowed down as well and moved over to the other side, bumping up the curb so that it was driving partly on the far sidewalk. It was obvious that they wanted to put as much space as possible between us and them.

It was an old freight truck—even older than my car. The

engine roared and smoke belched from the exhaust. There were three men in the cab, and I could see two more heads sticking above the wooden panels on the back. They were eyeing us as carefully and suspiciously as we were watching them.

I felt a rush of relief when they passed by.

"Let's get going," Herb said.

I pulled back out and accelerated away from them as I watched them in my rearview mirror, disappearing down the road.

"Do you think they were armed?" I asked Herb.

"They wouldn't be out here if they weren't. You have to assume that anybody we encounter is armed and potentially a threat."

"I've noticed a lot more old vehicles on the road the last few days," Todd said.

"I think people are getting them out of junkyards and putting them back on the roads."

"If enough old cars could be put back on the road, things could start moving again . . . you know, food and supplies," I said.

"I can only hope that's one small step toward the eventual renewal of home pizza delivery," Todd said.

I couldn't help but laugh.

"Pizza would be good," Herb said. "It would also mean more people having the mobility to attack the neighborhood."

I hadn't thought of that. There was so much that I hadn't thought about.

"I heard that there were fifty people in the group who

attacked the neighborhood when Mr. Smith was killed," Todd said.

"There were fewer than fifty men, son, a lot fewer," Herb said. "Stop here, okay? Do you see those cars up ahead?"

"I see lots of abandoned cars." Some of them had been tipped onto their sides.

"Those aren't just abandoned. They've been rearranged to block the road."

"Like a checkpoint?"

"Like a checkpoint." Herb told us to sit tight and wait until he gave the signal. "If I wave you off, then you drive home fast."

Before I could say anything Herb got out of the car and started walking toward the blockade.

"Should I go with him?" Todd asked.

"I think it's safer if you stay here."

"But he could need my help."

"I meant it's safer for *Herb* if you stay here. He has his shotgun."

"You really know how to build up a guy's confidence."

Herb moved toward the picket line of abandoned cars. He had the shotgun in front of him, leading the way, swinging it slightly from side to side as he walked.

"Do you see anybody?" Todd asked.

"Nothing."

Herb disappeared behind the first car, and I held my breath. What would we do if he didn't reappear? Would we drive off or would I go and—

At that moment he popped out and waved us forward. There was a lane between the cars, and I eased through it.

Herb motioned for me to stop and then climbed in. Quickly I pulled away.

"I guess it's only used at night," Herb said.

"Who set it up?" Todd asked.

"Probably the people in these subdivisions, just doing the same thing we're doing for protection."

"But we always have people at our checkpoints. Day and night."

Herb guessed the group that arranged the cars didn't have enough people or weapons to man the blockade all the time. I didn't care. I was grateful to be by it.

Quickly we came up to the highway, marking the edge of our suburbs and the start of the country. The open fields felt better, as if I could draw a fresh breath. What would it be like if we did move out here? Would the open fields and distance give us that little extra protection that Herb thought it would? Maybe it *would* be better to do what Herb had suggested.

After a few miles, we reached the driveway of the farm. I slowed down, made the turn, and slammed on the brakes. There was a man lying on his stomach across the track.

"Get down!" Herb said to us. He opened the door and jumped out, dropping into the woods beside the lane.

After a minute or two, he called out for Todd.

Todd climbed out the door and scampered over.

"Adam, keep us covered," Herb called after a moment.

Before I could even think to say anything, Herb got up,

leading with his shotgun. Todd jumped to his feet and followed behind, keeping low to the ground as he moved, the gravel sounding under his feet. Moving quietly wasn't one of his strengths. I aimed my gun through the window. What was I supposed to be aiming for?

Herb walked over to the man lying facedown in the dirt, aiming his shotgun at the motionless body and then fanning it around to the bushes on both sides.

"Let's take a look at him," Herb said to Todd as he aimed his weapon back at the body.

Todd didn't hesitate. He grabbed the man by the shoulder and flipped him.

The face was half gone! There was blood and mangled flesh, and the ground underneath him was stained dark. It was obvious that he was dead.

"Now we have to roll him into the ditch so the road's clear," Herb ordered.

I saw a slight panic in Todd's reaction, but that didn't stop him from acting. He flipped the body again and again, and the corpse, limbs flailing, rolled off the lane and into the ditch with a thud.

Herb praised Todd and then told him to return to the car.

Todd ran back and jumped in, his eyes glazed with fear. Herb motioned for me to drive, and I inched along the lane behind him as he walked forward. His shotgun was at the ready again. He held it chest high, swinging it from side to side as he walked.

"There's another one!" Todd hissed.

The second body was lying in the ditch beside the road.

There was a gaping hole in his side, and I could see flies buzzing around. I almost retched,

Is that what a shotgun would do to somebody?

Up ahead, angled across the lane and blocking the way, was an old flatbed truck with wooden boarding on the back. Both doors of the cab were open, the tailgate down. There was a third body on the ground, next to the passenger-side door.

"There's a gun!" Todd screamed. Herb dropped to one knee. I struggled looking for where it was and then I saw it, the barrel poking over the hood of the truck.

The barrel disappeared and Howie stepped forward carrying the weapon. Herb walked up to him, and Howie wrapped him up in a big hug. I pulled my car as far forward as I could, and then Todd and I climbed out and joined them.

"There were dozens of them!" Howie said. "They fired at us first, so there was no choice! They fled and left the truck behind."

"Is everybody all right?" I asked anxiously.

"Yes, yes, we're all okay," Howie said.

"Where is everybody else right now?"

"The Petersons are in the house, and Brett is covering the back, making sure the fire stays out."

"Fire?" Herb asked.

"The shed behind the barn was set on fire as a diversion," Howie said. "The fire spread to the barn, and we were lucky to put it out. You wouldn't believe what the rookie did."

"He had problems?" Herb suggested.

"No," Howie said, shaking his head. "He was the *solution* to the problems. He took charge. I don't know if any of us would be here if it wasn't for him."

"You never know how people are going to react under fire until they're there," Herb said. "I've seen some people who I thought would lead who just fell apart."

"I did my best," Howie said. "But I *was* afraid, almost paralyzed at first."

"You would have had to be an idiot not to be afraid. Do you know what people are most afraid of in those situations?" Herb asked. "It's not that they might be killed but that they might have to kill somebody."

"I don't think I *did* shoot anybody."

"But we saw at least three bodies," I said—instantly regretting my words.

"Brett. I think he shot them all."

"I'll talk to him and make sure he's all right," Herb said.

"You won't have to wait long," Howie said. "There he is."

Brett came around the corner of the farmhouse—a shotgun broken over his arm. He gave us a little wave and a big smile and walked toward us.

Herb offered him a handshake. "Howie was telling me that you did well last night."

"Just doing my job."

"It's never easy having to take a life."

"Better to take than have yours taken."

"Either way, thanks," Herb said. "Now I need you to go up and guard the entrance."

He saluted Herb and then headed for the truck.

"He seems to be doing okay," I said.

"People react to shock in different ways."

We went into the house and the Petersons rushed toward us. Lori, on the verge of tears, threw her arms around me, and then everybody started talking.

"Everybody, please!" Herb called out. "How about if we just sit down and let's take things slowly."

Herb sat down at the table, and Mr. and Mrs. Peterson and Lori took seats opposite him. Howie sat down as well. I eased over to the side, trying to remain unobtrusive, out of sight. Herb looked over at me, pushed out the remaining chair beside him, and gestured for me to join them, which I did.

"Just tell me what happened," Herb said.

"It was a mob, a gang," Mr. Peterson said. "I don't even know how many there were. Everything was quiet."

"I'd just gone out with my mother to bring everybody a hot coffee, and then we heard the sound of an engine," Lori said.

"That truck," Herb said.

"They just came pouring off and out of the brush as well," Howie said. "It was a coordinated attack. They came fast, lots of weapons, including rifles."

"And they started shooting right away, bullets flying everywhere," Mrs. Peterson said. "My daughter was in the middle of it all."

"I heard a bullet whiz by my head," Lori said.

"It's a miracle she wasn't killed," Mr. Peterson said.

"It's a miracle we didn't have *anybody* killed," Howie added. "Thank goodness Brett was there."

"I think he saved our lives," Mrs. Peterson said.

"I *know* he did," Howie added.

Mr. Peterson nodded in agreement. "I'm afraid of what tonight will be like," he said. "And that's why you have to take my wife and daughter with you when you go back today."

"Take us?" Mrs. Peterson said. "What about you?"

"I've got to stay to defend our home." He turned to Herb.

"Is it possible for me to have extra men to help guard the farm? I could offer them food and shelter."

"We don't have any other men to give you," Herb said. "We need them to provide security for the neighborhood."

"I guess I understand," Mr. Peterson said. "I'd rather the extra men were there to protect my family. They can go with you, right?"

Mrs. Peterson started to protest, as did Lori, but Mr. Peterson asked them to stop.

"They're welcome to stay at my house," Herb offered. "You have my personal guarantee of their care and safety."

"I'm not going anywhere without you," Lori said.

"You'll do what you're told, and we'll do what we can here to defend our home."

"What would you think about leaving the farm and coming with your family?" Herb asked.

"I can't do that," Mr. Peterson said. "What would happen to my animals?"

"We'd want you to bring them all, along with the tractor, tools, barbed wire, seeds, and anything else that could be valuable."

"You don't understand. This house is the place where my father and my grandfather were born. I can't just abandon it. Do you know what would happen if I wasn't here to defend it?"

"It would be overrun and looted."

"Exactly!"

"Which is ultimately the same thing that will happen even if you stay and try to defend it," Herb said.

"We defended it last night, and we can do it again," Mr. Peterson said.

"Maybe tonight or the next night, but not for very long," Herb said. "You have to leave."

Mr. Peterson jumped to his feet. "You have no authority to ask me to leave my own property!"

"You're right," Herb agreed. "I'm not trying to make you leave. I'm offering you an opportunity to go with us, with your family, and be safe."

"I'm going to stay here. Just give me a few more men and we can defend it, I'm sure."

"I've told you there are no more men to offer." He paused, and I had a sense there was still more to come. "In fact, I can't even allow those who are here to stay."

"You're going to take them away?" Mr. Peterson gasped.

"To leave them here is leaving them to die, too. I can't ask them to throw away their lives. We need them to defend the people in the neighborhood, which will soon include your family. You must come with us."

"This is my home, my place."

"Your *place* is with your *family*. It's not only too dangerous for them to stay, it's too dangerous for anybody to stay. You all need to come with us when we leave."

All the color had drained from Mr. Peterson's face. He turned away and slowly walked across the room until he was looking out the front window. I looked past him to what he was looking at. Stretched out before us was the farm, the side of the barn, the chicken coop, a small pond, and then the fields rolling out into the distance. We all sat there watching him in silence until finally he turned around.

"My wife and daughter will go with you. You can take the animals, all of them, and you are welcome to take any equipment you feel you may need, but I'm staying."

"You won't be staying for long," Herb said.

"Are you threatening to force me to leave?"

"No. You won't be *alive* for long. Things are moving even faster than I thought, deteriorating more quickly. This farm will be overrun within days. Staying here won't save anything. You're just throwing your life away."

"My father and grandfather and great-grandfather fought for this place. Do you know they're all buried on the property, right down there, and that one day I'll be buried here, too?"

"That day is going to be a lot sooner than you think," Herb said.

I could see the entire Peterson family recoil at that comment. Mrs. Peterson put her arm around Lori, who again looked like she was on the verge of tears.

"But, Stan, I'll make you a promise," Herb said. "I'll come back, and if I can find your body I'll bury it in the family plot." Herb got up and walked over until he was standing beside the farmer. "I respect your decision, I really do. It's just that your leaving here is only temporary. This will pass, and when that does happen you'll come back."

"Come back to what?"

"You'll come back to the land. And then you'll do what your ancestors did—you'll rebuild and go on."

"I just don't know," Mr. Peterson said. "I just don't know."

"Mr. Peterson, sir, if it's okay, could I add one more thing?" I asked.

"Go on," he said.

"What Herb is asking isn't about abandoning the farm, but about saving the lives of all the people in our neighborhood.

We have hundreds of people to think about. It's not just about security, but about being able to feed all of them, and the only way we can do that is if we turn every backyard and park and playground into a little vegetable garden or pasture."

"Do you really think you can turn backyards into cropland to grow enough food for that many people?" Mr. Peterson asked.

"We have no choice. We have to try. And we need somebody who can help us do that."

Lori spoke up. "It's not just your wife and daughter who need you, Dad. Lots of people need you."

He didn't answer right away. I hoped that meant he was thinking about it.

"You really aren't giving me a lot of choice, are you, son?"

I shrugged. "Sorry."

"Don't be sorry." He turned to Herb. "How many days do we have before I have to leave?"

"Not days. Hours."

"That's not possible!"

"It's going to have to be. We need to get to the neighborhood before dark."

"Then I guess we better get moving," Mrs. Peterson said as she jumped to her feet.

"You're doing the right thing." Herb offered Mr. Peterson his hand, and they shook.

22

I looked anxiously at my watch. It was almost five o'clock. We had three hours before sunset, but at the plodding pace we were going to travel it would take us a long time to make the seven-mile trip. We needed to arrive before dark, not just for our safety but for the security of the whole neighborhood. Herb had sent me back—along with Brett riding shotgun—to get permission from my mother for his plan. She'd agreed and sent another ten people and two vehicles to the farm to help. Until we returned the neighborhood security would be spread to the point of breaking. My mother had taken patrols and officers away from other areas to cover the neighborhood.

I walked along the farm lane, passing the assorted vehicles that formed our little convoy, our little parade. Leading the way was Judge Roberts's bright red '57 Chevy, driven by the judge himself. It *had* been in a lot of parades—local Santa Claus parades and events in little towns all around. It was loaded down with home-canned food, root vegetables, and kitchen equipment. Herb would be in the passenger seat, and it was going to be flanked by two motorbikes driven by armed officers.

Next came the tractor, driven by Mrs. Peterson, pulling

three farm wagons in a little train. Each wagon brimmed with seeds, tools, fencing, and livestock—chickens in cages and eight cows taking up one entire wagon by themselves. Getting them there was no small feat—a couple of them had balked at being driven up the ramp and into the confines of the rolling pen. Sergeant Evans and Officer O'Malley, with shotguns, had already taken up their positions in the front two wagons.

Behind that was a carriage, powered by the three horses, to be driven by Mr. Peterson, and loaded down with farm equipment, including the generator, and other electrical and technical things.

I was next in line in my car. My trunk and backseat were filled with stuff from the Petersons' house—clothes, pictures, a few keepsake items that meant a lot. My passengers were Todd and Lori.

Behind me was one more car—Mr. Langston's Camaro, with him at the wheel—and then at the end the abandoned flatbed truck, packed with the remaining farm equipment and more armed men, more than any other place in the convoy. Herb insisted that was the most likely spot to be attacked and so had to be the best defended. He said we had to be like a scorpion with lots of sting in our tail. Both Howie and Brett were in that last truck.

Herb barked out last-minute instructions, directions, and orders. Nobody argued with anything he had to say. I think people were starting to get used to him not only being in charge but being right. As things got more dangerous and risky it felt good to have somebody take the lead.

I knew Herb wanted to get going but was being patient as

the Petersons took care of last-minute things before leaving their home. How would I feel if I was going to say goodbye to my place?

They stood, the three of them, alone by the door of their house. They'd left behind most of what they owned. A lot of other things had been hidden in the barn. The root cellar had been stuffed with things, and then the trap door and the area around it had been covered with six inches of soil, in the hopes that no invaders would discover it.

I could see that Herb was itching to leave but was trying to give the Petersons as much time as he could.

"You've done this before, haven't you?" I asked him.

"Done what?"

"Arranged a convoy."

He held up two fingers. "Twice I've had to transport embassy and support staff and their families out of a country."

"Why did you have to do that?"

"War, civil unrest. It wasn't that much different from what's happening here. There was a breakdown of government, security, and the provision of basic human needs."

I looked up and the Petersons were walking toward us. Both Mrs. Peterson and Lori were crying. Mr. Peterson appeared to be fighting back the tears.

"Can I have everybody's attention, please!" Herb cried out.

The men in the hay wagons moved to the sides to be close to us, and everybody else came over until we were surrounded.

"I want you to know how *good* I feel about the people I have with us," Herb began. "I have no doubts about our *success*." He paused as people smiled and nodded in agreement.

"But I know that we're going to attract a lot of attention and that might also attract trouble. We have a great deal of what people want and need, and they might decide that they wish to take it. We will *not* let that happen. We will not initiate force, but we will meet force with greater force. We will overcome any hostile action with a greater hostile response. And, most important, you have to know that we are in this together. We start, we move, we stop as one unit. Together."

Again there was a nodding of heads and a mumbling of agreement. This reminded me of a pregame pep talk from a coach to his players. How many times had I been on teams when we got those talks before a big game? All those metaphors that coaches used—like "do or die," "life and death," "going to war," "take no prisoners"—now really meant something. At least potentially. Maybe this would be nothing more than a slow drive from the country and into our neighborhood. I could hope.

"People in the back, make sure you don't fall behind. We have to stay tight. Remember the signals." Herb pointed at me.

I remembered. One beep on the horn meant slow down. Two beeps meant potential danger. A long blast would bring the whole convoy to a halt, and we'd take cover and wait for orders.

"Now let's get going and let's be careful," Herb said.

People sprang into action. I held my door open for Lori. Todd climbed in after her. He gave me a forced smile. He was smart enough to be scared and brave enough to try not to show it.

All around me engines started as I settled myself behind

the wheel. I turned the key, and my engine sputtered and choked. I pumped the pedal, tried to give it some gas, but was afraid if I gave it too much it would flood. I tried again. It didn't want to catch. What would happen if my worry finally came true and it didn't start? Would they have to leave my car behind or—

Just then it started with a roar. I let out a sigh of relief. In front of me the carriage started forward and I inched along behind it, slowly bumping along the lane.

"I'm sorry," I said to Lori.

"Me too." She was working hard to fight back the tears.

I didn't know what to say. It was probably best that I didn't say anything. We turned onto the road.

"I wish we had an elephant," Todd said.

"An elephant?" I asked.

"Or two. Every parade needs an elephant. Or maybe a little car filled with clowns."

"I already have a car with a clown in it," I said.

"Adam . . . she's right here . . . That's such a terrible thing to say about Lori!"

Despite everything all three of us burst into laughter. Todd, the best kind of clown, had brought some comic relief. We needed that.

"I guess I should thank you," Lori said to me.

"For what?"

"For my father being here with us. He wasn't going to come, but you convinced him."

"That was mostly Herb's doing."

"No, my father said to us that it was you."

"I'm sure he would have come anyway."

"Why don't you just shut up and say you're welcome?" Todd said.

"I'm pretty sure if I shut up I couldn't say anything."

Lori laughed. "Thanks for that, too. I'm so glad you're here."

"I could get out and walk if you want to be alone," Todd offered.

If nothing else he'd given me a chance to regain my thoughts.

"Nobody wants you to get out and walk . . . although you could ride in one of the wagons with the other livestock," I suggested.

"Next time I'll make a point of that. I don't want anybody to say that I stood in the way of love."

Now everybody got silent. It was hard to believe that anything could have made this drive more uncomfortable, but we had managed.

"This is all pretty hard to believe," Lori said, finally breaking the silence.

"More like impossible," Todd added.

"Last night was the worst," Lori said.

"It must have been awful. I wish I'd been there to help."

"I'm so glad Brett *was* there," she said. "It was like a movie the way he came running in, firing his gun with one hand and sweeping me up with the other and carrying me to safety."

Great, just great. "I guess we're all lucky he's along for the ride today."

"It's good to know we're going to someplace that's safer." Lori went quiet again for a while. "Do you think I'll have a home to go back to when this is over?" she asked.

"I don't know, but at least this way you'll have a family. I just wish my father was with us."

"I am so sorry, I forgot about your father."

"I didn't mean to make you feel bad. My dad's fine, I'm sure. I know he's making his way back home."

We crossed over the highway. Now this dividing line seemed to mark something more ominous than the boundary between the country and the suburbs. This was where it became less safe. But really, with all these men and all this firepower, would anybody try to take us on? Then again, before last night would I ever think that a truckload of armed men would try to overrun the farm?

"This isn't quite the way I imagined it," Lori said.

"Imagined what?"

"You and me driving someplace together."

"And I never imagined I'd be the chaperone on your little driving date," Todd said.

"First off, shut up, Todd, and second, this is hardly a date," I said.

"But you have thought about us going out on a date?" Lori asked.

"I thought about it once or twice," I admitted—once or twice a day for two years.

"Once or twice?" Todd asked. "Okay, okay, I know—shut up, Todd."

"Then why didn't you ever do more than just think about it?" Lori prodded.

"You always seemed to be dating somebody else."

"Do you ever wonder how Chad is doing?" Todd asked.

I shot him a dirty look.

"Okay, this time I really will shut up. I promise," he said.

"I was dating other people because they asked me out. Was I supposed to wait for you to work up the nerve?"

"No, it's just that—"

I slammed on the brakes as the carriage stopped in front of me.

"What's happening?" she asked. "What's wrong?"

"It's probably nothing." Or it could be something.

I put the car into park. In my rearview mirror I caught sight of somebody climbing out of the back of the truck. It was Brett, shotgun at the ready, walking forward. He hesitated for just an instant at the open window of my car.

"I'll see what's happening," he said.

He was an action hero and I was sitting in my car, waiting, practically hiding.

"Slide over," I said to Lori. "You take the wheel. I'm going to check things out, too."

I climbed out and rushed after Brett, catching up to him as he reached Herb standing in front of the first car. Howie came up from behind. Ahead of it was the barricade I'd passed by three times earlier in the day. It was no longer unoccupied. Behind the cars I could see a few heads, and I thought I could make out rifle barrels. Suddenly I felt exposed. Maybe it would have been better to stay in the car.

"There was nobody there even when we came back to the farm with the extra people," I said.

"Doesn't look like there's many of them," Brett said.

"I don't know how many there *are*," Herb said, "only how many I can see."

"Look, we must have more firepower. We can take them," Brett said.

"Not without casualties," Herb warned. "I'll try to negotiate a way through."

"Wouldn't it be better if we just went another way? That road is open," Howie said, pointing to a side street.

"We don't know what's down there other than that the road is narrower and the houses closer together. It could be a trap that this barricade is directing us into. Besides, we don't have much time before dark. We have to get back. I'll go and talk," Herb said.

"You shouldn't go alone," Howie said.

"I'm not. Adam's coming with me."

"You're taking the kid instead of me or Howie?" Brett asked.

I had to agree with him—why me?

"It defuses tensions if we send an old man and a kid. It's the best chance we have. If there are problems, you turn this little circus around and make a run for it."

"But what about you two?"

"Don't worry about us. If something goes wrong you won't be able to help. Howie, I want you to stay up here, but first let people know what we're doing. Brett, you go and secure the rear of the convoy."

"I'm not turning and running away," Brett said.

"I'm not talking about you running. If this blockage is designed to stop us, we can be attacked and it's going to come from the back. I need you there to take care of it. Understand?"

"Okay, sure."

When they left us alone, Herb told me to run back and leave my gun in the car.

When I protested that this seemed like exactly the wrong time to ditch a weapon, he promised we were going to talk our way through this.

"The last thing you want to do is spook them," Herb explained.

I ran back along the line and pulled out my pistol as I got to the car. "Here, take this," I said as I handed it to Lori and ran back to Herb.

"Let's go." He put his hands up in the air and started walking forward, and I did the same thing.

We moved slowly. As we closed in I started to count. There were six men at the barricade, and at least three of them had rifles.

"You just listen and nod," Herb said. "Agree with everything I say."

"I wasn't planning on starting an argument with anybody."

"Neither am I, but if problems do develop, if there's gunfire, drop to your belly."

He stopped and I did the same.

"We're unarmed!" Herb yelled. "Can we come forward to talk?"

"Take off your jackets and shirts!" a man yelled back.

That surprised me. Herb took off his jacket, dropped it to the pavement, and then started to undo the buttons of his shirt. I pulled mine off over my head. Standing beside me Herb looked old, almost frail, and I felt exposed and vulnerable. Why had Herb taken me along? Why had I agreed to come with him?

"Okay, you can come forward!" a man yelled.

We raised our hands again. I could feel the sweat streaming down my back. We stopped at the first car. Two men advanced, their rifles pointed directly at us.

"Could we put our arms down now?" Herb asked.

"We'll tell you when you can do that," one of them barked. He was trying to sound confident, but I could tell he was scared. Herb was right.

"Sure, of course. I'm good at following orders or I wouldn't be here," Herb said. "I'm Herb, by the way. This is Adam."

The two strangers exchanged a nod. "Okay, get in here, Herb and Adam," the nervous one ordered.

Herb moved and I stumbled after him as we were escorted behind the barricade. My feet felt like they were weighted with cement, my mouth dry from fear. I was terrified.

There were five other men standing behind the cars. Only the first two guys had real rifles. A young-looking third guy had what looked like a pellet gun. The other four were all armed with clubs or knives. Two were at the barricade watching our caravan; the others were staring at us.

"We're here to deliver a message," Herb said.

"We're listening."

"We're willing to pay you a toll to let us by."

"What sort of a toll?"

"We have eight cows and are willing to let you have one of them," Herb said. "That would feed a bunch of people."

"And eight cows would feed us eight times as long," the nervous guy's partner said.

"Nobody is going to give you eight cows," Herb said. "But you know, we're going to be coming along this way a lot in the next few weeks. If you got one cow eight times, you would end up with eight cows and nobody would have to shoot each other. What do you think?"

"I think we need to talk among ourselves," our interrogator said. "Herb and Adam, don't move."

"Can we lower our arms and sit down?" Herb asked. "Please?"

"You just stand there and—"

"Let them," a guy with a knife interrupted. "The old guy looks like he's going to collapse if he doesn't sit down."

"Thanks so much," Herb said. He lowered his arms and slumped onto a picnic bench.

I eased onto the seat beside him and then lowered my arms as well.

"But don't try anything!" the knife carrier barked. "We have our eyes on you."

They backed away and formed a little huddle, glancing at us every now and then.

"You okay?" Herb said under his breath.

"I could be better."

"Remember what I said—drop flat to the ground if it goes bad."

"But it's going good, right?"

"Not so good. Listen."

I turned my head to try to make out what they were saying, but I couldn't hear any more than a stray word or two. I shrugged.

"I can't hear the words, but I don't like the tone," Herb whispered. "They're fighting among themselves, and when that happens the most aggressive voice usually wins."

The argument stopped and the men came toward us—at least three of them did—while two others ran off, including our friend with the knife. Why would they run away? There could only be one reason: they were going to get more people, and that couldn't be good.

"Get up!" their spokesman ordered.

I jumped to my feet and Herb slowly got up with a groan. He wobbled and I reached out to support him.

"Thanks," he said. His voice was weak. Was he all right?

"If you two want to live, you will do exactly what you're told to do."

"We will," Herb said. "Please don't hurt us."

"You won't get hurt unless you do something wrong. The kid stays here, and you're going to walk out and wave your people to come through the space we're going to open up."

"What if they don't come?"

"You better hope they do. If they don't come, you two are *dead*."

"You're going to kill us?" Herb asked.

"If we have to," the man said. "We want all the cows."

"Look, they're not just going to roll over and give you what you want. They have guns and they'll try to stop you," Herb said.

"We have weapons and the element of surprise, and we have you two, so that gives us the advantage."

"They'll fight. People will die," Herb said.

"People are going to die if we don't have enough food. We'll take that chance. Go out and wave them forward."

"I'm not feeling good," Herb said. "Can I have a drink of water or—"

The man pushed Herb. "Get going or you're going to be feeling a whole lot worse!"

"I can't—my chest—" Herb staggered and doubled over.

I grabbed him to stop him from falling down. We had to get him to a doctor or—

Suddenly Herb straightened up and spun around. He had a gun in his hand! I had no idea where he'd pulled it from. Maybe a holster on his ankle.

The leader started to raise his rifle.

"You move that another inch and you're done!" Herb yelled.

The man froze. They all froze.

"Drop your weapons," Herb ordered.

Nobody moved. Our captor cleared his throat and spoke up. "Look, gramps, there are five of us with three guns. You can't shoot all of us before one of us gets you."

"This is a fully automatic pistol that can fire its whole clip in three seconds. The first two shots are for you, the third is for the gentleman beside you with the twenty-two, and then I'll take out the young man with the pellet gun. Maybe he hits me with a pellet or two before I cap him, but I can live with a couple of dents in my skin."

"You think you scare us?" the boss man with the big rifle asked.

"If you're not scared, you're stupid. Shooting you might put you out of your misery."

"You really think you can kill somebody?" he asked.

Herb laughed. "How do you figure I got these cows to begin with? We're coming back from a raid on a farm up the road, you idiots. They're *my* cows now, and I won't even lose sleep over killing three *more* people today. You want to try me, go ahead—raise the rifle just a shade and see how fast you're dead."

"I'm putting mine down," the other rifleman said. He bent and placed his weapon on the ground. The man with the pellet gun did the same.

"Now I just have one target," Herb said. "Put it down *now* or die."

The man grumbled but then gave in.

"You two put down your clubs and come over here, too," Herb ordered, and the two men on the barricade dropped their weapons and reluctantly shuffled forward. "Now step back four steps, slowly, keeping your hands where I can see them."

They did what they were told.

"Now take off *all* your clothes."

"What?"

"Take off all your clothes, right now."

"I'm not taking off my pants!" the leader said defiantly.

"Do it or die," Herb said. "I don't care if you live or die, but *you* should."

"I'd rather die."

"You'll get your wish. Of course when the bullets start flying there's no telling who else might get hit." Herb swung the gun back and forth so it swayed from man to man.

"Just do what he says!" the youngest guy said.

Quickly they all started to undress until the five men were standing there, naked. They were being held at bay by an old guy and a kid, neither of whom was wearing a shirt. It was a pretty ridiculous scene, like a game of strip poker that was going horribly wrong.

"Now all of you roll that car away to let our vehicles by."

As a unit they rushed over to one of the vehicles. One of them jumped inside and the other four pushed the car, clearing a lane.

Herb told me to go out and get the caravan moving.

I raced away, passing the barricade and running into the open, waving as I ran. "Come on, come on, quick!" I screamed. When Judge Roberts's Chevy started in motion I grabbed our shirts and Herb's jacket and ran back to the barricade. The center car had been moved, making a big gap for us to pass through.

"Now all of you get going!" Herb yelled to his naked captives.

"We can leave?" our tormentor asked.

"Of course you can."

"And you're not going to shoot us in the back?"

"If I was going to shoot you it would be easier to just do it now instead of trying to pick off five moving targets. Go, before I change my mind."

They all hesitated for a split second and then they were off, bumping into each other, running away fast until they disappeared behind the fence and into their neighborhood. At that same instant the first car in our convoy came through the opening. Herb waved them forward.

I handed Herb his shirt and jacket. "Thanks. Now grab those rifles and get into your car!" Herb ordered.

When my Omega came through the gap with Lori at the wheel I jumped in on the passenger side, landing on the seat, the rifles under my arm. I pulled the door closed with a loud thud.

"You're okay!" Lori cried.

"Yeah, sure, I'm fine."

"What happened to your shirt?" Todd asked.

"They wanted to attack us, but we got their guns." I held up the two rifles, like they were trophies.

"That still doesn't explain what happened to your shirt," Todd said as I pulled my top back on.

"I'm just so glad you're safe, that we're all safe," Lori said. "Do you want to drive?"

"You're doing fine. I'll keep watch." I pulled one of the rifles off the floor.

What I didn't say was that my hands were still shaking so badly that I didn't think it was smart for me to drive right now. I'd just be a passenger—well, more than a passenger. Riding shotgun had a whole different meaning now.

23

It was a new experience to be woken up by a rooster, but there it was, in Herb's backyard, along with the chickens, eight cows, three horses, and Mr. Peterson.

I stood in my kitchen looking out through the window at the little farm beside us. I wanted to go over, say hello, and see how the animals were doing. Maybe I could say hello to Lori as well. But it was still too early, only six o'clock. I knew what I could do to kill the time. Last night I'd had my recurring dream about flying. Maybe I could do more than just dream: I could work on making that dream real.

I went out front. There were already people with their water containers heading to or from the creek. We'd had a couple rainy days in a row, and the water level was up. Mr. Peterson's tractor, the carriage, the wagons, and the flatbed truck were all on the street in front of Herb's house. Livestock in the back and tractor and carriage out front seemed like perfect symmetry.

I pulled open the garage door. There on the trolley was my ultralight, the wings lying on the ground beside the body, the engine attached but still lifeless. If Dad had been here, those wings would have been put on by now and we would have had our first flight. It was so close to being ready. If he had been here, it *would* have been ready.

We'd spent so much time on the plane I knew it like the back of my hand. Of course it wasn't just this little plane. I'd studied so much about flying. Not just the actual flying, but the science behind flight. If you didn't understand those principles, then you'd think that flying was magic. I often wondered what it would have been like for people in the early 1900s to look up and see those first flying machines in the sky. They would hardly have believed their eyes because what they were seeing wasn't believable. I had to laugh— when we'd seen that Cessna in the sky the other day I had thought my eyes were playing tricks on me. Flying had become amazing again because it was so rare. And if I was up there in the sky now, that would be *magical*.

What would be even more magical would be if my father had the ultralight with him. It was possible to fly an ultralight across the entire continent. It had been done. They weren't fast, but in twelve hours you could fly five or six hundred miles at a go. It would have taken my father only a few days to get home. Or, if I went to get him, I could have him here in five or six days.

Of course I couldn't do that. Where would I get gas? Where would I stop? Could I navigate that far? And even if I could get there, how would I find my father? It wasn't anything more than a fantasy.

"Good morning."

I turned around. Lori was standing there, smiling.

"Morning. You're up early."

"I'm a farm girl."

She walked into the garage. "Does it fly?"

"As soon as I bolt on the wings and do some minor adjustments, then she'll be good to go."

"Aren't they usually just one-seaters?"

"Usually. We built this one so my dad and I could go up together."

"I'm sure that'll happen."

"I hope. We spent hundreds of hours working on it." I paused. "When I'm out here it feels like I should just be able to turn around and he'll be standing behind me, ready to hand me a spanner."

"I could hand you a spanner, but I'd need to know if your ultralight is using SAE or metric."

"Metric, actually. I'm impressed."

"Like I said, I'm a farm girl."

She gave me a smile that made me feel like I was floating up into the air without the need for any machine.

"Since you have an extra seat, maybe I could even keep you company up there."

"I'm not sure how either of our mothers would feel about that."

"Maybe we don't have to tell them . . . After all, do you tell your mother everything you do?" Lori ran her hand along the frame of the ultralight. "But you *are* going to try to finish it, aren't you?"

"I want to but—"

"Good morning, kids."

We both turned around. Brett was standing there in full uniform. He flashed a big goofy smile. Lori smiled back. I worried that it was a bigger smile than the one she'd given me.

He walked into the garage. "This is one interesting little toy, Adam."

"It's not a toy," I said.

He put a hand against the plane. I had to fight the urge to brush it off. It wasn't the same as Lori touching it.

"I used to build models when I was a kid," he said. "Of course those planes had wings."

"But they didn't actually fly. This one can."

"*Can* fly, or *will* fly?" he asked.

"She'll fly, and I'll be the pilot," I snapped.

"There's no way you'd get me up into the air sitting on something that looks more like a lawn mower than an airplane."

I laughed. "A lawn mower you could handle, Brett, an ultralight you couldn't. Not unless you know how to fly a plane."

"Not me."

Brett suddenly looked anxious. That gave me an idea.

"Hey, I could take you up with me. It *is* a two-seater."

He took a half step away from the ultralight, as if he were afraid it might grab him and take off with him.

"No way he goes up with you—you're taking *me* up," Lori said. "You promised I could fly."

"Probably a good thing," Brett said. "I figure the only way this thing is going to fly is if it falls off its trolley." He stretched and yawned. "Anyway, I've been on patrol all night. I need to get to bed. I'm going to go crash on Herb's couch so the twins don't wake me up."

I was grateful to have him walk away. But now I was even more determined to get my plane in shape.

"You really want to help?" I asked Lori.

"You bet."

"Okay, let's wheel it outside. I want to attach the wings and maybe even start the engine up."

Lori answered with another one of those smiles. She helped me ease it off the trolley and onto its wheels. We rolled it outside onto the driveway.

"It looked a lot bigger in the garage," Lori said.

"Wait until we attach the wings."

I went back into the garage and picked up one of the wings. It wasn't heavy, but it was long and awkward. Carefully I carried it out and placed it on the ground, perpendicular to the body of the plane, right where it was going to be attached.

I went back in for the second, wishing my dad were here. In the first few days of the disaster, thoughts of him were floating around in my head almost all the time, but they'd been chased out for the last week or so. Maybe that was for the best. I felt awful when I thought about his situation and guilty when I didn't. There was no winning; it was just a question of which way was best to lose.

I came out with the second wing, but instead of putting it down I positioned it against the body of the plane.

"Could you help me with this?" I asked.

Lori took hold of the wing and was handling enough of the weight that I could nudge the end of it over until the bolts sticking out of it stuck in through the matching holes in the body.

"All right, if you can hold this here, I'll let go and get those nuts into place."

She nodded. Carefully I removed my hands, and Lori shouldered the whole thing. I pulled the nuts and washers from my pocket as well as a wrench, working quickly to tighten them up until the wing was secured.

"You can let go now."

She removed her hands and the wing stayed put.

"One down and one to go."

With Lori's help I picked up the other wing and got it into place. It attached just as easily as the first. With both wings on, the ultralight was now wider than the driveway.

"Now it looks like a plane," Lori said.

"It is a plane, I promise."

I climbed into the pilot's seat. The second seat was empty, but I could almost feel my father beside me.

Absentmindedly, almost instinctively, I hit the switch that fed fuel into the engine. It wouldn't hurt to start the engine, just to make sure it still worked. It would also impress Lori.

"Okay. Stand back, well back," I said to her. She retreated onto the lawn.

I hit the starter button and the engine roared to life. The propeller cut through the air, producing a breeze that blew back Lori's hair. I revved the engine and the plane jerked forward along the driveway. I eased off the throttle and put on the brakes.

My heart racing, I looked over my shoulder. I half expected my mother or Herb to come running out to see what was making such a racket. Instead there was just Lori, standing there, clapping and cheering. I decided I'd put on a little bit of a show for her.

I eased off the brakes and gave it more gas as well as applied the left brake pedal. Slowly I began to move forward again, and the front wheel eased off the driveway and onto the road followed by the left and then right rear wheels.

Giving it more brake, I turned it so I was in the middle of the road. Then I started to taxi up the street.

I looked over my shoulder, still expecting to see my mother running after me, but she was nowhere to be seen. Other people had been drawn out of their houses by the noise, though. Some waved and yelled out words I couldn't hear over the engine behind me. Reaching the end of the street, I put on the left brake hard to turn it around. In front of me was a straight, completely empty stretch of road. My wing-span was only twenty-eight feet, so as long as I stayed in the middle there was plenty of room on our car-less street. This stretch of pavement wasn't nearly long enough for a Cessna to take off, but it was definitely long enough for an ultralight.

I missed my flying lessons. I missed being up in the air. I missed my father. Being here behind the controls was as close as I could get to any of those.

No, there was one way to get even closer.

I took my feet off the brakes and gave it lots of fuel. The engine roared louder as the propeller pushed the plane forward and it rapidly gained speed. I tried to focus on the plane, but I couldn't avoid seeing the reaction of those watching. They were cheering, raising their arms, waving.

I gave it more and more gas until I was racing along, approaching takeoff velocity, the wheels feeling like they were just skimming along the top of the asphalt. I caught a glimpse of Lori off to the side, and right then I pulled back on the stick and I was flying!

I was in the sky, and it was fantastic—and a terrible mistake. *What was I doing?* I needed to set it back down, but there wasn't room. Up ahead the road ended in a cul-de-sac and there was a house, directly in my way. There was only one thing to do. I pulled the stick back even harder, gave it more gas, and climbed.

Within seconds I passed over the house and was above a field and then the highway, with the electrical towers looming ahead. Dead or alive, the electrical wires were a danger to any aircraft. I pushed the stick to the left, pressing the left rudder with my left foot, and the little plane responded instantly—almost too instantly. I eased off both controls.

Banking, I could see the highway clearly, a long curling stretch winding by our neighborhood and away into the distance.

To land, I had to come back over and approach our street upwind. I'd have to make a big, wide circle around the neighborhood. Below was the checkpoint at Erin Mills Parkway, and I was low enough to see the people. They waved and I waved back. I leveled off again and followed along the side of the neighborhood. There were more people below, and everybody seemed to stop and stare up at me.

I knew I should just do a tight circle and land, but I didn't want to. Besides, once my mother heard about this, I didn't think I'd be up here again, and it felt so amazing. I decided I'd just fly a little bit farther. My mom wasn't going to be any angrier if I was gone twice as long. My father would understand. If he were around, he'd be down there cheering me on.

I pulled back on the stick to gain height, while at the same time banking right and giving it more fuel to keep up my speed as I climbed. I needed more elevation. Height was safety. If the engine stalled out, the higher I was, the more time I'd have to glide until I found a place to land. That was something my father had drilled into me—a pilot should always have a backup plan, should always think one step ahead. Funny, that sounded so much like Herb as well.

There were also other benefits to gaining height. It gave me not only a greater perspective but even more space and separation from anybody or anything on the ground. Up here nobody could get me. I leveled off when the altimeter read out close to three hundred feet. I was high but could go higher if I needed to.

Beneath me I could see the houses and streets of other subdivisions. The main road was littered with abandoned cars. It all looked pretty normal except there was virtually no movement. It was like seeing a real-life painting instead of real life. From this height it was all calm and peaceful. Distance could be deceptive.

I kept traveling, retracing the route we'd done on the ground yesterday to bring the Petersons to the neighborhood. Up ahead was the barricade where we'd had all that trouble. I could see cars back in position, blocking the road, but couldn't see any people.

I crossed over the highway and left behind the houses and gained the fields and woods below, coming up to the farms. The fields were filled with the first shoots of crops that had been planted before this happened. That illusion of normalcy was once again so strong it was almost overpowering. I wanted that illusion to be real. Up here, for a while, it was. I just wanted to stay up here, fly until my tank was dry, and— *My tank! How much fuel did I have?*

I hadn't intended to fly, so I hadn't done any checks, hadn't even looked at the fuel level. I knew my father had been the last to put any in. He and I were working out the kinks in the timing of the engine. How long had that taken and, more important, how much fuel had he put in? Assuming he filled it up completely I would be fine, but there was no way of knowing. There was no gauge, and the tank wasn't accessible while flying. How could I be so stupid not to check? Really, I could have just done a turn and brought it right back in, but I hadn't. Instead I'd just kept extending the flight.

I banked hard to the right until the six lanes of Eglinton Avenue were below me. The road could be both my guide and my emergency landing strip if I needed it, although with the positioning of the stalled cars I didn't know if there would be space to put it down without running into one of them. Either way it was better to hit a car on the ground than crash into a house from above.

I tried to check off the variables in my mind. Height meant more safety if I did run out of fuel because I'd have more chance to glide to an open stretch of road, but climbing would cost me more fuel and make it more likely I'd need to find a safe spot to make an emergency landing. What I did know for certain was that speed sucked away fuel. The slower I flew, the farther I could go. I eased off the throttle and dipped down slightly—one compensated for the other so that I didn't lose any speed despite feeding the engine less fuel. I just had to stay above stall speed.

Now I had a close-up view of the ground racing by beneath me. Houses and stores alternately lined the route on both sides of the road. I caught split-second glimpses of broken windows or smashed doors. I could see where more than one building had been set on fire. Not all of those could have been accidents.

I could also see all sorts of people, looking around as they heard me coming, sometimes staring up into the sky before spinning to see me. I was so low that I could see their faces. They looked curious or amused, and always a little shocked. In a world where not much of anything mechanical was moving, I was flying! I was probably the only thing in the sky above the whole city. Now I just had to *stay* in the sky.

Then again, maybe I shouldn't even try. I should just bring it down while I could. If I could find a stretch of road long enough, I'd land, run straight to the neighborhood, and bring back my car, some extra gas, and enough support to protect us all. I'd just have to hope that my plane would still be there and in one piece. Of course, that was assuming that both of us were in one piece after I landed. I listened for the engine. It still sounded like it was getting enough fuel. I'd keep pushing forward.

As much as I was worried about crashing I was almost equally worried about my mother's reaction. I just hoped she didn't even know I was up here. Okay, that was being ridiculous. I'd taken off from our street in front of dozens of our neighbors, and I'd waved at a whole bunch of other people as if I were the Queen of England. If my mother didn't know right now, she'd know soon enough and I'd have to figure out what to say to her. But I couldn't think of that now. I needed to focus—did the plane's engine just flutter? Was I almost out of gas? I tilted my head to the side and listened. It didn't sound any different, did it? I gave it a little pulse of gas to rev the engine up. It sounded good.

Erin Mills Parkway appeared below, and I crossed over and started my curve into the neighborhood, heading toward my street. I accelerated a little bit more to compensate for the speed lost through the banking. I couldn't risk stalling out. Crashing because I had no gas would be unavoidably stupid, but crashing because I was coming in too slowly was just stupid.

Up ahead I could make out the individual houses. There were the two that framed my street, my landing strip.

Underneath me were houses in the subdivision just north of our neighborhood. I was so low I could almost reach down and touch their chimneys. The highway came up below. I was almost there. My street was just ahead. Even if the engine died now, I'd still have enough momentum at least to crash-land in the neighborhood.

I adjusted my course to correct for a slight crosswind, keeping the nose of the plane aimed right between my marker houses. All I needed now was just one more little squirt of liquid into the carburetor—heck, even the fumes should get me home from here.

I passed over the wall, so low I could recognize the sentries, and see their open-mouthed faces. I eased off the throttle even more, just keeping enough speed to avoid stalling. Fifteen feet up . . . ten feet. I leveled off a little to get across the intersection and onto my street. I looked forward and I could see my house—and Lori and my mother and Herb standing on the front lawn.

Deliberately I looked away from them and back to my task, focusing on the road coming up toward me. Less than ten feet, now lower than five. I had to touch down now or overshoot the street and end up on somebody's lawn. I pulled the stick slightly toward me to lift the nose up, and the wheels hit the road and bounced a little and then settled down. I eased off the throttle and put pressure on the brakes.

"Come on, slow down, slow down," I yelled at the plane, and it seemed to listen. It came to a stop, with five houses' worth of road to spare.

"Thank you," I said to the plane. I looked skyward. "Thank you as well."

I reached for the kill switch to turn off the engine, but before I could touch it the engine coughed, sputtered, and died. That could mean only one thing. I was out of gas. I undid my seat belt and climbed out as my mother, Lori, Herb, and a bunch of my neighbors rushed toward me. I wasn't sure exactly what I was going to say, but I knew I wasn't going to mention the empty tank.

24

"You shouldn't have done that!" my mother shouted. "You know that."

I nodded. There was no point in arguing. She was right. I stood there next to the plane, looking down, trying not to say anything to get her madder and embarrass me further in front of all the neighbors who were standing around watching. Then I saw the twins come barreling out of the house, shouting in excitement.

"I'm so angry and so relieved all at once I don't know whether I should hit you or hug you."

"I didn't mean to scare you. I just didn't think that—"

"You're right, you just didn't think!" she exclaimed. "What if you had crashed?"

"But I didn't. It flew, the way Dad and I knew it would."

"What do you think your father would say to you if he were here right now?" she demanded.

"He would have yelled at me, and then congratulated me . . . and then wanted to fly with me. *He* had faith in our plane and faith in my ability to fly it."

"*I* have faith," Danny said, jumping into the conversation. "Can you take me up?"

"Take me instead!" Rachel exclaimed. "You know you like me better than—"

"He's not taking either of you," our mother said, cutting her off. She let out a big sigh.

"It's not that I don't have faith, young man." She paused and I waited anxiously for what was going to come next. "Actually, I can't believe what I'm going to say. I need you to fly me somewhere."

"What did you say?"

"I need you to fly me somewhere."

"And then can he take me?" Danny asked.

She silenced him with a glare.

"Or maybe not," he said.

"Where do you want to go?"

"To the other precinct station."

I was so surprised I didn't say anything.

"Can you do it?"

"Um, I could get you there in thirty minutes, but I don't know if there's a place I can put down when I get there."

"I don't want you to put down. I just have to see it."

Herb stepped forward. "There have been rumors, Adam."

"What do you mean?" Lori asked.

"Let's talk in a little more private spot," my mother whispered. "Danny and Rachel, I want you to watch the ultralight."

She walked away and Herb, Lori, and I followed, leaving my ultralight—and the twins—behind. She stopped when we had separated from the crowd gathered around it.

"I really shouldn't say until I've got confirmation," Mom said. "I don't want to spread false information."

"It's only the four of us," Herb said. "Nobody is going to spread anything."

She didn't answer right away. Then she sighed. "I heard that it was gone."

"Gone? How can the station be gone?" I asked.

"Not gone. That's the wrong word. No longer in use . . . abandoned. I have to find out if that's true."

"You do have to find out," Herb said. "But maybe you shouldn't be the one to go."

"I can't send Adam there by himself."

"He won't be by himself. I'll go with him," Herb said.

"No, it's my responsibility. I'm the commanding officer."

"That's why you *can't* go. You need to be at your command. Besides, you're also a mother and you have children who need you, especially when their father isn't here."

"Adam needs me at his side, too," she argued.

"Up there you couldn't help him. Let me go. Have faith. In him and me."

She looked like she was going to argue. Instead she quietly nodded.

Thirty minutes later Lori watched as I put another tick mark on my preflight checklist—the bolts holding the wheels in place were solid. I'd already checked the bolts on the wings and the engine mounts, and of course I'd filled the tank to the top from one of the six-gallon plastic cans we had in the garage. Nobody had noticed just how much gas I'd put in. With the added weight of Herb aboard we'd be using far more fuel. If he'd been with me on that first solo flight it would have been the last of anything for either of us.

"Almost ready?" Lori asked.

I held up the checklist. "It's all checked and ready for another flight."

"So when do I get to go up?"

"Today's second flight is already booked."

"I guess we're never going to have that first date, are we?" she said.

"Were you just asking me out?"

"That's probably the only way it's ever going to happen," she said, "although technically I think I was asking you *up* rather than *out*. It would be so cool to be up there."

"And we wouldn't have Todd as a chaperone."

Herb rounded the side of his house. Trailing behind him were the twins. Danny was still annoyed that it wasn't him going up with me. Herb had binoculars around his neck, a big bag on his shoulder, and a scoped rifle slung over his back.

"Are you going hunting or flying?" Lori asked nervously.

"It's never bad to have a little backup in case somebody gets the idea of hunting us. Are you ready to go, Captain?"

"Safety check completed. Let's go."

"And I better go as well," Lori said. "Those cows aren't going to milk themselves."

"I could help," Rachel offered.

"And I could watch," Danny said.

"I'll take both offers," Lori said. She threw her arms around me. "Be careful up there."

I was too speechless from the hug to reply. She let go and walked away. The twins went with her and I was glad. I didn't want them to witness things if they went wrong.

"Funny, she didn't ask *me* to be careful," Herb said.

"I think she realizes you're too tough to be hurt," I suggested.

"If that were the case I wouldn't need these." He pulled two armored vests out of the bag he was carrying.

"Where did you get those?"

"It's amazing what's tucked away in my basement. Put it on."

"Do you really think that's necessary?" I asked.

"I'm not trying to make a fashion statement. Put it on."

It certainly couldn't hurt. I slipped it on and did up the clasps.

Herb put his on and then we took our seats. I turned the ignition and the engine caught. While it warmed up I slipped on my helmet and Herb did the same. In the helmets were headsets that would allow us to talk over the roar of the engine.

"Can you hear me?" I asked after we both had plugged in our communication cords to the console.

"Yes, or should I say 'roger'?"

"I think we can do without that. Clip on the harness."

"Harness?"

I reached down, took the belts, and clicked them in place. "There, now you can't fall out."

"I appreciate that. Did I mention that I'm afraid of heights?" Herb asked.

I laughed. "Nope. You do know I'm planning on flying higher than a few feet?"

"Yes, I gathered that. Let's get going."

I snapped my harness on, released the foot brakes, and fed the engine more fuel. It roared and the ultralight inched forward. All around us a crowd was gathering. It wasn't just people from our street but from other streets in the neighborhood who'd heard about our flight. They'd been moved back, well away from the road itself. Clipping one of them with a wing would have killed them and probably us as well.

I goosed the throttle and we picked up speed as we rolled down the road. I knew my mother had made a point of leaving to go back to her station and so wouldn't be there to watch. She wanted me to go, but she wasn't going to be there to see it happen.

We kept gaining speed, but not gaining any separation from the ground. The extra weight was making it necessary to reach even higher speeds before the wings would lift us up. Was this street going to be long enough?

I gave it more gas. This was no time to back off. The plane suddenly lifted off the ground, and I pulled back on the stick and gunned the gas. We started to climb, easily clearing the roofs of the houses at the end of the street.

I banked to the right, turning us toward the station and the city beyond. Herb reached out and grabbed my arm. "Not so steep if you don't mind."

"That wasn't very steep."

"Steep enough for me," Herb said.

"You being afraid of heights surprises me."

"People are all full of surprises and contradictions. It makes us interesting," Herb replied.

"You didn't have to come up here if you didn't want to," I said.

"It's important for me to be along. From my ham radio

contacts I know what's happening halfway across the country, but I don't know what's happening twenty miles away. What *is* your range?"

"It depends on weight, speed, and elevation, but six hundred miles is a possibility."

"That's a fair distance. Could you stay low, please?"

"It's actually safer to be higher. More elevation gives us a chance to choose a landing site if we need. Besides, it gives us separation from anybody on the ground."

"It doesn't give you separation from a bullet," Herb said.

"But it gets us farther away from whoever is shooting at us."

"Height isn't a deterrent to a high-powered rifle. Being high up just puts us in their sights for longer. Lower is better because by the time anybody sees us, we've already flown by and gotten behind cover. That's the way fighter pilots did it in World War One," Herb explained.

"And you brought the rifle along to fire back if we did come under fire?" I asked.

"If we needed to I could, but it's like I've always said, it's better to have a weapon and not need it than to need it and not have it."

We came up to the river, and the land beneath us dropped off. It was a big wide ravine and the slopes were steep, lined on both sides with grass and woods. The river cut a thick, dark line down the middle. I'd come to appreciate water. It was beautiful. All along the river I could see people, colorful water containers in hand, gathering water. Most of them stopped and looked up, and many pointed.

"If we bordered this river instead of the creek we'd never have to worry about water," Herb said.

"It's not that far. Maybe we could draw water from it if we needed," I said.

I pulled up so that we could clear the far bank. I was using the wide expanse of the highway as my guide to lead me to the other police station. The highway was cluttered with cars, but there was nothing moving. There was nothing moving anywhere. Where were all the people? I banked slightly to the right so that we could fly over the subdivisions that were south of the highway. Most houses looked to be intact, but an occasional burned-out home dotted the subdivisions.

"I understand looting, people grabbing things to survive, but what's to be gained in setting something on fire?" I asked.

"Some of these fires are accidental," Herb said. "And with no fire department even a little fire becomes out of control and destroys an entire house, or a row of town houses."

"But most of them aren't accidents, are they?" I guessed.

"Probably not. Arson isn't about gain. It's about frustration, anger, power, and control," Herb said.

"I guess there's a lot of that going on out there."

"More than yesterday but not nearly as much as tomorrow," Herb replied. "Do you see that?" He pointed in front of him.

I saw lots of things but wasn't sure what he was referring to.

"Below to the right. They've blocked off the streets leading in and out of that subdivision, and I think I can see guards at the street leading in."

I scanned the ground until I came to a fence line around

the subdivision, coming out to a street. It was blocked by cars turned onto their sides, and there were sentries standing at a little gap between the cars. Even from this height and distance I could make out rifles in their hands.

"Bank around the perimeter," Herb said. "I want a closer look."

I made the turn but also started to climb. I wanted more height.

"I'd imagine there were lots of other neighborhoods doing what we're doing, coming together for defense and survival," Herb said.

"That's good."

"And bad. Think about the barricade on Burnham. They weren't the friendliest of people."

"You handled that."

"I shouldn't have had to handle anything if I hadn't miscalculated to begin with. I was positive I could talk us through there. I put both our lives in jeopardy. I have to apologize."

"There's nothing to apologize for. I just couldn't believe what happened, the way you pulled out the gun. I didn't even know you had a weapon. You did tell me to leave mine behind."

"I did. I told you it was wise to have a gun only if you were planning on using it. I would have done what was necessary." He paused. "Thank goodness it wasn't, though. Of course, if it had ended well we could have formed some sort of partnership with that neighborhood . . . But maybe we can with this one."

"Like a treaty?"

"More like a trade agreement. I think we should try to meet with the people in this neighborhood."

"You want me to put it down?" I questioned.

"No, that's the last thing I'm thinking of."

That was reassuring.

"Let's just keep in mind that they're there, no more than a dozen miles from our neighborhood," Herb suggested. "How much farther is the police station?"

"We're almost halfway there. If I was higher I'm sure we could almost see it from here."

We hit some rough air and I had to concentrate on the controls to keep us steady. Herb went quiet for a long stretch.

"You're very comfortable up here," he said at last. "You're a good pilot."

"You're not a bad passenger either. You don't seem afraid of flying."

"I'm pretty terrified right now, actually. But I've learned that showing how you're feeling is usually not the wisest course of action."

"I guess you learned lots of things. Are you ever going to tell us exactly what you really did for the government?"

"I might have told you too much already."

"Todd is positive you were into some black ops sort of thing."

"Todd watches way too many movies," Herb said.

"He probably does, but that doesn't answer the question. Were you?"

"Black ops? In my business there was very little that was black or white. Most everything involved shades of gray and shades of right. Maybe this is a conversation best left for later."

"And if we talked later would you tell me?" I asked. "Would

you actually talk? Or is this just another way of not answering my question?"

He chuckled. "I guess we'll find that out . . . later. Can you see smoke rising up in the air ahead of us?"

I saw it. "It looks like something is burning." It was coming from a spot almost exactly where the station was. I followed the line of the highway beneath us. Had I been driving, I'd have gotten off at the next exit and turned north. From the sky I didn't need to wait for an off-ramp. I started my bank, curving to cut the distance but also to get a better view.

"It's a building. It's burned out and still smoldering," Herb said. I looked over. He was looking through the binoculars. "It's a low, level building, and there's a parking lot with lots of cars. Most of them have been vandalized or burned out. It's right at the intersection."

I felt my heart skip a beat. "What corner of the intersection?"

"Southwest."

"Those cars. Could they be police cruisers?"

"I'm too far to tell yet."

I pushed down on the stick. I wanted to be lower and faster. As we closed in I recognized the building—it *was* the police station! Wisps of smoke were rising from the roof—at least the parts of the roof that remained. Windows seemed to be blackened or missing completely, and as I curved around, we saw that where the building's entrance should have been was nothing.

"I can't believe it's been torched," I said.

"Not just torched," Herb said. "Those black marks around

the front aren't from a fire. Those are burn marks from an explosion. It wasn't just abandoned. It was overrun, attacked."

"But who would do that? Who *could* do that?"

"I don't have answers," Herb said. "I just know we have to get back to tell your mother. To *warn* your mother."

"Warn her?"

"Whoever did this here could do the same to her station. Do one slow circuit so I can see everything, and then let's go home."

I banked sharply away and pulled back on the stick. I'd do the circle, but what I needed was to get up and away and into fresh sky.

25

My mother walked into the elementary school gymnasium in full uniform. Herb had convinced her that it was important that she and the other officers look the part. It was about making a statement, putting on a show, and convincing everybody in the audience that she had the authority to make such an important decision for the community. It almost hadn't happened. It had taken an entire day to convince her and then three days to put the plan into action.

I watched people stare at her as she walked down the center aisle. Every chair from all over the school had been brought in and they were all filled, with more people standing at the back and along the sides. My mother joined Herb and me at the front. There were supposed to be nine hundred people—every teen and adult in the neighborhood who wasn't on watch or looking after the sick, the elderly, or kids.

The room was loud and hot and sweaty. All of those bodies pressed together were throwing out a lot of heat. Air-conditioning would have been great but impossible. I was just glad there were lights. Outside the side door sat a generator, its humming lost beneath the noise of the crowd.

"Well?" Herb asked.

"I'm all set," my mom said. "Let's give folks a couple more minutes to settle in. I could use the breather."

I knew she was exhausted. When Herb and I had returned from our flight we told Mom what we'd seen, and this then set in motion the chaotic days that followed. The last thing she'd wanted to do was abandon her station, but there was no choice. Herb had described what had happened to the other division—a full frontal attack by forces that had used a rocket-powered grenade launcher. She hadn't believed him at first, or wanted to believe him, but Herb had seen it before. He could tell from the scorch marks, the level of damage, and what he called the blowback from where the RPG was fired.

My mother had questioned where the attackers would get weapons to do that. Herb convinced her that the real questions were "Did they have more?" and "Was her station next?" Finally, reluctantly, she'd agreed. The police station and everything in it would be relocated inside our neighborhood. That was part of what was going to be announced tonight.

———

Earlier today, over the course of the afternoon, she and Herb had led a caravan to remove the final items from her police station and close it down. I was one of the drivers. We moved everything from the station that might be useful. Shotguns, rifles and pistols, all the ammunition, bulletproof vests, tear gas, bullhorns and walkie-talkies, shields, batons, handcuffs, and restraints. We also took along all sensitive papers, manual typewriters, batteries, office supplies, lightbulbs, chairs, and the portable generator.

We were lucky that the four officers who were living at the station all agreed to join our neighborhood. It wasn't hard finding them each a place to stay. Everyone Mom asked seemed happy to welcome a police officer into their household. Having a cop in the guest room probably made them feel safer.

"Are the newcomers in position?" Herb asked.

"Yes," Mom said. "They're on duty around the perimeter, along with the regular people at the checkpoints."

"I know this hasn't been easy," Herb said.

"I never thought I'd be in charge of stripping down the station. We even took down the Stars and Stripes."

"You took it down so that it can be put back up at the new station, once you decide where that's going to be," Herb said.

"When we have a station and we have a flagpole. Right now at least everything is in either your basement or mine, under lock and key."

"You did the right thing," I said to Mom, who looked so worried.

"It felt so wrong," she said.

"But it *is* the right decision," Herb said.

"I don't think there was a choice. I just hope that once things are restored the authorities don't feel that I've abandoned my duties," she said.

"You could get in trouble?" I asked. I hadn't thought of that.

"Very big trouble."

"There is always a risk in everything," Herb said, "but your actions will have helped to maintain lives while we hope that things are being restored. You've done nothing wrong, and I'll be the first to testify to that."

"Thank you. There's no point in worrying about it. We have to focus on the here and now." She scanned the room. "It looks like we have a full house."

"Except for those looking after kids, almost without exception everybody in the neighborhood who isn't at the checkpoints is here. They expect news, although I don't think most of them expect what's going to be said."

"So you think those to whom we've spoken kept quiet?" she asked.

"If they didn't, then we chose the wrong people to speak to," Herb said.

Over the past three days my mother and Herb had had meetings with dozens of people in the community: Judge Roberts, a councilwoman, all four doctors, a lawyer, Ernie Williams from the grocery, all of the police officers, a couple of engineers, and of course the Petersons. They discussed their plan and swore them to secrecy.

They were the people whom Herb had identified as leaders. They represented the lines of authority in the community—police, government, the legal and medical systems. Herb had explained that these people needed to be included, to give them a sense of ownership, so they would support the plan. If they lent their support, then others would follow. If they had argued against the plan, or even questioned it too loudly in this group, the whole message could have crumbled. And some had argued and had to be convinced. Today they would support it.

They were all seated in the first few rows of the gym with the exception of Judge Roberts, Councilwoman Stevens, the fire chief—also in full uniform—and Dr. Morgan. These four were all seated on the little stage, facing the audience. The two vacant seats would be taken by my mother and Herb.

"Now we just have to get all these people to understand and agree with our plan," my mother said.

"That's one hundred percent guaranteed," Herb said.

"I wish I felt that confident," my mother said.

"We have to exude confidence," Herb said. "These folks are looking not only for guidance but also for certainty. We have to be able to guarantee their safety if they agree to our plan."

"Can you really guarantee their safety?" my mother asked.

"I can guarantee that without this plan they have *no* safety. We better begin."

Herb and my mother stepped onto the little makeshift stage that had been constructed at the front and I moved over to the side of the gym. All of the seats were taken, but I didn't want to sit down anyway because I was feeling so anxious. Herb and my mother were going to present the plan, but it was still my plan. What if I was wrong?

I looked into the audience for Lori, who was sitting with some friends from school. A couple of times our eyes had met and she had delivered one of those incredible smiles. It was just plain stupid how in the middle of all of this something like that mattered so much to me.

"Could I have your attention, please!"

My mother's metallic, amplified voice bounced off the walls. The crowd, except for a baby crying, quieted immediately. Most of the eyes focused up front on my mother while others looked at the woman standing at the back, holding the crying baby. The baby continued wailing, and, looking embarrassed, the woman quickly walked out, and the sounds of the infant silenced as the door closed behind her.

"I want to thank you all for coming," my mother continued. "This shouldn't take long, and I want to reassure you that while you're here all your homes are safe. Patrols and sentries are in place, securing the neighborhood."

There was a spontaneous round of applause and cheering.

"In fact," she continued, "I wish to report that we have increased security. As of one hour ago my police station and its contents have been relocated and four additional police officers have been reassigned to this neighborhood. This neighborhood is now our only priority."

The applause came again, louder and more enthusiastically. I could see relief and joy in the faces of people as they cheered. My mother raised her hands to silence the crowd.

"It's been fifteen days since our lives have been turned upside down—since some kind of catastrophic virus has destroyed computers and rendered all forms of technology that rely on them totally obsolete," my mother began. "While originally we had hoped that this was localized, we are now fairly certain that this is not simply a national phenomenon but one that has probably affected the entire planet. As far as we can tell from the information we have gathered, the world has been plunged from the twenty-first to the nineteenth century."

Even though none of this was news to anybody in the room, there was a collective wave of despairing sighs and groans that washed through the whole gym and flooded over the stage in front. Mom raised her hands again.

"While we all had hoped that this situation would be fixed

quickly, it is clear that all the technology that has been rendered useless is the very technology that would have been used to solve the problem. There will be no short-term solution. In fact, it is more likely that the present situation will continue for many months."

The noise in the audience rose louder than ever before. I was grateful she didn't say what Herb was really thinking—that it could be years.

A man stood up. "You can't know that it will be months!" he said. "You can't know that it's everywhere around the world!"

Some stood up and yelled out similar sentiments while others disagreed, and the whole thing just got louder and louder. I expected my mother to use the power of the podium and microphone to get everybody to quiet down, or for Herb to step forward, but neither happened. She let them argue back and forth until finally they ran out of steam.

"At this time I'd like to introduce somebody most of you already know, Mr. Herb Campbell. He's going to update you on the situation and ask for your input about what we are proposing will happen next."

My mother sat down, and Herb walked to the podium and microphone. I was struck by how relaxed he seemed. Herb could be the principal welcoming us to parent/teacher night or a student play.

"Good evening," he began. "I know a lot of you, and a lot of you know me. I've certainly gotten to know many more of you over the past two weeks. I personally want to thank those who have made a contribution to keep our neighbors fed and our neighborhood safe. Let's give all of those people who have contributed so much a big round of applause."

Again, people clapped and cheered. I did the same but kept watching and thinking. I knew what Herb was doing. He wasn't just thanking them, but connecting with them, making them a part of the plan.

"Thank you," Herb said. "I understand how horribly difficult and emotional all of this is. Could I please have that first gentleman stand up again, the one who asked how we knew it could be months and that it was international?"

Reluctantly, slowly, the man took to his feet again. He looked uncomfortable.

"First off, I want to thank you for voicing your concerns and raising questions that many of us have, I'm sure."

"You're, um, welcome," the man stammered.

"I know that we're all dealing with an information vacuum here, so I was wondering if perhaps you personally have some knowledge of where the situation has been fixed or some gains that have been made in restoring services that would suggest that it's going to be over sooner."

Now the man looked even more uncomfortable. "Um, no, I guess I was just hoping."

"As we all are hoping!" Herb said. "Again, thanks for raising your question."

The man looked relieved and then slumped back into his seat.

"As to the second part of the question, through some limited shortwave radio contact I know for certain that the situation is nationwide. The entire country is paralyzed, so we can expect no help from our government. As for this being international, well, the fact that we're even here tonight is evidence of that," Herb said.

What exactly did that mean?

"Let me explain. Our country has many allies and enemies around the world. If this hadn't struck our allies they would have provided assistance, and none has come. If this hadn't struck our enemies, then I assume that they would have used our weakness to pounce on our country and we all would have been incinerated in a nuclear attack prior to this date."

I hadn't thought of that, and judging from the shocked expressions, neither had anyone else. Herb's words were logical. We were safe because everybody had been thrown back in time. There was no friendly country to rescue us but no enemy nation to destroy us either. I felt more reassured and more scared at the same time.

"We can count on nobody else to help us," Herb continued. "But we ourselves are not helpless. We have represented here your local councilor, the police captain, the fire chief, a judge, and medical authorities. And of course, I am a long-standing employee of the federal government. None of us has any information concerning what is being done to try to remedy the situation—although we all live with quiet hope. We know nothing but what we see with our own eyes."

The room was now so still that I didn't think Herb even needed the microphone to be heard in the back corner.

"Out there, beyond the borders of our neighborhood, is chaos. There is arson, looting, robbery, and murder. There are people going without food, water, medicine, or medical treatment. Those who have traveled beyond our neighborhood know that is not *rumor* but *fact*. Here, within our neighborhood, our people, you and your families, your children, have been eating, have fresh drinking water, and have been safe."

Another round of very loud applause thundered toward the stage. Herb let them cheer for a while and then silenced them with his hands.

"They have been fed and kept safe, *so far*," he said. "And I emphasize, *so far*. We have less than two months' supply of food. With the present level of security, that food, your possessions, and the lives of your families will be threatened or even taken by those who have nothing."

The crowd reacted once again—not with raised voices as before, but with shocked and scared expressions.

"However," Herb said, raising his voice, "we are prepared tonight to present to you a plan that will protect your families and homes, allow your children to eat and have fresh water. It is a plan that will allow us to survive."

"What if we don't want to be part of your plan?" a woman asked, rising to her feet.

"This is all voluntary. Anybody who doesn't wish to be part of it is free to walk away. This is your choice. Do you want to hear the plan?"

"Well, yes, I was just . . . okay." She slumped back into her seat.

"We have, in this room, a microcosm of our society. We have doctors and nurses to care for the sick, a pharmacist to prescribe the medications that we have stockpiled already. We have a dentist and even a veterinarian for your pets. We have people with the knowledge to convert our school yards and parks into cropland that can feed us.

There are engineers and mechanics and tradespeople who can maintain, create, reinvent, and retrofit what we need for survival. There are teachers who can educate your children, businesspeople who can help organize, and police and fire and military folks who can defend and protect this neighborhood."

There was complete silence, but almost in unison people were nodding, sitting forward in their seats to hear every syllable of what he was saying, and there was a look on their faces—hope.

"Adam, could you please come up here?" Herb said.

I looked over at him, startled. This wasn't part of the plan. He was staring directly at me and was motioning for me to come forward. I stumbled, trying hard not to trip on my own feet as I climbed onto the stage, realizing that every eye was on me. I joined Herb at the podium.

"The plan was first proposed by this young man. I think we need to acknowledge him before he speaks."

The entire gym burst into applause and cheers— Wait, did he say "speak"?

"I can't speak. I don't know what to say," I whispered to Herb.

"Just speak from the heart." Herb turned back to the crowd and raised his hands for silence.

I took a deep breath and the sound echoed out through the microphone and into the audience.

"Thank you for coming," I said. "I'm sorry, really sorry that you had to come out here to hear this—that any of this had to happen to begin with. But it did. We can pretend or wish things were different, deny or ignore what's happening, but that won't change any of it. Even if the electricity was turned back on today, if all the cars started working tomorrow, and if the water began running from our pipes again, it doesn't matter, because our world will forever be different due to what has happened."

I read the faces of the people in the front few rows. That hope I'd seen in their expressions was gone. I wasn't supposed to take that away. I had to think of what to say next to bring it back.

"I know that someday things will be fixed, but until then, we have to take care of ourselves. We have to take care of one another. Out there, beyond our neighborhood, things are getting worse, more desperate—more dangerous and more ruthless. We have to protect ourselves from those forces, but we don't have to become like them. We can construct our own world guided by justice and fairness, marked by caring and compassion. We can stand against what's happening all around us, persevere in what we believe. We have a chance. We can stand and succeed as a group or fall and fail as individuals.

"We can't do it alone. My family can't do it alone. Neither can my friends or the people on my street. But all of us, this neighborhood, together we can. I want to know, right now, today, who's going to stand with us. Who wants to survive? Who wants their family to be safe, to be fed, to live in a place where they'll be cared for and treated fairly?"

Herb stepped forward. "Stand up. If you're with us, I want you to get to your feet, *right* now."

I held my breath as the crowd seemed to be looking at one another, each of them afraid to be the first. Then a man and woman close to the front got up, then a family at the back, then others throughout the audience and then, almost all at once, like a wave the entire audience seemed to jump to their feet. Some were cheering and some climbed onto their chairs, followed by more people doing the same. They held their hands above their heads like they were reaching for the ceiling.

Herb shook my hand and then raised it above our heads. "And you were worried about what to say?"

"We did it," I said.

He kept smiling but shook his head. "No," he said. "You're wrong."

"But . . . but . . ."

"Words have been spoken; now we need action. The hard part is about to begin."

"I know it's going to be hard," I agreed. "But we can do it, right?"

He shrugged.

"You do believe we can do it, right?" I asked again, this time more emphatically so I could be heard over the cheering crowd.

"It doesn't matter what I believe," Herb said as he moved close and put his mouth against my ear. "It's what *they* believe that matters. And that's why I wanted you to speak. You have no doubts and that's what they needed. Certainty. You gave all of us what we need to have a chance at succeeding. Now we're going to see how big a chance it really is."

I looked around the room. Soon the crowd would quiet down again and they would want to hear about the details. We were ready for that; we knew what we were going to say.

But for the moment it was nice just to see the effect we were having. People had smiles on their faces, and they were patting one another on the back. They were people filled with hope. I just had to believe it wasn't false hope that I'd offered them.

26

Mr. Peterson made another pass with the tractor, changing the grassy field underneath the high-voltage electrical towers into a real field for crops. He was turning the soil on land that hadn't been planted or worked for fifty years or longer, since they first put the towers from a far-off power plant through this corridor to bring electricity to the people in this new community. Now, with no power in the lines strung above, it was once again being turned to what it had been before the first suburban tracts were built here—a working farm. The earth looked dark and black and rich. Mr. Peterson had said it would be productive soil.

Throughout the neighborhood, smaller patches—front yards and backyards and fringes of paved areas—were being turned over. There were nine rototillers and they were all in operation, but still a lot of the work was being done by hand—people with shovels and picks getting the land ready for planting. Every available space was being put into production to grow food. Because it was late spring, there was still time to plant for a fall harvest.

It hadn't taken long to get it all started. It had only been three days since that meeting. People kept coming up to me, offering thanks, telling me how much they believed in what we were doing. I tried to remain positive and confident.

I waved as Mr. Peterson rumbled by on his tractor. He raised a hand and then put his eye back on his work. The land he was tilling was on a slight slope and he had to work across the face of the hill so that when it was planted the furrows would hold the rain—and soil—rather than let it all erode and run down into the creek. The strip was long and narrow, blocked in on one side by the backyards of houses and on the other by the big steel-and-cement fence that separated the field from the highway. The fence had been built as a noise barrier to block out the roar of high-speed traffic on the road. Now it was a different type of barrier. It stood three times as tall as me, solid and thick and built atop a small hill. It now guarded the whole north side of the neighborhood.

At two-hundred-foot intervals construction teams were building ledges where sentries could stand and look over the fence. The ledges weren't much larger than what was needed for a sentry or two to perch. It all reminded me of the cardboard castles we'd constructed in elementary school when we were studying medieval times. This was a strange, real version though. I wished we had a moat so that we could build a drawbridge—but actually with two creeks forming part of our eastern and southern boundaries I guess we did, sort of.

Mullet Creek was so low from all the water that was being drawn upstream that it was now only a few inches deep. It would only protect us from invaders who were afraid of getting their feet wet. As I stood there, watching and thinking, I was continually passed by people going to and from the creek with water containers. It was mostly kids doing the work. Almost everybody said something to me as they passed. It could just be a simple hello or good morning, but some talked about my speech, about the plan, about what was happening.

In a neighborhood where I'd lived fairly anonymously my whole life I was now known by everybody. It was strange. Then again, what wasn't strange?

I walked along a thin strip between the turned soil and the edge of the creek where a defensive fence was being constructed. The sounds of pounding hammers and handsaws were mixed with loud talk and good-natured laughter. It was as if the people were focusing happily on the task at hand instead of the reality of why the task was necessary to begin with.

There were dozens of men and women at work. Todd's father had become one of the lead hands. He wasn't making furniture, but those same skills were being put to work in building the walls that would protect us. Todd was helping him and had been working so hard I hadn't even seen or spoken to him. Funny, up until this time, the only thing Todd had been able to do with a hammer was hit himself on the thumb, but he was showing some true skill. I guess the real upside to this was that it meant when he was wielding a hammer he wasn't obsessing about holding a gun.

I was impressed by how quickly the wall was going up. Half the gap between the last house and the highway was closed. The barrier was built of materials recycled from the fences that used to separate neighbors. It wasn't very high, and didn't look that solid, but it was becoming another boundary between us and the outside world. The fences were tying us together, making us into one group, separating us from everybody else.

Five families had chosen to remain independent and not join the effort, so their backyard fences remained. Their rights were being respected, although I didn't think everybody respected their decision. My mother had told me there had been rumblings about expelling them from the neighborhood, but she was adamant that their right to determine their own destiny was going to be protected. To do otherwise would have run completely contrary to what we were doing—trying to preserve an island of order in a sea of disorder.

I was glad the dissenters were down to only five families. Originally there had been eighteen that didn't want to accept our plan. In time I expected the last five to join as they realized surviving on their own was not a long-term possibility, although I guessed that's what they were hoping—that this wasn't going to be long term.

Hope was good. Unrealistic hope wasn't.

Just by the creek, Herb was standing on one of the platforms overlooking the highway, staring out. I wondered what he was looking at—what he was thinking. I wanted to talk to him, and he hadn't been the easiest person to find.

In the rush to help lead the effort to do things he seemed to be everywhere and nowhere all at once, and when we were together, there were so many other people that we really couldn't talk much. Now I wanted to get to him before anybody else did.

I walked quickly along the boundary. In the shadow of the highway fence I felt safe. It was so solid—cement and steel— that it inspired confidence. I just wished we had the material and skills to build a wall like it around the whole neighborhood.

Herb noticed me coming, waved, and motioned for me to join him. I was glad for the invitation. I climbed up the ladder—which had been borrowed from a house and was tied to the ledge. The platform sagged slightly under my added weight.

"It's pretty quiet out there," Herb said softly. "That's what they always say in old cowboy and war movies before all hell breaks loose."

"Do you think all hell is going to break loose?"

"Hopefully not until we're ready to handle it."

"And do you think that will be soon?" I asked.

"Soon that hell will break out or soon that we'll be able to handle it?"

"Both, I guess."

"I am pleasantly surprised by how fast things are coming together."

Our conversation was settling into a familiar groove. Me the optimist, him the pragmatist. Me asking questions, him not always answering them directly. "So you think we'll be ready?"

"I didn't say that," Herb said. "We're getting more ready every day, and we can certainly handle some things."

"But not everything."

"A large, organized, well-armed group could sweep along this highway, over these walls, and wipe us away like that," he said, snapping his fingers. "Think about what happened at the police station."

I didn't like to think about it, but he was right. People had attacked and destroyed a police station with frightening violence and terrifying weapons. If they attacked here, what would we be able to do to stop them?

I looked along the highway and was grateful to see only disabled cars. There were hundreds and hundreds of them stretching out as far as the eye could see in both directions. All had been abandoned midcommute, and while most remained intact, some had been vandalized. At least one looked like it had been barbecued.

"Our saving grace is that no large, organized, well-armed group has appeared on our horizon so far," Herb continued.

"Do you think we could stop them . . . the sort of group that attacked the police station?"

"Unlikely. I don't know who they were, but they had to be some sort of militia or even members of our own military."

"You think the army did that?" This suggestion jolted me. I still had hopes that the military would come to rescue us.

"We don't have enough information to know the answer for certain. You only have to know history to know that soldiers can become protectors or warlords, depending on their leadership and all sorts of other factors."

"And you think that's happening here?" I asked.

"Look around. Aren't we constructing a feudal kingdom to protect ourselves?"

"But that's to protect ourselves, not hurt other people."

"Not everybody has such noble ideals. Right now, even more than the walls, our best defense is our distance from the city, combined with the lack of modern technology. Lack of transportation and communication has meant that anybody who would attempt to attack us would find it difficult to launch an effective attack."

"I guess that's all good."

"Good for now, but don't forget that we're not the only ones getting organized. Challengers will soon appear on the horizon, and they're going to want what we have inside these walls," Herb explained. "The irony is that the better we prepare, the more force will be wielded against us."

"You mean the higher the fence, the more we build our defenses, the more people are going to think there's something here to defend." After weeks with him, I was getting good at understanding the guy.

"That's right, Adam. This neighborhood is going to be like a flame to moths. We're going to attract attention, if not attacks. But we have no choice. We'll prepare as best as we can. I'll be happier when all the walls are finished and all the trees and shrubs outside the walls are cut down."

Crews were working on the outside of the fence with chain saws and axes, cutting down and clearing anything that anybody could hide behind. The bigger trees were being cut into sections and hauled inside the walls. The wood would be stacked to dry and season and eventually be used for firewood.

"It's important that we have clear lines of sight if there's a firefight," Herb said.

I shook my head. It really threw me to even hear stuff like that.

"I understand it's overwhelming, but it's important that I keep being honest—at least with some people. For now let's just keep planning and working and preparing."

27

The committee was gathered in our living room for one of their nightly meetings. There were a dozen people, sitting on chairs and couches that had been pushed back against the walls to open up the center of the room. Herb and my mom were running the show. Howie was there, too. They'd put him in charge of the checkpoints and the guards on the walls. I pretended to clean the pantry, which was starting to look pretty cleaned out in general these days, listening in from the kitchen as they talked.

Danny and Rachel sat at the kitchen table, quietly playing a game of hangman on a scrap of paper. For a second I wished I could be like them, not really understanding the big picture.

The community's leaders were all there—Judge Roberts, Councilwoman Stevens, Dr. Morgan, Ernie Williams, Mr. Gomez, who was now in charge of salvaging teams, Mr. Peterson, Mr. Nicholas with his engineering skills, and Captain Saunders, the fire chief.

They were finishing up discussing the need for day care. There was so much work to do that there had to be a place for young kids to be cared for while the parents and older siblings were pitching in. So the committee agreed to open up a day care center and a school for kids twelve and younger. I thought that might be something Lori would be interested in helping organize.

Next they discussed the medical situation. The walk-in clinic was open for business, and half the pharmacy was being converted to be a small-scale urgent-care hospital, with space for eight beds. That would be ready within a week, with donations of beds, curtains, and furniture coming from houses all over the neighborhood. Dr. Morgan had even created a small operating theater where at least simple procedures could be done.

I couldn't help wondering whether Mr. Smith would have died had the clinic been up and operating. It had been over two weeks since he was killed, and his family had finally agreed to a funeral. Up to this point his body had been stored in the big freezer in Ernie Williams's grocery store. Ernie was here and seemed eager to get the body out of his one operating freezer.

Two doors down from the clinic, a dentist had already started seeing patients. All four—clinic, pharmacy, hospital, and dentist—were being powered by one generator. It wasn't enough electricity for full service but provided lights, a cooler for some medications, and, if other things were turned off, enough power to run a dental drill and the few pieces of medical equipment that were still operational and useful in a primitive setting.

Security was the next item on the agenda.

"We've divided the security detail into three units," my mother reported. "Each has sixty-five members. Each unit is on duty for twelve hours and then off for twenty-four."

I edged closer to the doorway so I could see into the room. This was the stuff I was more interested in.

"How many of those security people are trained?" Judge Roberts asked. He was sitting in my father's favorite reading chair.

"I guess that depends on the definition of 'trained,'" my mother replied. "We have ten police officers, three more retired officers, five former military members, six men who were trained as security guards, two private investigators, and eight firefighters or paramedics who have some parallel training. I have officers in charge of each unit."

"Are all of those people carrying weapons?" Councilwoman Stevens asked.

"All have some form of weapon, but so far we've limited firearms only to those who are fully trained."

"And the rest are being trained in the use of firearms, correct?" she asked.

"Training is taking place around security issues, the use of weapons in general, but even when they're fully trained we don't have enough firearms to equip everybody," my mother said.

"How many people could be armed?"

"We have enough pistols, rifles, or shotguns to arm one hundred and twenty people. I wish we had more weapons and ammunition."

"Should we be scavenging for those items outside our walls?" Mr. Gomez asked.

"The only way to get more weapons is to take them away from people who already have them, and they're not going to let that happen without a fight," Herb said.

"The most important question is, do we now have enough security to safeguard the neighborhood?" Councilwoman Stevens asked.

"There have been no intrusions into the neighborhood since we established the increased security and started constructing the perimeter fence," my mother said. "We are safe for now."

"For now?" the councilwoman asked.

"We will continue to become better trained, equipped, and fortified, keeping ahead of the curve of potential invasion forces," Herb said. He paused. "At least that's the hope."

That last sentence fell into silence.

While there was a whole committee of people who were in charge, it was starting to feel more and more like there were two clear leaders: my mother and Herb. Their opinions seemed to matter the most, their advice was taken, and they seemed to have divvied up responsibilities. My mother took care of the day-to-day security, and Herb tried to figure out what was coming next and get us prepared for it. I had started to think of it as a two-part system: she did the here and now, and he did the future; she did inside the wall, and he did outside. So far they hadn't disagreed about anything. I wondered what would happen when they did.

"With the ongoing training, the continued construction of the perimeter fence, and the communications we've established, we seem to be in solid shape," my mother added.

By now Todd's father had taken on a leadership role in building the perimeter wall—and Todd was at his side working. And it wasn't much different with Lori—although she wasn't working on the fence but on the farm.

The Petersons had moved into an unoccupied house

beside the park. The garage had become a chicken coop, and the land had become pasture for the cows and horses. Lori and her mother had been working hard to care for the animals while her father had been occupied plowing fields and planting throughout the neighborhood. Rachel had been spending a lot of time up there helping out, as well as taking the occasional ride on the horses with Lori.

"Can you tell me more about the communications?" Judge Roberts asked.

"We have equipped each sentry team with walkie-talkies as well as a way to signal if there are issues," my mother said. "Each section has a distinct signal they can use to signify trouble, and we can direct help to that quadrant."

"If a signal is sounded, then all off-duty security will be there within minutes to support the sentries and repel any outside danger," Herb added.

"That is reassuring."

The light on the percolator came on to show that the coffee was ready. Perfect timing. I'd bring out coffee—my invitation to go in and listen a little closer.

"Funny," Howie said, "what's bothering the people on the front line is the thought not so much of having to defend the neighborhood from hostiles but of having to turn away innocents who are coming every day."

"I don't understand," Councilwoman Stevens said.

"People walking by the fences who have to be turned away at the gates. Worse still, often these aren't just strangers. We're seeing people we know. They're asking for help, you know, food or water, or to come inside our neighborhood, and we have to say no."

"There isn't a choice," Herb said.

"I know that, but it doesn't make it easier," Howie explained.

I walked around the table putting down mugs in front of the committee members, who nodded or thanked me.

"You know, it might be possible that we could let some people in," Herb said.

"It is?" my mother asked.

"There are some people out there with specific skills that could benefit us. It would be wise to have a second farmer, a couple more builders, and another good mechanic or two."

"Do you want us to start asking people about their jobs?" Howie asked.

"We'll have to give it more thought, but there are certain skill sets that would be helpful and would legitimize the food and water they'd use."

"Speaking of water, is that being provided for?" Judge Roberts asked.

"Good progress," Mr. Nicholas, the engineer, answered. "We've been diverting gutters of houses to harvest rainwater from roofs into collection barrels. Or into swimming pools, if people have them. Pools make excellent storage tanks, and that water can be used for washing, flushing toilets, and cleaning and irrigation. In addition we're looking at ways to block off the sewers so that rainwater can be stored underground."

"Excellent work," the judge said. "And will any of that water be able to be used for drinking?"

"With the right amount of chlorine, almost any water is drinkable," he said.

"Just how much chlorine do we have?" Councilwoman Stevens asked.

"Enough to provide drinking water for the neighborhood for six months," Herb said.

"So, much more than we'll need," she said.

Herb didn't answer, although I knew he didn't see it the same way.

"It certainly wouldn't hurt if the scavenging parties can go into the pool supply store," my mother said.

"We've already explored that," Mr. Gomez said, "but it's too late. It's been stripped of every useful chemical."

I guess Herb wasn't the only person who'd figured it out—he just did it earlier than everybody else.

"I'm not so concerned about our quantities of chlorine as the potential for human waste contamination creating an outbreak of a waterborne disease," Dr. Morgan said. "We aren't equipped to deal with cholera or diphtheria."

"But that shouldn't be a worry, should it?" Judge Roberts said.

"There is always potential, but it should be minimal as long as the sanitation system continues to function," Dr. Morgan said.

"I guess we're lucky that the toilets are still operating if we pour in water," the judge added.

"It's an incredibly simple system," Mr. Nicholas explained. "It's all gravity based. Pour water down the toilets and it flushes away waste to a lower level. But if the system becomes jammed or clogged anywhere between here and the treatment center then the whole thing could back up."

"And then?"

"Then we'd have to find another way to get rid of our waste. And if the system is broken here, then it would be broken all over, including upstream from us. It would be almost certain then that the water from upstream would contain contaminants such as *E. coli* and other troublemakers."

"How about as a precaution, I do a regular testing of the water from the stream?" Dr. Morgan asked.

"Excellent suggestion, Doc, but we have to take steps to act on those precautions," Herb said. "If we wait until it happens, it will be too late. We need to start planning for waste disposal, and right now we need to start digging wells."

"Wells? Is that possible?" Ernie asked.

"Completely," Mr. Nicholas said. "The water table here is only a few feet below the surface. We wouldn't have to dig any more than ten feet if we choose the right location. I can put somebody to work on that tomorrow."

Herb smiled. "That's the sort of response I like to hear. People are often good at finding excuses for why they can't do something."

"I'm an engineer," Mr. Nicholas said. "My job is finding a way to make it work."

"Any more coffee?" Judge Roberts asked.

"Yes, sir." I topped up his cup.

"Thanks, son. That is certainly better coffee than we got at supper."

"Sorry, but it's hard to make coffee for a thousand people," Ernie said.

"No need to apologize. The meal itself was excellent!" the judge said.

"Lots of people to help there, and we will get better as we go along," Ernie said.

According to the plan, right now families were responsible for their own breakfast and lunch, either using up food they had in their homes already or relying on neighbors to share with them, and there was dinner for everybody, served at the gym, in shifts. We'd been lucky. Not only had we gone shopping just before this happened but Herb kept bringing over extra supplies. How much did he have in his basement?

"You have to know that we can all survive on far less food than the amount people usually eat," Herb said.

"Is the plan for us to have to survive on less food?" the councilwoman asked. "Are you saying we're going to have shortages?" She sounded panicky.

"We have food for now," Herb said. "Correct, Ernie?"

"Dried beans, rice, canned goods, other staples. For a couple of months at least."

"But we won't be able to harvest most crops until at least four months from now," Mr. Peterson said.

"We'll be supplementing our existing stock by scavenging and gathering from the surrounding areas," Herb said. "Things certainly went well today, right, Jeff?"

"Yes, it was a good day for scavenging," Mr. Gomez said. Along with a group of others, escorted by armed guards, he was making daily rounds outside the neighborhood looking for food and other things that were needed.

I knew what Herb was doing, redirecting them away from the question of food shortages and bringing in positive news. Nobody else seemed to notice, but I did. Food was going to be an issue, just like he'd talked to me about in the beginning.

"In one day, the scavenging team procured enough dog

food to keep all the neighborhood canines fed for the next few months," Mr. Gomez continued, "as well as bags of soil, fertilizer, assorted tools and, interestingly, some crossbows and bolts, and some bows and arrows."

"That is very successful," Herb said.

"Maybe tomorrow we can locate more human food," Mr. Gomez said.

"Although I know you wouldn't turn your back on any food supplies you can find, I think we have some other items on the list."

"What do you think we need first?" Mr. Gomez asked.

"Water will fall from the sky and food will spring from our soil. We need to prioritize about things that we can't replicate. We need to get sufficient fuel supplies to run our vehicles and generators."

"I thought the fuel truck that we dragged into the neighborhood would provide enough to last us," Ernie said.

"It never hurts to have more than we need," Herb said. "If nothing else we can always trade extra fuel to get additional supplies like food."

"So what do you have in mind?" my mother asked.

"I want to take all of the fuel out of the underground tanks at the gas station."

"Couldn't we just expand our perimeter defense to enclose the gas station?" my mother asked.

"Even if we could build fences it's never advisable to concentrate such a valuable resource and store it near the perimeter of your defenses. Not only does that make it more vulnerable, but it actually encourages somebody to mount an attack."

"But where would you store it?" Judge Roberts asked.

"That's the beauty of it," Herb said. "We transfer it to the gas tanks of cars throughout the neighborhood. Maybe those vehicles can't be driven, but they can store fuel."

"That makes perfect sense," my mother said.

"And we can also get more fuel and more storage by going out and getting vehicles that have stalled on the roads just outside the neighborhood," Herb added.

"Also," Mr. Nicholas said, "we'd be gathering tires that can be burned for heat, and metals and parts that can be stored for other use. It's amazing what the components on a car can be converted to."

"It sounds like you have some ideas. Would you like to share them?" my mother asked.

"I started thinking about the use of car parts, including alternators and generators, to construct small windmills to generate power," Mr. Nicholas said.

"You can do that?" Judge Roberts asked.

"We can. Renewable energy would free us of the long-term need for gas to fuel the generators," he explained.

I had the feeling that Mr. Nicholas probably had a better understanding than most of what "long-term" might actually mean.

"Excellent," Herb said. "Please start whatever is necessary to begin experimenting in that area."

"I'll be really happy when all those cars are removed from outside the walls," Howie said. "Right now they're nothing more than places that outsiders could use for cover in a gunfight or to set on fire. So our defense would be more solid once those are removed."

"It's a win-win-win situation," my mother added.

"And how would you move these cars?" the judge asked.

"We break a window, jam the ignition on, and then either push them or tow them in."

"I'm still hesitant to take possession of other people's property," the judge said.

"What if we list each vehicle by plate, vehicle identification number, and the person listed on the ownership papers, if the papers are in the car? Does that seem sufficient?" Herb asked.

"Works for me," the judge said.

It had been agreed that as a founding principle we would try to respect the rights of others, including those outside our community. Items taken were to be listed, and any other act on behalf of the neighborhood that could be interpreted as criminal had to be brought back before the committee for review and approval by the committee members.

"Mr. Gomez, can you take charge of gathering those vehicles?" my mother said.

"Of course, first thing tomorrow. I'll get another team together for that task. We have lots of people willing to help with almost anything."

"I can offer security," Howie said. "We can simply extend our guards to the other sides of those streets while that team is working on retrieving the cars."

"And I can free up people to help get the cars," Mr. Nicholas added.

"I appreciate that sort of enthusiasm from all of you," Herb said, and others nodded in agreement.

"The cars from Burnham could be hauled in and parked

in the school parking lot while those from Erin Mills Parkway could be stored in the mini-mall parking lot," Mr. Gomez said.

"Excellent, just excellent," my mother said. "Now, do we have anything further to discuss or can we allow everyone to get on with their work?"

"I have nothing else on my agenda," Judge Roberts said. "Let's adjourn and reconvene tomorrow at the same time."

28

"Cover up," Brett said.

We both pushed down the visors on the riot helmets we wore, and he took his nightstick and smashed out the window on a pickup truck. The glass shattered into a million little pieces, covering the whole bench seat of the truck. I popped up my visor and then reached in, unlocked the door, and opened it up. With a gloved hand I brushed off the driver's side.

"I never thought breaking into cars would be part of a police officer's job," Brett said.

He handed me the screwdriver. I jammed it into the ignition and turned it enough to unlock the steering wheel and transmission. Now I could shift the vehicle into neutral. Brett waved for the group of kids hovering by the side of the road to come over.

They raced in our direction, pushing and laughing as they came. Practically before I could climb out of the truck, two of them jostled to get into the driver's seat—the bigger of the two won the contest and pulled the door closed to seal the deal. He was somewhat older than the rest, maybe thirteen or fourteen. The other one joined his companions at the back of the truck. Funny how much older I felt than these kids. Actually I'd always felt older than everybody who was my age and quite a few grown-ups. Throughout this whole situation I'd been entrusted with information that almost nobody else knew, information that made me feel older, weighed me down.

"Make sure you get the tank filled up, and then get somebody else to steer it down the hill into the neighborhood," Brett said.

Each vehicle was being filled up at the gas station, with gas hand-pumped out of the big underground storage tank, and then it was steered down the hill into the neighborhood, safe and filled with precious fuel to be used for other working vehicles or for the generators.

"I can take it all the way!" the kid behind the wheel said.

Brett leaned into the truck and I could feel his glare without having to see it.

"You drive it to the gas station, and then somebody else, somebody who has a driver's license, drives it down."

"It's not like it has an engine that works or—"

"Are you arguing with me?" Brett asked. "You don't drive it."

"I won't," the kid said, although he didn't sound that convincing.

"I'll be watching," Brett said. He smacked the nightstick against the door and the kid jumped slightly in the seat. "This nightstick can do more than smash a window, understand?"

"Yes, sir, I do."

"Good. Now get going," Brett said. He turned to the other kids. "Get in gear!"

They put their shoulders into the back of the truck and started pushing it away. The kids were all still laughing and joking around. This whole thing had the feel of a charity car wash. I guess part of the reality check was the weapon I was wearing and the sentries posted along the length of the road, rifles in hand.

"A couple of those kids could use a swift kick to the rear," Brett said. "My father didn't take any garbage, and me and my brothers turned out the better for it."

I didn't reply. My parents didn't believe in physical discipline—my mother always said she hadn't met any violent offenders who hadn't had violence done to them by their parents.

"That was the last of the screwdrivers," I said, changing the subject. "I guess we'll have to wait until they bring back a few."

"How many cars have we taken?" he asked.

"At least forty."

"It'll be good to get this section of the road clear," Brett said. "I hope they're working as hard on clearing Burnham Drive."

"I guess we'll find out."

Brett walked over to the next car—a nice Buick. He took his nightstick and swung it at the car, and the front right headlight burst into pieces.

"Why did you do that?" I asked.

He shrugged. "I have to admit I like the sound of shattering glass. You sure you don't want to smash a few windows?"

"I think I'll pass on that."

"Don't say I didn't offer. You know, if they weren't dealing with all that paperwork crap we could be moving faster."

"They're just taking down the details, ownership, registration, VIN, that's all," I said.

"Let's get real—we're stealing cars."

"The judge said it was no different from cars being towed off the highway after a snow emergency," I said.

"No matter how you spin it, we'd still have some pretty angry people if they come looking for their cars," Brett said.

"I guess they would be mad," I agreed. "Although at least they'd have a full tank of gas."

"I just wish we'd stop pretending," Brett said. "To tell you the truth, I wish we were gathering something else."

"What did you have in mind?"

"Rumor is, there's a herd of deer down by the river. Do you know if there's any truth to that?"

"I've seen them," I said. "We used to play down there all the time when I was a kid."

"So you could show me where to go hunting for them," Brett said.

"I could show you."

"Have you ever done any hunting?"

I shook my head. "My only shooting has been at targets."

"Hunting is so much better. Man versus animal, a real contest."

"It would probably be a better contest if the deer had a gun," I said, using a line Todd had once said to me.

"It's a much more even contest if you use a bow and arrow," Brett said.

"You've done bow hunting?"

"Lots of times. It's much more personal when you're looking the animal in the eyes."

There was a strange look in *his* eyes. It wasn't just about hunting. But a deer would be meat for a whole lot of people. And if one deer would help, then two would be better and a whole herd might make a huge difference.

"You just stick with me, kid, and I'll make you a good hunter and a good police officer."

"I think I'll stick to being a pilot."

"Shame you don't have a real plane to fly."

"It's just about the most real thing in the air. Are you still afraid to go up with me?"

"I'm still too smart to go up with you." He laughed, then stopped suddenly. "Uh-oh. More people coming,"

I turned and looked around. It was a family; husband, wife, and two kids, both very young. The man was pulling a wagon loaded with possessions, and the woman was pushing a grocery cart.

"They look pretty harmless," I said.

"I think they should be turning everybody away when we're out here working."

"They're just trying to get somewhere. The patrol is giving them a break," I said.

"There's only one break I want to be involved in and it's this one." He smashed the side window on the car beside him, and one of the little kids screamed out in shock.

"Sorry," I said to the family. "We're supposed to be doing this."

The woman nodded and gave a hesitant, forced smile.

"We're moving them off the road," I added.

"You could do it without smashing all the windows," the man said.

"Do you have a set of keys for every car in the world?" Brett snapped.

"You don't need a set of keys if you have the right tools," he said.

"And you have those tools?"

The man set down the handle of the wagon and then pulled a thin piece of metal out of a toolbox on the rack underneath the cart.

"I've seen one of those," Brett said. "It's a slim jim. Car thieves use them."

"And mechanics and tow truck drivers," the man said.

"Are you a mechanic?" I asked.

"I can fix anything with a motor—at least anything with a motor that doesn't have a computer."

"Interesting," I said.

"Not as interesting as what's going on here," he said. "What *is* going on here?"

"Maybe I could have somebody explain it to you. Look, our whole neighborhood is having supper in about an hour. Would you and your family be interested in joining us?"

"We can't just let anybody in!" Brett snapped.

"Look, we don't want to cause any trouble," the man said.

"It's no trouble. Please join us for a meal." This was the exact type of person Herb had mentioned we needed.

"Are you sure you have enough to share?" the man asked.

"I think they can spread it to feed another four mouths. Besides, I have somebody I want you to meet."

29

As I'd thought, Herb had been very inter-
ested in the family I'd invited to dinner, and began asking
the father—his name was Paul Robson—questions about his
experience as a mechanic. After dinner, he had a quick discussion with key members of the committee, who agreed to
invite the Robsons to stay and found them a temporary
home with an elderly woman on my street.

Of course, the Robsons didn't have any way of knowing
that they'd be attending a funeral the next day, along with
what seemed like everybody else in the neighborhood. That
morning they were at the periphery of the procession—which
was where I bumped into them and they thanked me again.
I told them they should have been thanking the committee
and not me, but they just thanked me a third time.

I wanted to be at Mike Smith's funeral to pay my respects
even though I really hadn't known him that well. Sure, I'd
seen him around the neighborhood, but I hadn't spent any
time with him. When I closed my eyes I could still see him in
my mind, blood flowing from the wound, eyes clenched shut,
face distorted in pain.

His wife, son, and daughter followed closely behind the
casket, which was being carried by six men. The casket was a

simple, handsome pine crate assembled by the new carpenter's shop that had just gotten up and running this week. Once again Todd's father had taken the lead.

We had no funeral home or cemetery, and we didn't even have a church, a temple, or any other place of worship, although we did have a Methodist minister in the neighborhood. He was to lead the service.

It had been a long time since Smith's death, and the body had been stored in the cooler at the grocery store, the generator keeping the body on ice. It would have been better to put him in the ground earlier, but between the family and the committee there had been lots of argument about how and where he was going to be buried.

My mother said one of the differences between humans and animals was how we treated our dead. But I knew that we hadn't treated the dead very well lately. There were those dead men along the driveway at the Petersons' farm and those men killed trying to invade our neighborhood, but this was different. Mike Smith was one of ours.

There were hundreds of people. It seemed like everybody who wasn't on duty or working was here. It was as if it were more than just a funeral—more like a *wedding*—a ceremony to join together everybody in the neighborhood. Herb had said it was good to have a funeral because it reminded people what was at stake: life and death.

The line of people snaked along the edge of the field, underneath the lifeless power lines, down the creek, through an open gate in the fence, and beneath the highway overpass above the creek. It was strange to see all of these people— some really dressed up—negotiating the rough, narrow path.

Above their heads the highway was silent and empty; all of the abandoned cars had been harvested. It was a smooth, barren stretch of asphalt and cement. I thought about how it would be a nice landing strip for my ultralight or how even a Cessna could put down there. I wouldn't admit it to Brett, but I wished that's what I had. A Cessna could have taken me to Chicago and back, with my father at the controls for the return flight.

The spot for the burial had been chosen just on the other side of the highway. It was outside the neighborhood but still close. The soil was soft enough to dig, and most important, there was enough space for others to be buried there as well. When my mother had told me that last part it had sent a chill up my spine. We all knew there would be more bodies, but hearing her say it made it more real. How many more people would die before this was all over?

As the mourners assembled around the grave site, I took up a position well off to the side and to the rear. Still, I was close enough to hear the sobs of his family. The minister started talking, but I couldn't make out more than a word or two. I actually didn't care what he was saying. It wasn't like any words were going to make Mike come back or change what his family was feeling.

I looked away, back to the highway, and saw Herb atop the overpass, looking down at the ceremony. He had a scoped rifle strapped to his back. That made the whole thing more real and less real all at once. Here we were at a funeral for a man who was shot defending our neighborhood, and Herb was up there ready to defend the funeral itself. I realized that I wanted to be up there with him more than I wanted to be down here.

Slowly I backed away, leaving the Robson family behind, and then moved quietly through the underbrush. I scaled the side of the embankment and then climbed over the guardrail and onto the highway. Herb acknowledged my presence with a subtle nod. From this distance I could see everything but hear nothing. That detachment made me feel better.

"It's good to get him in the ground," Herb said.

"I guess it will give his family some comfort."

"I wasn't thinking about their comfort so much as the need to dispose of the body. It's never good to have bodies piling up," he said in typical Herb fashion.

"Nope, I guess not. At least we're doing the right thing here today."

"We are. Not just for the family, but for the neighborhood. All those people being here is part of us coming together. These are the events that bond us as a unit and prepare us for what is still to come."

"I think people are working well together," I said.

"That's to be expected in the initial stages." He looked off into the distance. "The scavenging team is out again looking for food."

"Is that where Brett is?"

"Yes, he's leading security on that team."

"Is he going to be in charge of security for all the trips outside the neighborhood?" I asked.

"Maybe not all, but many of them. His skills and temperament are better suited to *doing* than to standing and waiting." He paused. "You don't like him very much, do you?"

"It's not that I don't like him," I said. "It's just that I don't know if I really . . . well . . . I don't know how to say it."

"You don't know if you trust him?" Herb asked.

"I guess that's it. I don't trust his moods. He just seems so unpredictable," I said.

"He is a wild card, but I think he's better when he's acting than when he's thinking. We can put that to work for us. We'll see how that plays out."

"Makes sense. I guess even I'd feel more secure going somewhere if he was there with me."

"I'm going to ask a construction team to take down the walls on this side of the highway," Herb said. "We can use the material to extend our wall along Erin Mills Parkway and clear our field of vision across the highway and into the fields on the other side."

"Would you think of taking over those fields and planting crops over there?" I asked.

"I'm not sure we can extend our security across the highway to ensure that we wouldn't simply be planting to allow somebody else to harvest. There's no point in sowing without reaping, but we'll— Hold on."

Herb took the walkie-talkie that was strapped to his waist and raised it to his face. "I see a group of people, four or five, coming out of the woods to the north. Dispatch a team. Do you read me?"

"Roger, acknowledged," came the reply, full of static.

Almost instantly five men at the far edge of the funeral service broke off and headed north. Even from this distance I could tell by his size that one of them was Howie. He, along with one of the other men, was carrying a rifle. I didn't know why that should surprise me at all. In fact, I knew that they all would be armed, as would another two or three dozen people standing there.

I watched, fascinated, as they fanned out, two crossing back over the creek so that they were coming up on both sides.

"What are they going to do?" I asked.

"Just go and talk to those people, shoo them away. It's probably nothing."

"And if it is something?"

"Then they'll do whatever is necessary," he said. "That's what we all need to be prepared to do—whatever is necessary."

This time, it turned out to be nothing. Some hunters wandering close to our perimeter in their search for food. But I knew it wouldn't be long before that "something" happened. I just didn't know what or when—today, tomorrow, or a week from now—but it was coming.

30

Five days later, it came.

I woke from a dead sleep in the early morning to the horn going off and the faint recoils of gunfire. I jumped to my feet and headed for the door. Brett was already there, his rifle in hand. He was still sleeping in our guest room and had been off duty tonight.

"Two long blasts means that it's . . ." My head was still fuzzy with sleep. I couldn't remember what that meant. Was it the south wall or—?

"South wall bordering Burnham," Brett said.

The air horn kept going off, and I was sure that even in the limited light Brett could see that I was afraid.

"Where's my mom?" I asked.

"She's already out there on patrol, remember? Look, it's probably nothing, just a false alarm or something simple. The gunfire has already stopped."

I hadn't even noticed, but he was right. I was feeling panicky and Brett was thinking clearly. He seemed completely calm.

Rachel and Danny came down the stairs. They looked scared, which meant I had to try to look as calm as Brett actually seemed.

"Go back to bed," I said. "It's nothing."

"But we'll go out and check anyway," Brett added.

"We'll lock the door on the way out," I said. "You two need to go to sleep; you have school tomorrow."

"Well, now you're just being mean," Danny said.

"Go to bed."

They didn't move. Brett reached out his hand and pointed back the way they'd come, and they both turned around and headed upstairs. Why didn't they ever listen to me like that?

"Let's go." I reached for the doorknob, but Brett stopped me.

"Body armor," he said.

"Oh, yeah, of course."

He handed me a suit and slipped on a second himself. Somehow between the body armor and weapons this didn't really seem to shout out "Nothing to worry about."

The horn was still pulsing its warning as we climbed into the car. I was fighting to control the adrenaline flowing through my body when the horn stopped.

"Should we still go?" I asked.

"Aren't you curious about what happened?" Brett asked.

"I guess."

"Then let's go."

It quickly became apparent that we weren't the only ones who had responded to the alarm. Lights flashed around us, some steady, on vehicles, and others bobbing, obviously flashlights held by people heading for the wall. It was good to know that the neighborhood was reacting the way it was supposed to, even if it was for no reason now.

Maybe the people on the wall had overreacted to a

suspicious noise or something, and that was what the gun-fire was about. It wouldn't be the first time guards had panicked and fired at ghosts.

I pulled into the parking lot of the school. That was as close as I was going to drive. Brett jumped out before the car had stopped moving completely and ran toward the wall. I slammed the car into park, turned off the engine, and jumped out as well. I started to run as best I could in my clunky out-fit, but even though I was thinking it was a false alarm my legs were shaking so badly I had to slow down.

There was a lot of movement and a lot of noise. Voices were raised, lots of yelling and confusion. The wall was lined with people, and I could see Howie, standing head and shoulders above the rest in the middle of the group.

"Could I have your attention, please!" It was my mom on a bullhorn. She was standing beside Howie. I was happy to hear her, to know that she was safe. Now I just had to spot Herb to know he was okay. He had to be here, and there had been lots of bullets and— No, there he was; he was fine.

"I'd like to thank you all for responding so quickly," my mother said. "We had a disturbance outside the wall, but it's resolved."

A cheer went up from the assembled crowd.

"Nobody in our neighborhood has been hurt . . . It's all under control and there is no more threat, so let's all head home and get back to bed. And, again, thank you for your response."

There were lots of smiles, and I could almost feel the relief as the crowd started to disperse.

My whole body just melted in response. I *could* go home

but, still, I wasn't going anywhere until I'd spoken to my mother. Brett was right. I did want to know what had happened. I walked toward the wall as others started filing away, back to their homes and beds. My mother was standing with Howie, Herb, and Brett off to the side by the gate. They were so preoccupied that they didn't seem to notice me there. I would just wait for them to stop talking.

Looking past them, through the gate, I could see there was a truck out there, its shape outlined against the darkness. It looked like it had crashed into the wall on the far side of the road. That whole section of roadway had been cleared of cars, so nothing should have been there unless it drove up as part of what triggered the gunfire.

I listened closely—I thought I could hear an engine . . . Was it coming from that truck? Was its engine still running? I was too curious to wait any longer. I edged over and silently joined the conversation.

"So you're saying that the gunfire originally came from that truck," Herb said.

"That's what the men on the wall reported. They heard the engine and saw the truck, and then somebody inside opened fire on them," Howie explained. "Of course they returned fire."

"Was most of the gunfire incoming or outgoing?" Herb asked.

"I wasn't on this wall at the time, so I don't really know. I'm sure we gave at least as good as we got. It worked."

"Were there any other vehicles or men?" Herb asked.

"If there were, they fled," Howie said. "That one crashed or I'm sure it would have gone, too."

"Can you tell us anything more?" my mother asked.

He shook his head. "I'm sorry, I wasn't here when it began," he said. "I was patrolling up in the north section and—"

"And you were doing your job," my mother said. "Nothing to be sorry for unless you think you can be in two places at once or you're psychic and knew it was going to happen."

Howie looked relieved.

"Whatever happened, the people out there are no longer a threat," Herb said. "Do you know how many rounds were fired?"

Howie shook his head. "I'll check with everybody and give you a count."

"That can wait until morning. We'll take care of everything tomorrow," my mother said.

"I think it would be better to get the ball rolling tonight," Herb said.

"Morning light would be better," my mother said. "There's too much to lose and not enough to gain by rushing out."

"I don't want to rush out anywhere, but I do want to investigate," Herb said. "What if we're leaving an injured person out there to die?"

Those words produced thoughtful silence, although I was thinking that wasn't what was behind what Herb was suggesting. There had to be another reason.

"Under cover of darkness is the best time to go out," Herb said. "You have to trust me on this one."

Slowly my mother nodded. "I don't like it, but we'll do it."

"I'll get a patrol together," Howie offered.

"I was thinking of a very small group—me," Herb said.

"Just you?" my mother asked. She sounded surprised. "I think it would be advisable to take at least one other person. Even before all of this happened, we'd always insist on patrol cars at night going out with two officers."

"I could go with you," Howie volunteered.

"I need you inside to be in charge of the guards on the wall. Believe me, I'll be all right," Herb said.

"Sorry to pull rank," my mother said. "But I'm not letting you go out alone."

I could feel the tension between them for maybe the first time.

"Okay," Herb said. "You're in charge. How about if Brett comes with me?"

We all turned to Brett.

"I'm in . . . you know . . . if you say it's all right, Captain."

My mother didn't answer right away. Was she hesitating because she didn't think Brett should be the one, or was she going back and thinking that nobody should go out?

"Okay, but we're going to offer cover from the wall," she said.

"I want the cover but with a slight change," Herb said. "I want the guards pulled off this section of the wall and moved along to protect my flanks so that any men or vehicles that come along will be neutralized."

What a strange word. *Neutralized.* Not killed, or dead, but neutralized.

"What do you want us to do if you run into trouble?" Howie asked.

"Nothing. It's friendly fire I'm afraid of. People on the wall pulling the trigger again would just put me at more risk. I want you and the captain here by the gate. Leave it open in case Brett and I need to come back in a hurry."

Again my mother seemed to hesitate. I knew she really didn't want anybody to go out there, but she trusted Herb.

"Howie, go and give the orders to move the men as Herb. suggested," my mother ordered. He gave a little salute, then turned and headed off. Now Mom turned to us. She seemed to notice me for the first time and offered an unconvincing smile.

"Okay, Herb, tell me, why tonight, why now instead of the morning?"

"Howie doesn't know what happened out there. Nobody does. I think it's best we find out before everybody else does. I just want to investigate," Herb said.

"What's there to investigate?" my mother asked.

"I just have a feeling."

My mother stared at him, then nodded. "You go. We'll be right here, watching."

"We'll be fast," Herb said.

"Let's do it," Brett said. His voice was as calm and confident as Herb's.

———————

Herb headed out through the gate followed a few seconds later by Brett, who was on his "six," covering him from behind. They both were wearing body armor and carrying rifles, with Herb wearing his night-vision goggles.

Howie and my mother, both with rifles in hand, stood on either side of the open gate. I was a few steps back, trying to peer out into the darkness. I wished I had night-vision goggles. I had to admit that I felt better knowing Brett was out there to provide cover. The two of them together—Herb, the old spy, and Brett, the rookie cop. Although now nobody seemed to be bothering Brett anymore about being a rookie. He was one of the people Herb seemed to rely on the most.

I struggled to see, but with the cloud cover blocking out any stars or the moon the view was pretty dim.

"How long do you think this is going to take?" I asked.

"I can't imagine it will be long," my mother said. She didn't seem to mind that I was there, listening in.

"I'm still not sure why they went out there at all, why this couldn't wait until morning," Howie said.

"I don't disagree, but I think we've just come to trust Herb on these things," she replied.

"I trust him . . . I just know we didn't do anything wrong."

"Nobody's saying you or the guards did."

"It's hard," Howie said. "Being out here, watching, waiting, wondering what's in the dark and—"

There was a sudden *whoosh* and a burst of light. The truck was on fire! Herb and Brett were several paces away, and now they came back toward the gate, moving quickly, their figures lit by the flames behind them.

"What happened?" my mother demanded as they ran back.

"Not sure. The fuel tank had ruptured, so maybe leaking gas was ignited by the hot engine," Herb said.

"And the people inside?"

"All dead," Herb said.

"More than dead," Brett added. "They'd taken multiple hits—the truck was peppered with bullets."

The fire was getting bigger and bigger, and then there was an explosion. Involuntarily I jumped. Flames shot into the sky. It was like we were watching a scene from a movie.

"There's no more threat, but we should debrief," Herb said. "Brett, I want you to reposition the guards along the wall while we talk."

Brett nodded and left. Whatever was going to be talked about he already knew because he'd been out there. There was something in his expression and Herb's tone that made me think there really was something to talk about.

"So," my mother said, "the truck just spontaneously caught on fire."

"We gave it some help," Herb admitted. "It was important to hide the evidence."

"Evidence?"

"There were three people in the truck," Herb said. "An elderly couple in the backseat and a driver who looked to be in his late forties."

"I guess the others fled," Howie said.

"Nobody who was in that truck walked away. It was hit by over a hundred rounds of ammunition."

"Whoever else was there might have been in other vehicles or on foot," Howie countered.

"Did anybody see anybody else flee?" Herb asked.

"I don't think so, but it was dark and—"

"I don't believe there was anybody else, and neither do you," Herb said, cutting him off.

"I can't know that for sure, but they did fire first."

"They had a twenty-two, and it hadn't been fired."

"Are you sure?" my mother asked.

Herb was holding the gun. "You can check to confirm it hasn't been fired. We searched the vehicle thoroughly and found no other weapons," Herb said.

"Then the gunshots came from somebody else," Howie said.

"They did come from someplace else—from one of the guards on the wall. Those people in the truck were probably nothing more than innocents driving by."

"Oh my lord," my mother said.

"That can't be!" Howie gasped. "Are you saying we just shot three people for no reason?"

"That's half of what I'm saying," Herb answered. "Your guards shot three innocents, but for about a dozen good reasons. You know they were just trying to do the right thing."

"There's no reason good enough to explain what happened," Howie said. "Look, they're my guards, I'm in charge, so what happened is on me, not them. I'll tender my resignation and—"

"No you won't!" Herb snapped. He then turned to my mother. "Sorry, I'm overstepping. I know this is your call. It's just that it's not his fault, and we need Howie to be in charge of the guards."

"I agree," my mother said. "You've trained them well, Howie, and they have confidence in you."

"Obviously, I didn't train them well enough," Howie said. "And any confidence they did have will be gone when it's discovered what happened out there tonight."

"And that's why it's best that they don't find out," Herb said. "Nobody else knows about this beyond the four of us and Brett. Nobody else needs to know."

"What about the committee?" my mother asked.

"I don't know if there's any value in looping them in either. If anything, we could tell them later, but for now it should be known only to us."

"So what are we going to tell people about what happened?" Howie asked.

"I think we should tell them what they want to hear," Herb said. "We were attacked and our guards bravely fended off the attack."

"Won't that just encourage them to shoot at the next car that drives by in the night?" my mother asked.

"We'll find another way to stop that from happening," Herb suggested.

"And what will that other way be?"

"I'm not sure, but we'll figure it out," Herb said. He reached up and put an arm around Howie's shoulders. "You can't change what happened, but we can change what *will* happen. You're a good leader and, more important, a good man. The fact that this does bother you so much is why you need to keep being that leader."

31

I sat as quietly as possible as the committee members went over the day's events. They hadn't gotten to the last item on the agenda, which was the incident with the truck on Burnham two nights before. As I sat and listened it was reassuring to hear about the things that were going right in the neighborhood. The school and day care were up and running well. The dentist's and doctor's offices were functioning, as was the vet's.

The big supper meal was a huge success, and Ernie was coordinating the existing food supplies, reporting that things were surprisingly better than he originally thought. I should have seen that as a positive, but instead it was disconcerting—I didn't like surprises, even if they worked in our favor.

Walls and fences now covered almost ninety percent of the entire perimeter of the neighborhood. The last parts were the hardest, but the committee members figured within a week the workers would be finished. Then they'd go back and strengthen the walls wherever they thought there was a weak spot. There was a whole crew out disassembling the concrete walls on the other side of the highway and reassembling them as part of our perimeter. The more, the thicker, the higher, the better.

The gutters on every house now had been rigged to harvest

rainwater. After a heavy rain every pool in the neighborhood was filled to the top. The first well had been dug, and water was flowing from it. All drinking water was now coming from a central location—halfway between the creek and the new well—where chlorine was being added to make it completely potable. I had to admit that it tasted funny, but the important thing was that so far there had been no reports of any waterborne sickness.

The engineers, along with the mechanics, had been active in rejigging things. Aside from the rain collection, they'd converted three snowblowers into rototillers and another two lawn mowers into go-carts. The new tillers were already in use cultivating backyards, and the go-carts were given to the security teams to use for patrols. Mr. Nicholas estimated there were at least a hundred snowblowers and over three hundred gas-powered lawn mowers in the neighborhood. I had a vision of hundreds of go-carts streaking along Folkway like it was a little track.

Most interesting, a couple of moms who lived in the neighborhood had started a newspaper. It was called *The New Neighborhood News* and they were using an ancient mimeograph machine they had found in the school storage room to make copies. Herb spoke to the committee about the importance of communication, of giving people information so that they wouldn't be reliant on rumors and misinformation. It all sounded so good, so freedom-of-the-press-like. I would have been more impressed had I not known how much Herb wanted to make sure only *some* information got out. I couldn't help but think about what wasn't going to be printed about the attack the other night. Information could be controlled and given out to move people in the direction they needed to be moved. On some levels I knew what needed to be done, but part of me wondered how much of that was being *done to me* as well.

"We're down to the last items on the agenda," Judge Roberts said. "Stan, please provide an update."

Mr. Peterson got to his feet. "The larger fields, including the school yard and parks, have been completely prepared, and some have already been planted."

"Excellent," the judge said.

"We've made good progress. We're working on the backyards now. Those converted snowblowers are making a difference. Is there any chance of more of those being available for use soon?"

"Top priority," Mr. Nicholas said. "Count on one or two being made each day. That is, assuming that we can convince people to give up their snowblowers."

"Is that a problem?" my mother asked.

"People are still possessive of things they own," he said.

"I'll make sure that isn't a problem anymore," Councilwoman Stevens said. "I'll have people go door to door, secure the machines, and bring them to your workshop."

"And of course they'll be issued receipts and the confiscation of their property will be duly noted in our official records," Judge Roberts said.

The workshop was part of the backroom of the grocery store. As supplies were distributed, more space was opening up, and tools and workbenches were filling the openings. There the engineers and their crews could take advantage of the generator to make the power tools work.

"We'll do our best to put land under cultivation, but even then you have to realize that we won't be able to produce the quantity or variety of food necessary to feed sixteen hundred people indefinitely," Mr. Peterson said.

"What would make it possible for you to increase the quantity of food you can produce?" Herb asked.

"More land and a longer growing season."

"More land being put under cultivation is happening, but more land in general isn't a possibility right now. Yet maybe we can help with the growing season," Herb said.

"You mean I've been worrying about rain when you can control the weather?" Mr. Peterson joked.

"In a manner of speaking. Isn't that what a greenhouse does—extend the growing season?"

"Definitely, but we don't have any greenhouses, do we?"

"Not yet. How much more productive is a greenhouse than an open field?"

"At least ten times more productive than open land," Mr. Peterson said. "Are you planning on scavenging some greenhouses?"

"I think we can scavenge the components necessary to build some greenhouses." Herb turned to Mr. Nicholas. "What would we need?"

"Panes of glass and supports, metal or wood, and caulking, nails, or even glue."

"We need to put the scavenging teams on it," Herb said.

"Does anybody object to that?" the judge asked.

People nodded or said a few words in agreement.

"You'd mentioned limited varieties of food," Councilwoman Stevens said. "What exactly is being planted?"

"I'm concentrating on potatoes."

"Why potatoes?" she asked.

"We have the seed, it's a high-yield crop, and it is less dependent on rainfall. Besides, I can even get two harvests in this season."

"But we can't just live on potatoes."

"Actually, you can for a long time," Herb said.

"But that's not all that's being planted. There will be beans, cucumbers, tomatoes, carrots, and assorted squashes that I've already put in. And if there were greenhouses I'd be able to expand the range and the length of time they'd be available," Mr. Peterson said.

"You'll have those greenhouses," Herb said.

As far as I was concerned, Herb saying he would have them built was as good as them already being built.

"Excellent," the judge said. "Now, returning to the agenda: starting next week we will be convening a civilian court three afternoons a week to deal with internal disputes."

"Are there that many disputes?" Councilwoman Stevens asked.

"So far there have been a few, but we can expect many more to surface in the weeks to come," my mother said.

"What types of disputes are taking place?" the councilwoman asked.

"So far just minor things," the judge said.

"But it's inevitable that conflicts will arise when you put this many people together in such a confined space, and put them under pressure," my mother said. "What makes it more dangerous is that many of the people are now in possession of weapons."

"That sounds ominous," the councilwoman said.

"Actually," the judge said, "it would probably be good if you were willing to sit on the panel."

"I'd be more than willing to do that," she said.

"An excellent addition," Herb said, and my mother nodded.

"Now, shall we turn to the unfortunate altercation on the south of the neighborhood?" the judge asked.

"I think we successfully showed that we can defend the neighborhood," Herb said.

I looked over at Howie. His eyes were on the floor. He looked not proud but ashamed. I guess that look could have been interpreted in other ways.

"I applaud you for defending the neighborhood," the judge said, "but I never consider it a success when people are killed or injured. Three dead, right?"

"Three heavily armed men who attempted to attack the neighborhood were killed, and we have no idea how many were wounded and escaped," Herb said.

"An unwise tactic on their part," the councilwoman said.

"They probably didn't realize the extent of our defenses and the training of the people on guard," Herb replied.

"But there were no deaths on our side, correct?" the judge asked.

"Howie, do you want to answer that one?" Herb asked.

Howie looked up. "Nobody even wounded."

I knew our people had been in no danger unless they were shooting at each other.

"I think what we're doing in preparation has really paid off," the judge said.

"Obviously," Councilwoman Stevens agreed.

"There are, however, other issues that have significant

implications for the ongoing survival of our neighborhood," Herb said.

Was he going to tell everybody what had really happened?

"There was a terrible cost," Herb said. "A cost that nobody seems to want to mention."

My heart skipped a beat. He was going to tell them. How were people going to react when they found out we'd killed—*murdered*—people who hadn't even attacked the neighborhood?

"The sentries fired approximately three hundred rounds of ammunition," Herb said.

"That's a lot of ammunition," my mother said.

"We simply cannot afford to lose that many rounds every time there is an assault on our walls," Herb said. "If they continue to discharge that much ammunition every time we're threatened, we'll be in a position where we won't be able to defend ourselves in the future. I'm going to suggest that Howie, the captain, and I sit down and work out protocol around firing weapons. I think we have to limit how many rounds of ammunition are given to each sentry and to insist on nobody opening fire without permission."

"Counting the rounds is easy; training people to hold their fire is not so easy," Howie said.

"Not easy, but it can be done," Herb said. "I have every faith in you and know you can train them. I was also wondering if you think the attack could have been averted had there been enough light to see."

"Definitely," Howie said. "If there was light we could have seen them coming and probably they would have been less likely to attack."

"Then let me meet with our engineering people and see if

we can come up with a way to establish perimeter lighting to be turned on if needed," Herb said. "Mr. Nicholas, does that sound workable?"

"If we only needed it for short bursts, like spotlights, we could draw power from car batteries."

"We have plenty of those available out there," Mr. Saunders added. "We just need lights."

"Another item for the scavenging team to procure," Mr. Gomez added.

"We may not have to go outside the neighborhood to get those lights," Herb said. "Let's look internally first. I have an idea about where we might find some. Other than that, I was wondering if you could give us an update on what the sentries are seeing from the walls."

"There are still lots of people out there, generally moving either west or north, away from the city and toward the country," Howie said.

"Mainly families?" Herb asked.

"Family groups and what we're calling wolf packs."

"What's a wolf pack?" Councilwoman Stevens asked.

"Groups, mainly young and male, who look like they're up to no good."

"Often groups divide themselves into two categories, prey and predators," Herb said. "Are you seeing more weapons?"

"Almost everybody seems to have some sort of crude weapon, but there are also many more guns visible."

"That's to be expected," Herb explained. "If somebody has a gun they want to display it to let people know they can defend themselves."

"We're also noticing more vehicles," Howie said. "Old cars

and trucks, motorcycles, minibikes—basically anything that can still move seems to be out there. Also, there are lots and lots of bicycles."

"Anything else you've noticed?"

"We're continually being asked for food or water," Howie said. "I know it's hard on the guards to say no, especially if it's women and children."

"That is hard," Herb said.

"They just seem so desperate," Howie said.

"They are desperate," Herb said. "But you have to remember we're just a lifeboat."

Howie looked puzzled.

"This neighborhood is a lifeboat in a storm we can't stop. Only so many people can be in our boat, no matter how many swimmers you see bobbing about in the ocean. If you try to pull in too many, you sink. You save nobody, including those who were in the boat. Our priority has to be those who are in the boat, because we can't save all of those who need to be in the boat. Our only exception has been when those on the outside can make our lifeboat stronger and more self-sustaining."

"I guess that makes sense," Howie said.

It did. That just didn't make it any better.

32

The movie ended and there was a smattering of applause throughout the gym from the several hundred people gathered there. It was an old romantic comedy made long before I was born and it had been shown on a Super 8 projector donated from somebody's basement. Still, it had been pretty good.

But the gym had gotten so hot it was almost steamy. This confined little space wasn't meant to hold so many people for this long, stacked so close together. I knew I was sweating. I hoped I wasn't smelly as well.

"Let's go out this way," Lori said.

She took my hand—my sweaty hand—and led me through the crowd and out the side door. It felt good, being hit by a wave of cool, fresh air. It was now near the end of May and we'd had a nice stretch of spring weather.

"What did you think of the movie?" I asked, hoping to start some small talk.

"It was all right. I guess it is the best one around right now."

"I'm sure it's the *only* one."

Lori laughed.

I watched some kids riding around on their bikes, like it was an ordinary evening.

"So are you going to walk me home now?" she asked.

"Of course."

She continued to hold my hand—which made it even sweatier—and led me away through the crowd, which had spilled outside.

Todd was off to the side talking to some other people. He smiled, gave me a thumbs-up, and blew me a kiss. He was a big goof, but he was almost as happy about me being with Lori as I was about it. That's what made him such a good friend. I felt bad that we didn't seem to be able to spend much time together. He and his father had completely enclosed the neighborhood with their fences but now were going back, making them higher and stronger.

Lori started leading us in the opposite direction from our houses. "Shouldn't we be going the other way?" I questioned.

"It sounds like you don't want to spend any more time with me than necessary."

"I'm okay, you know, with a *little* more time."

We left the crowd behind, circled around the school, and were almost alone.

"It's good to get away," she said.

"It was crowded in there."

"Not just that. It was tense. Didn't you feel it?"

"I guess. People are just anxious about everything. Danny was telling me there have been a lot of fights at school," I said.

"I think it's hard for everyone not to feel really hemmed in," Lori said.

We kept walking. It was a cloudy night and pretty dark out. We were coming up to Burnham. I'd made a point out of not going this way since those people had been killed. I didn't like to even think about it. I'd stayed up in the north part of the neighborhood, and the only times I'd left were by air. Even then I'd always flown in and out from the north. I'd gone up on a couple more short flights with my mother's blessing. I hadn't gone far or long but with each flight she had more faith—in me and in the machine—and I was able to see from up there what a dozen patrols would have trouble viewing from the ground.

"How about if we turn here?" I suggested.

"Let's keep going along the fence."

"We can walk around all night if you want."

"I think my father would have something to say about that," she said. "Although he does seem to trust you."

"I've been told that I'm very trustworthy. Besides, you certainly are safe. We're surrounded by armed guards."

"Will they protect me from you?" she asked in a flirty way.

"I am not that much of a threat," I said. For some reason, saying this made me aware of the weight of the pistol I was carrying in its holster. I didn't feel comfortable being without it anymore.

We closed in on the wall and I started to deliberately make more noise with my feet. The last thing I wanted to do was surprise anybody who was on guard. I'd seen what could happen.

Of course the new protocols had been put into place. Nobody except the officer in charge had more than three bullets loaded in their weapons. The guards had more ammunition but it could be loaded only after they were given permission. Herb hoped that would stop what had happened from happening again.

"Those guard towers are really coming along," Lori said.

"Better security." The towers poked well above the dark outline of the wall. They were also one of the recommendations. Better sight lines of what was out there meant a better chance to react, or not react.

"Hello!" I called out as we continued toward the wall. A few shadowy figures turned to our direction. One of them was significantly bigger than the others—Howie.

"How are you doing, Adam?" he called out.

"I'm good."

I'd always liked Howie and I thought he liked me, but now we had a shared bond, a shared secret, and that seemed to make it feel like we were closer.

"You two are just in time."

"In time for what?" I asked.

"I'll show you. Come on."

He walked toward the gate and we trailed behind. The gate was open. "You need to come outside to fully appreciate it."

I felt myself hesitate. Inside was safe. Outside was dangerous, and that danger could come from our own people.

"This will be the first time I've stepped out of the neighborhood since I got here!" Lori said. Holding my hand, she dragged me along and through the gate until we were standing by Howie.

I looked up and down the empty street, grateful that there was nothing I could see. That didn't stop me from seeing things that weren't there anymore or imagining other things that could be hidden in the darkness.

"What are we supposed to see?" Lori asked.

"Turn them on!" Howie yelled.

Suddenly we were bathed in light. All along the length of the fence there were strings of bright Christmas lights.

"It's beautiful!" Lori exclaimed.

I wasn't amazed as much as I was disturbed. We were outside the fence, standing in the bright lights, perfectly visible, surrounded by darkness that could contain anything, where anyone could see us without being seen.

"This is the first section that's been hooked up," Howie said.

"Merry Christmas!" Lori said.

"And Merry Christmas to you, too!" Howie laughed.

"They work well," I said. "Can we turn them off now?"

"I guess we should," Howie said. "Turn them off!" he yelled.

There was a slight pause and then we were in darkness. It took a few seconds for my eyes to adjust.

"Let's get back inside the wall," I said.

"Can't we just stay out here for a while?" Lori asked.

"No, we have to get back inside."

Lori looked at me, a little surprised. My words had come out more forcefully than I had intended.

Howie backed me up. "He's right. It is safer inside. Nobody is supposed to go in or out without permission."

We headed in. This time I was the one pulling her along. The gate closed behind us, sealing us inside. I felt myself relax.

"That worked well," Howie said. "Nobody is going to be sneaking up on us again. If we sense anybody is out there, we just throw on the lights."

"Wouldn't it be better to leave them on all the time?" Lori asked.

"They run off car batteries," Howie explained, "so running them all the time would drain the batteries and then we'd have to use the generators and fuel to repower them. We don't want to draw that much power."

"Or draw too much attention," I added.

Even in the darkness I could see Lori's questioning expression.

"In a dark world those lights can be seen from a long way away," I explained.

"He's right," Howie said. "Somebody might figure if we have lights we have other things they might want, and, well, we could end up getting into fights instead of avoiding them."

"Avoiding them would be best," I said.

A sudden drop of water landed on my cheek. I looked up.

"It's starting to rain," Howie said. "That will keep things quiet as people look for shelter."

"Thanks for the tour, Howie. We better get to shelter, too."

"It's just a sprinkle. We could keep walking," Lori suggested.

"We can do that," I said.

"Well, I hope you two enjoy your stroll," Howie said. I heard him chuckling as we walked away. "My wife and I used to do a whole lot of strolling when we were your age."

"Good night, Howie," I said.

"That's how it all started with me and my wife!" he called out.

"Good night, Howie!" I yelled out over my shoulder.

Lori giggled. "Funny, we haven't even kissed and he already has us getting married."

"I think he's getting things a little out of order."

"You're right. Let's put them in the *right* order."

She stopped and turned, and we kissed. I was kissing Lori! How long had I thought, dreamed, and fantasized about this happening?

"There," she said.

"I guess the first step is finished."

"Are you asking me to marry you?" she questioned.

"No, of course not! I was just—"

She started laughing. "Don't worry—I don't expect you to have to marry me because we kissed." She reached up and kissed me again.

We started walking home, hand in hand, paralleling the wall. I was grateful for the darkness. I felt awkward, needing to say something, and I had the perfect something to say.

"Would you be interested in going for a trip outside the neighborhood tomorrow?" I asked.

"Wow, first kiss and now a date. Where are we going?"

"Not far." I paused for dramatic effect. "We're just going for a little flight."

"In the ultralight?"

I nodded. "Your father gave permission."

She squealed in delight and threw her arms around me.

"I can't wait to get up in the air!"

I didn't have to wait. I was already three feet off the ground.

33

"There's nothing to be scared or worried about," I offered over the headset inside my helmet.

"I'm not worried, and I'm certainly not scared," Lori replied.

"Good to know. Most people are at least a little nervous their first time up in an ultralight. There just isn't enough plane around you for you to feel secure."

"I like the wind in my face."

"So do I. A lot. I'm going to bank to the left now."

"You don't have to tell me every time. I'm good. Really."

I'd done a full circuit of the neighborhood just to make sure Lori was okay with flying. She seemed more than just okay.

It looked beautiful down there. The sun was out and, aside from the rooftops and paved streets, the neighborhood was filled with green vegetation, brown tilled soil, and bright blue swimming pools. It had rained a lot last night after I got back home, which was good for everything. It had watered the crops, filled the swimming pools, and swollen the little creeks. Never before in my life had rain been something to care about except if it canceled a baseball game. Now it was essential.

My eye was also caught by the glint of sun reflecting off glass from a couple of the little greenhouses that were going up throughout the neighborhood. The scavenging teams had been bringing in windows from abandoned houses and car windshields, and construction teams had already gotten busy. As soon as they had been put up, they'd been filled with plantings. Mr. Peterson said they'd quickly outpace the crops that had been planted outdoors.

I completed a pass along the north boundary of the neighborhood, and we made the turn—a little more gently than I normally would—and headed south. I wanted to keep Lori from feeling scared. I was hoping she could accompany me regularly. It wasn't the usual burger and a dance, but a date was a date. Spending time with her was the best thing I did, and it made all of this craziness seem less bad—in fact, it almost felt impossible not to be happy when I was around her. She seemed to wipe away the awful reality everywhere else.

We slowly banked again—once more toward my side of the plane—and headed east into the still-rising sun.

We were up here for a mission that Herb and my mom had sent us on. I had been thrilled when Lori's father had said it would be okay for Lori to join me. Any day, my ultralight beat the heck out of Chad's BMW.

"Is the target far from here?" she asked.

"Not too far. It's on the other side of the river. Are you comfortable?"

"I'd be more comfortable if I was wearing a parachute instead of body armor," she said. "Do we really need to wear this stuff?"

"It's just a precaution. Nobody is going to shoot at us. Besides, it helps keep you warm."

"I must be keeping really warm because I can feel the sweat running down my sides," she said.

"I bet you say that to all the boys."

"Not all of them. Just out of curiosity, what would happen if we crashed?"

"We're not going to crash. The worst thing that would happen is I'd have to put us down. One of the advantages of an ultralight is that I don't need much space to land."

I looked down at the road below. It was cluttered with abandoned vehicles. Not much open landing space. Between the vehicles I could make out people already up and about, walking along with pails and buckets. Life went on, and gathering water was the most basic activity.

"This is so different from being in a big plane," Lori said. "I feel more like a bird than a passenger. How high can this fly?"

"My ceiling is around eight thousand feet."

"How high are we now?"

"Just over fifteen hundred feet. Do you want to go higher?"

"This is fine, unless you need to go up. Could you do a loop-de-loop?"

"Depends on if I wanted us to die or not."

"Wouldn't the harnesses hold us in?"

"Yep, they'd keep us inside the ultralight all the way to the crash landing."

"That's too bad." She sounded genuinely disappointed.

"But I think I could do a barrel roll."

"A barrel roll?"

I motioned with my right hand, turning it over. "But it's pretty dangerous—we might prefer to live."

Lori laughed. "How long can we be up for?"

"It depends on speed and fuel consumption. At this speed, about four hours, but if I added an auxiliary tank we could be up for twice as long and travel twice as far."

"How far?"

"With the extra tank we could go six hundred miles, as long as I stayed well under our top speed of seventy-five miles an hour."

"Are we traveling that fast right now?"

"Just over half that," I said.

"It doesn't seem that fast."

"That's the thing about height. Lots of things aren't the way they seem from up close."

We were quiet for a stretch, just enjoying the view and each other's company. At one point, we passed over a deserted strip mall where the stores had all clearly been looted and burned.

Lori sighed. "You can see so much from up here."

"I can see our target up ahead," I said.

"All I can see is houses and more houses."

"We're aiming for those houses just ahead and to the south. The cement highway fence is their boundary, just like it is for part of our neighborhood. Do you see some tipped-over cars blocking a street leading off the main road?"

"I see it. That's the Olde Burnham Hills neighborhood. I've been there before all this happened. I've got a couple friends from over there."

Thank goodness Chad wasn't one of them. He lived way south of our neighborhood in one of the bigger houses by the lake.

Olde Burnham was a relatively new subdivision, a gated community with a wall around the whole development and a front gate with a gatehouse. It was significantly smaller than our neighborhood, just a few hundred people.

As we closed in I could also see guards—sentries at the gate. I banked sharply to the right, and Lori grabbed onto her seat with both hands.

"Sorry," I said.

"I thought you'd changed your mind and were doing a barrel roll!"

"That I'd warn you about."

We crossed above the cement wall and soared over the tops of houses and streets. Down below, people were looking up, pointing, waving, running along to try to keep us in view longer.

"Hang on again," I said.

I banked hard to the left. The turn cost us speed and height. I leveled off at less than fifty feet and came in low and flat toward the guards at the gate.

"Okay, there's your target!" I said.

Lori reached down with one hand, undid the Velcro holding the parcel in place under her seat, and pulled it free. The package contained a letter from Herb asking for a meeting the next day and a small gift—thirty chlorine tablets—enough to purify a lot of water.

Lori lowered the parcel over the side and after a moment or two let it go. I banked again, sharply to the left—the better to avoid passing over the guards and to see the parcel with its homemade parachute drifting down.

I held our turn while Lori kept an eye on the parcel. As long as it didn't land in a tree or on a roof, our mission would be accomplished.

"Direct hit!" she shouted, and then narrated as it landed on the pavement in the middle of an intersection and was mobbed by a group of people.

I pulled back on the stick, banked right, and goosed the gas all at once in an attempt to gain speed and height simultaneously while pulling us away from the area.

"I'm still not sure why we had to do it this way," Lori said.

"Unexpected face-to-face meetings can be open to misunderstanding, and misunderstanding can lead to bad things." I couldn't have sounded more Herb-like if I'd tried.

"How will we know if they agree to the meeting?"

"If they agree, they'll show up tomorrow at ten in the middle of the big bridge over the river."

"Seems like a strange place for a meeting."

"Herb explained it's the best place for a meeting. Nobody can sneak up on anybody. Herb asked for just two of their people to walk across and meet two of our people in the middle."

"Herb is a different sort of guy," she said. "Don't get me wrong—he's always supernice to us. It's just that sometimes I get the feeling that, well, this sounds crazy, but that he could be dangerous."

I laughed. "Believe me, he could be very, very dangerous. But he's always thinking of what's best for the neighborhood."

A gust of wind shook the wings and bounced us around a bit. She laughed, too, which was like music to my ears. I wished I could do a barrel roll just for her, but really, that was too risky. I'd had some dates that crashed and burned, but not the way that could happen in a plane.

She reached out and placed a hand on my hand. It felt good. *Really* good. Maybe better than I deserved to feel with everything that was going on around us.

34

I stopped at our side of the bridge and turned the car off.

"Do you think they'll show?" I asked.

"I guess we'll find out soon enough," Herb replied.

Behind us, the rest of our convoy came to a stop. Howie was leading a dozen guards. They were all armed, as were we.

"Sorry I couldn't be up in the air to provide an eye in the sky." It was too windy to risk a flight today.

"You can only do what you can do. I'm glad to have you here."

"I thought you might want Brett here instead of me."

"He is here."

I looked around. "Where?"

"He's on the edge of the cliff, on the opposite side of the bridge. He has a rifle with a scope."

"I thought we were just going to talk."

"That's my plan, but it might not be theirs. You know how I feel about a backup plan."

Herb always had a contingency plan. I wondered if his contingency plan had a backup plan as well.

There were a few random travelers straggling their way across the bridge. Closest was a family—a man, a woman, and four children, including a baby. They eyed us warily and then passed, trying to keep as much space between us and them as possible. I didn't see a gun, but there was no question the parents would be carrying a weapon of one sort or another.

Two trucks pulled up and stopped at the opposite end of the bridge. From its bright orange color I thought I recognized the bigger of the two from my overhead pass yesterday.

"Is that them?"

"Looks like it."

"So do we go now?" I asked. We were doing the old-man-and-boy routine again. My mother knew all about the meeting except for the fact I was going out onto the bridge with Herb. If I didn't ask, she couldn't say no—better to ask for forgiveness afterward than permission that might not come.

"No weapons." Herb pulled out his revolver and put it on the dashboard of the car.

"At all?" I questioned, wondering if he had a backup gun on him somewhere.

"No need. Like I said, we have friends in high places . . . up on the cliffside."

I removed my pistol. Somehow I felt undressed without the weight of it in the holster on my belt.

We climbed out of the car. Herb turned to Howie. "Nobody comes onto the bridge until we get back."

"You can count on it."

As we started onto the bridge Howie and the guards walked over and sealed it off. There were a few people still in the middle coming toward us. They'd be allowed to leave, but nobody else was going to come on from our side. I'd noticed they were blocking the other side as well.

I looked across to the far side and saw two figures coming toward us from the trucks.

"Not too fast," Herb said. "We don't want to look anxious or threatening. We're just here to talk."

"I'm just here to listen."

Slowly we approached them, passing random people on the bridge. Those who had now noticed both ends blocked off looked scared. Herb offered them reassurance.

"It's just a meeting," he said to one family. "No need to be afraid."

The two men from Olde Burnham looked like they were my dad's age. Both were bigger than Herb and me. Both were empty-handed, as far as I could tell. I tried to read them. They looked like two guys reluctantly shopping at the mall with their wives—kind of annoyed, not really wanting to be there.

"Remember," Herb said, "big smile, look as friendly as possible."

Another part of the deception. Herb had told me that assassins often had smiles on their faces to disarm their targets. Is that what we were—assassins? Or were we the targets? I flashed a phony smile. I just hoped they couldn't read the fear in my eyes.

"Any problems, any gunfire, and you hit the deck and wait for Howie to come and get you in a vehicle," Herb said.

"Okay."

"Now, stay right here, I'm going the rest of the way on my own."

I took another half step before his sideways glance stopped

me completely. As much as I didn't want to be here and didn't want to go any farther, I wanted to be by his side.

He kept walking, eyes forward. The two other men hesitated in response, exchanged a few words, and then did as we had done, one waiting and the second going forward.

"Good afternoon!" Herb yelled out. "I assume you fellas are from Olde Burnham. Glad you could make it."

The other man said something to Herb that was too quiet for me to hear. The two met in the middle and shook hands, probably exchanging introductions. I stared at them but also tried to look past to the man standing farther behind. He was shuffling his feet nervously.

Herb turned and gestured for me at the same instant the other man was called forward. A surge of adrenaline jumped through me. I worked to contain the energy and walked calmly, timing my steps so that I'd arrive at the same instant that the other guy did.

"Well, it's your meeting, Herb," the first man said. "What can we do for you?"

"I guess I just wanted to be neighborly," Herb said. "We're from the settlement west of here."

"Eden Mills?" he asked.

"You know about us."

"We have been sending out scouts to see what's going on out there. Are you the leader?" he asked.

"I'm a representative," Herb said, "but I'm able to make decisions. And you?"

"I'm one of the leaders for Olde Burnham. We have a lot of people to look after in our neck of the woods."

"And we can defend ourselves," the second man added.

His statement was threatening, but his voice was hesitant, catching over the last words. He was scared.

"I would imagine you've had the same problems we've had," Herb said. "Have you been fending off any attacks?"

"Until we came together there were some *incidents*," the first man said. "Since then we upped our defenses. Now whenever we see some threatening groups of people pass by and give us the eye, we make sure they move on."

"We've had the same. So far they're only targeting the weak and defenseless."

"And we're neither," the second said. Again, not that convincingly.

"We're aware of your size and relative strength," Herb said. "After all, we did do a couple of flyovers."

"That ultralight gives you a real advantage," the first guy said.

"It does. My young friend is the pilot."

"And there's been another plane flying over as well—is that yours, too?" he asked.

"We've heard reports of a plane," Herb said. "We think it's some sort of Cessna."

"I've seen it," I said, "but just once."

"We've seen it a few times, but never as low as you flew. That little thing of yours certainly was a surprise," the first man said. By his tone, he clearly meant it wasn't a nice surprise.

"Dropping a package seemed like the best way to extend the invitation without risking a misunderstanding," Herb said.

"A couple of the guys wanted to take a shot at the ultralight, but I told them not to," he said.

My eyes went wide at that remark, as I thought about how I'd naively reassured Lori that we were perfectly safe up there.

"I think my young friend here and his girlfriend are particularly glad you didn't," Herb explained.

"To be honest, it's hard to get control over people," the second man said. "I think the reason nobody did shoot was because they couldn't get a bead on you and we're trying not to waste the limited—"

"Shut up," the first man snapped.

"Look," Herb said, "we all have limited quantities of the necessities, whether it's ammunition, medicine, food, or chlorine to disinfect water supplies."

"Oh, we thought you might have more chlorine," the guy in charge said. "That's why we're here."

"Those tablets are pretty valuable. We don't have an endless amount, but we do have enough that we can share some more with you. Could you use another hundred tablets?"

"That would be great, but what do you want from us in return?"

"Like I said, we don't have unlimited quantities, but chlorine is something we could talk about sharing more of. Think of it as one neighbor trying to help another."

I knew that Herb had something up his sleeve.

"If it was up to me," he went on, "we'd just be helping each other, but it's not my decision. The committee that runs things at Eden Mills isn't going to be happy about me giving away something for nothing, so if you can think of anything you have that you could offer back, something you have in big quantities, then we can talk about doing more."

The two men from Olde Burnham looked at each other.

"Vehicles," the second guy said, and shrugged. "We have vehicles."

"We have some vehicles, and I'm sure you'll need the ones you have."

"No," he said, shaking his head. "For some strange reason we have a huge posse of mechanics in the neighborhood. We've made trips to the nearby junkyard and were able to scavenge and repair over a dozen cars and trucks. We probably have a truck to trade."

"Or maybe you could just lend us one of your mechanics to help with our conversions. We're turning lawn mowers and snowblowers into go-carts and rototillers."

The two envoys looked at each other. "We hadn't thought about doing that," the second guy commented.

"If you have a mechanic or two who can help us with the conversions for a few days, then we'll be able to show them how it's done. That's the sort of exchange I think can help us both," Herb said.

"We'll talk to our people. We might be able to do that," the first guy said.

"That would be great. I also want to invite you two to come to our community for a midday meeting and a meal," Herb said. "If you have anybody who needs to see a doctor, you should bring them along with you."

"You have a doctor?" he asked.

"We have four doctors and a medical clinic, as well as a dentist and a vet. Luck of the draw—you got mechanics and we got doctors. Any of your people or pets who are in need of treatment can come to our community and receive it."

"Can you really make that offer?" the second man asked as his partner gave Herb a hard stare.

"You have my personal guarantee."

"Well, thank you so much," the nicer guy said. "I just don't know what to say."

"Just say you'll accept our invitation. Why don't you go back to your people and talk this over? We'll expect you tomorrow, around noon."

"That's so generous. It's just that . . . that . . ."

"You don't know if you can trust us, correct?"

Both guys nodded.

"We're not at war with you, my friends," Herb said. His voice was soothing and soft and reassuring. "We are two little pockets of civilization. We can't let this situation, the things we've all seen and had to do, take away our basic humanity. We are surrounded by savagery, but that doesn't mean we have to become savages. We can become good neighbors. You have my word."

Herb shook hands with both men, and I did the same. It looked like the second man was on the verge of tears.

"Come in off the gate on the south end," Herb said. He gave them directions. "I'll be waiting there for you at noon."

"We'll be there." The second guy paused. "We'll bring *two* of our mechanics. And if it's okay, could we bring nine or ten people, mainly women and children, who need to see a doctor? Is that too many?"

"You bring whoever needs to be seen, even if it's double that amount, and we'll make sure our doctors are ready and that everybody has a good meal. See you tomorrow, and remember, despite what's going on out here," Herb said, gesturing around, "you have friends in Eden Mills."

We turned and walked away.

"That went really well," I said.

"It had some positives."

"Extra mechanics would be a big boost to us. That's a really big positive."

"It's important for us to be able to do it, but I can see the potential for terrible problems," Herb said.

"What sort of problems?"

"They're not the only ones who have been fixing old vehicles and putting them on the road. The more mobile people are, the more there is potential for them to come out here, in large numbers, and present a threat to us. And with more vehicles the demand for fuel goes up, and there's still no ability to refine more. There will be more competition and conflict over the supplies that do exist."

"I hadn't thought of that."

"The first thing we have to do is go out and secure all the fuel we can find from every source and store it for both our own use and for trading."

"And the second thing?" I asked.

"We have to become more fortified, build better walls, secure more arms, and be more able to defend ourselves from the assault that *will* come, sooner or later."

"You sound so certain," I said.

"I'm just not certain that it *won't* happen. I do know human nature and believe there's potential for things to get much worse before they can get even a little bit better."

"Did you believe them, what they said?" I asked.

"There was no deception. I believed them."

"And did you believe the things *you* said to them?"

"I'll keep my word, you know that."

"Not your word, but what you said about being friends, helping each other?"

"I think calling them friends was overstating for effect, but I know we can be allies and we can help each other. Besides, it's only in our best interests to have communities out there like ours in both the short term and the long term."

I gave him a questioning look.

"Short term, it's good to have people who we can trade with, but also to share any danger that's out there. It's best that we're not the only target. Anybody coming out from the city along Burnham is going to see them before they get to us."

"And long term?"

"Society isn't coming back together fast, and it isn't coming back complete," Herb said. "It's going to be in smaller chunks, neighborhood by neighborhood." He paused. "Although I'm starting to think that you're having a bad effect on me."

I snorted. "Me? How?"

"I really do *want* to believe that people will do the right thing. I blame that on you. For example, I wanted to believe that that meeting would go well."

"And it did."

"It did, but I still also had a scoped rifle aimed at their heads," Herb said. "I'd like to believe, but I don't want to have to rely on that faith for my life, or for the lives of those in our community. We can't give up our faith in humanity, but we can't let that faith blind us to what might happen." He laughed. "I've got to make sure I don't get too infected by your faith in people."

"M-A-P, map . . . with the 'P' on a double letter score . . . so that's ten points," Todd said as he put down his tiles.

"That's not bad," I said. "You're catching up."

"I'm catching up to you but not to Lori. She's killing us both."

"What can I say? I'm more than a pretty face," Lori said.

The three of us had been hanging out at Lori's place, trying to distract ourselves from reality. I, for one, wanted to not think about the meeting that had taken place that morning, about whether people wanted to do the right thing or not.

"I'm not surprised I'm doing so crappy," Todd said, "but I expect more from you, Adam."

"It's just not my night."

I usually did do better than this in Scrabble, but tonight the tiles didn't seem to be falling in the right order and when I did have a word that I could use I didn't want to. My mind kept trying to arrange my letters to say things like "death," "kill," "cheat," "destroy," and "betray." Herb was worried about me infecting him, but it was more like he—or, to be fair, the situation—was infecting me. I would have loved to put my mind somewhere else. Even Lori being here wasn't enough. Even being up in the sky didn't always work. It seemed like I needed that double dose of her beside me up in the air to feel better. But even then I felt guilty about having a little escape that nobody else did.

And what about my father? He was so far away, in the midst of what was probably worse than what was happening here. And he was alone, if he was even alive.

"Adam?"

I snapped back to reality and saw Lori looking at me, a little worry in her eyes visible in the candlelight we were using to play.

"It's your turn."

I looked down at my letters and at the board. I'd hardly registered what words they'd put down. I built off the letter "F" and put down "A-T-H-E-R" and felt my heart hurt.

"Nice one," Todd said, in a way that made me think he understood where my head was at.

Lori counted the points. "The 'E' is on a double letter and you get a double word score, so that's worth twenty-six points. That's easily your best score of the night."

"Do you know what would make Scrabble a better game?" Todd asked.

"What?" Lori questioned.

I knew better than to ask him.

"It needs to have either sex, action, or violence."

"And how would you suggest that—"

"Please don't get him going," I said.

"Too late. I'm going already. What if you got to punch your opponent? You know, just as he was getting ready to lay down a big word score you get to pop him or at least give him a slap on the top of the head?"

"That would add an element of drama," Lori admitted. "What about the sex part?"

"You could make it like strip poker except with Scrabble tiles."

"And how exactly would that have worked out tonight?" I asked.

He looked at my score, his, and then Lori's. "Not well. Not only would Lori have gotten to keep all her clothing but

I think she might have added a coat. And me, well, I'd be butt naked . . . In fact I'd have had to pull out a couple of teeth."

I started laughing. I pictured Todd standing there, shielding his privates with one hand and with the other holding a pair of pliers trying to remove a molar, and the image just seemed so hilarious that I couldn't stop laughing. I doubled over and laughed louder and longer until I felt tears coming out, and then I realized the other two were just sitting there staring at me, not laughing. Todd and Lori looked worried.

I wiped my eyes, took a deep jagged breath, and gave them a goofy smile.

"I think I better call it a night," I said. "I really need to get some sleep."

"Clearly," Lori said.

Todd shook his head. "You poor thing."

I wished them both a good night and hurried away, leaving them hanging out in Lori's basement.

They weren't the only ones who were a little bit worried about me.

35

I pulled back on the stick and the plane rose up, clearing the houses at the end of the street and lifting up into the sky. We were on our way to Olde Burnham, where Herb wanted to discuss a few things with their leaders.

"That didn't bother me nearly as much as the last time," he said.

We kept gaining elevation and I banked to the left. I'd made it a habit to always make a pass over the neighborhood whenever I took off. It was reassuring to look down and see the progress below, especially in this past week. Each time there were more changes. The whole forest to the north was being harvested. We were using the timber for reinforcing the fence and even making some rough lumber. There were dozens and dozens of people working, saw blades and chain saws shimmering in the sunlight.

"This is much faster than driving and, I hope, much safer," Herb said.

"That sounded like a vote of confidence! You have to learn to trust me more."

"I trust you with my life. And you have to trust me."

"I do. And, more important, our friends at Olde Burnham trust you."

"It's been a good partnership," Herb said.

Over the last week there had been a lot of contact between us and them. Our doctors had helped take care of more than two dozen of them with things as simple as aches and sprains to as complicated as resetting a broken leg. There was even a minor surgery scheduled for next week. Our dentist had done a couple of fillings and an extraction, and the vet had seen some sick dogs. In exchange they had sent over two mechanics every day who were helping retrofit lawn mowers. I had a vision of a whole fleet of go-carts buzzing through the neighborhood.

Herb had also given them a long-range walkie-talkie from the cache of supplies taken from the police station. The systems weren't great and there was a lot of static, but we actually could communicate between the two neighborhoods. It was good to know that we weren't alone in this. We could actually make a *call* to somebody, sort of. We had friends—or as Herb liked to say, allies. I knew there was a difference, but still some of them actually *were* friends. There were half a dozen kids I knew from school or from being on the same baseball team. It just felt nice to be flying *to* something, to some people I knew, instead of feeling like I was continually traveling across hostile territory. Now, if I had to put down for emergency reasons, there was another place I could land and be helped.

"I'm glad we've gained their trust. Now if only I could get you to trust me around things that you might not necessarily agree with."

"What sort of things?" I asked.

"Well, Brett for starters."

"What makes you think I don't trust him?" I said.

"Adam, remember who you're talking to. We've had this conversation."

It had sort of slipped my mind, but really, even if we hadn't, there was no point in trying to lie to Herb.

"And it's not just that you don't trust him, you don't like him."

"I just don't feel comfortable around him," I admitted. "It's like since this has started he's changed."

"Crisis doesn't change people; it reveals them," Herb said.

"You know, if you're going to keep trying to sound like the Buddha you're going to have to stop carrying two guns."

"Even the Buddha would carry, given the circumstances," Herb said.

"Okay, Mr. Buddha with a Gun, so what is that supposed to mean about crisis?"

"Brett is leading the patrols to protect the scavenger hunt. He's shown himself to be brave, almost fearless, willing to take risks. That is very much who he is."

"And he doesn't like to follow orders or have much respect for authority and thinks he knows everything."

"And those things sort of go together with the other characteristics. But he already was all of those things. This has allowed him simply the chance to be who he is, for you to see it."

"But he always seemed so respectful, you know, especially to the higher-ranking officers and my mother."

"'Seemed' is the right word. He never had much respect for anybody, and now he can show how he really feels."

"So maybe that's why I don't trust him."

"Trust comes from being able to predict. I can predict him, so I can trust him. Because I know how he will react, I can control him. Besides, there is a need for him. Can you think of anybody else who could lead the away teams?"

I tried to think of somebody but couldn't.

"What he's doing is important, essential, for the survival of the neighborhood."

"We can survive without him," I argued.

"He's doing a vital job. As long as he's directed, controlled, and supervised he is an asset. In times like this, we need people like him."

"People like him? How about people like you?"

"And like me. I know him because I've been him."

"And you were needed before for things that needed to be done?" I asked.

"They were done," he said matter-of-factly.

"I just don't know what he's capable of doing," I said. "And I don't mean that in a good way."

"He's capable of doing almost anything. And I mean that in both a good and bad way."

"That's not reassuring."

"He's the sort of person you'd rather *aim* than have aimed at you. In 400 BC the Chinese general Sun-tzu said, 'Keep your friends close and your enemies closer.'"

We got hit by a sudden burst of side wind. The plane bucked and I saw Herb stiffen up beside me and dig his fingers into the seat. He was so good at hiding his emotions that I'd forgotten he was afraid of heights.

"Sorry about that," I said.

"Not your fault."

"Back to what you mentioned. Are you saying Brett is an enemy?"

"Not an enemy and not a friend. I'm not sure Brett has friends."

"He's friendly with a couple of the guys."

"Friendly isn't the same as having a friend. I can be friendly to people I despise if it serves a purpose. Brett is an asset to be used to help all of us."

"Were you used?" I blurted out before I thought better.

"I was almost used up." He turned to me. "When we get there I want you to land right on Burnham, by the gate."

"Roger, that. I'll put it— Whoa! Do you see that?" I asked.

"See what?" Herb asked. There was alarm in his voice.

"There on the horizon, it's not much more than a dot, but it looks like a plane."

"Are you sure?"

"Pretty sure."

"In that case follow it," Herb said.

"Really? What about the meeting?"

"This is more important. How fast can this thing go?" Herb asked.

"Not fast enough to catch anything else except another ultralight."

"Maybe that's what it is. Try," Herb said. "Open it up."

I opened the throttle and pushed forward on the stick at the same time, nosing us into a descent to use gravity to increase our air speed. It responded quickly.

"I still don't see anything," Herb said.

"It's about twenty degrees above the horizon, at ten o'clock, moving north to south."

"You've got younger eyes. I can't see anything, but as long as you can see it . . . What do you think it is?"

"It's small and can't be too complicated. I don't think I'd be able to see it if it was an ultralight. Maybe it's the Cessna. That's the only thing we've seen in the air since this all happened."

We passed over the top of Olde Burnham. They'd been expecting us so probably were surprised when we didn't stop and went shooting by. We were so low that there was no question that they could see us, because we could see them clear enough—not just houses and cars but people on the streets.

They'd been following our lead, and more and more of their yards were being put into cultivation, a couple of greenhouses were being built, and in the center of the development a well was being dug—I could see the pile of freshly excavated soil. People waved as we passed, and I waved back.

I focused again on what was in front of me. Now, where was that plane? I did a quick scan of the horizon and couldn't pick it up immediately. Then I saw it, still moving from the north toward the south. It was going to cross our path but way, way in the distance. I couldn't even guess how far ahead—that depended on its height, its speed, and the course it had plotted.

"How far have you gone in this direction before?" Herb asked.

"I've gone to the edge of the city and then south from there and down to the lake."

"Perhaps since we're racing along in this direction we should go right into the city."

"Really?"

"We have our body armor, weapons, and more than enough fuel. It's well within your range, isn't it?"

"We could do five round-trips to the city."

The dot on the horizon wasn't getting any bigger, but it didn't seem to be getting any smaller. I knew that the Cessna had a low stall speed. If he wanted to save fuel or was scouting the ground he could have been deliberately cruising just above that speed—which was a lot slower than my top speed.

I followed the path of the plane with one eye and kept a second on our route. We were less than a hundred feet in elevation, with Burnham just below us. There were still abandoned cars on the pavement and people moving between them, walking, carrying water, pushing carts, or pulling wagons. One of the wagons was being pulled by a horse. All of the people below looked up; some stopped walking and waved. I could see that many of them were carrying weapons. There was an occasional vehicle moving along beneath us.

We passed over a stretch of parkland that formed the rough dividing line between the suburbs and the city. Here was a big expanse of open land that could have been used to grow food, but nothing was being grown. I guess unless you could defend it there was no point in growing it.

In the far, far distance were the office towers of the downtown core, so tall that they were visible even from this distance. Closer now were the houses, apartments, and smaller office buildings that seemed to occupy every inch of the ground. Numerous blackened buildings—houses and apartments—dotted the landscape. I was close enough to the ground to see the shattered windows of stores, the vandalized cars, all sorts of destruction.

Here, too, was no sign of any cultivation. I didn't know how many people were still down there, but none of them seemed to be trying to grow food. If communities were coming together, they weren't visible from the air.

The airplane ahead was descending, getting lower and lower. That was why it wasn't moving that fast—it was coming in for a landing. I knew the city well enough to know that there was no airport downtown, so I had to assume that the Cessna was doing what I'd been doing, using a stretch of road as a runway.

As it continued to descend I started to gain elevation to keep it in sight. That wouldn't last much longer. It was definitely landing. If I could mark the spot where it set down and continued in that direction, I could pass right over. Even if I couldn't immediately see the plane, I couldn't miss a runway from this height, whether it was a dirt strip or, more likely, a road. Who knows? I thought. Maybe I could even set down and we could— No, I didn't need Herb to tell me we weren't going to do that. It would be far too dangerous to land not knowing who the people were.

But once I knew where it was we could always go back, drop a message, establish communication the way we had with Olde Burnham. That had worked out well, so we could hope that this could work out, too. It would be great to have another pilot on our side, not to be alone and vulnerable in the air.

"I've lost it," I said as the plane dropped below the horizon. "I'm going to aim for the last spot I saw it go down."

I adjusted course, dead-reckoning to a location I thought was about five miles east and a mile south of our present location.

"I'm disappointed in what I see," Herb said. "I thought there would be more, and instead there's much less. I'm not sure how people are able to survive down there."

"How many people do you think are still living in the city?"

"It would have been almost a quarter of a million people before this happened. Now it might only be thirty or forty thousand."

"That few?"

"Possibly even less. But unless there's more than that here, I just don't see enough development to support ongoing survival."

"I've noticed that, too. Nobody seems to be growing anything. Where did all the people go?" I asked.

"You've seen them stream by our walls, migrating out of the city," Herb said. "You've also seen the bodies. The death rate has undoubtedly continued to soar."

I couldn't help but think how we'd managed to escape that in the neighborhood. There had been three deaths: one on the wall—that first shooting—and two from natural causes, a man who'd had a heart attack, and an elderly woman.

"Up ahead, do you see it?" Herb asked.

I did. There was a long, wide stretch of pavement and on it was an airplane. It was a shiny white Cessna. It looked like the one I'd seen overhead before.

"We found it . . . and more."

All along both sides of the pavement were vehicles—trucks and cars—and people, lots and lots of people. The place looked like an industrial compound surrounded by a high metal fence, and it seemed like a whole army of—

I saw the flash of a muzzle and then felt a bullet rip into the wing above my head.

"Turn!" Herb yelled.

Before the word had escaped his lips I'd already started to bank sharply to the right. I heard another bullet whiz by my head and I pushed down on the stick, dropping behind the row of stores that lined the street. I was so low I was practically skimming along the asphalt.

"They shot at us! Why would they shoot at us?" I screamed.

"Just stay focused, stay calm. We have to get away."

"We're safe now—they can't even see us," I said.

"What if they send the plane back up to get us?" Herb asked.

"It's a Cessna, not a fighter jet."

"Do you think we're the only ones who carry a rifle?" Herb asked.

I hadn't even thought of that. I pulled up enough to be above the level of the rooftops but not high enough to be visible. If that plane was coming after us I couldn't outrun it, but I could try to hide among the buildings.

Quickly I had to figure this out. The Cessna had landed coming from the north. If it was going to take off they'd have to taxi it around and aim back into the wind, taking off to the north. I banked to the south, putting more space between us and where it was going to have to make its turn. How long would it take to get it back into the air? Probably the pilot had already left, so they'd have to scramble him back into the cockpit. If the plane had been out for a while they'd have to refuel, and even if they didn't have to refuel I'd still have a good five minutes before it could get to where I was now. I pressed against the throttle, trying to eke a little more speed out of the engine.

I caught sight of Herb looking backward.

"Do you see anything?"

"Nothing. Not yet anyway. How much faster is the Cessna than we are?"

"At least twice as fast."

"What's its range? How far can it fly?"

"With a full tank it can go three times as far as my ultralight."

"What can you do better?" Herb asked.

"Not much. It can carry more people and more cargo, can handle more g-force, has a much higher ceiling, and can go up in weather that would keep me on the ground."

"There must be some advantage."

"Because I'm so much slower, I can make tighter turns."

"So you're more maneuverable."

"I guess so, and my stall speed is much slower."

"Explain that to me. Quick," Herb said.

"I can go slower without stalling out, without crashing."

"Interesting. So the Cessna is much faster, but it can't go as slow. That could be an advantage."

I didn't see how going slower was much of an advantage.

"What else?" Herb asked.

"I can also land or take off on a much shorter strip."

"Again an advantage, but right now our best advantage is probably not being seen. Can you take us down even lower?"

"I could, but I think the best thing to do is take evasive action—and I need to be higher than the houses for that."

"Do whatever you feel is best. You're the captain."

I banked us sharply to the west. I was going to make a big looping sweep and come back toward the neighborhood from the west. I had enough fuel.

I glanced over at Herb. He was looking up at the wing, and I noticed what he was doing. He had his finger in a hole in the wing, the bullet hole.

"That is a really big hole," I said.

"It was a large bullet. I think it came from a fifty-caliber rifle."

"That is big . . . bigger than anything we have."

"I have two rifles that match that caliber."

"Did you pick those up at the shopping mall?"

"They're from my personal collection. I have a few interesting weapons in my basement, including some grenades."

"Where did you get grenades?"

"I have—I *had*—certain connections. I just wish I had utilized those connections more. Those weapons I saw on the ground in that brief pass looked to be military grade," Herb said.

"I didn't see much except men and vehicles."

"Including two armored vehicles, and lots of weapons. Obviously they have large-caliber firearms. I wonder if they have rocket launchers."

"Like what was used to destroy the police station?" I asked.

"Exactly. I didn't see any, but they had some heavy-duty equipment."

"Where would they get stuff like that?"

"I guess they have their connections, too. The army has weaponry like that, and I'm sure they weren't able to keep custody and control over all of their equipment. Or who knows? They could be members of the armed forces who've gone rogue."

I hadn't even thought of anyone from the army being *against* us.

"We bring this discovery to the committee, but we tell nobody else," Herb said. "Unfortunately, I think things have suddenly gotten more interesting. And more dangerous."

36

I ran my hand along the new section of the wing. It felt a little different, but it certainly was stronger and better. The place where the bullet had gone into the wing created a hole the size of a quarter. Where it had come out the top side had been a jagged opening big enough to stick my fist into. Herb had said that exit wounds were always much bigger.

It had shocked me when I'd seen it after landing. It was probably better I didn't know the extent of the damage until we'd put down. Of course that didn't matter now. Mr. Nicholas had put a metal patch on and it was as good as new. It wasn't bad to have a bunch of engineers to help.

It had seemed strange not being up in the air for a couple of days. No, *strange* wasn't the right word. It felt wrong. It wasn't just that I loved flying but that I felt a greater need to be up there, watching, guarding over us, keeping an eye on the ground, to be aware of everything or anything going on around us. And now I was needed up there even more.

We now also knew that there were other communities out there that had a lot of men and more dangerous arms than we did. This was what Herb had talked about all along. It wasn't that I didn't believe him, but now I'd seen it for myself, had the evidence fly by my head and wound my precious ultralight. If that wasn't hostile intent I didn't know what was.

Herb had said that they might have been frightened by our sudden appearance and just reacted, that I shouldn't necessarily take *that* as being a definite indication that they were dangerous to us. He was right. When they'd first seen us, the guys at Olde Burnham had said they'd thought about shooting at me.

But while Herb said that to me to be reassuring, he had also pressed the committee to put more resources into fixing the defenses and doubling the efforts to reinforce our walls. I couldn't help but wonder how any of our walls would do if a grenade or rocket hit them. Really, there wasn't much to wonder. Even the high cement walls by Highway 403 would be blown to pieces. It was also significant that Herb hadn't suggested going back to the city, either in the air or on the ground, to try to establish contact with whoever those people were.

Also, an order had to be given to all the guards to keep an eye upward and to report any sightings of the Cessna. None had been reported—at least not from the guards in our neighborhood. From the folks over in the Olde Burnham subdivision we had a few reports of the plane making a closer pass. They were situated closer to the city than us, so that wasn't surprising.

Of course we told them about what we'd seen during our encounter, warned them to watch for the plane, and suggested that they work to improve their defenses, too.

One other thing had been constructed in our neighborhood. I was standing under a canvas hangar that had been built over the top of my driveway to house my plane. I was grateful to be able to work out of the sun, and on days when I couldn't go up the ultralight was protected from rain and wind. The ultralight was remarkably strong—strong enough to have a hole punched through the wing and still fly—but also very delicate. A large gust of wind could flip it over and crush it, but now it was much more protected. Herb said he wanted it protected from the elements but also hidden from any other plane flying over.

Of course anyone flying over would have a lot more things to see than my little plane. Circling in the distance, a pilot wouldn't see anything much different than any other subdivision, with houses and roadways. But, from directly above, he could see the greenhouses, cultivated fields, and the thick walls that ringed the area. It was obvious from the air that something good was happening here. Something worth stealing. Something worth killing to get.

I sensed somebody behind me and turned to see Herb, studying me and the plane.

"So how do you like your new digs?" Herb asked.

"Very nice. Thanks for having them do this."

"We have to take care of our assets, and your plane is one of our greatest, along with its pilot. How are you both doing?"

"The wing is as good as new."

"And you?"

"Fine, I guess, although I still can't believe that somebody took a shot at me."

"Sir Winston Churchill said there is nothing so exhilarating as being shot at and missed."

"It certainly was a rush of adrenaline."

Herb walked over to the plane. "Just out of curiosity, if I wanted to shoot you down where would I aim?"

"Well, not that I've thought about it much, but I guess you'd try to hit either the gas tank or the engine."

"Or the pilot, I would imagine," Herb added.

"Definitely the pilot. Why, are you thinking of trying to shoot me down?" I joked.

"I'm actually trying to figure out how to make it harder for somebody else to shoot you down. Can you work with Mr. Nicholas to try to build more protection, perhaps a second layer of metal to surround both the engine and the gas tank?"

"I guess we could. The only thing is that every extra pound reduces my top speed and range."

"That might be a sacrifice worth making. See if the two of you can figure out how it could be done," Herb said. "I would also imagine that the Cessna is the same as the ultralight— the best places to aim would be pilot, engine, and gas tank. Do you know where the gas tank is on a Cessna?"

"It's here in the tail section. Would you try to shoot it down if it comes over us?"

"I'm not planning on doing that, but still it's better to have that knowledge if needed," Herb said. "Besides, if I do shoot at it, I have to do more than *try* to knock it out of the air. We can't afford to get those fellows mad at us. If we start something, we better be able to finish it."

"A Cessna can fly over at a height where its pilot or

passengers could see what's going on down here, but we wouldn't have a chance of hitting him," I said. "In fact, if he was really high, that plane could have passed over without us even noticing."

"I've thought about that. They could be well aware of our existence, but I'm pretty sure we're safe for now."

Herb assuming anything seemed out of character.

"Why do you think we're safe for now?"

"Think about it. If they flew over they'd see fields that are starting to grow food. There'd be no point in coming now. They'd be far better off to let us do all the work, grow the food, and then take it from us."

"I guess that does make sense. It's reassuring and upsetting all at once. Do you really think they might come and try to do that?"

"It should be upsetting, because it's real. We need to continue to be prepared, and that preparation includes asking about things like shooting down a Cessna."

"But just because they fly overhead doesn't mean they're a threat," I said. There was a code among pilots to look out for each other. That could be me or my father up there.

But then again they had shot at me already! In times of war, the code disappeared. Is that what this was? Were we at war? Would we have to try to shoot it out of the sky?

"They might not be a threat, but we have to assume that they are. If we assume they're hostile and we're wrong, then they're dead. If we assume that they're friendly and they're not, then we're dead. Which would you rather it be?"

"But they could become our allies, like Olde Burnham." I needed to at least think there was a way out of this that didn't involve us trying to kill each other.

"They could become allies, but there's a big difference. I initiated contact with the Olde Burnham neighborhood knowing that we were clearly bigger and stronger. If they started something with us we could finish it with them. They weren't a threat to us."

"But we could have been a threat to them," I said.

"We could have *destroyed* them," Herb said. "Just like those people we discovered could destroy us."

That thought sent a chill up my spine.

"We present a very attractive target. Our job is to make us a *hard* target. We have to make it too expensive, too costly, for them to try to overrun us. If we are well enough defended they might try a nonmilitary approach. We might be able to offer them food."

"So we would trade with them."

"Well, if you consider us giving them food and them not killing us a trade, then I guess we'd be trading," Herb said.

"But that's like blackmail, like extortion."

"It's survival. Of course it's a fine balance. If we gave away too much food we'd be in trouble anyway."

"A lot of grumbling about food has started already."

"Everybody has run out of their own personal food by now," Herb said.

"Almost everybody," I said. Herb had stocked so much canned and packaged food that he was still doling it out to my family and the Petersons. I had been shocked when I had seen all the full cupboards and shelves in his basement, but now that I was spending so much time with him, I wasn't really surprised. He must have been through a lot to be so cautious. "I guess I should feel a little guilty."

"No you shouldn't. It's my food and I can share it with whomever I choose. Besides it's not like anybody is starving. There's enough food from the community kitchens for everybody to live on," he said.

"That was a pretty good stew last night," I admitted. "It was very tasty, although I guess I really don't want to know what the meat was."

"Ernie would be the person who would know best. You could ask him."

"I think I'll pass on that." I knew what the possibilities could be. I'd noticed that there were far fewer squirrels in the neighborhood and fewer stray dogs outside the walls, which sort of gave me more information than I wanted to know. I knew that whatever people were able to catch or trap was being added to the meals.

"I'm hoping that tonight's meeting will help people understand why there's a need to restrict and ration our food," Herb said.

Each week there was a large town hall meeting at the gym for all who wanted to attend. That, along with the little newspaper, was the best way to pass around important information.

"I guess the big question is, how much are you going to tell them?"

"It's a fine balance, a delicate dance. We have to give them enough information to get them scared but not enough that they're terrified."

"Are you going to tell them about the other settlement, the one with all the weapons?"

"There's no need. Not yet. That's still classified and

restricted to the committee members. You are going to be at the meeting, right?"

"I'll be there as long as you don't make me talk again."

"I think that should be avoided. You're not the best person to talk when we might have to shade the truth."

37

I awoke sometime before dawn to the sound of thunder. Funny, the skies had been clear when I went to bed and I didn't hear any rain on the skylight. Maybe the rain was coming but hadn't arrived. It would be good for the crops if it did rain.

Then I thought about my plane. It was in its little canvas hangar, but if there was a storm coming there could be big winds. I should get up and make sure it was okay. I sleepily pushed back the sheet and then jumped at the sound of pounding on the front door.

I leaped up and grabbed my revolver. I'd gone no more than a couple of steps when something lit the way down the stairs. My mother was already heading down, a flashlight in one hand, a shotgun in the other. Rachel and Danny came out of their rooms, too. I didn't need much light to see the scared look on their faces. I hoped they didn't see the same expression on mine.

There was more pounding on the front door—stronger and even more insistent.

"Open up!" It was Herb.

My mother threw open the door.

"Olde Burnham is being attacked!" he exclaimed.

There was another rumble, but it wasn't thunder.

"Explosives," Herb said. "They radioed to say they were under heavy attack."

"What do we do?" my mother questioned.

"I've already sent Brett to get the away team ready to go out—with your permission of course."

"Of course. Shouldn't we send more people if we're going to help fend off the attack?" she asked.

"They're going in that direction, but we can't commit them to do anything until we know what's out there."

"Shouldn't you be back on the walkie-talkie, then?"

His expression turned even grimmer. "I can't get a reply."

"Have they been overrun?" my mother asked. "Is it over?"

"If it was over, the explosions would stop."

"So we should get every available person to offer assistance and—"

"We need to know what's happening. We need to sit tight and wait for Brett to report in."

"There may not be time! We have to go right away if there's any chance to offer assistance," my mother insisted.

"We need to get ready to go, but we can't go," Herb said. "If we rush into the unknown, in the dark, we might only get ourselves killed and save nobody."

"But it could take hours for him to get there and back and—"

"What if I flew there to see?"

"You're not equipped for night flight, are you?" Herb asked.

I shook my head. "I could do it . . . but not really."

"Then let's just get ready for action, but not take any right now," Herb said. "Agreed?"

My mother hesitated. "Agreed. It's hard to just sit back and wait, but I know you're right. Let's get ready," my mother said.

The explosions had stopped long before there was enough light to fly. Waiting, we'd made some preparations, getting ready to go. I took off, with Herb beside me. I'd sat in my plane waiting until the first thin ray of light had allowed me to fly. The whole neighborhood had been awoken either by the explosions or by other people who had heard them. It was eerie being out on the street, silently surrounded by others, everyone listening, waiting, wondering, and thinking the worst. It had been a relief finally to be allowed to get the ultralight in the air. The sun was just up above the horizon as I started to circle Olde Burnham. With each circle I got tighter and tighter. The air was still, and smoldering fires were sending smoke straight up into the sky, rising and fading until it dissipated and disappeared. Herb, beside me, studied the ground with binoculars. I needed to stay focused on flying.

Herb continually told me what he saw. The neighborhood was deserted. He saw bodies, but he hadn't seen any signs of life. Over three hundred people had been living there. I could always make out movement before when I passed over at this height. Now there was nothing moving except for the rising smoke. I couldn't even conceive that they'd all been killed. Some must have run away, and others might still be hiding in the houses where we couldn't see them.

With each pass we could see more of what was on the ground. It was so obvious that I didn't need binoculars. Large sections of the perimeter wall had been broken down. The gate blocking the street entrance was completely smashed. Houses scattered throughout the subdivision had been burned down or had gigantic holes in them or were missing an entire side. Vehicles were burned and the roadway was covered with debris—smashed brick from the collapsed houses, and bodies, lots and lots of bodies. I couldn't see those, but Herb was narrating what he was seeing for me.

"Okay, I want one more pass," Herb said. "I want it low and slow."

"How low and how slow?"

"Make it just above the roof level and just above your stall speed."

"Do you see something?" I asked hesitantly.

"If I did we wouldn't be flying so low. Just one more pass to be sure. If there's a problem we can certainly have some help pretty quickly."

The away team, along with two dozen other armed guards, was divided into two groups, one just west and one just south of the community. They were waiting to hear from us if it was safe for them to proceed. Brett was leading one group and my mother the other, behind the wheel of my car. She had insisted on going out this time. I would have been happier to have her back at the neighborhood. It was bad enough to risk one of us.

Our neighborhood was on full alert, and the guards on our walls had been doubled. Everybody knew something had happened, but they had no idea yet that our friends had been wiped out. *Wiped out.* That echoed in my head.

I made the final turn and aimed straight across the subdivision. I eased off the accelerator. I wanted us to be slow but still well above stall speed. Stalling out from that low an altitude would leave no room for error, no time to restart the engine, and no time to find a safe place to let down.

As it was I didn't know where we *were* going to put down. The streets inside the subdivision were filled with debris, and I didn't want to put down on any of the streets surrounding it. Funny how in the last couple of weeks I'd felt safe when I was down there inside their walls. Now the walls were ruptured and breached, and my sense of safety had just as many holes in it.

We came in so low that I could see which houses needed their roofs patched. Others just didn't have a roof anymore. There were multiple homes that had been gutted by fire and some where I could clearly see the blast marks from explosives. It looked like there wasn't one car remaining that hadn't been set on fire. I knew they had had a lot more vehicles. Those must have been used for escape or taken by the attackers.

What hadn't been taken were the bodies that littered the streets. Now, at this height and speed, I could see them for myself. There were dozens and dozens. Some were by themselves, away from other bodies, alone in death, but there was also a mass of bodies all clustered together, fallen into one heap at the end of a street. They must have stood and fought there and been cut down by a barrage of fire. We passed beyond the back fence, or what remained of it.

"I didn't see anything," Herb said. "No movement. Pull it up and I'll radio down."

Simultaneously I gave the plane more gas, pulled back on the stick, gave it left rudder, and banked to the left.

"You can proceed," Herb said into the radio. "Be cautious. We'll reconnoiter and then land. Can you clear a space for us to land inside the area, please?"

"Will do." It was my mother. "Keep safe."

I straightened out so that we were parallel to Burnham. "How far do you want me to go?"

"Go five minutes. Far enough to make sure nothing is coming, but well away from the city, from their base of operations."

"Are you sure it was them?" I asked.

"I think what I saw down below fits with what I saw when we flew over their compound. They have the men, machinery, and weaponry to do that sort of damage. I'll keep an eye on the ground, and you keep an eye on the sky. I don't want any surprises from above."

I'd been so focused on the ground that I'd momentarily forgotten about the sky. That's where the real danger for us would come from. We could outrun or hide from anything on the ground. A shot or two at most and we'd be past, hidden or out of range. A Cessna could go farther, faster, and higher. I wouldn't be able to outrun or outdistance it. With renewed anxiety I scanned the horizon and above, looking for anything else sharing the sky with us. All I could see were a few birds. No danger there.

"The road is definitely clear," I said. "There's nothing and nobody; but you could hide dozens of people along here and I'd never see them from this height. Do you want me to drop down or double back?"

"No, keep going."

As we traveled I started to catch glimpses of movement on the ground. There were people moving along Burnham.

On both sides, on the little streets there were more people, going about their business. I wondered how much they knew about what had happened just a few miles away. Life went on. What was more important was what we didn't see. There were no convoys of trucks, no masses of armed men, coming along Burnham toward our away team. Of course I hadn't really expected to see anything approaching us, but I thought we might catch a glimpse of them moving away.

"Do you want me to go farther?" I asked Herb.

"This is far enough. You can go back and put down."

"Shouldn't I stay in the air to keep watch?"

"I need to be down there. Besides, I think it's better that you're on the ground. Maybe you can see more from up here, but you have to remember, the more you can see, the more you can be seen."

That sounded ominous, maybe because it was so right. There was no way of telling who on the ground was watching us.

I banked again, losing altitude and gaining speed. I wanted to get back and down as quickly as possible. It wasn't long before we came up to Olde Burnham again, and I could see movement. It was our vehicles and our people spreading out. One of the streets—the place where I usually landed—had already been cleared. I corrected my course until my front wheel was aimed right down the center of the street. Slowly, I brought us down, lower and lower. There was a slight bounce and then we touched back down, the road rumbling underneath the wheels. I had flown over hell. Now I was landing in it.

We slowed and came to a stop. I turned off the engine,

and the motor gurgled and then the roar faded away. Herb and I both undid our buckles and climbed out of the plane. As Herb walked away, I went to the back of the plane. Gently I grabbed the tail and lifted it, walking around and turning the plane until it was aimed back down the runway. I wanted to be ready to take off.

I rushed after Herb, catching up just as he reached my mother.

"What can you tell me?" Herb asked.

"We've found a few survivors," she answered.

"A few? But there were over three hundred people living here," I said.

"We've already counted more than one hundred bodies," she said.

"They had fewer than thirty people with weapons," Herb said.

"It's not just the guards who were cut down. There are women and children dead. They must have been caught in the crossfire."

"Where are the survivors?" Herb asked.

"We've brought them to that house right there," she said, pointing to one of the buildings that seemed to have escaped unscathed.

"Keep looking for other survivors," Herb said. "There are probably more, but they're hiding, afraid to come out. Be careful—they must be terrified, and terrified people with weapons might mistake you for somebody else. Were there any bodies that didn't belong here?"

"What do you mean?"

"Did any of the attackers get killed?" Herb asked.

"I'm not sure if we can initially identify a body as being one of the attackers," my mother said.

"If it's the people we flew past, they're in darker clothing that almost looked like a uniform."

"They might have taken their dead with them," my mother said, "but we'll look around."

"And do any of the bodies have weapons?" Herb asked.

"None that I've seen. It looks like the dead have been picked over. Some of them don't even have shoes. Those were taken, too."

"That fits. They've probably taken everything of value they could find. What they couldn't take they destroyed."

"That doesn't make sense. Why destroy things?" my mother asked.

"If you attack an enemy, you are best to destroy that enemy. Now nobody here is in any position to pose a threat to them, to even try to enact any revenge. This sort of thing has been done by conquerors since the dawn of time. Right now I want you to search for the people you know, the leaders of this community. I need to know if they are dead or still alive or—"

Almost on cue, out of one of the buildings a group of people emerged. There was a man, three women, and a few children. The man was carrying a rifle. It was hanging down at his side. There was something about the way they were moving, as if they were drunk or drugged, and then I looked at their faces. Each held the same expression—empty, open eyes reflecting fear and shock and disbelief.

My mother identified herself and the rest of us.

One of the children started crying, and another was swept up into his mother's arms.

"They're gone," my mother said. "You're safe."

She said that with no confidence.

"They just came so suddenly," the man said. "We couldn't stop them . . . we . . . we . . ." He started crying, large sobs from deep in his chest.

"There was just so much, so many," one of the women said. "Bullets and rockets and—" She started crying as well, and that set off the child in her arms.

"My wife, have you seen my wife?" the man asked. "Is she okay?"

"We're still getting all the survivors together," Herb said.

"We'll take you all back to our neighborhood, where you're safe," my mother said.

"Are you afraid they might return?" one of the women asked. Involuntarily she stepped back and looked all around. She looked terrified.

"They're gone," Herb said. "They're not coming back, not now. We just want to take you to safety, provide medical treatment if it's necessary."

"Come with me," my mother said. "It'll all be okay."

She led them away. They didn't put up any opposition.

"Stay close," Herb said.

I fell in beside him.

"The blast patterns on the walls indicate that they had multiple RPGs and weren't afraid to use them," Herb said. "I count dozens and dozens of explosions, which would mean they must have so many rounds that they don't even need to count."

"Maybe they just lost control."

"No, this is very controlled and deliberate. There are

multiple explosions but not multiple explosions on individual buildings. One hit per building. It's the same with the external walls of the neighborhood. They were breached in a very specific pattern, right where the guards were posted along the wall."

There were bodies along the crumbled sections of the wall.

"They simply launched an RPG at any section that was firing at them," Herb said.

"How do you possibly defend against that?" I asked.

"You don't."

We continued to move, past more bodies scattered along the road. We walked along and Herb stopped, looking at each one. Not looking, *studying*. He turned a body over and I gasped. Herb looked at me.

"That's Sam. I know him from school. Is he . . ."

I let the sentence trail off. It was so obvious there was no point in asking.

"Judging from the wounds it was fast," Herb said. "Your friend didn't suffer."

"He wasn't really my friend. I just knew him."

"It's harder when you know them. We're going to know many of them. You don't have to do this. You can wait by the plane."

I shook my head. "No, I'll come. I've seen bodies before."

Was that really me saying those words? What was I trying to prove to Herb or myself?

"Stay right by my side," he ordered.

We started to walk again. I was aware of the bodies but tried not to look at them as we passed. Herb stopped and examined each one. With a few he reached down and felt for a pulse, searching for life where the wounds hadn't obviously killed the person. Each time he stood up and walked away.

Up ahead there was a mass of bodies. Somehow there being more bodies made it less upsetting, like I couldn't focus on an individual. I started counting to make them into a number instead of people. There were eleven men who had fallen so close together that they were practically intertwined, gaping holes visible in them. Already there were flies buzzing around.

"These men were executed."

"What?"

"They were lined up against the wall of this house and shot. Look at the wall and you can see the bullet marks."

There were marks, chips in the brick.

"Each man was shot in the chest, and then a second bullet was put into the back of the head. See?"

I did see, but I just couldn't believe.

"Those bodies on the perimeter and on the street were killed in battle. These men had already been captured. The attackers weren't interested in taking prisoners. They didn't want to leave anybody behind. Do you notice that there are no wounded?"

I hadn't noticed, but he was right.

"There had to be people wounded in the battle," I said.

"If they found anybody wounded, they just killed them," Herb said. "Wounded are inconvenient. Depending on the wound it could have been merciful, although I suspect there is little mercy with the people who did this. It was all very cold-blooded. They didn't even take their own dead with them. Judging from the uniforms, I've counted nine of their dead."

"Subtract those from the bodies we've counted and that means that there should be more survivors. More people must still be hiding or escaped."

"Or are dead in the burned-out buildings," Herb said.

"Herb!"

We spun around. It was Brett, running toward us. "We found one of their men. He's badly wounded, but he's alive."

"Take me to him so I can ask some questions."

"He's not going to be answering many questions. They left him for dead because he's almost finished."

"Then get him into a vehicle and back to the neighborhood. We have to save him."

"After what these people have done we should be putting a bullet into his head," Brett snapped.

"We need him to live. Get him back right away. We need information. We need to know about them, and more important, we need to know what they know about us."

38

We lifted off straightaway. I felt a wave of relief wash over me as we gained height and put more distance between us and what had happened at Olde Burnham. I didn't want to even think about it, but I couldn't shut the images out of my mind. There were bodies and more bodies. The final count was close to two hundred, and of those there were almost two dozen who had obviously been executed. That same pattern, shot in the chest and the back of the head. I knew some of them, either by name or face. I couldn't help but think about what it would be like to be standing there, hands up to surrender, and then realize that men with guns were going to kill me anyway.

Whoever these people were they were ruthless and uncaring. Human life didn't mean anything to them.

In the end we had found thirty-five survivors, people who had been hiding in the rubble or in basements or had scrambled away and then come back. They were all being taken to our neighborhood. That left close to fifty people who were still unaccounted for. Had those people escaped, or were they still hiding? Or were they buried in the rubble?

I was flying the most direct route back, right along Burnham. Almost immediately I flew over our trucks and cars going back to the neighborhood, carrying the survivors.

Before I could say anything, Herb reached out and put a hand on my arm. I looked over.

"That doesn't have to be our fate," he said.

"Really?"

"There are times I haven't said everything, but I've never lied to you or your mother. This is serious, deadly serious, but we have time. I just hope that man doesn't die before I can get more information."

"He deserves to die!" I exclaimed. "Even if he doesn't die from his wounds, he should be killed, and I think I'd be willing to kill him myself!"

"No you wouldn't," Herb said. "And I wouldn't let you, even if you could. Taking a life takes away part of your soul and—"

I let out a scream. Out of nowhere the Cessna had appeared, right beside us. I dove and banked as it raced past us and in that instant I saw the brilliant flashes of weapons fired toward us from the side window of the plane. I'd turned too quickly, the harness holding me in place as we slid sideways, and the g-forces were practically pulling me out of my seat. I had to think. I had to act quickly.

I pulled the stick up and gave the engine as much gas as I could to power it to counter the spiral and get us upward. I felt the plane buckling beneath me, could sense the wings straining against the body as if the force was going to rip them free, and then it stopped and we leveled off.

"There it is!" Herb said.

The Cessna was well ahead of us, but it was starting to bank. It was moving so much faster than I was that it needed more distance to come back around. I turned much more quickly, putting distance between us. But that wouldn't last long. I strained my mind, trying to think what to do. My head was practically charged with electricity. I wanted to run away, to hide, to land, but none of those options were possible. I couldn't go higher or faster or farther, and there was no place to hide in the brilliant blue sky.

"It's made its turn," Herb said, looking backward. "It's coming back toward us."

I tried to look over my shoulder but couldn't see it.

"Which side?" I asked.

"My side. It's coming fast."

There was no way I could outrun it. I looked over my shoulder again and this time saw it racing toward us, eating up the air between us. It would be right on top of us in less than ten seconds. I put my hand on the throttle to open it up completely, to give it all the gas we had to get all the speed we could—and then thought better of it. I instead closed the throttle, and the engine almost stalled as we slowed down to almost nothing.

The Cessna shot by so fast, but so close, that I could see the people in the cabin—all four of them—and the weapons they were holding, but I figured they weren't able to fire at us because I'd caught them by surprise.

I banked hard again, almost forgetting to give the plane more gas to counter the drag of the turn. If I hadn't remembered, we might have stalled out. We picked up speed and executed a complete turn while the Cessna was still banking, trying to come back at us again.

"That was a good move. Do that again," Herb said.

"He'll be ready for it this time," I said. "He'll probably slow down as he approaches."

"But he can't slow down as much, right?"

"His stall speed is almost twice as much as mine."

"Good, just get me in position to take a shot at it."

He reached down and pulled up his rifle. If they were the cat and we were the mouse, we were at least a mouse with teeth.

Below us was the river and its valley. I dove down the side of the valley and at the same time opened up the accelerator to gain even more speed. If he was trying to slow down to try to match my speed, I'd open it up enough that he wasn't able to catch me. My top speed was much more than his stall speed.

I saw him over my right shoulder. Still far away, but he was closing, and not nearly as quickly as before. As I'd expected, he had significantly reduced his speed. That would give him more time beside us to take more than one shot. He wasn't going to let my slow speed be as much of an advantage. He was still curving, coming at me from about seven o'clock. If he came in from that angle Herb might get a shot, but only after they'd had a good long time to take shots at us first. I didn't want to trade shots.

"Do something unexpected," Herb said.

"What does that mean?"

"I don't know. You're the pilot. Do whatever he doesn't expect you to do."

There was only one thing he completely wouldn't expect.

I banked hard to the left, as hard as I could to bring the plane right back around, then aimed directly at him. We were going to play chicken. We raced toward each other, and then I pushed back on the stick and he soared over the top, so close that I could see the rivets in the bottom of his cabin.

There was a loud explosion. Herb had taken a shot at the Cessna with his rifle as it passed.

"Did you get it?" I exclaimed.

"Not even close. Everything is too fast, but you certainly surprised him. Did you see the expression on the pilot's face?"

"I didn't see anything except the plane."

"If I'm to have any chance of hitting him, I need to have a clean, level shot."

"I can't do that without him having a shot at us first."

"Then that's what we're going to have to do," Herb said.

"What?"

"What choice do we have? He can keep coming back at us until we crash, run out of fuel, or get shot down. Just do it."

I nodded. I knew what to do. I just didn't want to do it.

I banked again, pushed down on the stick, and hit hard rudders. I kept the turn until I was almost parallel with the bank of the valley on my left and then kept dropping until I was just below the top of the ridge. I wanted him to have to come up on the right, on Herb's side. Next I adjusted my speed. I needed to be going slowly but well above my stall speed to force him to fly as slowly as he could to try to match my speed. I had to focus on the contours of the valley as it jutted in and out. I wanted to make sure I was so close that he couldn't come up on our left, but that meant flying dangerously near the side of the valley.

"Tell me what he's doing," I yelled at Herb.

Herb's head was swiveling around, trying to find the plane. "He's there, almost right behind, slightly to the right, slightly higher."

"How fast is he closing?"

"He's closing but not quickly."

"How far is he?" I demanded.

"Two hundred yards or even less than that."

"Keep watching. I need to know when he's about twenty-five yards behind."

"Okay. I'll count it down," Herb said. "He's less than a hundred . . . closing quickly . . . seventy-five."

"Get ready to fire," I said.

"I'm ready. Forty . . . Thirty-five . . . It looks like he's slowing down even more . . . Thirty."

"Is he still to the right?"

"On the right, almost level with us and farther out."

I couldn't see him, but I could *feel* him there in my blind spot. I had to fight the urge to swerve, bank, dive, climb, or speed up.

"Twenty-five!"

I pulled back hard on the stick and eased up on the accelerator. We slowed, and the Cessna roared by us again. I opened the throttle fully and dove, and suddenly we were not only on the tail of the Cessna but gaining on it. It had all happened so quickly that the pilot hadn't adjusted to the speed.

Herb fired again and again, the bullets finding their targets in the tail and fuselage of the Cessna—six, seven, eight, or more spraying along the top of the plane. The Cessna jerked to the side as the pilot tried to shake us and more bullets hit into the top of the cabin—and then it dropped sharply.

We soared past, and I knew what was going to happen next. There was an explosion, louder than the roar of our engine. The Cessna had crashed into the valley wall.

Herb strained to look back at the wreck. I kept my eyes focused ahead, both hands on the stick, and slowly started to turn, putting the bank at a safe distance.

"We got him," Herb said with hardly any emotion.

I understood. I should have felt happy, maybe even thrilled. Instead I just felt drained, worn out, worn down. I cut the turn and plotted a sight course back to our neighborhood. All I wanted was to get home, and get on the ground, and I wanted to get there without passing by the crash site. I could already picture it too sharply in my mind without my eyes having to see it. But still, I couldn't look completely away. There on the far side of the valley, almost at the top of the cliff, thick black smoke rose into the sky. Whatever was left of the plane and its crew was burning away to ash and bone and twisted metal.

I banked again so that I couldn't see it and then gained elevation and climbed up and over the Burnham bridge, flying above it as a convoy of our cars passed over it. The bridge was so far above the river that it almost looked like they were flying, too, and I had the irrational thought that I should bank away again so they couldn't chase after me.

Slowly I brought the plane around, coming in from the north. I'd land and get something to eat and drink. It was funny how, despite it all, I was so hungry and thirsty. After what I'd seen, what had just happened, all I could think about, all I was worried about, was my stomach. I'd witnessed so many people who were never going to have to worry about eating again. There were hundreds of dead on the ground and the four in that plane.

I aimed the front wheel for the middle of the strip the way I always did. I passed over the highway, the walls ahead, the heads of guards poking over the top, slower and lower until I could have seen their faces if I had looked directly down. We dropped beneath the height of the houses and the little bit of crosswind that had been present was blocked out completely. I focused on the landing and eased the plane onto the road, smooth and perfect. We rolled along and slowed down, finally coming to rest almost directly in front of our houses.

I turned off the engine.

"Nice touchdown," Herb said.

"Better than the Cessna made."

Herb gave me a concerned look. "Adam, there was no choice."

"I know that." I hadn't fired the weapon, but their blood was still on my hands.

"We did what we had to do."

"I know that, too. I just want to eat." I unbuckled my belt and Herb grabbed my arm.

"I killed those people, not you."

I laughed and, judging from Herb's expression, it surprised him as much as it surprised me.

"Herb, I know you fired the gun, but I know I'm just as responsible. And you know what? I don't care. I just want to eat."

39

"Do you remember what you're supposed to say?" Herb asked.

I nodded. I remembered. I hoped I could pull it off. After three days' rest, hanging out with Todd and Lori, who both worked hard at trying to distract me, trying to blunt the horrors of that day, I was ready to do what I could do to help. And that meant getting information from the enemy.

"You look so honest that he'll believe you. You could fool anybody."

I hoped he was right. If this didn't work, though, Herb would simply try to convince the man to provide information through interrogation. He said it was best to try this first in case he wasn't willing to cooperate.

I opened the door and walked in carrying the tray. Herb slipped in behind me, staying out of sight behind the curtain, and I stepped around it. Inside, recovering from his surgery, was the man—the enemy. He was propped up in bed, both wrists handcuffed to the rails of the bed. He eyed me suspiciously.

"Afternoon." I gave him my best attempt at a friendly smile.

He gave a semi-smile back. Smiles meant nothing. Not mine and not his.

"I've brought in your lunch. Are you feeling like you can eat?"

"I could, if I had a free hand." He held up his right hand and the handcuffs rattled loudly.

"I'm going to undo one wrist." If he was right-handed, I figured it was better to free his left hand to eat. I tapped the revolver strapped to my belt. "Don't make me use this."

I undid the cuff on his left hand. I leaned back, away so that he couldn't reach my gun, but I was still glad to have Herb standing by behind the curtain.

"You shouldn't complain about anything. You're one of the lucky ones," I said.

He gave me a questioning look.

"At least you're alive. We retaliated last night. We killed almost everybody. We stopped counting when we reached three hundred bodies."

He looked shocked, and then that look gave way to one of disbelief. "I don't understand. We overran you—there was only token resistance."

"That wasn't us," I said. "But they were our friends. They radioed to us when you attacked. We couldn't get there in time to save most of them, but now we got almost all of you."

"I don't believe you," he said, but he didn't sound confident.

"I don't care if you do," I said. "But think about it. How do you think we got you?"

He didn't say anything. I knew my words were raising doubt as they sank in.

"And the others who were wounded, are they here?"

"We have a few others," I lied. "Four, including you."

"Where is this?" he asked.

"You're in our hospital."

"But where?"

"Don't you know?"

Again, he looked like he was thinking.

"We call this place Eden Mills," I said.

"The neighborhood at the corner of Burnham and Erin Mills?"

"You know about us?" I asked.

"We know."

I tried not to react. This was just confirmation of what I feared. They knew about us, which put us in danger. That was one of the two questions we needed to ask.

"And we know all about you. We've been watching you from the ground and from the air," I said.

"The ultralight belong to you?" he asked.

For a split second I thought he meant me personally, but of course he meant our community.

"The ultralight is ours."

"We didn't know that. Nobody thought that you'd have enough people and weapons to do that to us, to be a threat. We just thought that you were going to be our next—" He stopped.

"Target?" I asked. "We were going to be next?"

He nodded.

"That might have changed if you had known that we have over four hundred people in arms."

"We have closer to six hundred and fifty men and—"

"Not anymore. There *were* more of you. We destroyed dozens of trucks and even shot down the Cessna."

Again he looked shocked.

"I guess it was you and your group that destroyed the police station," I said.

"We needed what they had. A few cops with revolvers and rifles isn't much of a match against grenades, rocket launchers, and machine guns."

That now answered the remainder of my questions, but I couldn't resist reacting. "So you just killed them."

He shrugged. "Dog eat dog."

"Those weren't dogs—they were people, and you just killed them."

"It's a war out there."

"It doesn't have to be, but you wouldn't know about that." There was nothing else I needed from him. I turned to leave.

"Hey!" he called out. "So what happens to me now . . . to those of us you captured? Are you going to, going to . . ."

"Kill you?" I asked.

He nodded.

"After what you people did, we should kill you." I paused. "But we don't do that. We're not savages. We value life."

Herb stepped out from behind the curtain. "Especially the lives of those who cooperate."

"And if I do cooperate, what then?"

"We might let you go," Herb said.

"Go where? I have no place to go."

"Then we might let you stay here as a free man," I added. I could tell he was pondering.

"If I do cooperate, how do I know you'll keep your word?"

"You don't," Herb said. "But you have to think about it. We kept you alive even after what you were part of. We had our doctors operate on you and save your life. If we wanted you dead all we had to do was just let you lie there where we found you. Do you want time to think about it?"

He shook his head. "I'll tell you whatever you want to know."

"Good."

Herb motioned me to the side of the room for a conference. "Do you want to stay for this?" he whispered.

"Is it all right if I leave?"

"You've done enough. More than enough. I want you to go and find that girlfriend of yours and spend some time relaxing, being a kid again. At least for one evening."

40

The next night, my mother and Herb called a committee meeting at our house.

Herb stood in front of the group. I sat on the floor at the back of the room, crowded in along with another two dozen people. They weren't members of the committee, but they were important in the community and it was essential that they be here.

Bringing the survivors and the wounded into the neighborhood meant that everybody had heard at least something about what had happened to Olde Burnham, some version of the truth, and in every case it wasn't something good. There was enormous fear, almost a sense of panic, that could be felt as you walked through the streets. Nothing else was being talked about.

"Thank you all for being here," Herb said. "Obviously there is only one thing that we're going to talk about. We have to replace rumor with fact, panic with plan, fear with a direction."

Herb's words were calm. He was always calm, but I couldn't help noticing the little quiver in his voice and the slight tremor in his hand when he took a sip of water. He was looking older—the last two months had aged him.

"We have been confronted with an enemy that is much larger, has more equipment and weaponry, and from what we've seen is well organized. From interrogation of the prisoner, we know they are a combination of a reserve military unit that went rogue, former military men they recruited, and an assortment of random criminals they've incorporated. They are ruthless, without mercy. The rumors that they executed many of those they captured are correct. We have discovered that they are very much aware of our presence, and have already discussed an attack. We are a target."

Howie jumped in. "But a well-defended target!"

Herb shook his head. "Not well enough. We have walls, but they have rocket-propelled grenades that can knock those walls down. We have armed people, but they have four times as many. We have weapons, but they have more sophisticated weapons. We cannot withstand a direct attack."

"Are you suggesting that we surrender?" Judge Roberts asked.

"Surrender would only result in death. They showed no mercy to the members of Olde Burnham, and from what the prisoner has told me, none to other communities or individuals they have attacked, so they will show no mercy to us."

"Could we negotiate with them?" Councilwoman Stevens asked.

"From what I've learned from the prisoner, they have never negotiated with anybody because it removes the element of surprise. They simply attack in force, overwhelm their victims, and take what they want—and they want what we have."

"But if we can't fight and we can't negotiate, then what

are you suggesting? Do we have to run?" The councilwoman stared fiercely around the room.

"Running would also result in massive deaths. Abandoning the neighborhood before the harvest would leave people with insufficient food to survive the winter."

"What if we waited until after the harvest?" Mr. Peterson asked.

"They're going to be here sooner than that. Possibly two or three weeks, according to the information we obtained."

A heavy silence filled the room.

"So you're saying we can't stay and we can't go," Judge Roberts summarized. "There must be something that we can do."

"There is," Herb said. "There's only one option. We have to attack."

The entire room erupted in noise, voices raised in question and concern. Herb stood, immobile, no expression on his face, no reaction to the upheaval he'd caused.

"Please, everybody, silence!" Judge Roberts called out, but the noise didn't subside.

Brett stood and yelled, "Everybody, quiet!"

The noise suddenly shut off.

"Let the man speak," Brett said.

But Howie went first. "If we have fewer men and fewer arms, wouldn't it be suicide to attack them?"

"It would be, if they knew we were coming. We'll hit them completely by surprise, because the last thing they expect is for somebody to attack them," Herb said. "We have the element of surprise. Plus we have Adam."

Everybody turned to me.

"An ultralight flown by a teenager is our advantage?" Howie asked. "No, offense, Adam."

"No offense taken." I understood completely.

"Having eyes in the sky provides strategic advantages," Herb said.

"And you really believe we could win if we attack," the judge said.

"No, it's almost certain that we wouldn't win."

Again the room erupted, and again it was silenced by Brett.

"Look, I'll go into any battle you want me to," Brett said. "You know that. But you want us to attack when you think we'll lose?"

"Not lose, just not win. What I'm suggesting is only the first battle. The war will come next. I have a plan, and I need everybody's agreement and cooperation for that plan to succeed."

"But you think we *can* succeed?" the judge asked.

There was a hushed silence as everybody seemed to stop breathing, waiting.

Herb answered with only one word.

"Yes."

41

I brought my plane in for a landing and rolled along the street, finally coming to a stop right in front of our house. Herb was waiting, along with some of the committee members. I turned off the engine, and they surrounded me before I could unbuckle.

"The groups are in place," I said.

My mother, Howie, and Brett were each leading a group of thirty people. They had spent the day in twos and threes and fours, moving into the positions where they were going to wait out the rest of the day and into the night.

For the week after the committee meeting, all we had done was plan for this moment. Rachel and Danny basically camped out at the Petersons' place so that we could turn our house into a war headquarters.

The attack was scheduled for four the next morning.

"Is there any sign of any of the enemy out there?" Judge Roberts asked.

"I couldn't see anything coming along any of the major roads."

"Good . . . good."

"They're like a snake," Herb said. "They fed on the other neighborhood and they've been lying low to digest what they gorged on."

"I just wish we didn't have to count on that," the judge said. "We're practically defenseless right now."

"We have the wall, and there are still people on it. Nobody out there knows that there aren't many weapons in their hands," Herb said.

"We are too vulnerable."

"There's no choice. We need to send enough men into battle to sting them hard, to destroy as much of their men and equipment as we can."

"So what now?" Councilwoman Stevens asked.

"Are the escape groups all ready?" Herb asked.

"As ready as they can be."

As always Herb had a backup plan—a plan nobody hoped would ever have to happen. The community had been divided into thirty-two groups. Each had been given food, supplies, and equipment that they would take with them if the neighborhood had to be evacuated. Herb was with my family, Todd's family, and the Petersons, along with Howie and his family and Brett. Our little group was the best armed and, along with a second group led by Sergeant Evans, was going to try to fall back to the Peterson farm, attempt to negotiate with the people who were there, or simply recapture it if negotiating failed.

If we did end up at the farm, we would be executing Herb's original evacuation plan that I'd stood up against. I wondered if we should have just listened to him to begin with.

"How did the plane handle?" Mr. Nicholas asked.

"Sluggish, but okay. It's more like driving a tank than flying an ultralight." The cockpit, engine, and fuel tank had been covered in metal to offer more protection from bullets, and the whole thing had been painted a dull gray to blend into the sky.

"Slower but safer," Herb said.

"Unless we run into another Cessna."

"Have you seen one?" He sounded alarmed.

"Nothing. I own the sky."

"How long will it take for us to get into position?" Herb asked.

"At least thirty minutes."

"Then we'll leave at three-fifteen in the morning to allow us a fifteen-minute margin for error."

"I'll be ready. Is everything else ready?"

"I'll make sure it is," Herb said. "It looks like you have somebody else who wants to talk to you."

I turned around. Lori was standing off to the side, waiting, trying to look casual. She didn't look casual. She looked beautiful.

"I'll see you later." Herb walked away, bringing the committee members along with him, and Lori came over.

"So how are—"

She kissed me. Suddenly, what I was going to say didn't seem that important. Nothing seemed that important.

"I don't want you to go," she said.

"I have no choice."

"I know." She looked like she was going to cry. "I wish we could go up in your plane, you and me, and just fly away, go up and up, and when we came back down everything here would be the way it was before all of this happened."

"I guess we all have things we wish for," I said. "I already got one of the things I wished for, for the longest time."

"What?"

"I think you know."

She laughed. "I guess that it didn't quite happen the way you had planned it."

"Nobody could have planned this nightmare," I said.

"People wake up from nightmares."

"Let's hope." I sighed. "I'm sorry, but I have to prepare the plane. Can you hang around for a while?"

Now it was Lori's turn to sigh. "I wish, but I have guard duty on the wall right now—with so many people gone, I volunteered. You have to promise me you'll stay safe."

"I can't prom—"

"No, you have to promise me!"

"I promise, but if it doesn't go the right way, then you have to promise me that Rachel and Danny are with you, that you and your family will take care of them."

"They'll be with us; I promise."

"And then we'll meet at the planned spot. Agreed?" I asked.

"Agreed."

This time I kissed her.

———

I pulled the night-vision goggles down. Herb pulled his down at the same time. The world took on a soft green glow, and I could see the road ahead of me. I gunned the engine and we rolled down the darkened strip. Faster and faster, we were coming up to the two lights, guards holding flashlights to mark the end of the road. I wanted to be in the air well before I reached them. I gave it full gas and pulled back on the stick. We jumped off the strip and soared. I held the throttle fully open and kept pulling back.

The plane still felt sluggish. Between the protective plating that had been fitted on the plane, Herb, and the equipment and weapons we were carrying, it was well above the weight it normally would be.

I started a long, slow bank, trying to see through the darkness. If we could have waited an hour or so, there would have been a little light on the horizon instead of complete blackness. Below, looking ghostly, was my neighborhood. In the day, I could have seen the lush green plantings, the pools sparkling with water, the hundreds of secure houses, all contained within the high, strong walls that surrounded it. It was beautiful and precious and fragile and vulnerable. I couldn't let anybody harm it or the people in there. They weren't just my neighbors anymore—they were part of my tribe.

Herb was quiet beside me. In fact, over the past few days, he had been much quieter than usual. I knew he'd been busy supervising all parts of the whole plan, but still there seemed to be part of him that wasn't there even when he was standing beside me. There were questions I'd wanted to ask him, but I didn't want to trouble him when he had so much on his mind. Or maybe that was just my rationalization, because I was nervous about some of the answers I might get.

Darkness was our ally, and in a world where there was so much against us, it was nice to have nature on our side. There was one more thing that had been installed in the plane that might help. Atop the controller, a carpenter's level had been screwed into place. The little luminous ball that glowed in the dark would show me when I was flying level. Flying low, without light and the ground obscured below, it could be the only thing that would let me know I wasn't tilting toward the earth. We were moving slightly up, still gaining altitude.

"Are you okay?" Herb asked.

"As okay as I can be, I guess." I paused. "Will this work?"

"It will work better than doing nothing except waiting for them to attack us. We have a chance."

"A big chance?"

"Maybe a bigger chance than I deserve."

"What do you mean?" I asked.

Herb remained silent.

"This is no time not to answer," I said.

"I'm just trying to figure out what to say. Look, I can think of at least two dozen times I should have been dead," Herb said. "And more than that, I can't stop thinking that after the sort of things I've been part of, maybe it would have been fair if I had died."

"I don't understand."

"Karma. Good things happen when you do good things. Bad things happen when you do bad things. I deserve some bad karma for all the things I've done."

"I'm sure you've always tried to do the right thing," I said.

"No, there were times I did things that I *knew* were wrong but that had to be done. I tried to justify it by thinking I was just following orders."

"But you were, weren't you?"

"Just because I was following them didn't mean I believed they were right. Do you believe in God?" Herb asked.

I hadn't seen that coming. "Sure, yeah, of course."

"I'm almost afraid to believe. I've broken more than a few commandments in my time. If there is a God I certainly deserve to be punished."

This was the most personal conversation I had ever had with the man, and I wanted to make sure I said the right thing. "I know that without you, a whole lot of people we just left behind on the ground wouldn't be alive."

"I guess we'll see how long they'll still be alive."

We flew along in silence after that. I was usually the one pressing for Herb to be completely honest, and now I would have welcomed a reassuring lie and false confidence. Maybe that confidence had to come from me.

"Herb, I don't know what you did in the past, but I know what you've been doing over the past couple of months, what you're doing now. Maybe all those times you were kept alive, there was a reason, and that reason is this, here, now, to keep all of us alive."

"That's a nice theory, although no lives have been saved yet. In fact, a lot of lives are going to be lost tonight. There always is a reason for killing. When I was working it was us against them, and 'they' were the evil empire or the threat to democracy, or our way of life, or our ideals, or our very survival."

"But this *really* is about our survival," I said.

"Actually it's about more than just our survival," Herb said. "This is about the very survival of a way of life, of the ideals that we believe in. The people we're fighting are destroyers, tearing down any attempts for civilization to ever reestablish itself. What we're doing today isn't just about us—it's about so much more. Right is on our side."

Now Herb was sounding more like his old self. "And right always wins," I said.

"Not always, but just maybe, this time. You know, I'm an old man. I've lived my life. Whatever happens to me doesn't matter that much."

"It matters to me. It matters to my family. It matters to the people of the neighborhood. So I want you to do me a favor."

"Favor?"

"Yeah, stay close to me so I can keep an eye on you."

He laughed. "Since they can't shoot down half of the ultralight, I think we have no choice but to watch each other."

"And we'll watch everybody else, too," I suggested. "We're the eyes in the sky."

"How long before we get over the top of them?" Herb asked.

"At this speed no more than fifteen minutes."

Timing was crucial. I knew we couldn't arrive at our objective early or we might tip them off that an attack was coming.

I banked toward the south and reduced the throttle until it was only half open. Herb was right. There was no need for speed.

"Our objective"—it sounded so clinical, sanitary, almost harmless. It was none of those. We were going to attack a group that was four times bigger than we were, more heavily armed, better trained, and completely ruthless. We were going to sneak into their stronghold during the night and try to destroy as much equipment as possible, kill as many men, and retreat without being wiped out ourselves. The odds weren't good, but we had surprise. They couldn't even think that anybody would be crazy enough to attack them.

Herb had said that their strength was their biggest weakness and that we had to exploit that weakness. If we couldn't, it would mean the death of lots of people today—and it would mean the end of our neighborhood and the deaths of most of the people who lived there.

I'd seen, up close, what these people were capable of.

Herb was right, this was more than just about *our* survival. These people had committed *evil*. We had to stop them. Or die trying.

There was a burst of light on the horizon, and then a loud explosion shattered the silence of the night.

It had begun.

42

"Hold on," I said. "This is going to be a rough ride."

Off to the left I could see a blaze of light and flashes of explosions. I banked sharply and aimed right for the middle of the light. I opened the throttle up full.

There was another explosion, and then one more, bigger than the first, shot up into the sky.

"It looks like our people have managed to infiltrate the perimeter defenses," Herb said. "Those are fuel tanks going up, so they got to the vehicles."

"Will we be there in time?"

"Just get me close enough and low enough to do some damage."

I dropped down and leveled off at around fifty feet.

"Just about perfect. We can afford to come in low because they won't be expecting an attack from above."

We were closing in fast. Along with the light from the fire there were bursts of light—guns being fired—and headlights sweeping this way and that as vehicles were swerving around inside the compound.

Herb had pulled up the bag, placed it on his lap, and opened it. I couldn't see inside, but I knew what it contained.

There were two dozen hand grenades and another dozen Molotov cocktails—simple bottles of gasoline with a wick. Herb would light them and drop them, and they'd set fire to whatever they landed on. It was great to have this arsenal of explosives and flammables—unless a bullet hit one of them before it was dropped. Then we'd be instantly incinerated. At least it would happen so fast it wouldn't even have time to register before we were dead.

We were now so close that the sounds of gunfire punctuated the roar of the engine. There was a hailstorm of bullets flying through the air—just hopefully none of them high enough to hit us.

Flames were shooting up into the sky, some almost as high as we were flying. It was so bright that I could clearly see figures running around, scrambling away from vehicles and buildings that were on fire. We were coming in at full speed, but it was as if everything were slowing down. Herb had the bag on his lap and two grenades in his right hand. As we raced overhead he pulled a pin and dropped a grenade, and then did the same with another and another and—

The light from the explosions reached us before the noise.

I pulled up and banked hard, both hands gripping the yoke to stabilize us as we were rocked by another explosion. Herb tossed more grenades over the side, and the sounds of explosions overwhelmed the roar of the engine. We sailed away from the light and were swallowed by the predawn darkness.

I took a glance over my shoulder as I continued the curve. I could see the whole scene playing out. There were more flames, more light, and more chaos.

"Do you want me to make another pass over the compound?" I asked.

"No. Come along hard and high. I want you to come in right over the top of the road," Herb said. "Do you see those lights?"

"I see so many."

"There are vehicle lights, going along Burnham. That's them chasing after our squads."

"Where are our people?"

"Somewhere in front of those lights, driving as fast as they can, or scrambling on foot to disappear into the surrounding houses," Herb said. "Catch those lights. I want to get to them before they get to the first ambush site."

I wanted that, too. I banked hard. If we could stop them in their tracks they couldn't pursue our people, or even get to where my mother and her squad were waiting in ambush. Todd was with that group. They had been situated to protect the retreat of the attacking squad led by Brett. I could picture Brett down there acting like an action hero. I was grateful to have him on our side.

The compound came into full view off to the left as I completed the turn. I could see dozens of vehicles and half as many buildings on fire.

"As you close in on the vehicles I want you to come in low and slow," Herb said. "They'll be so focused on the chase that they won't be expecting to be attacked from the air and from behind."

I straightened out as we came over the road. There were seven or eight vehicles up ahead. Despite being almost at full throttle I wasn't closing very fast. Our extra weight was slowing us down.

"How soon before they hit the spot where the ambush is going to happen?"

"Soon. Less than two miles," Herb said.

We'd catch them before that. We were coming up to the last truck in their convoy. If they looked back and up they'd see us and we'd be a sitting duck—or at least a low-flying duck. I had to hope that Herb was right about the surprise.

I pulled back on the stick, gaining some more height and slowing us down in the trade-off. Herb wanted me to come in slow, anyway. The altimeter read seventy-five feet.

My eye was distracted by a flash of light. I looked over. Using a little cardboard box as a windshield, Herb had sparked his lighter and lit the wick on three Molotov cocktails. Now we'd no longer be invisible in the dark sky.

"Get me closer."

I pushed down on the stick until we were right over the top of the last truck, keeping exact pace with it. Then Herb dropped the flaming cocktail and as I shot ahead there was a burst of light from behind and the plane was bathed in the glow. We kept on flying, passing the second truck and a third, as Herb dropped his other two gas bombs over the side, followed quickly by a couple more grenades. The explosions and percussion waves pushed against the plane, bucking and rocking us.

The rear lights of the trucks ahead blazed as the two lead trucks slammed on their brakes and the three cars behind smashed into the back of them.

We raced past the first truck and were caught in the upper edge of its headlights. I pulled up, trying to avoid the glare, and gunned the accelerator.

Herb lit another Molotov cocktail and dropped it over the side. I could picture it shattering and exploding onto the road beneath us.

"I want them to think hard about going any farther," Herb said.

He lit another one and dropped it to the pavement.

"Take one more pass," Herb said. "But this time they'll be looking for us to come in head-on. We're going to hit them from the side."

I banked sharply to the right. I wasn't positive, but I figured they might have seen my turn. That meant that if anything they would be expecting us to come in from the north. I wasn't going to do the expected. Herb had said the side, but he didn't say which side. I reduced the turn. I was going to go long and curve completely around them in a big circle so that I could attack from the south. As I continued to bank there were a number of pools of light on the road. Two were the Molotov cocktails Herb had just dropped on the road itself. The others had to be trucks on fire. There were no more headlights. The drivers had finally figured out that they should turn them off, and with my goggles there was still enough light on the road for me to see the darkened shapes moving along . . .

But wait, they were retreating!

"They're driving away!" I yelled.

"They don't have much stomach for a real fight," Herb said. "Let's finish them. Make the pass."

They were moving fast, and I had to try to time my pass to make up for their speed. I increased my bank and aimed for a spot ahead where I hoped I could intercept them. In the distance I could see their compound, fire and smoke and light shooting up into the sky.

"I won't be able to get to them until they're almost back home," I said.

"Perfect. They'll think they're safe and relax. We'll show them they're wrong. I'm going to drop the entire bag, all the remaining grenades and the Molotov cocktails. This is going to be one incredible explosion. I don't want to miss, so get me in as close as you can," Herb said.

"The closer I get, the more the chance they'll see us."

"I *want* them to see us. They know we have an ultralight. I want them to *know* that it was us that attacked them."

"If you want I'll get you in so close that you can hand the bag to somebody."

"Not that close, but I want to drop it right on the roof of one of the lead vehicles if I can."

I nodded. I'd do what he wanted even if it was the last thing we did. Then I realized it *might* be the last thing we did. We were going to dive-bomb a convoy of heavily armed men who knew we were up here somewhere, who could be scanning the sky looking for us. I couldn't think about that. I needed to focus on what I was doing. There were enough ways to kill yourself flying in an ultralight before dawn without worrying about people trying to shoot you down as well.

I was high and to the south of the convoy. They were running dark without headlights, but they were still visible, darker shadows against the dark pavement. I had to think that if they were visible to me, maybe I was visible to them.

I wanted to intercept the first truck, come in from the side at about two o'clock and then pass by, low, and disappear behind the stretch of houses on the north side before they could react and direct accurate fire on us.

"Less than twenty seconds," I said to Herb.

"I'm ready." He had the bag in his lap and was holding a grenade in one hand, prepared to pull the pin.

"I'm going to come in slightly from your side to give you a target."

I took a deep breath. "Here we go." I pushed back on the stick, and we dove toward the ground and the fast-moving trucks. Was I going to shoot over the road before they arrived or would they zip past before I reached the intercept point? I did a slight adjustment to correct for their speed and— There were muzzle bursts from one of the shadows! I felt the plane buck and realized that we were being hit. I fought the urge to pull back or swerve to the side even as there were more bright bursts from weapons.

"Bombs away!" Herb yelled as he pulled the pin, and in one smooth motion put the grenade back in the bag and dropped the whole thing. We zoomed past the second truck in the convoy and I pulled up hard on the stick, and then there was an explosion. The plane rocked upward and I could feel a wave of heat engulf us. I struggled with both hands to control the tilting, rocking plane. We slid sideways and for a second my hand slipped off the stick. I regained my grip and pulled hard, and then we were flying flat and level, the plane back in my control.

I started to climb. The plane responded, but slowly. It was like everything was heavy when it should have been light. We'd lost a ton of weight with what Herb had dropped over the side.

It didn't matter; slowly climbing was better than quickly crashing.

"That was the shock wave of the explosion," Herb said.

"You should see what I can see. The middle trucks are gone. Just gone, almost disintegrated by the force."

"I wish I could have seen it."

"There are people down there who wish they hadn't. The people who lived aren't going to ever forget what they saw. And they're not going to forget us, forget the ultralight."

"And that's good, right?"

"Sometimes you have to poke the tiger with a stick to get him to do what you want him to do. If you can't avoid a battle, it's always best to have it happen when and where you want. Especially when your opponent doesn't know you decided those things. Today we set the direction they'll follow. But now we have to get home."

"You don't need to tell me twice." I corrected course. "All I want now is to get on the ground in one piece."

"How is the plane flying?" Herb asked.

That was an unusual question. Why would he ask that? "It's fine . . . a little slow. Why?"

"Just curious about how important the tail is to turning and landing."

"It's important, but— How bad is it?"

"Some of it's still there."

I turned around to see what wasn't there, but in the dark, blocked by some of the plating, I really couldn't see it. Besides, I had to focus on flying—especially now.

I leveled off. We didn't need any more height. I was almost straight over the top of Burnham, and there were long clear stretches of open road not too far ahead. Maybe I should just land it when I could. No—if we were going to crash, it was better to be closer to our clinic and Dr. Morgan.

"Radio in and let them know to light up the walls along Burnham," I said.

I was sure Danny and Rachel would be waiting for me when we landed. So would Lori. I needed to get home, lie down in my bed, and go to sleep, maybe for a few days. Did we have a few days?

"How long before you think they might attack?"

"It could come as early as tomorrow morning," Herb said. "We stung them. They're going to want to sting back. As far as I'm concerned, the sooner the better."

"Are we ready for an attack?"

"I guess we'll find out."

In the distance the multicolored Christmas lights appeared. Despite it all I couldn't help but smile. I pointed at them. "Merry Christmas, Herb."

He laughed. "Merry Christmas, Adam. I think we've already gotten part of the gift we were hoping for."

43

After a few hours' sleep, I was back up, thinking about this new day. Would the group from the city be able to organize a counterattack as quickly as Herb thought they might? The feeling throughout the whole neighborhood was electric—we'd all been shot at and missed . . . and now we were all waiting to be shot at again. Everybody seemed to be talking too fast and asking too many questions, and I just needed to be left alone. That was why I was so grateful to be outside and away.

It was only a five-minute drive from our neighborhood to the bridge. I was happy to have Lori in the passenger seat beside me. I was also happy that I had a rifle in the backseat and just plain grateful for the ground under my tires. The landing after the attack, with only half a tail, had been difficult. No, not difficult, terrifying. It was a classic case of the old saying "Any landing you can walk away from is a good landing." With the nearly missing tail, I'd come in too hard and done some damage to the landing gear. Mr. Nicholas was confident they could repair the damage and have me up in the air again by noon.

Lori reached over and took my hand, and my whole body tingled. I hadn't told her everything about the attack yet, and she'd been thoughtful enough not to ask. I always needed time to think about how much I should unburden myself to her. Right now she had enough to be worried about without knowing what I'd seen and done and how close those bullets had come to my head.

In some ways we were all just dodging bullets. And rocket-propelled grenades, because that's what they were going to fire at us. If they came—*when* they came—they were going to come in hard and mean and merciless. There was going to be little time to escape and few places to hide.

About a mile north, Herb had secured a small house—previously abandoned—and sealed up the garage. In it was a working truck, extra ammunition and weapons, some fuel and food. Nobody else knew about it except me and my mother. I hadn't even told Lori. She didn't need to know unless we needed to use it. From there, once things had settled down, we'd make our next move, trying to reestablish ourselves out at her family's old farm.

It wasn't that we were abandoning the neighborhood. We'd be there to fight to protect it, but if we had to flee, if we were overwhelmed, the first stop was at the secure house. Herb knew that if people were captured it wouldn't be long until they told everything they knew. The men from the city would want to find our leaders and kill them. They might be particularly interested in finding the pilot of the ultralight. I was a marked young man.

Our people had closed off Burnham at the bridge, blocking it on both sides where it went over the river so that nobody—no cars or people—was allowed on this stretch of road, except for people from the neighborhood.

I slowed down as we came up to the roadblock. There were a dozen vehicles parked to the side and two dozen armed guards manning the makeshift blockade, which was made of half a dozen overturned cars thrown across the lanes of the bridge.

"There's your mother and Herb," Lori said.

We got out of the car and joined them.

"I was hoping to see you up there," Herb said, pointing to the sky.

"They're still working on the tail. Mr. Nicholas said it might be ready by noon."

"Personally I like having my son with his feet on the ground," my mother said.

"I like him right here as well," Lori agreed as she squeezed my hand.

"Up there is better for everybody. We need to see them coming," Herb said.

"Do you think it's possible they won't come?"

"They're going to come. It's only a matter of time."

"Maybe we inflicted so much damage they're not able to mount an attack," I suggested.

"We didn't disable them. They still have hundreds of men and more than enough vehicles to get them here."

I knew our own casualties—four killed, two wounded, three missing and presumed dead.

"I guess we should just hope it isn't today," Lori said.

Herb shook his head. "The longer they wait, the more potential they have to get stronger. We have to hope that if it isn't today we can provoke them into attacking tomorrow."

"How would we provoke them?" I asked. I was almost afraid to ask.

"We'll put snipers around their base and pick off their men and drop some more bombs on their position. Are you ready for another flyover?"

"I'll do whatever needs to be done."

"Shouldn't we want them *not* to attack us?" Lori said.

"We know they're going to attack," I explained. "We want to control the timing and the location. Rather than wait for them to attack our neighborhood when and where they want, we need them to come right along here, right across this bridge, where we'll be waiting for them."

"What if they take another way?" she asked.

"There are only three routes. Here, to the north along the 403, and Dundas Street. Three ways, three bridges over the river. We're prepared whichever way they come, but this is the most direct, and they seem to like direct."

I looked past the overturned cars on this side of the bridge. All along, the narrow stretch of road was littered with wrecked cars. They had been positioned to slow down anything coming across the bridge. I didn't see Brett anywhere and wondered if he was over there or out on patrol somewhere. He never did like guard duty even if it wasn't on the wall.

I'd heard what he'd done last night. He had led his men right into the enemy compound, set fire to a dozen of their vehicles, taken lives, and managed to get his squad out with minimal losses.

"You should probably head back to the neighborhood and see how the plane is—"

There was a crackle on the radio and then an excited voice called out, "They're on the move! They're on the move!"

44

Herb, Lori, and I jumped into our vehicle and raced back to my house, where Mr. Nicholas was making final adjustments to the tail. We all leaped out and rushed to the plane, Herb yelling that we had to get up into the air.

I grabbed the tail with both hands and started pulling it to test it. The whole plane moved toward me, the new tail section staying exactly where it should be.

"It's good?" Herb asked.

"It looks okay, but we really won't know for sure until we're up in the air. Maybe it would be better if I went up by myself first."

"There's not enough time for a test flight," Herb said. "Besides, I've been up there already when you had only half a tail. How much worse could this be?"

I climbed in and Herb climbed in beside me with a canvas bag that I knew was filled with more grenades and Molotov cocktails. The cocktails could be readily made, but I was surprised at just how many grenades he had in his basement. I wondered how many he had left. Then again, if this didn't work it didn't matter.

I started the engine and revved it fully. I wanted to feel

the vibrations. There was shaking, of course, but nothing different from what there would have been normally. I had the same feeling in the pit of my stomach that I'd had the first time I'd soloed.

"We have to get up in the air," Herb said. "We haven't got long."

"Where are they?"

"I just got a report that they've left their base. It took them a bit to muster up into a convoy."

Herb had arranged for a series of scouts who used walkie-talkies to be positioned at intervals to relay messages all the way back here.

"We just have to hope they're coming our way," Herb said.

That wasn't what I hoped. I released the brakes and started us forward. There was nobody to watch us take off. Everybody was either out on patrol, on the walls, or at the bridge. Or they had fled for already-designated safe houses—small children, some older folks, people who didn't have any weapons. The emergency plans had some people believing that we thought we weren't going to win, but it was more important that they be safe just in case we couldn't stop the enemy at the bridge. Lori would be leaving shortly, taking Danny and Rachel with her and her mother.

We rolled down the road, rumbling and shaking along the asphalt until the wheels lifted off and we were in flight. Gently I pulled back on the stick, slowly gaining height. Up ahead the dead high-voltage electric towers were looming, the useless wires still strung between them, still a danger to my plane. I stayed low and flew under the wires. I banked, again slowly, turning toward the east.

"How is the plane responding?" Herb asked.

"Good so far. I'm just not going to push it too hard. At least not yet. How many of them are there?"

"Reports are that they have more than thirty vehicles, so it could be five hundred men."

"It sounds like we didn't do as much damage as we thought we did," I said.

"We did a lot. Surprisingly, sometimes people are remarkably easy to kill and in other cases they show remarkable resiliency and are incredibly hard to dispatch. But today we'll do better."

What a strange thing to be talking about—how we hoped we'd kill a lot of people today.

I gave it more throttle again, gradually increasing our speed and monitoring the plane's reaction. If there was more vibration than usual it wasn't significantly different.

"Can you go faster?" Herb asked. "We need to get to them as soon as possible."

So much for gradual increases. I gave it full throttle and the plane roared in response.

"And more height would be good. They're going to be looking for us now and throwing up lots of lead if they see us."

"I can give you as much height as you want. You just name it."

"Keep climbing."

Burnham was below and to the right. This was the best position for Herb and his binoculars. Farther south was Dundas. I could make it out but couldn't see any movement along it.

"What if they decide to come along the 403 or Dundas instead?" I asked.

"I don't think they will, but we're prepared as long as we know what they're doing."

"But we really can't see all three routes from here."

"We know they started along Burnham, and we know how many vehicles left their compound. I'll count how many are in their convoy when we sight them."

"Do you think they might split up?"

"I think they're going to stay together and come right at us, right along Burnham. So far there's been nothing subtle about the way they work. They count on overwhelming force, and they wouldn't want to dilute that force by separating into different columns."

We were over fifteen hundred feet and still climbing. Burnham was a black line stretching out in front of us.

"I see them!" Herb yelled out.

"Are they all there?"

"I'm counting." He had his binoculars up. I was only able to pick out a line of vehicles moving west.

"Twenty-six or twenty-seven," Herb said.

"But weren't there more than thirty vehicles?" I questioned. "Are some going a different way?"

"They might just be lagging behind. It's hard to keep that long a convoy together. We need them to be bunched together as close as possible when they hit the bridge. That's where we come in."

"Are we going to attack them?"

"That would be suicide. I just want to get their attention and slow them down."

I started to bank to the right, coming around until Burnham was right underneath us. We were now coming up on them from behind.

"There are the other vehicles," Herb said. "They're not far behind the larger part of the convoy. Keep going, stay high, and go right past them. I want to get in front of them."

We quickly passed the last trucks and started gaining on the major part of the convoy.

"Do you think they see us?" I asked.

"Probably, but believe me, I'll make sure we get their attention."

I didn't like the sound of that.

"Just keep our height until we're well ahead of them, and then get down low, fast. I need you to be right above the road."

We came up on the main convoy. They were far below and tightly bunched together. We quickly passed over each vehicle, far below, until we got in front of the lead truck and kept moving. Satisfied there was now enough separation from them, I started to descend. I pushed down on the yoke and we dropped quickly, the road rushing up at us.

"How low?"

"The lower the better."

I kept dropping until I reached thirty-five feet and then leveled off.

"And slow down. Speed makes this more challenging," Herb said.

I eased off the throttle. The road below was littered with abandoned cars.

Herb had already pulled out a couple of Molotov cocktails, which he was balancing on his lap. Using his little homemade windshield he lit the first and dropped it over the side of the plane.

"Got it!" he yelled.

"Got what?"

"I dropped it on an abandoned car." He lit and dropped the second. "And that was a miss."

Again and again he lit and dropped cocktails over the side of the plane.

"Hopefully it will slow them enough to get them to bunch up."

I pulled back on the stick and we gained some height. Up ahead I could see the bridge with its blockade of overturned cars. Between the cars were bricks and stones and pieces of wood embedded with nails designed to puncture tires. Wires and cables had been strung between the bridge supports, and some of them had been booby-trapped—work that had all been done in the days before we launched our attack. The question remained, though: Would any of this stop them or even slow them down?

The other end of the bridge came up. It was blocked off as well, piled even higher with overturned cars and logs wedged between the cement supports to form a solid wall. I waved at the people below, and they waved back. I knew my mother was down there somewhere, but I couldn't pick her out among the people lining the barricade. There were guards, sentries, and snipers all along the bank ready to fire on the convoy as it crossed.

If they crossed the bridge, if they broke through the barricade and got past, there was nothing but a clear stretch of pavement leading them right to the walls of the neighborhood. If they weren't stopped here, they weren't going to be stopped.

I banked sharply, accelerated, and pulled back on the stick to gain height.

"Do you think they're ready down there?" I asked.

"They have to be."

"I just wish we could ask."

We couldn't. Any attempt to use the walkie-talkie would just give information to anybody else who might be listening. Surprise was still almost all we had. ·

"Swing extra wide," Herb ordered. "I want to come back toward them from the valley, right as they're crossing the bridge."

I banked to the left, still climbing, giving it almost full throttle.

As we gained height I could see our neighborhood in the distance.

Eden Mills. I guessed it was as close to Eden as anyplace that existed anymore. Would it still be Eden in a few hours? Would it even still exist?

We came back around, and I could see the bridge ahead but couldn't see down the road itself.

"Can you see them?" I asked Herb.

He was peering through his binoculars. "Not yet. My view is still blocked so I can't—"

A truck burst through the barricade, sending abandoned cars and timbers flying up and into the air! It was followed by a second truck and a third and a fourth! They rolled across, pushing the abandoned cars off to the side, bumping and rumbling over the rocks and obstacles strewn along the bridge.

"It's not stopping them!" I yelled.

"But it's slowing them down. Get me closer, aim right for the lead truck."

I didn't hesitate. I dropped down and hit the left rudder, trying to aim for where the truck would be by the time I got to the bridge, but if it wasn't slowed down, it could be over the bridge before I got there.

I opened up the throttle all the way. We were streaking toward the bridge, dropping down on it like a dive-bomber. More and more trucks were rumbling onto the bridge. There were at least a dozen, and each few seconds another started over.

There were flashes—muzzle blasts—we were taking fire . . .

I dropped down and—

"Keep it level!" Herb yelled. "I may need to take a shot!"

Herb had the rifle out and was aiming at the lead truck. I felt his gun discharge, again and again, as he fired. I eased off my rudder, slowing down. I had to adjust and— I felt something strike the plane—we'd been hit. I struggled to keep the plane straight and in control, but I could feel us starting to slide.

There was an explosion, and flames engulfed the lead truck. It must have hit a trip wire with a grenade attached. It now blocked the way, but the second truck pushed on, knocking the flaming vehicle through the guard rail and off the side of the bridge, charging forward, followed by the third. The whole top of the cliff lit up with muzzle flashes from our side's guns, trying to slow them down.

"Come on," I said. "They're all on the bridge now, don't wait any longer."

The lead truck was almost over, bearing down on the second barricade, when there was a tremendous explosion, and a second and a third. The whole bridge trembled and a shock wave rushed out and bucked the plane upward. I struggled to regain the controls as the second and third waves washed over us. One of the gigantic pillars of the bridge started to disintegrate. The pavement began to buckle and then it just melted, flowing into the valley, the lead truck and the second tumbling with it!

Everything just slowed down. The thin black ribbon of asphalt, the whole bridge shattering, falling, the whole structure collapsing, all of the vehicles on it falling into the valley, twisting and turning as they plummeted!

I pulled up on the stick and we rose, practically flying *through* where the bridge had been only seconds before. It was gone. They were all gone. I soared through the open air. Another shock wave hit the plane, throwing us up and off to the side. I struggled to retain the controls in my hands and pulled back on the stick as we were buffeted by the explosion from below.

And then we stopped shaking and flew steadily through clear blue sky. I looked back over my shoulder. I couldn't see much behind and below except gigantic clouds of dust and smoke. I was just happy to see that the tail of my plane was still there.

"The charges took down the bridge!" I screamed. "It worked!"

"Bring us back around," Herb yelled. "Bring us around!"

I banked hard to the left, the plane tilting to the side, and eased off on the throttle, slowing down to allow a tighter turn. We soared up and over the edge of the river valley, and I looked out. In the distance I could see the edge of our neighborhood. There behind those walls were my brother and sister, Lori, her family, and almost every other person in the world who meant anything to me, and I knew something that they didn't know. We were going to live.

I came around hard and fast until I was facing back at the bridge—at where the bridge used to be.

In its place was a haze—a cloud of dust and dirt and smoke rising up into the air, two of the thick concrete pillars still intact, soaring toward the sky but holding up nothing, while the rest were gone—collapsed and crumbled under the force of the explosives that had been wrapped and wired around them.

"The bridge is gone," I gasped.

"And everybody who was on the bridge is gone with it."

I looked down and tried to see through the cloud. There, through the haze, I could make out the shattered hulks of vehicles, trucks littering the valley floor, some half hidden in the river itself. I could see them, but they didn't look real—it was like they were little toy trucks. Dozens of trucks, hundreds of men, and all of their weapons were at the bottom of the valley, shattered and crushed and finished. They couldn't harm us anymore.

"We're safe."

"We are safe," Herb said. "At least for today."

ERIC WALTERS,

a former elementary school teacher, is a bestselling children's author in Canada and has published over eighty books. He lives in Mississauga, Ontario, and is the founder of Creation of Hope, a charity that provides care for orphans in the Mbooni district of Kenya.